"We married with the intention of building an alliance—and a family."

Synnamon couldn't argue with this assessment of their marriage—it *had* been far more partnership than romantic passion.

Then Conner went on calmly. "Then you changed your mind and wanted a divorce, and because that was a decision that affected only the two of us, I went along."

"Exactly," Synnamon agreed. "And we also, if you'll recall, made an agreement to be civilized, amicable, about the whole divorce."

"That was before we so *amicably* created a child."

"Conner," she said desperately, "you can't force someone to stay married."

His eyes darkened. "Can you honestly tell me, Synnamon, that you love me any less today than you did on our wedding day?"

Dear Friends and Readers,

Fifty books. I can hardly believe it.

Fifteen years ago, when I was still feeling puffed up about the publication of my first book, my husband—The Great Visionary—said, "The day will come when you'll have written fifty." And I said, "Yeah, right."

Now, fifty books later, I'm still happy about each and every love story. I laugh and cry with my characters, and I hate to say goodbye when their story ends. But I'm no longer puffed up about writing and publication; in a lot of ways I believe I know less now than I thought I did fifteen years ago.

Those years have brought lots of changes for my husband and me—a move, an empty nest, three wonderful grandchildren. And one of the most beautiful blessings I could receive—the hundreds of new friends around the world who have written to me about my books and shared important pieces of their own lives.

Thank you for following this long road with me. I'm looking forward to a hundred, one book at a time.

With love,

Leigh

P.S. Leigh loves to hear from readers. You can write to her at P.O. Box 935, Ottumwa, Iowa, 52501-0935, U.S.A.

The Perfect Divorce!
Leigh Michaels

Harlequin Books

TORONTO • NEW YORK • LONDON
AMSTERDAM • PARIS • SYDNEY • HAMBURG
STOCKHOLM • ATHENS • TOKYO • MILAN
MADRID • WARSAW • BUDAPEST • AUCKLAND

ISBN 0-373-03444-X

THE PERFECT DIVORCE!

First North American Publication 1997.

Printed in U.S.A.

CHAPTER ONE

THE Contessa was dying.

Synnamon felt the announcement sinking into her bones like lead into water, and she hardly recognized her own voice. "But I thought she was better! Just last month, after her surgery, she told me—"

The voice at the other end of the telephone line was almost diffident. "I'm sure she didn't want to worry you right then, Mrs. Welles, when you'd just lost your father. But the doctors told her, I believe, that it was only a matter of time."

That made sense, Synnamon thought. With everything that had been going on in Denver in the past few months, it was no wonder the Contessa hadn't wanted to add her bad news to Synnamon's burden.

As if not being prepared would make it easier to lose her, Synnamon thought.

"You won't tell her I called, will you, Mrs. Welles?"

"Of course not, Hartford. I'll be there as soon as I can get on a plane."

She could hear relief in the weary voice. "We'll make arrangements for you and Mr. Welles to be met at the airport."

Synnamon kept her tone steady with an effort. "I don't think Mr. Welles can get away."

There was an instant of shocked silence. "But if you were to come alone, she'd suspect I'd called you. I thought if I could tell her that you and Mr. Welles were coming for a long weekend, sort of sneaking off for a second honeymoon...'

Second honeymoon. If only Hartford knew how deliciously ironic that was! But he was right, of course. The Contessa adored Conner. If he was there, she wouldn't ask uncomfortable questions about exactly why he *wasn't*.

And if there was one thing Synnamon didn't want to explain to her dying godmother, it was that she and Conner would never have a second honeymoon, or even a first anniversary—because in a matter of weeks they'd have a divorce decree, instead.

Synnamon bit her lip and sighed. "I'll see if he can clear his calendar," she said. "I'll have Annie call you back with the flight number."

She put the telephone down and noted with detached interest that her hand was trembling. It still looked shockingly bare, too. Though she'd worn her diamond solitaire for less than a year and the matching wedding band for little more than eight months, there hadn't been enough time since she'd taken them off for the indentation at the base of her ring finger to disappear.

She punched the intercom button. "Annie, book two seats on the first plane to Phoenix, and see if Mrs. Ogden is still at my apartment. If she is, ask her to pack an overnight bag for me, and send a car out to get it. And call Mr. Welles's secretary, please, and ask if he can see me right away."

Annie's voice held a hint of hesitation. "Do you want him to come here?"

"Of course not. I'll go to his office. And if there's anything that needs my signature before the end of the week, can you have it ready in the next hour?"

"I'll check, but I'm sure I can."

"Thanks, Annie." Synnamon turned off the intercom and pulled open the door of her tiny closet to check her hair and makeup. It was silly, perhaps, to still want to look her best for Conner....

Now what had made her think that? She wasn't trying to impress him. It was long-ingrained habit for Synnamon, as the daughter of a cosmetics baron, to always make sure she looked as attractive as possible. And maybe, too, she was trying to postpone the instant she'd have to walk into Conner's office and ask for a major favor.

Which was sillier yet, of course, because in the month since they'd agreed to go their separate ways, they'd gotten along quite well. Not that they'd been pals, exactly—they'd never been that—but they'd discussed their business matters without a hint of acrimony. In fact, Synnamon had almost enjoyed the night they'd had dinner with both their attorneys. They'd been so civilized that they'd settled the entire division of property over the appetizers, and then the four of them had spent the rest of the evening amicably discussing theater and politics.

She straightened her hair, tucking a few ash-blond wisps into the neat French twist, and touched up her mascara even though it was the new brand they were testing—guaranteed to stay on through water aerobics, rainstorms and lifeboat rescues. Then, with nothing else to delay her, Synnamon walked down the hall to the chief executive's office.

The hallways of the Sherwood Cosmetics complex were deeply carpeted in the rich royal blue that was the company's trademark color. Carved into the thick plush at regular intervals was the stylized letter S that Silas

Sherwood had sketched on the first lipstick tube he'
manufactured thirty years before.

His monument, Synnamon thought wryly. He'd calle
it the symbol of an empire built on vanity. Though he'
been talking about the women who used his products
Synnamon had always thought that when it came to de
fining vanity, her father's own egotism was an even bette
example.

The marketing director was sitting in the waiting roon
outside Conner's office, and Synnamon started to tak
a chair nearby.

But Conner's secretary waved a hand toward the doo
to the inner office. "Go right on in, Mrs. Welles. He'
waiting for you." The surprise in her voice was faint
but Synnamon could hear the signs.

In the time they'd both worked at Sherwood, she'
never been one to pop into Conner's office or encourag
him to dash into hers. The rule of business etiquette dic
tated a polite call before dropping in on a co-worker
She'd seen no reason to violate that rule when the co
worker was her husband, and felt even more strongl
about it now that the relationship was in name only. An
since Synnamon's job was in customer relations, he
business was seldom so urgent that it couldn't wait fo
the chief executive officer to finish what he was doin
and get back to her.

No wonder Carol was surprised today, not only b
Synnamon's request for immediate attention but by th
fact that Conner had put her ahead of the marketin
director.

He's waiting for you. Synnamon wondered if tha
meant Conner had something on his mind. It must b
close to a week since they'd run into each other. Yes, i
had been in the staff dining room, last Friday. She'

said a polite hello, and he'd returned it. She'd picked up yogurt and a bagel, and he'd selected a chicken salad plate, and they'd moved almost automatically to tables on opposite sides of the room....

But there couldn't be anything important going on, or he'd have sought her out and brought it up. They had agreed to be civilized about this whole thing, after all.

Synnamon tapped twice on the door and pushed it open.

The chief executive's office was huge, so big that even the overstuffed couch and love seat seemed to be tucked into a corner. A wall of windows looked out over downtown Denver to the faint blue line of the Rocky Mountains beyond.

Conner was sitting at the enormous ebony and glass table that served as his desk. His profile was silhouetted against the mountain skyline, and the telephone was at his ear.

He looked at Synnamon and murmured into the phone, "Excuse me just a second, Nick."

"I'm sorry." Synnamon's voice was unsteady. "Carol must not have realized you were busy."

"No, I told her to send you in. Sit down, I'll be off in a minute. Ask Carol to bring coffee, if you'd like."

Synnamon shook her head, but Conner didn't seem to notice. He swiveled toward the window and put the phone back to his ear.

She chose the chair squarely across from him and sat down, idly smoothing the rose-pink tweed of her skirt as she watched him. He seemed to have forgotten her presence, or else he was completely undisturbed by it. He'd picked up his conversation crisply, almost in midsentence. Something about the chemical composition of a new product, she thought.

Not that she expected him to be uneasy with her around, any more than she was nervous with him. They were like strangers, really. No, more like longtime casual acquaintances who no longer had much in common. She hadn't even really looked at Conner in weeks—since the day not long after her father's funeral when she'd told him she wanted out of their marriage, out of Sherwood Cosmetics.

Synnamon eased back in her chair, curved one slim leg around the other and watched Conner's profile against the hazy gray-blue of the winter sky. He wasn't conventionally handsome—his face was too craggy for that, his dark hair a little too wiry. But his eyes were quite nice, so blue they were almost purple, surrounded with long black lashes that could turn an ash-blond like Synnamon green with envy. And his smile could be attractive. In fact, just the other day she'd overheard a couple of production-line workers discussing Conner's smile—and other things—in terms that might have made Synnamon blush if she'd still been his wife in anything but the legal sense. *Gorgeous* was one of the terms they'd been tossing around. And *incredibly sexy* ...

They were probably right, she admitted calmly, if one was interested in that sort of thing. She could take it or leave it, herself.

She wondered if Carol was the one who made regular appointments for his haircuts these days. Conner certainly was better groomed than before he'd moved into this office.

And the office was different, too, she noticed. The changes since Silas Sherwood's day were subtle—as if Conner were still feeling his way. Or perhaps there were more important things than decorating on his mind.

Silas's favorite Andy Warhol print had given way to a soft watercolor of a sailboat passing under a suspension bridge. The overstuffed furniture was the same, but the couch and love seat had been pulled around into a less formal arrangement. The desktop was clear except for a couple of folders, much as Silas had always kept it, but the new coffee table held a bit of clutter, papers Silas would never have allowed to gather. And the putting green that had been her father's favorite tension reliever was gone.

Conner put the telephone down and stood, and for the first time Synnamon realized he was wearing a long white lab coat. That was different, too. She couldn't remember ever seeing her father wearing one, though he had a doctorate in chemistry, just as Conner had. That was one of the reasons, no doubt, that Silas had taken to Conner Welles the moment he'd walked into Sherwood Cosmetics and applied for a job as a research and development chemist.

"What's wrong, Synnamon?"

She must have looked startled, for Conner's eyebrows went up slightly. "I'm not claiming to be psychic," he said dryly. "But when I asked if you'd like to move over to the couch, you didn't hear me. And you've been nibbling at your thumbnail since you came in. Keep it up and you'll have eaten your whole hand by dinnertime."

"Oh." She jerked her hand away from her mouth, feeling color flare in her cheeks. She'd given up biting her nails when she was twelve. What Silas would have said about a relapse didn't bear thinking about—but then she had only herself to please now. "Thanks for seeing me, Conner. I'm sorry to interrupt, and I won't take long, since Larry's waiting outside."

"That's all right—he'll wait."

Synnamon stayed in her chair. She'd completely forgotten what he'd said about moving to the conversational corner, because she was trying to find the words to begin.

After a moment Conner perched on the corner of the glass-topped desk. "I knew if you asked to see me it must be important."

Synnamon searched his voice for sarcasm, but she could find none. Of course not, she told herself. There was no reason for him to be sarcastic. He'd made a simple statement of fact. He knew she wouldn't bother him about trivia.

"It's the Contessa," she said. "Hartford called to tell me she's very ill. He doesn't expect her to survive another week. I'm going to Phoenix this afternoon, as soon as Annie can get me on a plane. And—" She paused and cleared her throat. "Hartford thinks you should come, too."

"He does, does he?" Conner wasn't looking at her but at his shoe, swinging idly back and forth. "What do you think?"

Idiot, she told herself. As if Conner would take his orders from the Contessa's butler! Of course, he wasn't any more likely to take them from Synnamon. Not that she was trying to order him to go to Phoenix, she reminded herself. She was asking a favor, that was all.

"I mean," she went on steadily, "that he doesn't want her to suspect that he's sent for me, which she will if I go alone. And I..."

Conner finished the sentence. "You don't want to tell her about the divorce."

"She's dying, Conner. What good would it do?"

He didn't argue. "Why didn't Hartford tell us before that she was so ill? Or the Contessa herself?"

"She didn't want to worry me."

He looked vaguely dissatisfied. "Why? Are you sure she doesn't know about the divorce?"

"Not from me." Synnamon's voice was sharper than she'd intended, and she regretted it instantly. *You're civilized*, she told herself. *There's no need to shout.* "I intended to go down in a couple of weeks, to break the news to her."

"Well, I certainly haven't told her. I haven't even talked to her."

"I wasn't accusing you. I'm sure she had her reasons for not telling me what the doctors said. They can be wrong, you know."

"But apparently in this case they weren't."

"She might not have wanted to admit it even if she realized the end was coming. Maybe she wants to die with the same grace she's carried all her life, without a whole lot of people standing around her bed."

"And just maybe..." He stopped. "Go on."

"And of course, with my father's heart attack coming just a few weeks before she got this bad news..."

Conner nodded. "That I can understand. But I wouldn't be so certain she doesn't have an inkling what's happening up here. So what's the plan?"

"Hartford wants to tell her we've managed to find a free weekend and we want to get away. The weather's so nice in Phoenix right now that it makes sense." She didn't think there was any point in mentioning what Hartford had said about a second honeymoon. Conner wasn't apt to find any more humor in that than she had.

"And if we both show up, obviously we're still in the throes of love?" Conner didn't sound convinced. "All right. When does the plane leave?"

"Annie's getting tickets. I'll ask her to call Carol with the times." Synnamon slid toward the edge of her chair. "Conner—thanks. This is very kind of you."

For a moment, she thought he wasn't going to answer. "Don't mention it," he said finally. "I'd like to see the Contessa one last time myself."

"I hope it won't interfere too much with your plans."

He shrugged. "Sherwood can run without me for a couple of days."

"That wasn't exactly what I meant. I thought you might have—" she paused and added delicately "—plans for the weekend."

"If that's a request for information about who I'm spending my free time with, Synnamon—"

"It isn't. Not that I'd mind, of course, if you were seeing someone—but I'd be sorry about your plans. I just want you to know that I appreciate how civilized you're being about this."

"From you, my dear," Conner said, "that is the highest compliment possible."

The flight seemed to take forever. Synnamon turned down the snack the attendant offered and stared out the window as she sipped her glass of white wine, trying to ignore Conner in the seat beside her. Not that he was attempting to gain her attention. That was obvious. He philosophically munched his airline peanuts, drank a single Scotch and water, and then leaned back, eyes closed, arms folded across his broad chest.

Synnamon had no idea if he was napping, meditating or contemplating a complex chemical formula, and she didn't care. She wasn't bothered by his presence, either, not really. It was just that he seemed to occupy all the space and consume all the air in the cabin. Thank heaven

Annie had booked them into first class. Synnamon hated
to think what this flight would have been like if Conner
had had to fold his six-feet-four into a narrow coach
seat. She'd have been practically sitting in his lap.

She hadn't been so close to him since her father's funeral, and that day she'd been too numb to notice much.
She remembered that he'd been unobtrusively beside her
every minute, offering an arm for support. She hadn't
needed it, of course, but it had been some comfort to
know he was there.

And it would help to have him there when she saw the
Contessa, too. The Contessa had fallen in love with
Conner at first sight, and he could help bridge any
awkward gaps that might arise. It wasn't going to be
easy to see a woman she loved in the state Hartford had
implied. . . .

Synnamon sighed.

Conner didn't open his eyes. "I'd suggest you wait
till you get there to start mourning."

Synnamon stared at him. His lashes, long and thick
and black, lay heavily against high, strong cheekbones.
"That's a pretty heartless attitude."

The seat belt sign came on, and Conner shrugged and
sat up straight. "Not really. I was just imagining the
Contessa flinging open the front door and saying,
Surprise!"

"The Contessa would never go along with such a cruel
practical joke, much less plan it. Besides, why would she
have Hartford tell me she's dying if she's not?"
Synnamon handed her half-full wineglass to the flight
attendant and returned her seat to the upright position.

"Because that announcement got us both down here.
And if my suspicions are right and she wants to have a
little talk about our marriage—"

"Our marriage—our *former* marriage—is none of the Contessa's business."

"You can try that line on her. As the former advice queen of the nation, she might see things differently."

"Etiquette was her specialty, not straightening out the lovelorn. Has anyone ever told you you're a cynic, Conner?" Below the plane, the city of Phoenix spread out almost to the mountain ranges that surrounded the flat valley. The minutes were ticking by, and Synnamon's heart began to pound. "What if I don't know what to say to her?" She wasn't talking to him so much as to herself. "I've never seen anybody who was dying...except for my father, of course. But he went so suddenly that there wasn't time to think about it."

"Silas never did have any patience with being kept waiting," Conner said.

Synnamon bit her lip. That was typical, she thought. It wasn't often she forgot herself enough to confide her fears, but when she did, the answer was glib. Just as it would have been if it had been Silas instead of Conner beside her—except, she thought, she'd never seen any indication that Silas possessed a sense of humor.

She turned toward the window once more. The pitch of the engines changed as the runway rose to meet them, and the slight vertigo she always experienced on landings rocked her stomach.

"Synnamon."

She didn't look at him. "What?"

"Follow her lead." His voice was almost somber. "If she wants to talk about dying, let her. If she doesn't, tell her what you remember most—remind her of the good times you had together."

Synnamon hesitated, then nodded. But she didn't turn away from the window, and a moment later the plane's tires screeched against the runway.

A uniformed chauffeur was waiting at the gate with a sign that said Welles. Synnamon handed him her overnight case, and he led the way across the terminal to a white Cadillac limousine.

Conner raised an eyebrow. "Do you ever consider taking the middle-class way, Synnamon? Like a taxi?"

"What good would that do?"

"A rhetorical question if I ever heard one." He handed his bag to the chauffeur and opened the back door of the car for Synnamon.

As the chauffeur slid behind the wheel, she leaned forward to make sure he had the Contessa's address. She braced her left hand on the jump seat and swore under her breath when she realized that her finger was still bare. "My rings," she said. "I forgot all about the rings, and no matter how sick she is, that's exactly the kind of little touch the Contessa is bound to notice. I suppose I can tell her they're at the jewelers being cleaned, but—"

Conner reached into the inside breast pocket of his blazer and dropped a small black velvet bag into her palm. "I wondered when you'd remember."

Synnamon tipped the contents into her hand. Even in the subdued light that passed through the limousine's tinted windows, the full-carat diamond solitaire flashed fire, and the matching wedding band, crusted with tiny stones, sparkled like a fresh snowfall. Almost reluctantly, she slid them onto her finger, the wedding band first, closest to her heart as tradition dictated, and then the solitaire to stand guard.

"I wouldn't have thought you'd have time to get them," she said. "But of course if you went home to pack—"

Or perhaps he'd kept them closer at hand.

But why would he? The rings were no more pleasant a memory to Conner than they were to Synnamon. It was a foolish idea, probably born of the fact that the platinum bands were warm from his body—as if that meant he'd carried them for the past month. The truth was, until this instant she wouldn't even have bet that he'd kept them.

Almost as if he'd read her mind, Conner said, "They were in the office safe. It's a whole lot more secure than leaving them in a hotel room. And I didn't have to go back to the hotel to pack. I've gotten in the habit of keeping some clothes in the office."

"That's certainly handy," Synnamon said crisply.

Conner shot a sideways look at her. "What does that mean?"

"Nothing. My father obviously thought it was a good idea, or he wouldn't have built a closet and a dressing room into his executive bath. That's all."

"Well, it's one thing Silas was right about. How did you manage to pack, anyway?"

"I didn't. Mrs. Ogden threw some things together, and one of the couriers made a detour and picked my bag up."

"What will you do after the end of the year, Synnamon, when you don't have all of Sherwood's resources to draw on any more?"

She looked at him levelly. "Are you afraid I'll still demand perks after I leave the company? Don't worry about me, Conner. Even after our division of property, I won't exactly be poverty-stricken." Deliberately, she changed the subject. "Mrs. Ogden asked about you just this morning, by the way. I think she misses you."

"How kind of her. Perhaps when I get an apartment she'll come to take care of me on the days she's not working for you."

Was he serious? But why shouldn't he be? "That would be tidy," she agreed. "Of course, I have her come in most days, so she doesn't have much time left for anyone else. Why are you still living in the hotel, anyway?"

Conner shrugged. "When you're starting from scratch, it takes time to find an apartment and furniture and appliances."

And he'd given up most of his things when they'd married. Not that he'd had much, Synnamon thought, so if he was suggesting it was her fault he had nothing in the way of household goods...

But of course he wasn't. She'd asked him, over the appetizers the night they'd agreed to terms, if he wanted anything in their apartment, and he'd made it clear he didn't.

The limousine purred through traffic, smoothly negotiating the beginnings of rush hour, and pulled up at a wrought-iron gate. Beyond it lay a long, curving row of elegant town houses, set at angles that increased the sense of privacy, each surrounded by a lawn so plush and unusually green—given the desert surroundings—that the grass looked artificial.

The guard at the gate checked his list and passed them through, and the limousine pulled up smoothly in front of the Contessa's home.

Thought it was technically a town house, Synnamon had always thought it was more like a villa. This was no mere two-level apartment, as most town houses were. It spread out lavishly at the end of the complex, and the front door, behind a colonnaded entrance, silently invited them to approach.

After the gray day they'd left in Denver and the tinted windows of the limousine, the Phoenix sunshine was harsh and brilliant. Synnamon stood for a moment outside the car, blinking, not quite sure if it was sunlight or tears that made her eyes hurt.

Conner signed the limousine bill and joined her on the sidewalk. "You know," he said, "you never have told me how the Contessa got her name."

He was trying to distract her, Synnamon knew. It was kind of him to bother. "It started as a joke when she was a child," she said. "She was the elegant one in a big and rowdy Italian family. Some of her brothers and sisters called her prissy. Then when she grew up and became the arbiter of proper behavior—not quite as famous as Emily Post, of course, but just as respected and obeyed—she cultivated the image of the Contessa. Now hardly anyone remembers her real name."

Synnamon took a deep breath and braced herself as the front door opened, revealing a woman in her sixties wearing a black dress and a crisp white apron.

The woman's eyes were swollen and red, and her lower lip trembled. "Oh, Mrs. Welles," she said, her voice shaking. "I'm so glad you're here!" She held out her arms, and Synnamon took a step forward and gathered the woman close.

Over her shoulder, she cast a glance at Conner, who looked a bit subdued. So much for his expectations that the Contessa herself would greet them, in perfect health and high spirits at having pulled off a prank.

But Synnamon had to admit that despite her knowledge of the Contessa she'd been hoping against hope Conner might be right. Now that last flicker of wishful thinking faded into darkness, and a chill settled deep in her heart.

She patted Mrs. Hartford on the shoulder and looked over the woman's head toward the butler, hovering in the hallway. "Take us to her, please, Hartford," she said. "We've left it too long as it is."

Midnight found her beside the Contessa's bed. A favorite book from her childhood lay open on her lap, but it had been long minutes since Synnamon had looked at the pages. She was watching the Contessa instead, searching the dear and familiar face, studying each line, each shadow and trying to figure out which ones were new. The Contessa's skin had always been luminous. Now it was almost translucent. Her eyelids, closed in a shallow sleep, seemed paper-thin. Her breath was faint. Her thin body seemed so fragile that Synnamon feared even the weight of the blanket might crush her.

As if there had been no interruption in the conversation, the Contessa sighed and said, "I'm so sorry, my darling. You came for a weekend getaway, and I'm ruining it. I can't help being glad to have you here, but it's terribly rude of me to spoil your holiday."

Synnamon couldn't keep herself from smiling at the slightly querulous tone. The voice of conscience, Synnamon had called it in her youth.

Mrs. Hartford came in with a medicine cup and a glass of water, and the Contessa waved a fragile hand toward the door. "Don't let me be so selfish, Synnamon. Go to your husband now. That's where you belong." Her hand dropped as if the effort had exhausted her.

Mrs. Hartford nodded. "She'll sleep for a while," she said softly. "And I'll sit with her."

Synnamon knew better than to argue. Perhaps the Contessa would rest more easily if she wasn't trying to talk. "You'll call me if she wants me." It wasn't a question.

"Of course. Or Hartford will—he's sleeping now, but he'll take over in a few hours."

Synnamon walked slowly across the balcony that divided the Contessa's bedroom from the guest quarters, pausing to look down into the enormous living room below. The scent of roses, freshly arranged in a crystal vase on the baby grand piano, tugged at her senses. She wondered when Mrs. Hartford had found the time for flowers, but she knew why she'd managed it. The Contessa loved roses—and if she gathered enough strength to walk out of her room again, there would be roses waiting for her.

Synnamon was still holding the book she'd been reading to the Contessa. She looked at the intricately drawn leaves on the cover and remembered what the Contessa had said when Synnamon had opened it to the first chapter.

"*The Secret Garden*," she'd murmured. "I feel somehow that I'll see that garden very soon."

Synnamon closed her eyes for a moment and swallowed hard, and then walked deliberately across to the guest suite. She did her best to be quiet, in case Conner was already asleep.

But the lights were on, and he was lying atop one of the twin beds, reading the *Wall Street Journal*. The spread had been turned back, but he hadn't bothered to get between the sheets. He'd simply stretched out across the blankets.

Perhaps, Synnamon thought, that was because he wasn't exactly dressed for bed. He was wearing jogging shorts and a T-shirt, as if he'd expected to be summoned to the Contessa's room. Or maybe it was all he had. No doubt Conner didn't keep pajamas in his office closet any more than Silas had. Though there had been talk about Silas sleeping in his office....

She noted and tried to ignore Conner's long, strong legs, the powerful breadth of his chest, the muscular arms under the short sleeves of the tight shirt, and turned toward the rack at the foot of the other bed, where Hartford had placed her overnight bag.

Twin beds. She almost hadn't noticed.

Well, that was a benefit she hadn't counted on. The last time they'd visited the Contessa—the only time the two of them had shared this room, shortly after their wedding—the beds had been pushed together and made up as a single king-size unit.

"How is she?" Conner asked.

"Worn out—and fading, I'm afraid, even since you saw her. I think Hartford was optimistic when he said it might be a week."

"I'm sorry," he said gently.

Synnamon nodded. She couldn't say anything. She was afraid if she tried she'd break down.

The only nightgown she could find in her bag was the flimsiest and laciest she owned. Mrs. Ogden's doing, of course—the woman loved lacy lingerie. That, Synnamon thought, would teach her to be catty about Conner's lack of pajamas!

By the time she came out of the bathroom, he'd turned off the light above his bed, leaving only the small lamp near hers, and the moonlight that filtered through the sheer curtains, to illuminate the room.

Synnamon slid between the sheets and turned off the lamp.

It was almost worse than being alone, to know that he was across the room. In the dark, the demons seemed to grow and taunt her, and she couldn't even cry, or he would know.

She was losing the most precious person in her world, the one who had always understood and loved her no matter what. The Contessa hadn't been required by the bonds of family to love Synnamon. She'd *chosen* to care about her—and that made her more valuable than anyone else had ever been.

Now—in a day, maybe two, but certainly not much longer—Synnamon would be entirely alone in the world.

The tears started as a silent trickle and grew into a flood. And though she tried fiercely to be quiet, the sobs could not be smothered. They wrenched at her chest, at her throat, at her heart.

"Synnamon," he said, and she heard his footsteps, soft as they were on the deep carpet. His hand passed over her hair, so tentatively that she could barely feel his touch—but it seemed as if his gentle gesture had reached deep inside her and flipped a switch.

She reached for him, tugging him down to her, as if by holding onto Conner she could cling to all that was sweet and precious in her life and keep it from slipping away.

"Hold me," she whispered. "Help me forget."

"Are you sure you know what you're asking Synnamon?"

"I'm sure."

Slowly, his palm cupped her chin and turned her face and he bent his head as if to kiss her temple. A kiss of pity, she thought—not at all what she needed just now. She twisted frantically in his arms till his lips, instead of brushing the corner of her eye, met hers like sparks striking gunpowder.

She could taste his strength, his warmth, his desire. He couldn't hide the truth, that in this instant he wanted *her*—only her—and the knowledge fed her longing.

"Make me forget it all, Conner," she said against his mouth. "Everything."

He didn't make her forget...at least, not quite. Perhaps nothing could have done that. But by the time the world exploded around her, the pain of impending loss had receded to a thin shadow at the corners of her mind, overwhelmed by the pure sensuality of his touch, the fire of his fingertips against her skin, the velvet of his lips against hers, the whisper of two bodies communicating in the wordless language men and women created long before the dawn of time.

He held her, afterward, the two of them curled together on the single narrow bed. Neither of them spoke.

With her body still throbbing, Synnamon forced herself to lie still, to breathe normally, to stay quiet, to pretend to sleep.

But deep inside her mind, as the shadows crept back, she was shrieking, *What have I done?*

CHAPTER TWO

THE sky was starting to lighten when Hartford knocked on the door of the guest suite to summon them, and before full daylight the Contessa had gone into the secret garden she had talked of, where her beloved roses would never fade or lose their scent.

Synnamon stayed beside the bed for a long time, hands folded, watching the still, peaceful face. When she finally came downstairs, Conner was sitting at the grand piano, picking out a melancholy one-fingered melody. Without a word, he moved across the room to a silver tray on a low table and poured her a cup of coffee.

She held it, hardly feeling the heat radiating through the china and sinking into her fingers. "Perhaps you'd call the airline," she said finally. "I can be ready to go in an hour or so."

Conner frowned. "Go where?"

"Denver. Home. Where else?"

"But what about the arrangements?" he asked quietly.

"The Contessa took care of that long ago." Synnamon smiled a little, but it took all the strength she had. "She had definite views on the rudeness of leaving that sort of job for someone else to do. And since she didn't want any sort of funeral service, just cremation with her ashes scattered in..." Her voice began to tremble as the reality once more hit home.

She half-expected Conner to reach for her, or at least to extend a hand. Her body tightened, and embarrassment flooded over her at the memory of her unin-

26

hibited behavior last night. The way she had responded to him, demanded, pleaded, begged . . .

But Conner didn't move. He simply stood quietly in the center of the Contessa's elegant living room, looking at her.

Thank heaven, Synnamon thought, *he's sensitive enough to understand that last night was an aberration.*

"Are you certain you want to go home just now?" Conner asked. "I should get back, I suppose, but there's really no reason for you to rush."

Synnamon shook her head quickly. "Oh, no. I'll be better if I'm busy." Too late, she realized that meant she'd be flying back with him. How easy it would have been to wait till tomorrow, or even to take a later plane today.

Had he meant that he didn't want her to come along? Surely not, she told herself. The flight would be so brief it couldn't matter, and then they would both be free to plunge into their jobs, into real life. "Besides," she went on firmly, "the Hartfords need a rest, not someone else to take care of."

"I'm not sure they'd agree with you. They might even like the distraction. I think I actually hurt Hartford's feelings this morning by telling him not to bother with breakfast." Conner pointed at the cup in her hand. "Drinking that, instead of only holding it, might do you good, Synnamon."

"And if I don't drink my coffee, Hartford will really be hurt?" Obediently she raised the cup to her lips. He'd put in half a spoon of sugar, exactly the way she liked it. She was vaguely surprised, until she realized that if the roles had been reversed she'd have remembered how to fix his, too—with just a touch of cream.

"Well, I wouldn't be surprised if they both feel a bit threatened just now."

Synnamon shook her head. "The Contessa arranged a pension plan. And I've already told them they can stay here as long as they like."

"You'll keep the town house, then?"

"Oh, yes. I can't imagine dividing up her things...." Her voice began to shake again, despite her best efforts, and she had to take a couple of deep breaths before she could say, "I just want to go home."

"Synnamon..." He paused. "I'll call the airline."

She set her cup on the silver tray and tugged the rings from her finger. "Here," she said as she held them out to him. "So I don't forget them later."

Slowly, Conner raised a hand to take the gleaming bands from her. "Are you sure this is a good idea?"

She frowned. "Why not? I doubt the Hartfords will notice. And they'll have to know about the divorce sometime, anyway. Now that the Contessa's gone..." She drew her elbows close against her body. "Conner, I want to thank you for—" she hesitated "—for consoling me last night. I'll be fine, really."

He said levelly, "I'm sure you will." He looked at the rings, the stones sparkling against his palm. "I always thought diamonds were perfect for you, Synnamon, but I wasn't quite sure why. Now I know. They're every bit as brilliant and hard as you are."

Synnamon toyed with a bread stick and tried not to look out the window. A mid-December snowstorm was venting its fury on Denver, and from twenty stories above the street, atop one of the city's premier hotels, all she could see was a gray-white cloud that shifted and rolled and twisted till her stomach threatened to rebel. To make it worse, the Pinnacle was a revolving restaurant, and though the constant and slightly jerky motion normally didn't bother her, today she felt like she'd been stranded on a carnival ride.

But the restaurant was her attorney's favorite, and when Morea had called yesterday to set up a lunch date so they could talk about the progress of the divorce, Synnamon hadn't hesitated to accept the invitation. Of course yesterday she hadn't been thinking about the predicted snow.

Morosely, she snapped another bread stick in two and played with it. The wind seemed to whistle around the glass and steel tower.

The maître d' swept across the room and with a flourish pulled out the chair opposite Synnamon's. Morea Landon settled into place with a sigh, tossed the end of a fringed red silk scarf over her shoulder with an elegant flourish and leaned forward to touch Synnamon's hand. "Darling, how are you?" Her voice was low and husky. "I haven't seen you in two weeks, at least."

"I'd be better if it wasn't snowing horizontally."

Morea smiled sympathetically and glanced at her menu for all of three seconds before tossing it aside. "It does look a bit like a Rorschach test out there, doesn't it? Want to split a bottle of wine?"

"No, thanks. I'm dizzy enough with the rotation and the snow."

"Club soda, then. And turn your back to the window. Or else watch the snow more closely—that might help. I remember my dad got me used to thunderstorms by treating them like a video game and making me tell him what I thought the lightning looked like."

"Sort of like searching out pictures in the clouds?"

"Exactly. See that little eddy right there? It resembles the governor on a bad hair day, don't you think?" She sobered. "I'm dreadfully sorry about the Contessa, Synnamon."

"Thanks for the note you sent."

"You were planning to go down for Christmas, weren't you?"

"Actually, I'd planned to be there about now. I didn't want to break bad news to her on the holiday." Synnamon glanced at her menu, more for the sake of a moment to reassert her self-control than because she needed to refresh her memory, and looked at the waiter. "I'll have the seafood salad, with house dressing."

"And I'll have the scampi with a double order of garlic toast." Morea smiled sweetly. "I'm spending the afternoon in conference with my opponent in a divorce case that is not likely to be as easily settled as yours. I figure he might be more willing to negotiate if it's the only way he can escape the garlic."

"Is that what they teach you in law school?"

"Oh, no. In law school I only learned which books to look things up in." Morea raised her glass of club soda. "I have a date for you, finally. Here's to your divorce, which will be final in the middle of February. On the fourteenth, to be precise."

Synnamon almost dropped her glass. "Valentine's Day? But that's—"

"Your wedding anniversary, I know. At least it's tidy," Morea pointed out. "You'll never have any trouble remembering the date of your freedom. And you can go to the Valentine's Have a Heart Ball as a single woman with an absolutely clear conscience."

"I doubt I'll be celebrating," Synnamon murmured.

Morea set her glass down. Her voice was suddenly serious. "Look, darling, if you have any doubts about whether this divorce is what you want—"

"Of course I don't have doubts. It's the only answer. This marriage was a big mistake for both of us."

"Well, you're probably half right."

"What does that mean?"

"Conner's come out of the whole thing rather well, hasn't he? You know, Synnamon, you don't have to give him the earth wrapped in gold tissue paper in order to get out of this marriage. If you want to fight to keep what's yours—"

"All I want is a clean, fair finish."

"That," Morea murmured, "is exactly what I'm talking about. Especially the *fair* part."

Synnamon ignored the comment. "It's not as if Conner doesn't have any right to Sherwood Cosmetics. My father made him president of the company and a full partner."

"Silas was an idiot. Besides, that doesn't mean you have to meekly hand over the rest."

"I'm not. I'll still have a good share of Sherwood when it's done, as well as the apartment and everything in it. Morea, whose side are you on, anyway?"

"Yours, darling—and the little oath I swore when I passed the bar was to give you, my client, my very best advice."

"Consider it done, all right? My mind's made up."

The waiter brought their food. Synnamon picked up her fork, but somehow the salad—as delightful as it had sounded—wasn't inviting any more. The scallops piled atop the bed of lettuce seemed to quiver with the motion of the restaurant. They almost looked alive, Synnamon thought.

Morea crunched a crisp bit of garlic toast with evident delight. "I can't wait to see Ridge Coltrain's face when he gets a load of this," she murmured. "Best garlic toast in the world. So, if we're finished talking about the divorce, what are we to discuss? Oh, I know—what are you doing for Christmas? If you're not going to Phoenix, why not come and celebrate with us?"

"I didn't say I wasn't going to Phoenix," Synnamon said.

Morea frowned. "You didn't? I'd have sworn...."

Synnamon relented. "Actually, I'm not. But I've already made plans for Christmas Day."

The fact that her plans included staying quietly at home alone, sleeping late and watching old movies was really none of Morea's business. As the Contessa would have said, as long as one didn't actually lie, there was no need to tell the entire truth on every occasion. And in a case like this, Synnamon would much rather be alone than at the fringes of Morea's crowd, where everyone seemed to be half of a twosome.

"With somebody interesting, I hope? Maybe it's a good thing after all that you and Conner are being so decent about the whole thing. If one of you wanted to make a fuss about who the other one's seeing, it could get rather unpleasant."

"Why? Who's Conner seeing?" The words were out before Synnamon could stop herself.

Morea wagged a gentle index finger at her.

"Not that I care, you understand," Synnamon said.

"Of course not. In any case, how should I know? I hear things now and then, but I haven't seen Conner since the night we all had dinner together and you practically shoved money at him. Not that I'm trying to reargue the case now," Morea added hastily. "It's just been a long time since I've had a client who was more interested in giving property away than in keeping it."

"Morea—"

"Bear with me, darling. In another eight weeks the divorce will be final, and I promise I'll shut up about it forever after. But in the meantime, just in case you change your mind, I want you to know where I stand. Just don't wait too long, all right?" She stabbed a shrimp. "Now then. If you won't come for turkey, how about later? A bunch of us are going up to Telluride the week after Christmas. If you don't feel like skiing, you can always sit in the whirlpool and flirt with all the hunks who get hurt on the slopes."

"Thanks, but that's the last week I'll be working, so I think I'd better stick around the office. Conner still hasn't hired anybody to take over my job, so—"

"Does he run the rest of the business with the same degree of foresight and care? No wonder Silas thought he was perfect."

Synnamon couldn't help but bristle a bit. "Don't be sarcastic, Morea. It's not Conner's fault the job hasn't been filled."

"I'm charmed to hear you defending him."

"He turned the interviews and the decision over to me, and I haven't found anybody who's really qualified." She pushed her salad away. "In fact, I have an appointment to talk to him this afternoon about that."

"Are you sure you want to give up your job?" Morea asked idly.

"Oh, yes. I've been in customer relations since I joined Sherwood three years ago, and I'm a little tired of it."

"No doubt. Who wouldn't be, dealing with complaints all day? What I really meant was that perhaps you just want a change. You should have had the top job, you know, instead of Conner."

"Me? Why?"

"Well, you *are* the only remaining Sherwood."

"You think that mattered to my father? He never thought I could do anything." Synnamon regretted letting the bitter tone ooze into her voice, and she masked it as quickly as she could. "That's partly why I didn't mind giving so much of my share of the company to Conner. If he's going to have all the responsibility—"

"I still think it was foolish of you. Conner's got a majority interest in a very profitable cosmetics firm. And you've got—"

"A nice guaranteed income, without working another day in my life."

"So what are you going to do instead?"

"I'm not sure. Maybe I'll grow poinsettias."

Morea sighed. "Well, at least make it pink ones, darling. Red's the wrong color for you. Or won't you take my advice on that, either?"

At one minute to three, Synnamon took a seat in the waiting room outside Conner's office. "It's going to be a while," Carol warned. "He's pretty thoroughly tied up."

"I'll wait." Synnamon opened her portfolio and started through the stack of applications again.

It was a full twenty minutes before the office door opened and the head of the research and development division came out, stopped to shake Conner's hand, nodded to Synnamon and went off down the hall.

Conner leaned against the doorjamb and sighed. Then he said, "Sorry I'm running late, Synnamon. Come on in. Carol, I could use a cup of coffee, after that."

Synnamon pushed the applications into her portfolio. "Problems with research and development?"

"You might say." He closed the office door behind her and gestured toward the couch in the corner. "Anderson just announced his intention of retiring at the end of the year."

"You mean this year? That's a bit abrupt—it's only two weeks off." Taking a seat on the couch could be interpreted as issuing an invitation. Synnamon chose the love seat instead. She sat in the precise center and put her portfolio on the low glass table.

"It does add a little extra spice to the holidays, having to decide who gets the job. Oh, well, I wasn't planning to go anywhere for Christmas, anyway."

"I suppose you'll be promoting one of the senior people?"

"They're all well-qualified."

"I know."

Conner settled onto the end of the couch and stretched one arm across the back. "But you sound a bit doubtful."

"Not really. It's just that some of those people have been with the company for twenty years—almost as long as Anderson has. Perhaps some new blood would be a good idea."

Conner frowned, but just as he started to answer, Carol knocked and wheeled in a small cart. By the time she'd poured the coffee and gone out, Synnamon had thought better of the impulse to express her opinion. In two more weeks, she, too, would be leaving Sherwood Cosmetics. After that she'd be no more than a silent partner, so she'd better get used to keeping her ideas to herself.

Not that it would be a difficult change, she thought. Silas Sherwood had certainly never solicited her opinion. In fact, the main difference between Conner and her father was that Silas wouldn't have bothered to listen before doing exactly as he pleased.

She stirred sugar into her coffee and leaned forward to open her portfolio. "But of course you're the boss. As you requested, I've brought a list of the best applicants for my job." She frowned at the neatly typed page atop the stack of applications. "The trouble is, none of them are all that good. The top candidate was so busy assuring me of his qualifications that he never let me tell him about the job. I suspect he'd be like that with our clients, too, not even listening to their needs."

"Not the kind of customer service we want to provide," Conner agreed. "I see your point. What do you want to do? Run the ad again?"

"No." Synnamon took a deep breath. "You may think this is shortsighted—"

Conner shook his head. "No—Anderson giving me two weeks' notice is shortsighted. Knowing you, Synnamon, I can't imagine you'd make a proposition without having figured out every possible consequence."

She wasn't quite sure if she'd been complimented or insulted, but she decided not to test the question. "I want to hire Annie."

Conner's eyebrows flew up. "Your secretary?"

The incredulity in his voice reminded her painfully of Silas, and she had to fight the urge to duck her head and apologize for having wasted his time. "She's already half-trained for the job," she pointed out.

"That's quite a promotion, don't you think?"

"Yes, and I think she could handle it beautifully. But of course the decision is yours."

He leaned back against the cushions, long fingers stroking the strong line of his jaw, watching her thoughtfully.

Synnamon waited patiently for rejection, wondering what reason—if any—he would give. Why had she even bothered? Secretaries didn't get promoted to department head status in one leap.

Abruptly Conner rose, walked across the room to his desk and keyed the intercom. "Carol, ask Mrs. Welles's secretary to come to my office immediately."

Synnamon blinked in surprise. "You mean—"

"Let's wait till Annie gets here, shall we?"

Chastened, Synnamon sipped her coffee. The silence lengthened uncomfortably, and finally she said, "Morea told me the divorce will be final in about eight weeks."

Conner looked thoughtful. "Valentine's Day," he said.

It hadn't taken him long to calculate that. Synnamon wondered if Morea was right and he was seeing someone already.

I don't care if he is, she told herself. *It's curiosity, that's all*.

There was a tentative tap on the door and Annie came in. She looked, Synnamon thought, like a kid who'd been summoned to the principal's office and didn't have the slightest idea why. "You wanted to see me, Mr. Welles?"

"Have a seat, Annie. How do you like your coffee?"

Annie perched on the edge of the love seat next to Synnamon. "Just black, thanks."

He handed her a cup and saucer. It rattled a little as she took it, and she didn't even pretend to drink.

Conner settled back on the couch. "Mrs. Welles has found the person she feels is just right to take over her job."

"Yes, sir?"

"You."

The saucer tipped alarmingly. "I— Me, sir?" Annie cleared her throat. "Sir, I know I should jump at the chance. But I'm not sure—"

"Exactly," Conner said. "I'm not sure, either. Annie, I have a proposition for you, if Mrs. Welles will go along with it."

Warning bells went off in Synnamon's head, but before she could argue, he'd gone on. He wasn't even looking at her, but directly at Annie.

"I'm offering you the job as head of customer relations on a trial basis for a ninety-day period. During that time, Mrs. Welles will make herself available to you for advice and consultation."

Synnamon gave him a stony stare.

"At the end of the trial period," Conner went on, "the three of us will sit down again and decide if the plan is working. If it is, we'll make the promotion permanent."

And if not, Synnamon thought, *it's quite apparent whose neck will be on the line.*

"Is that agreeable to you both?" Conner asked.

Synnamon nodded curtly. She could hardly disagree, since it had been her idea. Though what could he do to her, after all, if Annie failed? And Annie wouldn't fail.

Conner said, "Then let's shake hands on it." He extended a hand to Annie, and then to Synnamon.

There was no way to politely refuse, though she wanted to. She hadn't touched him since that night in Phoenix when she'd thrown herself at him with such embarrassing abandon. On the flight to Denver they hadn't even sat together. The plane had been almost full—but she'd wondered at the time if he'd arranged the separate seats on purpose.

His hand was firm and warm, the palm as smooth against hers as it had been against her breast that night almost four weeks ago—

And that is enough of that, she told herself. The sooner that night was entirely forgotten, the better.

She stood up. "If that's all, Conner, Annie and I have a lot of work to do."

He smiled. "No particular hurry. You have ninety days, Synnamon, so surely you can take a minute to finish your coffee."

Christmas had a habit of never going quite as one expected, Synnamon thought. She was alone, just as she'd planned. The telephone was quiet, as she'd planned. Her nontraditional holiday feast was spread out on the glass-topped dining room table, as she'd planned—caviar and pâté and quails' eggs carefully arranged on a picture-perfect plate.

But the only thing that looked good was the toast points.

"Isn't it just my luck," she said, "to have to share Christmas dinner with a virus?"

She munched a bit of toast and stared at the only ornament in the apartment, a big glass ball Annie had painted to look like carved marble. It looked terribly lonely, perched on an antique salt cellar in the middle of the dining room table.

"I know you're not much in the mood to celebrate this year," the secretary had said when she'd brought it into Synnamon's office last week. "But I wanted you to have a reminder that I'll be thinking about you. And if you change your mind and want to come over, just call."

It was a good thing she hadn't, though, Synnamon thought. Annie had two small children, and she wouldn't want to give this virus to them. It was funny, though, how this thing seemed to come and go. She could be exhausted and miserably nauseated—and half an hour later feel energetic enough to go dancing.

She picked up the marbleized ornament and cradled it in her hand. This would certainly be a Christmas to remember—despite her best efforts to make it completely forgettable.

"And that's quite enough feeling sorry for yourself," she said firmly. "It was your decision to be alone, after all."

And not just for today, either, but altogether. She didn't doubt that if she hadn't asked for her freedom, things would be going along now just as they had for the first six months she and Conner had been married. All very pleasant and decent, but...lacking. The trouble was, she didn't quite know what was missing.

The holidays had never been the season of shimmering happiness for Synnamon that they seemed to be for other people. Last Christmas, with a brand-new diamond solitaire sparkling on her ring finger, she'd had hopes of feeling that incredible joy.

But the day had turned out much the same as every other holiday she could remember. She and Conner had had dinner with Silas. The men had talked business till she'd wanted to scream, and when she'd excused herself to retreat to the kitchen, they hadn't even seemed to notice. But Silas's housekeeper, horrified at her request for something to do, had shooed her back to the living room. Silas had eventually remembered it was Christmas and handed her the usual envelope with the usual sizeable check....

No, she couldn't regret not having a repetition of that. The trouble was, she wasn't so sure what she wanted instead.

Today, with Silas gone, she and Conner would probably have gone to one of the country clubs for the luncheon buffet. A holiday dinner just for them was too much trouble, and Mrs. Ogden wanted the holiday with her own family, anyway, instead of with her employers.

But next year, Synnamon thought, she'd put up a tree no matter what. She might even cook a turkey—who cared if it was just for herself? At least, she'd make a stab at having a normal Christmas, the kind Annie and other people talked about.

Her stomach protested the idea of food, and she had to swallow hard to keep it in place. Hoping to distract herself, she wandered through the big living room and down the hall, as if she was seeing the apartment for the first time.

The apartment was too big for one person. It had been large even for the two of them. But then she'd expected that someday there'd be a child.

Synnamon had chosen the apartment, but it had been Silas's wedding gift, and she'd had as much fun decorating and furnishing as if she'd been outfitting a full-size dollhouse. She hadn't realized till later that Conner hadn't seemed especially interested in any of it.

She opened the door to his den for the first time in weeks. It was still as perfect as the day she'd put the final touches in place. It smelled like leather and—despite Mrs. Ogden's constant cleaning—just a little like stale dust. He'd never really used it. He'd never even seemed to live here. Last fall, when he'd moved out, he'd taken only his clothes. Nothing else had changed.

It was as if he'd been only a visitor in her home, in her life.

That might have hurt, if she'd ever been foolish enough to believe that Conner had fallen in love with her. But he was too much like her father for that. She'd found that chemists were something like engineers—level-headed and logical, wanting everything to have a sensible explanation.

No, Conner's behavior had never been that of a young man in love. But then she'd never expected it to be. She'd always been aware that any man would find himself at least as attracted to Sherwood Cosmetics as he was to Synnamon herself. If she'd needed any further evidence of that, she'd have found it in Silas's reaction to the news of her engagement. He'd been delighted, excited beyond anything he'd ever expressed before—at least where Synnamon was concerned. And before the week was out he'd announced that Conner would be his successor as president of the company.

Their marriage might have been a chilly sort of bargain, but Synnamon had seen no reason they couldn't make it work. Even the Contessa had told her, through the years, that love was greatly overrated, that there was a lot more to a successful marriage than a heady rush of emotion. "A level head will carry a match much farther than a case of hormones can," she'd said.

And they certainly both could gain from this alliance. Through Synnamon, Conner would get Sherwood Cosmetics—signed, sealed and delivered. Through Conner, Synnamon would gain independence and perhaps even some value in Silas Sherwood's eyes. She wouldn't simply be his awkward daughter anymore.

It had started out all right, she supposed, and if it hadn't been for Silas's death, they might have rubbed along reasonably well together for years. Lots of married couples didn't have a great deal to say to each other. Her parents had certainly never talked much, so why should she and Conner be different?

They didn't fight, and they weren't incompatible in bed. She might not even have noticed how rarely Conner came to her room. They weren't living in a soap opera, after all—they were ordinary people.

But when Silas died, everything slowly began to come clear. It seemed to Synnamon that she'd been living in a frosted bubble for more years than she could count, but on the day of her father's funeral the fog had begun to dissipate. And she didn't like what she saw.

Things had come to a head a few weeks later, when Conner had come home one night and suggested that perhaps they should take a week off and get away, since people were starting to comment about how tired they both looked.

"No, thanks. Who cares what people think?" Synnamon had looked straight at him and added calmly, "We don't have to pretend any more, you know. In fact, I've been thinking that it would be best for both of us if we called a halt to this farce. You have what you wanted, Conner, and you don't need to worry about losing Sherwood. You're welcome to it. All I want is peace and quiet."

He had said, finally, that perhaps she was right, and he'd moved out the next day.

It had been the best thing for both of them, Synnamon knew. It was at least the honest thing. That was what she'd planned to tell the Contessa.

And as for her hopes of a family... Well, she'd survive without a child. Perhaps she'd adopt someday, or perhaps...

Suddenly there was a brassy taste in her mouth. Synnamon looked at the wreckage of her thumbnail. She'd unconsciously chewed off all the polish.

She wished she could convince herself that accounted for the chemical flavor on her tongue, but she knew better. That nasty taste had an entirely different source. Its origin wasn't oral at all, but mental—born of shock.

Now everything suddenly made sense. Her lack of appetite, the way the Pinnacle's motion had affected her, the virus that came and went, the sudden unbearable tiredness.

She'd have to go to work early in the morning and stop in the employees' shop for a quick manicure and a set of replacement nails. That way only the manicurist would suspect how nervous Synnamon was—and even she would have no way to know the reason behind that uneasiness.

But even before that, she'd have to run another errand. She'd stop by the nearest pharmacy for one of those home-testing kits. And as soon as she was alone, she'd find out for certain whether she was pregnant.

CHAPTER THREE

AND if she was...

It wouldn't change anything, Synnamon reminded herself. She was perfectly capable of raising a child. She had the financial resources, and now, with her job almost finished, she would have all the time in the world. She could take on the responsibility of a baby. *All* the responsibility of a baby.

She might as well be talking about the weight of the universe.

But there was a good chance she was only imagining things, she told herself firmly. It wasn't as if she had any real knowledge of what morning sickness felt like. And wasn't every woman different, anyway? Maybe her upset stomach was only a combination of a kooky virus and a mind made suggestible by a bad case of loneliness.

And the suspicion that she might be pregnant wasn't exactly a logical one, either. She and Conner had lived together for eight months, so perhaps it was foolish to think that on one single, desperate night they might have created a new life.

It wasn't impossible, of course—but it was improbable. Incredible. So unlikely that she was certainly not going to drive herself crazy by worrying about it.

But she wished it wasn't Christmas, and that she didn't have to wait till tomorrow for a pharmacy to open, so she could know for sure.

* * *

Synnamon's newly manicured hands shook as she locked herself into the half-bath off her office and ripped open the home-testing kit. The instructions seemed a mile long, and she had trouble concentrating. But eventually she had followed all the directions, and she held her breath as she waited for the results.

She was quite certain what she wanted the answer to be, she told herself. The last thing she needed to complicate her life right now was a child. And yet...

The test strip slowly, inexorably, turned pink.

She stared at it, stunned by the evidence that she would not be spending next Christmas alone after all—for by then her baby would be four months old.

She bit her lip hard and sat down on the tiled counter next to the sink, still holding the test strip. What a tiny thing it was to change a life!

Two lives—hers, and that of the child she carried.

Panic threatened to overwhelm her. It was one thing to consider solitary child-raising in the abstract, but it was a bit different to contemplate a real-life, breathing, screaming baby.

Annie tapped on the bathroom door. "Mrs. Welles? Are you all right?"

Synnamon had to swallow hard before she could answer. "I'm fine, Annie. Be right out."

Her hands were still shaking as she hurriedly gathered up all the paraphernalia and dumped it into the Tyler-Royale shopping bag in which she'd smuggled the kit into the building. She shoved the bag into the cabinet under the sink and said, as she came out, "I've got just a little upset stomach—I think I celebrated a bit too much yesterday."

Only then did she see who else was waiting for her. Conner was leaning against her desk with his arms folded across his chest, the long fingers of his left hand drumming gently against the sleeve of his deep charcoal suit.

"Mr. Welles is here," Annie said unnecessarily.

Conner, Synnamon thought desperately. How on earth was she going to break the news to Conner that in a well-meaning act of consolation he'd fathered her child?

What, she thought half-hysterically, would the Contessa advise? No matter how thorny the situation, the queen of etiquette had always had an answer. But what would she say about this tangle?

"Sorry to rush in on you," Conner said briskly, "especially at this hour of the morning. But I'm on my way to Fargo because there's been a contamination in one of the production lines at the plant up there."

"Contamination? What—"

"Nobody knows yet how it happened. I just wanted to let you know that you're apt to be getting some questions from customers when the rumors start to fly. As soon as I know what's going on I'll give you a call, and you can put out a statement. But in the meantime if you can just try to keep a lid on the speculation..."

Synnamon nodded, and her heartbeat steadied a little. "I'll take care of it, Conner."

"Of course you will." There was obviously no doubt in his mind. Synnamon supposed she should consider it a compliment.

Conner turned toward the door and then swung back abruptly to face her. "Are you all right, Synnamon? Really?"

Half of her wanted to blurt out her news right there and have it over and done with. But with Annie in the room, and Conner obviously anxious to be gone, it would hardly be fair to drop a bombshell like that.

Besides, she wanted a little time herself to come to terms with this complication before she let the rest of the world in on it. She *needed* a little time. Surely it wasn't cowardly to want to think it over first?

"I'm fine," she said steadily.

Conner's smile didn't quite reach his eyes, Synnamon noticed. But then she suspected hers didn't, either.

"And pigs fly, too." He nodded toward her hands. "Biting your thumb now and then is one thing, but when you're wearing a full set of fake nails, Synnamon, it's a dead giveaway."

She raised one hand and stared at the offending fingertips. The acrylic nails looked just fine to her—perfectly natural and elegantly shaped. She'd have said this new product was by far the best adhesive nails Sherwood had ever produced. They were even lightweight and comfortable. But if Conner could tell at a glance...

She said wryly, "Maybe the real question you should be asking is how to improve the nails so they don't look fake."

"Oh, they wouldn't to most people," Conner assured her. "I'm just particularly attuned."

To the nails? Synnamon thought in sudden panic. *Or to me*?

"Don't forget I supervised the last research trials on that brand," he went on. "I'd recognize them a mile away."

She started to breathe again.

"If the problem is that you're already missing your job, Synnamon, I'm sure we can work something out."

"I'll certainly keep that in mind," she said dryly. "Don't let me make you miss your plane."

After he was gone, Annie said, "I'll start working up a standard answer for any questions, if you'd like."

Synnamon nodded. "Good idea."

Annie's voice was hesitant. "Mr. Welles is right, you know. If you should change your mind and decide to stay—well, I just want you to know I completely understand."

"Don't worry about it. It's not going to happen." Synnamon swallowed hard and sat in the overstuffed chair next to her desk. "In fact, you may be handling the job even earlier than you expected, Annie. I don't think I'm fine, after all."

She didn't want to tell him.

There's no reason to, a little voice at the back of her brain argued. It wasn't as if this incident would make a difference in the course of Conner's life. The responsibility was entirely hers. She was the one who'd invited this disaster, and she was the one who would have to deal with the consequences.

The divorce might not be quite final, but the marriage was long over—and that meant the days of expecting loyalty whether in sickness or in health were already past.

If she'd walked out in front of a truck and been injured, she wouldn't expect Conner to come running to her assistance. Well, this accident wasn't his fault, either, so why make a point of bringing him into it?

Because it's different, she told herself wearily. She couldn't keep a pregnancy hidden forever.

Or could she? If she finished her work and announced that she was moving away...

There was nothing keeping her in Denver. It was quite logical, with all the stress and changes in her life this year, that she'd want to start over somewhere else. She could sell the apartment and go to live in Phoenix for a while—in the Contessa's town house—while she made up her mind.

Except for one minor detail, she recalled. She'd promised to give Annie ninety days of support and training, and she could hardly do that over the telephone.

No, she'd have to tell Conner. It was only fair to do so, anyway. She'd simply have to be careful how she did it, to make it clear that she didn't expect anything from him.

Annie tapped on her office door. "Mr. Welles is on the phone. Are you enough better to talk to him?"

"Of course." Synnamon glanced at her watch. Conner had been in Fargo for just a few hours. She pushed the damp washcloth off her forehead and sat up straight. After spending most of the day in the chair, she was a bit light-headed.

Annie looked concerned. "Shall I bring another cool cloth?"

Synnamon stood and had to reach for the corner of her desk to steady herself. "Not just now." She took a deep breath and reached for the telephone. "Conner?"

"There's good news and bad news," he said. "The contamination is bacterial."

And therefore it would be particularly nasty to combat, Synnamon deduced.

"But we think we've already found the source, and if that's confirmed, we can steam-clean the whole production line and start it up again. By the end of the week everything could be back to normal."

She was jotting notes. "And there's enough product in the warehouses to take care of demand in the meantime, right?"

"Yes—except we'll have to test every batch in order to be certain the contamination didn't sneak in earlier than we think."

"All right. I'll tell everyone that there may be minor delays in shipment because we're taking no chances with customer safety."

"That's good. I'm going to stay here till it's all cleaned up, just to be certain."

"That will look reassuring to some of our customers and suspicious to the rest, Conner."

He laughed. "Use your best judgment on who to tell."

Synnamon was startled by the genuine amusement in his voice. She hadn't realized how long it had been since she'd heard anything of the sort.

He sobered. "Are you feeling better?"

"Some. Conner—"

The word was out before she could stop herself, but immediately Synnamon thought better of it. To tell him like this, when he was two states away, would truly be the coward's way out. Not that she was looking forward to telling him face-to-face, either—but she needed to be able to see him when he heard the news. Only then could she judge his reaction and respond appropriately, by re-assuring him that she didn't blame him at all and that she didn't expect him to be bound by this mistake.

"I'm fine," she said. "I think I just got some bad pâté at the deli. But everything's smooth here."

She put down the telephone and dropped her face into her hands. Phoenix and the Contessa's town house looked more inviting than ever.

With the mess in Fargo finally under control, Conner was due back in Denver in the afternoon of New Year's Eve.

Synnamon couldn't make up her mind whether she wanted him to come to the office or stay away till after the holiday. She was pleased to have the production problem solved, of course. She'd spent most of the week on the telephone, soothing nervous corporate accounts. But the closer she came to the time when she would have to confess her secret to Conner, the more jittery she grew.

At least physically she was feeling better. The morning sickness still came and went, but at least—unlike the day after Christmas—it no longer persisted around the clock or kept her from working.

The weather on the final day of December was almost as gloomy as Synnamon felt. The sky was so heavy and dark it was hard to tell where the clouds ended and the mountains began. If she was lucky, she thought, the predicted snow would materialize and the airport would close, stranding Conner in Fargo for the holiday.

As each hour ticked by and she did a few more things for the last time, Synnamon's sadness grew. From now on, when she spent time in the office it would be as Annie's assistant and adviser. This would no longer be her private retreat.

She had spent three full years within the four walls of this room—at least the most meaningful part of each day had found her there—and it wasn't going to be easy to give it up.

She'd had to fight for the opportunity to make a place for herself at Sherwood. It would have been far easier to go to work somewhere else, but deep inside, Synnamon had known that only if she could prove herself at Sherwood Cosmetics—in the family business—would she really believe in her own worth. And if along the way she could prove a thing or two to her father—well, that would be the icing on the gingerbread.

That was why, on the day after she'd graduated from college, she'd appeared in the waiting room outside her father's office, determined to sit there until Silas gave her a chance. Eventually, he'd grown tired of her persistence, and he'd assigned her a job.

Customer service wouldn't have been Synnamon's first choice, for she felt that her talent lay in juggling numbers, not people. But she'd been in no position to quibble. In fact, Synnamon had always thought Silas had sent her to customer service because he believed she'd soon be so discouraged and stressed by handling questions and complaints that she'd quit altogether. But then, Silas Sherwood had never known his daughter very well.

The first year had been especially tough, as she felt her way like a blind man through a mine field. Many of Sherwood's clients had been reluctant to deal with her, convinced she was a dilettante daughter with a manufactured job. She'd worked ferociously to develop relationships with the clients, to carve out enough authority so she could actually handle their problems, to figure out when to be sympathetic and when to be assertive.

Assertiveness still didn't come naturally to her. The difficulty of her own struggle was one of the reasons she'd agreed to help Annie with her adjustment. If there was one thing Synnamon fully understood, it was the feeling of being inadequate for the job.

Perhaps that was why, with Silas gone, the whole thing no longer seemed to matter. Though she felt sadness at the idea of leaving Sherwood and fear of the great unknowns that awaited her after she left the only job she'd ever held, there was also relief. She'd made a success of a difficult assignment and she no longer had anything to prove.

Now she just had to pack up the trivia of her life.

Synnamon picked up the silver-framed photograph of her mother from the credenza behind her desk and looked thoughtfully at the young, beautiful face of Rita Sherwood. By the time Synnamon had been old enough to recognize her mother's beauty, it had been overlaid with a veneer of hardness. The bitter dregs of unhappiness had taken the lively glow out of Rita's eyes and thinned the sensual lips to the sharp line Synnamon remembered.

She understood now that Silas had been no happier than his wife. Theirs had been a marriage that would have been better dissolved, but Rita's religious beliefs had not allowed divorce. So they had stayed together—not through thick and thin, Synnamon had heard her mother tell a friend once in an acid moment, but through thin, thinner and thinnest.

Only now did Synnamon really understand what Rita had meant, and she thanked heaven that she and Conner had had the good sense to see what lay ahead and get out before the unhappiness marred them both for life, while they could still break up without battling. At least, she thought, they had the advantage of being civilized about it. They were splitting decently, without recriminations or resentment or hard feelings, without argument or sharp words or fights over bits of property. In short, theirs was the perfect divorce.

Synnamon wrapped the frame in tissue paper and reached for the small Russian lacquer box that had stood next to the photograph. There were a thousand of her possessions in the office. She'd be the rest of the day packing them all up. She hadn't realized how many of her personal things had crept into her work space—almost more, she thought, than her apartment held.

Annie punched the button that turned off the speakerphone on Synnamon's desk and swiveled her chair. "How did that sound?"

"You did just fine," Synnamon said, and tried to soothe her conscience. It was only a tiny white lie, after all, to imply that she'd been listening intently to every word of the conversation. It wasn't the end of the world to have let her mind wander. If Annie had stumbled, she'd have heard.

"Thanks. You don't know what that means to me— knowing that you're there to back me up. Don't worry about packing everything today. There will be plenty of time later."

"But as of Monday morning it will be your office. And you'll want your own things around."

"Actually, I think I'd find it more comforting to have some of yours for a while." Annie's smile was wry. "That way I can pretend I'm only using your office temporarily while Sandra borrows mine. Do you think she's going to work out?"

"She has potential," Synnamon said carefully. "But be careful to treat her as an employee, not a friend. Especially until you have a little more experience as a boss, it's better for everyone not to get the two things confused."

Annie sighed. "I know. There's so much to remember, and it's so easy to slip up."

"You'll get the hang of it. It just takes practice, and getting in the habit of thinking before you start talking." Synnamon looked around. "I thought I had another box somewhere."

"No—that was the last of them. There's a shopping bag in the bathroom, though. I just noticed it this morning." Annie bounced out of her chair and went after it.

Synnamon's eyes widened in shock. How could she have forgotten to dispose of that damned bag and its telltale contents? But she knew how it had happened. Between juggling phone calls all week and feeling ill at the least convenient moments, she'd put the test kit out of her mind. Besides, she admitted, she'd *wanted* to forget the whole thing—to pretend that it wasn't real.

Annie was back in a moment, brandishing Synnamon's Tyler-Royale bag. "I thought it was empty, but there's something—" She dumped the bag's contents onto the desk blotter.

Synnamon knew the instant the brand name emblazoned on the box registered in Annie's mind. The woman had two small children herself. There was no doubt she'd recognize a kit for a home pregnancy test when she saw one.

"Oh, my," Annie murmured. "I had no idea."

Synnamon braced herself. Would the reaction be delight? Congratulations? Shock? And did this mean she'd better rush to tell Conner, before the grapevine got hold of the news? She didn't question Annie's discretion—but if Annie had spotted that bag, the janitorial staff might have, too.

Annie's face was absolutely expressionless. She didn't even look at Synnamon. "I noticed when I came back from lunch," she said, "that Mr. Welles is in the building now."

She sounded as calm, Synnamon thought, as if she was really changing the subject. Which of course they both knew she wasn't...not really.

Synnamon's heart was thumping. She hadn't expected him back quite this early.

Of course, she didn't have to rush down to his office right this minute. She could wait till next week to tell him, and at least keep Sherwood Cosmetics out of it.

Right, she told herself dryly. *It'll make everything so much easier if I just phone him up on Monday and ask him to lunch. And over the hors d'oeuvres I'll just casually mention that we're having a baby!*

"If you can take care of the rest of those calls," Synnamon said, sounding much calmer than she felt, "I'll go and check in with Mr. Welles."

There would never be a good time to tell him, she reminded herself as she walked down the hall. She'd have to be careful how she handled it, of course—but no matter what his reaction, at least that much of the difficulty would be behind her.

But Conner couldn't see her. "He's tied up," Carol said, "and I don't even have a good idea when he'll be free. I'll call your office, if you like, as soon as he can fit you in." She must have seen the strain in Synnamon's face, for she added gently, "I'm sorry."

"That's fine," Synnamon said. "I'll catch him later."

She supposed she should have expected it. After a week away, Conner's in-basket was probably brimming with problems to handle and calls to return. That was exactly the reason she'd made the rule for herself to always phone for an appointment before going to his office. It was a rule she had broken today without even remembering it.

She had worked up her nerve for nothing, and now she felt as if there was a rock lodged in her throat—a dry, crumbly, dusty piece of limestone that was likely to stay there until the deed was done.

She didn't want to face Annie just yet, so she wandered down to the staff dining room, got a bottle of orange juice and sat down to drink it. A caterer's crew was working in the kitchen, putting the final touches on the office New Year's party. The bustle made her nervous, and with the half-full bottle in her hand she started toward her office.

As she passed the executive suite, the door of Conner's office swung open, and she caught just a glimpse of him. She knew he couldn't see her, standing in the hallway outside the waiting room, but the rock in her throat suddenly felt even larger. He seemed taller—or was it just her fear of facing him that made him seem more imposing?

She heard him laugh, and then she saw the redhead who was standing beside him with her hand placed confidingly on the sleeve of his jacket. The rock suddenly grew into a boulder, almost choking off her air supply.

"I'll talk to you later, Nick," he said. "Think it over, and let me know."

Nick. The name seemed to echo in Synnamon's head, but why should it sound familiar?

Finally she recalled his telephone conversation on the day she'd gone to tell him about the Contessa. Hadn't he been talking to a Nick that day? It had been a business conversation, Synnamon was sure, and she'd assumed it was a man he was talking to—but it might have been this woman instead. She could be a supplier, a customer, an ad agency representative... any number of things.

What was it Morea had said about Conner seeing someone? That she'd heard things, that was it. *Maybe,* Synnamon thought, *I should have asked her exactly what it was she'd heard.*

On the other hand, she reminded herself, there was no point in acting like an idiot. It wasn't as if she had any rights where Conner was concerned, or even any real interest.

But she couldn't help noticing that he looked more alive, somehow, right now—with the redhead's hand on his sleeve—than Synnamon remembered seeing him in months.

Before she could move, he'd closed the office door once more, and the redhead came across the waiting room. As if she had radar, her gaze focused on Synnamon.

Almost as if she recognizes me, Synnamon thought. It made sense, of course, that a woman who was interested in Conner would have an idea of what his wife looked like and be curious about her. Conner might even have described her.

Now there's a comforting thought, she told herself wryly.

She gave the redhead a cool, polite nod—the same as she would to any stranger she met in the halls—and went to her office.

The shopping bag had disappeared, but Annie had come up with another box and was carefully packing the things Synnamon had already wrapped in tissue. "Carol called just a minute ago," she said, "to say Mr. Welles was free now. But I didn't know where you were, so—"

"It doesn't matter, Annie." Synnamon's lips felt stiff. "It's not important any more. In fact, I think I'll just go on home, since there's really nothing left for me to do here."

Annie sounded shocked. "And miss the party? But—"

"I'm not much in the mood for a party." Synnamon forced herself to smile. "I wouldn't want to keep everyone else from having fun by being a grump."

"But you can't! I mean, you're never a grump, and besides..." Annie drew a deep breath. "Carol will kill me for telling you this, I suppose. But you see, Mrs. Welles, it's not just a New Year's Eve celebration, it's going to be a farewell party for you."

Synnamon's heart sank. It was one thing to skip an ordinary office party, something else to miss one given in her honor. The questions her absence would raise didn't bear thinking about. She was stuck.

"That's very thoughtful," she managed to say. The Contessa, she thought, would have been proud of how calm she sounded.

She stayed in her office as long as she conscientiously could, and by the time she arrived the party was already in full swing. Synnamon asked the bartender for ginger ale in a champagne flute, and she was just turning away from the bar when Conner—with the redhead beside him—came up and asked for two Scotches with water.

How cozy, Synnamon thought, that they liked the same drink. But what in heaven's name was the redhead doing there in the first place? She had to bite her tongue to keep from asking Conner just when he'd decided to open Sherwood parties to dates as well as employees.

"Synnamon," he said, "I'd like you to meet Nicole Fox. Nick helped sort out the problems in Fargo."

Fargo, Synnamon thought woodenly. Conner had sounded happy when he was in Fargo. She remembered thinking that she hadn't heard that note in his voice in months. Was this woman the reason?

"Is that where you're from, Nicole?" she asked, politely holding out a hand.

"No, I'm based here in Denver." Nicole's handshake was warm and firm. "Conner and I are old friends." She smiled at him.

A meaningful smile, Synnamon thought. One that contained all sorts of hidden messages.

"When he called to ask my opinion of the contamination, I happened to be free," Nicole went on, without taking her eyes off Conner's face. "So I flew up."

"Nick was a tremendous help." Conner handed Nicole her cocktail glass and raised his own in a casual salute. "In fact, I've offered her the position as head of research and development."

Synnamon was stunned.

Think it over and let me know, Conner had told the woman at his office door just a couple of hours ago. Obviously this was what they'd been discussing.

She told herself it could be worse. She just didn't quite, at the moment, see how.

She swallowed hard and made some feeble comment. Conner's eyebrows went up, but before he could comment Annie called Synnamon over to present a gift from all the employees.

It's none of your business who he hires, she tried to tell herself as the party wore on. But the truth was that, however much she'd like to deny it, she was still involved. Even though she was no longer formally employed by Sherwood Cosmetics, she was still a stockholder, and she would always feel a responsibility to her father's employees. And this, she knew in her heart, was a very bad decision for everyone.

She couldn't square it with her conscience not to bring her objections to Conner's attention before it was too late for him to change his mind. Whether it would do any good was another question entirely, but she had to try.

But by the time she was free, Conner was nowhere to be found. She sought out Carol, who said, "I wouldn't be surprised if he was going to do a little more work. You might try his office."

The wing of the building that held the executive offices was hushed and only dimly lighted. Synnamon hesitated outside Conner's closed door. What if he wasn't alone? She hadn't seen Nicole at the party in the last half hour, either, and if they'd retreated to his office together...

Until this moment, Synnamon had almost forgotten the rumor that one of the couches in Silas's office unfolded into a bed. She'd heard the whispers in her first months at Sherwood, but the talk had always been quickly suppressed when she appeared, and she'd never known if there was any truth to the story. She wouldn't have been surprised to know of a mistress—in fact, she'd have been far more amazed if Silas had continued to be faithful to his marriage vows through the long and miserable years. But somehow a fold-out bed in his office didn't seem quite like Silas. A cozy little penthouse at the Brown Palace, on the other hand...

But if there *had* been a bed in the office, it was still there, since Conner hadn't changed the furniture. And the suite was awfully quiet.

Synnamon knocked, but there was no answer. Almost as an afterthought, she turned the knob and was surprised when the door opened. The office was dark, however, and obviously deserted.

She started to back out, but suddenly nausea overtook her and she rushed toward Conner's bathroom instead.

She was over the worst when the bathroom lights snapped on. She put up a hand in self-defense against the blinding glare, and Conner said, "Somebody should have warned you that punch Carol makes will get you every time."

"I didn't even try the punch."

"Oh, that's right. You were drinking champagne. To what do I owe this honor? It isn't even the closest bathroom."

Synnamon pulled herself to her feet, ignoring the hand he offered, and reminded herself that much as she'd like to take a swing at him it wouldn't get her anywhere. And telling him about the baby wouldn't be a great idea at the moment, either. She had a real and solid reason to have sought him out, and it would be foolish to let herself be distracted—no matter how annoying he was.

"I'm not trying to interfere, Conner, but..." She paused and patted a tissue across her temple. "Do you mind if I sit down?"

"Oh, please do." He led the way into the office and snapped on the lights. "Carol said you were anxious to talk to me this afternoon, but then you changed your mind. Have you changed it back again?"

Synnamon glanced from the couch to the love seat. Which one of them would be most likely to hold a mattress, tucked away from casual sight? *I don't care*, she reminded herself.

"Believe me," Conner said, "I'm delighted to know you don't intend to interfere. So what did you want to talk to me about?"

Synnamon smothered a sigh at the faint irony in his voice. "Nicole Fox. I don't think you should make her head of research and development." She sat on the love seat.

"Oh? It was your idea, after all." Conner perched on the arm of the couch.

"Mine?" Her voice was little more than a squeak.

"Yes. You're the one who suggested we bring in new blood, all that sort of thing."

"Well, I didn't suggest it be hers!"

Conner's eyebrows soared.

Oh, great, she thought. *Now I sound jealous*! "I don't have any idea what her qualifications are—"

"That's right. You don't."

"But it doesn't matter. Naming her—or any other woman—to that job would be a big mistake."

"I'm listening."

Synnamon took a deep breath. She had one chance, and she'd better make it good. "Putting a woman in charge of those right-wing men would be asking for disaster. I don't have anything against Nicole Fox, in particular—"

"I'll certainly keep that in mind, Synnamon."

"In other words," she said tartly, "you've already decided."

How long had he had this move in mind? Conner hadn't really said, when Anderson made his announcement last week, that he was going to offer the position to one of the current people. Had he planned even then to hire Nicole Fox?

"What else?" Conner asked.

Synnamon was taken aback. "What do you mean, what else?"

"What else is bothering you? You've obviously had something on your mind since this afternoon, and it can't have been Nick, because you didn't know about her till the party. And since you don't seem to be drunk after all . . ."

If she'd been feeling better, Synnamon might have kept her head. But she was far too irritated to think before she spoke. "Oh, it's nothing much," she snapped. "I'm just pregnant, that's all."

He drew in a short, harsh breath, and wary silence descended on the room. Synnamon could hear her own heartbeat throbbing unsteadily.

Instantly, she regretted letting her temper get the best of her. What had happened to her resolve to be decent, amicable, civilized—no matter what? Breaking the news to him so harshly was no way to get along.

"I'm sorry, Conner," she said quietly. "I had no idea that little encounter in Phoenix would end up in such a mess."

He was so still that she wondered for a moment if he'd even heard her.

"It's nothing for you to worry about," she offered finally. "I'll deal with it."

"You'll *deal* with it how? An abortion?" He sounded perfectly calm, as if—once the moment of shock had passed—he'd had no trouble at all reaching a decision.

Synnamon was stunned. Did he honestly think she was capable of destroying a life? Even though she didn't want this child any more than he did...

No, she realized, that wasn't quite the case. It was the pregnancy she didn't particularly want to deal with, and the complications it represented—complications like Conner's attitude. But as for the *child*...

Something she'd never felt before surged through her body—a combination of heat and emotion that threatened to engulf her. Was this, she wondered almost in awe, what it felt like to be a mother? This almost overpowering desire to protect—at any cost—the tiny helpless being inside her?

Thank heaven, she thought, it was really none of Conner's business what she did. She certainly didn't need to convince him, or even let herself be drawn into an argument about it.

"Well, it is the perfect answer, don't you think?" Synnamon said, with a calm that matched his own. She pushed herself to her feet. "Sorry if I've upset your evening, Conner—I probably shouldn't have bothered you with it at all." She managed a note of solicitousness. "You won't lie awake tonight worrying about it, will you?"

She didn't wait for an answer, though. She was out the door before he moved and home before she stopped shaking. She paced the floor in her living room, muttering, cursing him. How *dare* he accuse her of wanting to destroy a child?

Eventually, however, she calmed enough to see that however unflattering his attitude, there were certain advantages for her. Perhaps it was just as well Conner felt that way. There would be no question of him wanting to be involved, and her life would be a great deal simpler because of his detachment. She could bring up her child in peace, without having to deal with a reluctant, part-time second parent. There wouldn't be any quarrels over schools or methods of discipline, over visitation rights or child support, or even whether the kid should have hockey skates or dancing shoes. Yes, they would be better off this way, all three of them.

Eventually, she started to feel calmer, and after a while she even began to see things from Conner's point of view. Not about the abortion, of course—there was no understanding that. But she could appreciate his shock— heaven knew she'd felt that herself. She could comprehend the consternation he'd felt, the instant panic over what she might demand from him.

His reaction was partly her fault, anyway, Synnamon admitted. She could have broken the news a great deal more smoothly than she had. She could have reassured him, made it clear that she was telling him only out of a desire for fairness, not because she expected—or wanted—anything from him.

Instead, she'd dumped the facts on him like a load of gold bars. No wonder the man had been stunned. He might even have thought for a moment that she was going to suggest they resume their marriage.

In the silence of the apartment, the click of a key in the front door lock seemed to echo like a gunshot. Synnamon swung around and stared through the small foyer just as one of the double doors swung open.

Conner was standing there, his trench coat draped over his arm, pulling his key from the lock.

She hadn't thought to ask him to return his key. She hadn't even considered changing the locks after he'd moved out. She'd never felt physically unsafe with him, and it wasn't the sort of divorce where one of them would hide assets or make off with personal property in a desire for revenge.

"What are you doing here at this hour?" she managed.

One dark eyebrow tilted and he said evenly, "I couldn't make it any earlier, I'm afraid. I had a few things to finish up before I could leave."

"That's not what I—"

He closed the door with a firm little click. "I must say it's very thoughtful of you to have waited up, Synnamon, so we could take up our discussion where you so rudely broke it off."

CHAPTER FOUR

SYNNAMON had trouble finding her voice. "*I* was rude? And what, exactly, were you?" She realized that approach was likely to end in nothing but petty squabbling, so she took a deep breath and tried again. "I don't think we have anything at all to discuss. I'm sorry I bothered you with this, Conner. It's not your problem, after all—"

Conner shook his trench coat out with a snap and hung it in the hall closet. "It certainly sounds like a problem to me."

"It's a complication, yes. But it has nothing to do with you," Synnamon said stubbornly.

"Because you're going to end the pregnancy." It was not a question.

"And you're obviously worried about it. Why, Conner? Are you afraid I won't go through with it?" The tremor in her voice was a far cry from the bravado she was trying for. "Well, whether I do or not, it still isn't any of your concern." She raised her head proudly. "I lied, you know. I was trying to shake you up."

"You succeeded," he said dryly. "Are you going to tell me now that you're not pregnant after all?"

Synnamon wasn't listening. "This isn't your baby. It has nothing to do with what happened in Phoenix. I don't know why I told you that. Desperation, probably. But—"

He actually smiled, but there was no matching sparkle in his eyes. "Oh, no. It's a little late to try that approach.'' He took two steps toward her, and despite her resolve to stand her ground, Synnamon backed away from him and collided with the edge of the French door between the foyer and the living room. Only half-conscious of the bump, she rubbed her arm and stared uncertainly at him.

''If I had any reason to believe you wanted me back,'' Conner went on thoughtfully, ''I might be convinced you'd made up a story about being pregnant, or conveniently assumed I was the father of a child who might actually be someone else's. But the fact is, you don't have any reason to lie about the baby being mine, because you *don't* want me back.''

He stripped off his suit jacket and draped it over the back of the nearest chair.

He might as well be planting a flag of conquest, Synnamon thought bitterly.

''So I'm afraid there's only one logical conclusion,'' Conner went on inexorably, ''and that's to believe you told the truth the first time around—that you *are* pregnant, and it *is* my baby. Now, shall we cut out the nonsense and get down to business?''

Synnamon bit her lip. ''If you want to be technical,'' she conceded, ''you've got it right. But I was the one who was careless, and I'll deal with the consequences. All the consequences.''

The silence seemed a living thing. The air positively sizzled. Why, Synnamon wondered, hadn't her declaration eased the tension as she'd intended it should? Her knees were shaking, and she had to lean against the French door to keep herself upright.

Conner's forehead wrinkled. ''You shouldn't be standing.'' He stepped forward, a hand outstretched. ''In fact, you should be in bed.''

"I would have been, if you hadn't turned up," Synnamon pointed out. She pushed herself away from the door. "Look, Conner, why don't you just go away and forget I said anything?"

"And leave the loose ends to you."

Perhaps she shouldn't have been so annoyed at the idea that to him the baby was no more than a loose end, a minor annoyance to be destroyed with as little thought as he'd clip a dangling thread. She tried to remind herself that the less interested he was in the child as a person, the less trouble she'd face in the long run. But why couldn't she seem to convince Conner that she didn't want anything from him?

Strain and exhaustion and the aftermath of nausea combined to make her head spin, and suddenly she was just too tired to argue any more. Why should it matter what he thought, anyway? Conner's opinion wasn't going to change her plans.

"Leave your key on the hall table," she ordered. "And lock the door behind you."

Synnamon kept a hand on the wall to steady herself as she walked down the hallway to the master bedroom. She didn't look over her shoulder, but she knew he had followed her as far as the foyer and that he stood there watching until she reached her bedroom and firmly closed the door.

Her sleep was restless, at best, and Synnamon woke to a gray Denver day with a headache to match. What a way to start out a new year, she thought, and considered pulling the pillow over her head and staying in bed.

But she wasn't likely to be able to sleep. Her mind was running in circles, and her stomach was churning. Some food might help, unappetizing as the idea of eating was at the moment. Coffee, on the other hand, was positively inviting.

The longing for caffeine pushed her upright. She shoved her feet into the most comfortable old slippers she owned, wrapped herself in a terry robe and started for the kitchen.

It was only her imagination, of course, that made Synnamon think she could smell coffee. Mrs. Ogden had taken the holiday off. But the imaginary scent reminded her of the earliest days of her marriage, when Conner had occasionally brought her coffee in bed. She told herself sternly that she had better things to do than dwell on a few good, sentimental memories.

She was yawning as she walked into the kitchen, and for a moment, with her eyes squeezed almost shut, she didn't see him. When she did, Synnamon had to blink twice before she could focus.

Conner was standing at the range, the snow-white sleeves of his shirt rolled to the elbow, coating an omelet pan with melted butter. His hands were steady and his gaze was fixed firmly on his task. He looked up at her only briefly before turning to the bowl full of eggs next to the pan.

She stared at him. "I thought I told you to leave your key on the hall table," she said ominously.

"And I will. When I'm finished with it."

"Oh, you're finished, all right."

Conner shook his head. "We never completed our discussion. Besides, you didn't seem in the best condition to be alone last night, so I thought I'd better stay."

It was no longer his obligation to be concerned about her—but it was an odd mixture of annoyance and comfort that tumbled through her veins. Synnamon thrust her hands into the deep pockets of her terry robe.

"Well, I hope you didn't have any trouble finding your way around!"

The barb seemed to bounce off him. "Not at all, thank you." His voice was perfectly calm. "I used the guest room so often in the last few months I lived here that I felt right at home."

There was no answer to that, of course. Obviously, with her head aching, Synnamon was going to be no match for him this morning. At least she hadn't been dreaming the coffee. She moved past him and across the narrow kitchen to get a mug. "There's no cream," she said, almost defiantly. "I haven't kept it on hand since you left."

"I noticed. I had the doorman bring some up."

"Oh, that's great. Now the whole building will know."

"That I spent the night? And why should anyone care? We are still married, you know. Would you care for toast?" Efficiently, he buttered two slices and offered her one.

Synnamon took it. It was her loaf of bread, after all. He wasn't doing her any enormous favor to have dropped a slice in the toaster.

He bit into his own toast. "Or have you been in the habit of entertaining overnight guests, and now the whole building is watching to see who's next?"

"Of course not."

Conner smiled a little. "I didn't think so."

Too late, Synnamon wondered if she should have lied. Perhaps it still wasn't too late to persuade him that the baby wasn't his. *Dreamer*, she accused herself.

He tested the pan's temperature and stirred the eggs once more. His hands were perfectly steady as he poured the mixture into the sizzling butter. "Besides, I asked the doorman if you'd been seeing anyone—and he said you hadn't.''

''You—'' Synnamon was almost speechless with fury. She took a deep breath, and then another, before she could control herself. ''All right, dammit,'' she said. ''Let's take this from the top. How many times do I have to tell you this baby is not your business?''

Conner reached for a spatula and lifted the very edge of the omelet to let the uncooked egg run underneath, against the hot pan. The motions were smooth and easy, as if he had nothing else on his mind. And yet there was a wariness in the set of his shoulders, in the way he held his head. ''About this abortion—''

Synnamon sighed. He'd know the truth soon enough, anyway. Maybe it would be better to sort everything out now. ''I'm not going to do that, Conner.''

''Then why did you say you were?''

''Because you made me furious by assuming that would be my first reaction.'' Synnamon sat at the breakfast bar, cradling her coffee mug between her hands. ''But no matter what you want, I can't do that.''

''Well, that's something.'' He cut the finished omelet into two pieces, slid half onto a plate and surrounded it with fresh buttered toast before setting it in front of her. Then he fixed the other half, filled his coffee cup and sat down with his plate. ''Why the hell did you think I was standing guard?''

''Because you *didn't* want me to?'' Her head was reeling. ''Oh, that's rich. As if I could run right down to the corner drug store on New Year's Eve . . . Well, I'm glad we got that settled. You can stop worrying about me destroying the baby, and I can get on with my life.''

''Not so fast. What *are* you going to do?''

"How many choices are there?" Deliberately, she let irony drip from her voice. "I'll keep the baby, of course. What else can I do?"

"And bring it up the way you were raised?"

There was something about his tone that made the hair on the back of her neck stand on end. "What does that mean?"

Conner picked up a bit of toast and systematically shredded it. "There's more than one way to destroy a child, you know."

"Are you implying I'm incapable of being a decent mother?"

"Your upbringing wasn't your fault," he mused. "But if that's what you intend, this kid is going to be neurotic from the outset."

"Just like me, I suppose you mean?" Synnamon said icily.

"There's going to have to be some balance from somewhere."

"And I suppose you feel obligated to provide it? Look, Conner, it's downright decent of you to offer, but—"

"Thank you. You don't know what that does for my ego."

Synnamon ignored the interruption. "But I've told you and told you there's no need for you to be involved. It's only going to cause unnecessary complications if you insist on playing any part in this child's life. You're being shortsighted and completely unfair to yourself, to me *and* to the child—"

"If you want to get into a quarrel about unfairness, Synnamon, let me warn you—"

"No," she said quickly. "I don't want to quarrel about anything. I just want to get the rules hashed out right now, so nobody's confused about where we stand."

"I'm listening."

"You don't need to worry that I'll be calling you up to come to dance programs or piano recitals, so we can pretend to be a normal family." Her voice dripped irony. "And I won't expect you to follow the rules on visitation times, either."

"That's perfectly all right with me. I don't find anything particularly inviting about taking over a kid for every other weekend and a month in the summer."

The level voice was almost frightening, Synnamon thought. Not only hadn't Conner reacted to her sarcasm, which surprised her, but he sounded as if he hadn't even heard it. As if he had a different agenda altogether.

"And I don't plan to baby-sit while you're out on a date, either," Conner went on easily. "So don't even think about asking."

"Don't worry, I won't." She took a deep breath. "So what are you suggesting instead? That you drop by once a year or so, when it's convenient for you? Look, Conner, if you want to do something nice for this child, why not make it easy on us all? I'm asking you one last time. Let's cut things off clean right now and pretend this never happened."

He looked at her levelly over the edge of his coffee mug. "I didn't say I wouldn't see the child regularly, Synnamon. I said I wouldn't be satisfied with the normal schedule for divorced parents."

Synnamon tried to tell herself she was furious, but she knew better. The ache deep inside her wasn't anger, it was pure fear. "Then what do you want?"

He crunched a bite of toast. "I want this child," he said simply. "And I will not settle for less."

Synnamon's heart felt as cold as the omelet that had congealed on the plate in front of her. She stared across the breakfast bar at him.

She didn't feel hurt, exactly, or even surprised. Her chest ached, she told herself, because she'd been idiot enough not to see what was really going on. She should have realized that Conner wouldn't turn his back on a child, no matter how unwanted or unplanned that baby was.

But this declaration was even more than that. He had matter-of-factly proclaimed that this child was his and his alone. It was just one more way he was like Silas Sherwood.

Her voice trembled. "If you're going to try to take the baby away from me—"

"It wouldn't be my first choice. Even an inadequate mother is better than none at all."

Relief flickered through her, to be drowned almost instantly by fury. He might as well have come straight out and said she was nothing more, in his eyes, than an incubator! "Then I really don't see what you mean."

"Don't you?" His voice was almost gentle. "You must not want to see, then—because you're certainly not stupid."

Synnamon could feel her heartbeat. It was an irregular, dull thud deep in her chest, and it hurt.

Conner picked up his empty plate and carried it to the dishwasher. Efficiently he loaded it and the omelet pan, filled the detergent cup and pushed the button to start the cycle.

As if, Synnamon thought, he'd been doing it all along. As if he thought he had the right.

Over the hiss of the water, he said, "Whatever had happened last night, Synnamon, I wouldn't have left.

Because, you see, I'm here—in this apartment, and in your life—to stay."

The expression in his eyes, she thought, was almost sympathetic.

"In fact," he went on softly, "for want of a better word, you could say I've come home."

Synnamon sat at the breakfast bar long after Conner had left the kitchen. The irregular rush of water in the dishwasher mimicked the flow of blood through her body, sometimes surging with anger and adrenaline, sometimes slowing with fear and lassitude.

Home. The word rasped like sandpaper in her brain. It was bad enough that he'd come back at all, but to lightly announce that he was moving in and staying, that he'd come *home*—as if this had ever really been his home.

He couldn't get away with it, that was all. The first thing she'd do was call her attorney. Morea Landon, Synnamon was sure, wouldn't mince words about Conner's behavior.

She left her untouched plate on the breakfast bar and headed for her bedroom and the most private phone she could find. Beyond the open door of the hall bath, she heard an almost tuneless whistling and saw a neatly arranged array of brass and rubber pieces laid out on a spotless white towel at the edge of the sink.

Despite herself, she paused outside the door. "What are you doing to the faucet?" she accused.

"I'm stopping it from dripping. Are you objecting?"

She'd be a fool if she did, Synnamon knew, since she'd reported the leak twice already to the building superintendent. "How kind of you to make yourself useful," she said sweetly.

Conner didn't even look up. "I'm sure you'll find all sorts of ways I'll come in handy."

Why, Synnamon wondered, did she bother to bait him? It was a waste of time.

She dialed Morea's home number from memory and lay back against the satin bolster on her bed to wait for the call to go through. From the wall opposite, above a low chest where Synnamon stored her sweaters, the Contessa watched her. A much younger Contessa, painted by one of the most renowned artists of the day, wearing her trademark strand of perfect pearls—the pearls she had given Synnamon to wear on her wedding day.

What would the Contessa think of this mess?

Loss and loneliness engulfed Synnamon. What she wouldn't give to be able to put her head down in the Contessa's lap just once more and confess what an idiot she'd been.

The telephone clicked, and Morea's breezy answering machine message reminded Synnamon that her attorney had said she was going skiing after Christmas. They were going to Telluride, Morea had told her—and Synnamon couldn't remember if she'd even mentioned when she'd be home.

Synnamon put the phone down without leaving a message. She'd call Morea's law office tomorrow, and if she wasn't back yet...

I can't last till tomorrow, she thought suddenly. The longer Conner had to entrench himself, the more difficult it would be to dislodge him. She'd better do something, and fast, before he convinced himself that she'd invited him to move in and supervise her life.

She found him in the small television room, flipping channels on her tiny set. "Watching the parades?" she asked.

Conner shook his head. "Waiting for the football game to start."

"Good, I'm glad to know I'm not interrupting." She perched on the edge of a chair. "Let's try this once more, shall we?"

"Is there something left to say?"

"Surely you don't actually believe you can just move in here like this."

His brow furrowed. "Why not? I've done it."

"We are not going to have any continuing relationship."

"Now that's where you're wrong. As long as we share a child, neither one of us can exactly pretend the other doesn't exist."

"All right," Synnamon admitted. "You've got a point there, but don't you see that the baby is a different thing altogether? We can't, personally...the two of us, I mean..." She was stammering.

"Live together? Why not?" He put the television remote control aside. "We intended to, when we married."

"Well, yes. But that's all over now."

"The important facts haven't changed at all, Synnamon. We didn't go into this marriage all dazed with romance and passion. We did what sensible people have done for hundreds of years—we chose, with our eyes wide open, to be partners. We married with the intention of building an alliance—and a family, if that was meant to be—that would last a lifetime."

She couldn't argue with the assessment of their marriage. It *had* been far more partnership than romantic passion. But the appraisal made her insides freeze none-theless. She'd always known he'd been as attracted to Sherwood Cosmetics as to Synnamon—but had Conner really not found her even minimally appealing on a per-sonal level?

"Then you changed your mind and wanted a divorce," Conner went on calmly, "and because that was a de-cision that affected only the two of us, I went along."

"Exactly," Synnamon agreed. *Now*, she thought, *we're getting somewhere.* "And we also, if you'll recall, made an agreement to be civilized about the whole divorce. We haven't gotten bogged down in fights over petty things yet, so surely there's no reason we can't settle this reasonably, too."

"A child is not exactly a petty thing."

Synnamon took a deep breath and tried to keep her tone reasonable. "I didn't mean to imply it was. I was just trying to make clear that under the circumstances, I'm quite willing to take full responsibility for what hap-pened. Since it really doesn't involve you, there's no reason to quarrel about it. We'd already agreed to an amicable divorce, so—"

"Of course, that was before we so *amicably* created a child."

Synnamon was speechless. She was amazed he could enunciate so clearly when his jaw was set like concrete.

"If there had already been a child when you first asked for a divorce," Conner went on, "I wouldn't have been so willing to go along. I would have reminded you of the bargain you'd struck, and I'd have held you to the contract between us." He settled a little deeper into his chair, as if staking a claim.

"Conner," she said desperately, "you can't force someone to stay married."

In the dim light of the television room his eyes had darkened to pure, passionate purple. "Can you honestly tell me, Synnamon, that you love me any less today than you did on our wedding day?"

She gasped. "That's not fair, Conner. Love never had anything to do with it."

"Exactly. And everything else about our contract is still precisely the same, too. Except now there *is* a child— and so the divorce is off. You're my wife, Synnamon. And you're going to stay my wife."

The flat calm of his voice was more convincing than any amount of shouting or arm-waving could have been. He was dangerously gentle. In fact, she thought with a twinge of panic, he sounded as if he could afford to be compassionate—as if they were playing a life-size game of chess and only he could see the board.

There was no point in arguing with him, of course— or even answering. That would have to be Morea's job, she concluded. Synnamon had done everything she could do.

But neither, she decided, would she avoid him. It was her apartment, after all. *He* was the one who didn't belong, so why should she shut herself in her bedroom? Instead, she rummaged through a stack of magazines and curled up on the couch to read, with the subdued bustle of the pregame show as a background.

On a normal holiday, she couldn't help but think, she'd probably have brought a briefcase full of work home with her. There were always customer inquiries to answer, new-product data to read, problems to research—and the constant ringing of the telephone in her office made it difficult to concentrate there.

Now all that would be Annie's job, and Synnamon was reading magazines.

A roar from the television warned her that someone had scored a touchdown. Not Conner's team, she concluded, sneaking a quick look at him over the top of her magazine, since he was frowning.

Or was he thinking of other matters, and not the game at all? The man couldn't be happy at the turn his life had taken in the last twenty-four hours. Facing impending and less than welcome fatherhood created enough tension all by itself. Moving into the apartment and resuming the appearance of a marriage would be even worse...except, of course, that he wasn't actually going to do either of those things. Morea would put a stop to that soon enough.

She thought idly about what he'd said last night when he first came into the apartment. *I had a few things to finish up*, wasn't that it? She wondered what those things had been. Had he, for instance, told Nicole Fox about the baby?

The very thought made her feel hollow. *With sympathy*, she told herself. Poor Nicole must have seen her future swept away by Conner's single careless act and his quixotic decision.

Of course, if she'd just be patient for awhile... Maybe, Synnamon thought, she should make it a point to talk to the woman.

"Hungry?" Conner asked.

Her thoughts had been so far away that she had to consider the question. "No."

"You can't live on coffee, you know."

She couldn't quite keep the tart edge out of her voice. "Don't you mean the baby can't?"

Conner shrugged. "Same thing." His gaze wandered to the action on the field.

She sniffed and buried her nose in her magazine. That was an unpleasant harbinger of things to come, she thought. If he was planning to be her shadow all through the pregnancy so she didn't damage *his* baby...

From a corner of her subconscious so deeply buried that she'd been unaware of its existence floated a hazy memory. Her mother had been ill one winter....

Rita Sherwood had just come home from the hospital, in fact, and Synnamon, who'd worried for days about her absent mother as only a four-year-old can, had slipped away from her baby-sitter to make sure Rita was all right. She was hovering on the landing when Silas came out of his study, and instead of running down into her mother's arms, she'd slipped into the shadows at the turn of the staircase.

The conversation she'd overheard hadn't meant anything to her then, and she could recall only the haziest of phrases. Silas had said something that sounded like *criminal carelessness*, and later he'd referred to *my son*.

Now the meaning was all too clear. By that time, Rita had obviously held value in her husband's eyes only for the son she might produce, and when her second pregnancy ended without Silas's longed-for heir, even that bit of worth had vanished like the morning mist.

And now, it seemed, it was happening all over again.

Maybe I should pray for a girl, Synnamon thought. Conner hadn't said anything about the baby's sex. Maybe that meant it didn't matter—or maybe he was enough like her father that only a son would do. Maybe he hadn't even considered the possibility that his child could be a girl.

If that was so, and the baby was a daughter, he might vanish from their lives, after all. As, for all intents and purposes, Silas Sherwood had turned his back on his daughter.

It had been so simple, Synnamon thought wearily. It had all made such perfect sense. She and Conner didn't want to be married, so the sensible thing—the only civilized thing—was to split. But there would be no recriminations, no anger, no fights. No bitterness, no resentment, no tugs-of-war over money or possessions. Theirs would be the perfect divorce.

But now, because she had stupidly lost control of herself in a moment of pain and loneliness and created a life that would link the two of them forever, their perfect divorce was falling apart.

CHAPTER FIVE

SYNNAMON didn't get out of bed on the morning after New Year's Day before she reached for the telephone and called Morea Landon's law office.

Morea's secretary sounded doubtful. "She's due in court this morning, Mrs. Welles, and she may not even come to the office first. But the moment she arrives I'll tell her you called."

"Tell her," Synnamon said firmly, "that it's urgent."

She felt a little better knowing she'd done everything she could for the moment. And her morning sickness seemed to have taken the day off, she discovered when she cautiously stood up.

She rummaged through her closet for jeans and a sweater. It felt strange to dress so informally on a weekday morning, when her normal attire would be a tailored suit and heels and panty hose. In fact, she was tempted to stick to her terry robe and scuffed slippers, just to make the point to Conner that she wasn't going out of her way to look her best for him. Except, she thought, he probably wouldn't notice.

He was still in the apartment, Synnamon had no doubt of that. She could feel his presence, even though it was past the time he usually arrived at the office.

Mrs. Ogden was back from her holiday, and when Synnamon reached the kitchen the housekeeper was just setting a plate of waffles and sausage on the breakfast bar in front of Conner.

"That looks wonderful, Mrs. O," he said, and the housekeeper beamed.

"Don't let him fool you into waiting on him," Synnamon murmured. "He's perfectly capable of taking care of himself."

Mrs. Ogden clicked her tongue in reproof. "But where's the fun in that, Mrs. Welles? And what would you like for breakfast this morning?"

"Just fruit and coffee. I'll get it myself."

Mrs. Ogden poured Synnamon's coffee, however, and set it on the breakfast bar directly across from Conner's plate. She took the opportunity to top off Conner's cup, as well. "Yes," she said with a broad smile as if picking up a conversation where Synnamon had interrupted it. "It certainly is nice to see you back where you belong, Mr. Welles. Such a nice young couple you two make."

Behind the open refrigerator door, Synnamon rolled her eyes heavenward. She was selecting a grapefruit when the telephone rang, and Mrs. Ogden reached it first. "One moment, please," she said disapprovingly, and held it out to Synnamon. "It's that Ms. Landon, for you."

Conner's eyebrows lifted, but he didn't comment, just cut another bite of waffle.

Synnamon seized the phone. "Morea, I'm on the cordless phone, but let me run to another room, all right?"

"Only if you hurry," Morea said. "I'm sorry, but I've got just two minutes before I have to leave for court. I would have put you off till afternoon if Cindy hadn't said it was urgent, because the unbearable Ridge Coltrain is waiting for me."

Synnamon let the kitchen door swing shut behind her, but she still wasn't far enough from Conner and Mrs.

Ogden to feel safe. "Did you put garlic in your scrambled eggs this morning just for him?"

Morea sniffed. "Why bother? I had heartburn for a day and a half after that episode, and he didn't even turn a hair. Then just as our conference was ending he complimented me on my new perfume. Can you imagine? Why do you have to leave the room to talk on your own phone, anyway? Is Mrs. Ogden spying for the opposition? What's wrong, darling?"

Synnamon had reached the relative safety of the big living room. "I'm pregnant, Morea."

Fifteen seconds of dead silence ticked by before Morea said, "That's urgent, all right. I'm afraid I can't speed up the divorce, though, if that's what you're calling about. We're locked into that timetable unless everybody agrees to move things up, and I can't just go to Conner's attorney without giving a reason for the hurry, so—"

Synnamon took a deep breath and interrupted. "It's not that at all, Morea."

"Oh? I assumed you'd want to marry the father as soon as possible."

"Not exactly," Synnamon said dryly.

"Surely you aren't asking *me* to tell Conner? As a matter of fact, there's no reason for him even to know—"

"I've already told him. And there was every reason."

There was another brief silence. "Oh, no," Morea said wearily. "I don't think I want to hear this."

"It...just sort of happened. When we were in Phoenix."

Morea sighed. "Have I ever told you you're the single most difficult client I've ever dealt with, Synnamon Welles? No, I take that back—not because it isn't true, but because that sort of comment is unethical and unprofessional and could get me censured if you complained to the bar association."

"I wouldn't."

"Now that's an isolated example of good judgment. Nobody else would take you on. Dammit, Synnamon, if you'd been scheming to take a simple divorce and mess it up, you couldn't have done a better job!"

"Believe me, this wasn't *my* idea." A vague doubt flickered momentarily through Synnamon's mind, but she promptly dismissed it. She was being silly—far too suspicious for her own good. Conner couldn't have planned this set of circumstances any more than she could have, and if anything he would have had less reason.

Morea had regained her self-control. "All right. I really have to go to court this instant, but I'll meet you for lunch at the Pinnacle and we'll talk it over."

"Not the Pinnacle," Synnamon pleaded. "Somewhere I can keep both feet firmly on the ground. Can we make it Maxie's instead?"

"All right. One o'clock."

"Thanks, Morea."

"And Synnamon—don't do anything idiotic between now and then, all right?"

"Like what?"

"I couldn't possibly recite a full list," Morea said wryly. "So let's just say, don't do *anything*."

The phone clicked in Synnamon's ear. She turned the receiver off.

"How's Morea?" Conner asked pleasantly.

Synnamon jumped a foot. She wheeled toward the foyer to see him leaning against the French door. "How long have you been standing there?"

"Long enough. But don't worry, you didn't say anything incriminating, or even suggestive. Actually, I was just waiting till you got off the phone to tell you goodbye, as any good husband would."

"Oh, cut out the role-playing," Synnamon said crossly. "Or get some acting lessons, if you want to be credible as a loving spouse."

"I'll keep that in mind." His voice was calm. "So what did your attorney advise?"

"Do you think I'm going to tell you?"

"Of course not. But you might think about it long and hard before you talk to her again, Synnamon. This isn't a rag doll we're talking about, you know—it's a real little human being who deserves the best start in life we can give him."

"Or her," she said sweetly.

Conner didn't comment. "I happen to believe that includes two full-time parents. And I also suspect that if you'll let yourself simmer down long enough to really think about it, you'll admit I'm right." Conner reached into the closet for his trench coat.

"Two full-time antagonistic parents, you mean? At each others' throats all the time, and wretchedly miserable?"

"Of course not. I'm not expecting us to act like love-birds, any more than we ever did. But look at it this way, Synnamon. If we could agree so easily to a cool and civilized divorce, surely we can agree to resume a cool and civilized marriage."

"It is *not* the same thing," Synnamon argued.

He raised his eyebrows a trifle. "Is there someone in your life that I should know about?"

"I don't have to have another man on the string in order to want a divorce, Conner."

He smiled. "I didn't think there was."

Synnamon didn't know if she was more annoyed at herself for taking the bait or at him for the implication that she couldn't possibly attract another man. And before she could decide, Conner was gone.

She swore under her breath and went to the kitchen for her grapefruit and coffee.

Mrs. Ogden was cleaning the breakfast bar. "It does my heart good to see that man back where he belongs," she said once more. "I suspected you were regretting the decision you'd made, the way you've moped around the place for the last month or so."

"Moped?" Synnamon said coolly.

Mrs. Ogden nodded. "Ever since the Contessa died, I've wondered if you weren't having second thoughts about asking Mr. Welles to leave. That's the kind of thing that certainly makes one think, a loss like that. And then when you told me you were quitting your job, I said to myself this was in the wind, that you'd finally seen how much more important your husband is than that work of yours."

Synnamon stared at her, bemused. She'd always known Mrs. Ogden was a romantic, but she'd never realized how rosily unrealistic the woman could be. Had she honestly been unaware of the tension in the kitchen this morning?

"What shall I make for dinner, do you think?" Mrs. Ogden rinsed out her dishcloth and started to work on the range. "Oh, I know—my beef bourguignonne is Mr. Welles's favorite, and I can leave it to simmer when I go home, so all you'll have to do is dish it up." She gave Synnamon a conspiratorial smile. "And don't worry about cleaning up the mess afterward. Shall I put candles on the dining room table, or would you rather eat by the fireplace?''

Synnamon pushed her coffee away. It had gotten cold, and she'd lost her taste for it, anyway. ''Whatever you like. If you'll excuse me, Mrs. Ogden, I have to go change my clothes.''

''For what? You look fine to me.''

Synnamon paused in the doorway. ''Because I'm going to work after all, that's why.''

Mrs. Ogden's mouth fell open, and instantly Synnamon regretted her sharpness. Being annoyed with Conner was one thing. Taking it out on the good-hearted Mrs. Ogden was something else.

Then the housekeeper smiled. ''I think it's cute,'' she said, ''that you just can't stand the idea of not seeing him till dinnertime.''

Morea Landon was already at Maxie's Bar, stirring a glass of tomato juice with a celery stick, when Synnamon dropped into the chair across from her.

''Sorry I'm late,'' Synnamon said. ''An impossible client.''

''Now why does that problem sound familiar?'' Morea murmured. ''I thought you were finished with impossible clients. Don't tell me Conner still hasn't hired anyone to fill your job.''

Synnamon waved a hand. ''As a matter of fact, he has, but I'll tell you all about that later. Am I the reason you're scowling at that poor glass of tomato juice?''

''Aren't you enough cause? I come back from a wonderful week on the ski slopes to find my only straightforward case has suddenly taken on as many twists as a plate of noodles. To tell you the truth, I'm wishing the tomato juice was Ridge Coltrain's blood, but we can save that story for later, too. Tell me what on earth made you lose your mind."

Synnamon sighed. "I was upset about the Contessa, of course. It was the night before she died, and Conner was right there, and I just wanted to—"

"I didn't mean I wanted the details about *that* bit of insanity," Morea said hastily. "I have an imagination, after all. But why didn't you tell me before you went blabbing the news to Conner?"

Synnamon shrugged. "It just seemed the fair thing to do."

"I'm your attorney, Synnamon. How can I advise you if—"

"And he's the baby's father, Morea. Doesn't that give him some rights?"

Morea looked a bit abashed.

More gently, Synnamon went on, "Besides, you were in Telluride—and I thought Conner would be reasonable."

"But he wasn't, of course. What did he say?"

"It wasn't what he said," Synnamon said carefully, "so much as what he did. He moved in."

Morea dropped her celery stick into her glass, and tomato juice splashed across her cream-colored sweater. She didn't seem to notice. "Into the apartment, you mean? And you let him? Synnamon—"

"A lot I had to say about it," Synnamon said acidly. "I just blinked and there he was. Now I want to know how—"

Morea shook her head and stared over Synnamon's shoulder, her wide, dark eyes intent.

There was no missing the message. Synnamon bit off the rest of her sentence and turned to look over her shoulder.

The maître d' was seating a solitary guest at the next table. Synnamon sighed. ''Fancy meeting you here, Conner.''

''Hello, Synnamon—and Morea, too.''

He was trying, she thought, to look just a trifle worried. Synnamon wasn't convinced for a moment. There was no doubt in her mind he'd overheard her this morning arranging to meet Morea at Maxie's. The only question she had was how he'd been so certain of the time.

''I hope my presence doesn't blight your conversation,'' he said. ''I *could* ask for a different table, I suppose, but as busy as the restaurant is today...''

''Oh, come on over and join us,'' Morea said. ''Let's take care of this right now.''

Conner moved without apparent haste, but so smoothly that before Synnamon could gather the words to protest he'd taken the chair next to hers and was signaling the waiter to bring him a glass of water. ''You don't know how happy this makes me, Morea,'' he said earnestly.

Synnamon's inner alarm system was shrieking warnings. What did he have to be happy about?

Morea said dryly, ''I'm sure you're going to tell me why, Conner.''

''I know, you see, that last week the three of us couldn't have had any sort of formal conference. We'd have needed my attorney present to protect my rights.''

''True enough,'' Morea said. ''And furthermore, we *still*—''

''So, since you invited me over to chat, that must mean that you're no longer Synnamon's attorney.'' He smiled. ''And since I fired my lawyer this morning, too—'' He reached for Synnamon's hand.

She moved it just in time. He was a better actor, she thought, than she'd given him credit for being.

"The least I can do to celebrate," he went on, "is to buy you both lunch. Oh, and send your bill to me, Morea—I'll settle it up immediately, and then we can simply be friends again."

Morea stared at him for a few seconds, then turned to Synnamon. "I apologize," she murmured. "Now I see what you meant about *letting* him move in. Stopping him is like arguing with an influenza germ."

"I'm glad you realize it," Conner said. He turned to Synnamon. His eyes were dark and intense. "So the divorce *is* off, then?"

Synnamon closed her menu with a snap. "You can't force me to stay married to you, Conner."

"I can certainly make it costly for you to divorce me."

Morea frowned. "No more than it already has been, I'd say."

"Perhaps not, if all you're talking about is money. But since that's not the only question now..."

Synnamon's heart twisted. "You told me you wouldn't ask for custody. Fool that I was, I believed you!"

"I said it wouldn't be my first choice," he corrected. "But if you force me, Synnamon, I will do whatever is necessary. I will not be reduced to a footnote in my child's life." He shook his napkin out with a snap and draped it across the edge of the table. "It's your choice, Synnamon. Let me know what you decide. I don't think, however, that I'll stay for lunch after all."

He left behind a silence thicker than Maxie's famous cream of mushroom soup.

Finally, Synnamon asked, "He *can't* get custody, can he?"

For a moment, she thought Morea wasn't going to answer. Then the attorney sighed. "It's hard to tell. The fascination of the law, of course, is that there are two sides to every question, and you never know what a judge will decide in a particular case. Even when there's clear precedent for a mother's request—"

"Thanks for the encouragement," Synnamon said wryly.

"Sorry, darling, but I'm just doing my job. If I guaranteed results, I'd be crazy." Morea added thoughtfully, "And probably disbarred, too."

"If you'd tell a judge the things Conner said just now, the threats he made..."

"What threats? All I heard him say is that he intends to be involved in his child's life, and I can't think of a single divorce-court judge who wouldn't burst into applause at that announcement. Besides, I can't exactly testify to anything, because I'm not only your attorney but a prejudiced witness. It would be pretty easy for the court to dismiss my opinion."

"Then what do I do? Just go on with it and take my chances?"

Morea's eyes narrowed. "There is one possibility."

"I'm willing to try anything."

"It might not solve the problem entirely, of course. But if Conner were to change his mind—"

Synnamon started to laugh. "Oh, please. That's what you call a possibility? If Conner set out to empty the Pacific Ocean with a soup ladle, I wouldn't bet against him. Morea, if that's the best you can do—"

Morea shrugged. "It's the only thing I can think of. The whole idea of divorce makes people do strange things. I've known couples who hated each other, but they simply couldn't keep their distance because the joy each of them got from annoying their partner was more satisfying than having a scrap of peace for themselves."

"I don't see Conner being that sort."

"No, but the principle still applies. You want him to move out of your apartment but also to give up the idea of custody, right? Well, arguing about either matter is only going to make him more determined about both. I've seen it happen in a hundred cases, with men a lot less stubborn than Conner is. But if *he's* the one who gives up the idea of staying married, if he's forced to admit that this grand idea of his simply won't work..."

The silence drew out into forever while Synnamon thought about it. "And just what do you think I can do to make that happen?"

"At the moment," Morea admitted, "I haven't a clue."

Annie looked pathetically glad to see Synnamon. "I'm glad you're back," she said. "This afternoon there have already been half a dozen people who wanted to talk to you. And one of them—"

Synnamon hung her suit jacket in the closet. "That's easily explained." Her voice was matter-of-fact. "Once they find out I'm gone, they'll be quite happy to have your attention instead."

"You mean one head of customer relations is just the same as another?" Annie asked skeptically.

"Well, perhaps not quite. But all you need is the benefit of the doubt for a few weeks till you have a chance to prove yourself, and they'll be eager to talk to you."

"I wish I believed you were right. But one of them hung up on me just now when I explained you weren't with the company any more—and I think he was going to call Mr. Welles directly."

"Who was it?"

Annie reached for a pink message slip, but she didn't look at it. The name was obviously engraved on her brain. "Luigi." She sounded like the voice of doom.

"The one who owns the string of beauty spas?"

"There can't be more than one with a single name and an Italian accent thick enough to slice, can there?"

"I hope not. Luigi's an original—a truly self-made man. His real name is Harold Henderson, and my father told me once that he was born in the south Bronx. I wouldn't worry about him, Annie. I'm sure Mr. Welles will be up to the challenge of dealing with Luigi."

"You don't *mind* if he talks to Mr. Welles? It's not you he'll be complaining about, of course, it's me, but—"

"I wouldn't be so certain of that. Luigi has a tendency to take everything personally, so he's probably feeling insulted by the fact I'm leaving."

"Oh, now that's a real comfort," Annie said wryly.

"Relax. It's just part of his stereotypical vision of how a temperamental Italian should behave."

"Well, it doesn't change the fact that his account is the size of the national debt, and if he calls Mr. Welles and makes a fuss about how I treated him . . ."

"It's not you, Annie. He just hates change. He complained about me when I first took the job, too."

"I suppose that should make me feel better," Annie admitted. "But since that was before Mr. Welles's time . . . Does he know about Harold Henderson and the south Bronx?"

"I'm sure he does, but I'll remind him."

"Would you? *Can* you? I mean . . ."

"No doubt," Synnamon said dryly, "Conner and I will exchange words from time to time."

Annie sighed. "Then you're still... Even with the baby... Sorry. I didn't mean to be nosy."

Synnamon started to announce that of course there would be no change in plans. Instead, she heard herself saying softly, "I'm not sure what's going to happen."

The sudden uncertainty startled her, but she had to admit it was the only honest reaction she was capable of just now. She was too confused to know what to do.

She knew, intellectually, that Morea was right. The only way Synnamon could achieve her long-term goals was for Conner to change his mind. Arguing obviously wouldn't accomplish that. It was likely to make Conner more stubborn. But reasoning with him wasn't going to work, either. She'd already tried that approach. And if she simply went along with what he suggested, and resumed their farce of a marriage... Well, Conner had seemed perfectly comfortable in that role before, so what was to prevent him from settling down into it once more?

Synnamon was the only variable—or at least the only one she could control. She'd have to make sure he wasn't so complacent this time around.

An idea stirred to life at the back of her mind and slowly took shape. What would happen if *she* became the complacent one—or, at least, if she appeared to be? If she seemed contented with the situation, placidly accepting how things had worked out, might Conner begin to feel restless? Uneasy? Even, perhaps, eager to be free?

"Hand me the phone," she told Annie.

"Are you going to call Mr. Welles about Luigi?"

Synnamon had forgotten all about Luigi. "Why not?" she murmured. "He'll make a lovely excuse. But first..."

Conner was waiting for her. The door of his office was open, and he was perched on the corner of his secretary's desk, signing letters, when Synnamon came into the waiting room.

To a casual observer, she thought, he would appear perfectly at ease. Even Carol probably couldn't tell the difference. But Synnamon could feel the tension in the lean lines of his body. And of course the fact that he was in the outer office at all was a dead giveaway.

He's eager to talk to me, she thought, and her pulse went into overdrive.

She hadn't told Carol what her business was, just that she needed a little time with Conner. She'd been counting on having a couple of quiet minutes to gather her thoughts before confronting him. Now, robbed of that island of serenity, she felt her mouth going dry with anticipation.

He signed the last letter, handed the clipboard to the secretary and stood up. "Hold my calls, please, Carol. Synnamon..." His gesture toward the open office door was a wordless invitation.

She accepted it silently and told herself it was foolish to be anxious. Either this idea would work—eventually— or it wouldn't. If it didn't, she would be no worse off than she was at the moment.

Still, she couldn't quite stop her insides from quivering.

Conner waved a hand toward the couch. "Make yourself comfortable. What can I do for you?"

Synnamon settled into the corner of the love seat. Her pastel tweed skirt slid slowly upward. Her fingers twitched with the urge to pull it down, but she forced her hands to stay still, folded in her lap, instead. To give her skirt a nervous tug would carry a twofold message. It would say first that she was jittery around him—which was true enough but was hardly a thought she wanted to cross Conner's mind. Second, it would imply that she expected him to be watching, and perhaps even wanted him to be interested in the view of her knees—which was far from the truth, and again not something she wanted Conner to be thinking about.

"What can I do for you?" he asked.

She raised her gaze to his face. "Have you talked to Luigi lately?"

She wasn't disappointed. Surprise flickered in his face, and his eyes shadowed from blue to intensely purple. She had to admire his control, however. An instant later there was no evidence he'd been so much as startled. "Not for a couple of weeks. Why?"

She told him about Annie's encounter with the spa owner. "He threatened to call you, and naturally she's concerned that you might blame her for upsetting him. I told her you understood Luigi's point of view—"

"Without a doubt."

"And his history, and that you wouldn't have any trouble handling his complaints."

"Your confidence in me is touching, Synnamon. I'll certainly give it my best effort. Thanks for the warning."

"My pleasure."

"Is there anything else?"

"No, I don't think so." She stood up. "Oh, yes—there is. Something I've always wondered." She paused, letting curiosity have a chance to grow. "Is there really a bed built into this office?"

To her disappointment, Conner's eyebrows didn't even twitch. "If so, it's too well hidden for me to find. Or are you suggesting that I install one?"

"Certainly not for my sake," Synnamon said politely. "I was just wondering. You won't be late tonight, will you?"

She thought she saw wariness creep into his eyes, but all he said was, "I was planning to stop by the hotel first, pick up my clothes and check out."

He hadn't already done that? So he hadn't been nearly as sure of himself as he'd been acting, Synnamon thought, and annoyance chewed at the corners of her mind. Perhaps, if she'd held firm just a little longer instead of acting on Morea's advice...

"But I'm sure that will take only a few minutes," Conner went on smoothly.

It was too late to back out, Synnamon knew. She was embarked on this new path, and she'd have to see it through. "It's beef bourguignonne," she said. "Mrs. Ogden and I decided since it was your favorite..."

"Then I'll try to hurry—" he paused "—home."

"Good." Synnamon allowed herself a smile. That tiny hesitation of his had spoken volumes. Her self-confidence took a gigantic leap. All she had to do was be sweet, innocent and accommodating—up to a point— and before long Conner would be choking on his grand idea.

"Because I've invited a guest," she went on. "She'll be there at seven o'clock."

"She?" There was a note of distrust in Conner's voice.

Synnamon had to make an effort to hide her delight at the reaction. "Yes," she said gently. "Since she's going to be working here at Sherwood, I thought perhaps I should get to know her better. I hope you don't mind spending an entire evening with Nicole Fox?"

CHAPTER SIX

THE apartment was dim and quiet when Synnamon let herself in. The thin gray daylight was gone, as was Mrs. Ogden. But true to her promise, the housekeeper had left the bourguignonne simmering in the oven, and its scent wafted down the hall to greet Synnamon.

She was happy to see that Mrs. Ogden had opted for the dining room instead of setting up an intimate meal before the fireplace. The table was covered with starched white linen and half a dozen candles. Two silver service plates had been polished to a gleam and laid at a corner of the table, ready for the dinner plates to be put in place.

It was very thoughtful of Mrs. Ogden to arrange it that way, Synnamon decided, so it would be possible for the two diners to stare into each others' eyes without blinding themselves with the candlelight. And the housekeeper had added white ribbons, and something that looked like orange blossom.

Synnamon shook her head with wry humor as she got another service plate from the cabinet and set it at the opposite end of the table from the other two. The idea of inviting Nicole Fox was looking better and better. Set for three, the dining room had a pleasant party atmosphere. As a twosome, it would look positively bridal—which of course was exactly what Mrs. Ogden had in mind.

Synnamon frowned. One thing she and Conner hadn't talked about was whether he intended to move into the master bedroom as well as the apartment.

Surely he wouldn't even suggest it, she thought. He'd hardly spent any time there when the marriage was still a real one, and now that it was purely a nominal relationship...

She frowned again as she went to the kitchen to stir the bourguignonne. She was just sliding the dish into the oven when the doorbell rang. It was seven o'clock on the dot, and standing on the welcome mat was Nicole Fox.

She looked just a bit pale, Synnamon thought, and very wary. Of course, that was no surprise. She'd been practically speechless this afternoon when Synnamon had phoned her to issue the invitation.

Nicole stepped into the foyer and gave up her coat with what Synnamon couldn't help but interpret as reluctance. Her gaze darted across the hall into the obviously empty living room, and Synnamon had no trouble following the path of her thoughts. As a matter of fact, she was thinking the same thing herself. *Where was Conner?*

Surely, she thought, he wouldn't leave her to entertain Nicole Fox alone. It wasn't that he'd feel obligated to appear, exactly. She could even imagine him saying that since she hadn't consulted him before inviting a guest, she could hardly rely on him to help her entertain.

But she didn't think it likely he would risk it, under the circumstances. He couldn't know what she might have planned for the evening, and surely he wouldn't dare leave the two of them without a buffer.

However, Synnamon supposed she might have miscalculated. Perhaps he had enough faith in Nicole to leave

her on her own with the problematic wife. They might
have been together somewhere just now, snatching a few
moments of privacy and making plans for how to handle
Synnamon. She could almost hear the conversation.

"What's she up to, anyway?"

"I don't know, we'll have to just play along."

"Maybe she suspects?"

Oh, stop it, Synnamon told herself. She was starting
to sound like a bad spy movie!

"Conner isn't home yet," she said lightly as she led
Nicole into the big living room, where the gas fire was
already giving off a pleasant wave of warmth. "He had
some things to do after he left the office, I think. Would
you like a Scotch and water?"

The redhead nodded. "What a beautiful view you have
of the mountains."

Mrs. Ogden had left a tray on the cocktail table,
Synnamon noticed, something she hadn't done since
Conner had moved out. Before that, it had been a daily
routine, even though much of the time the tray had gone
untouched. After Conner had left, Synnamon had told
the housekeeper to stop. It was one more reminder she
didn't need.

The scary part, however, wasn't that Mrs. Ogden had
so easily returned to the routine of the old days, but that
Synnamon had turned automatically to look for the tray.
Perhaps it would be easier than she thought to slide into
the old ways. Not that she wanted to, of course. But
maybe Conner wasn't so far off track about thinking
this cool and civilized marriage could work.

Nicole held the cocktail glass Synnamon handed her,
but she didn't take a sip.

Synnamon poured herself a champagne flute full of
club soda and dropped in a wedge of lime. She settled

into a wing chair by the window and gestured to the matching one opposite her. "Please sit down. It *is* a wonderful view, isn't it? I think that's what made me choose this apartment over every other one I looked at before Conner and I were married."

Nicole nodded and obediently sat, but she didn't answer.

For nearly twenty minutes Synnamon kept the conversation going, moving from one innocuous subject to the next—but it was some of the hardest work she had ever done. Nicole seemed to consider every response at great length.

Synnamon heard Conner's key the instant it clicked into the lock, and a wave of relief swept over her. She was puzzled for an instant by her reaction. She certainly wasn't particularly happy to see him. His presence wasn't going to make the situation delightful or her own role any less guarded. In fact, the tension level could only increase with him there. And that was why she'd planned the evening in the first place, wasn't it?

But at least she wouldn't be stuck trying to pry a few words out of a silent dinner companion. And at least she'd be able to add a little discomfort to his life as well as her own, and if she was lucky, that uneasiness would make him start to question his decision.

"Hello, dear," he said calmly as he came across the living room. "Good to see you, Nick." He bent over Synnamon's chair before she had considered what he might do. Almost reflexively she jerked her head, and his lips brushed across her hair. Synnamon was annoyed with herself. He'd intended to kiss her temple, she was sure. It wasn't as if he'd planned some passionate display. She ought to have stayed perfectly still, not tried to dodge him like a nervous virgin.

He shook Nicole's hand, and smiled.

Synnamon was greatly impressed with his self-control, less so with the way Nicole's eyes widened and fastened on him as if she was a drowning sailor who'd just glimpsed a life belt.

"Shall I fix you a drink, darling?" Synnamon asked solicitously.

"No, thanks."

She tried to sound casual, perfectly normal, as she launched the next element of her plan. "Then if you'll excuse me, Conner, I'll leave you to entertain our guest until dinner. The bourguignonne needs just a bit of last-minute attention."

Leave them alone, she'd decided, *and see what happens*. Of course, she wasn't naive enough to think that they couldn't arrange to meet anytime they liked. There were opportunities aplenty for that. But the idea of being alone together with the troublesome wife just down the hall had a piquancy that Synnamon thought they could not ignore.

"Is the bourguignonne what I'm smelling?" Nicole asked just as Synnamon left the room. Conner must have nodded, for she went on, "It's a wonderful aroma. Just think of the potential if we could reproduce that for a kitchen air freshener, Conner."

She was laughing a little, but there was a catch in Nicole's voice when she said his name that sent a quiver up Synnamon's spine.

Synnamon told herself it was nothing out of line, exactly. It was so subtle that if she hadn't been listening for something of the sort, she probably would have passed it over. It wasn't as if Nicole was in obvious pain...

She began to feel a little ashamed of herself for dragging Nicole into this. It might not have been smart of the woman to get involved at any level with a man who was still technically married—but it wasn't exactly her fault, either. Who could have predicted this twist of events?

Synnamon served the broiled grapefruit appetizer, and when she went into the living room Conner and Nicole were talking about the research and development team. There was something a bit strained about the conversation, Synnamon thought, but at least Nicole was talking.

Conner held a chair for Nicole and then came around the table to help Synnamon, but she'd pretended not to notice and had already seated herself. "How has the response been from the other chemists?" she asked as she spread her napkin carefully across her lap and picked up her grapefruit spoon.

"There's been some grumbling," Conner said. "Not as much as you expected there would be, however—mostly because, with your warning in mind, I made it clear from the start that I wouldn't tolerate it."

The note of approval—almost appreciation—in his voice startled Synnamon.

"I think even that will die down once Nick really gets started." He smiled at the redhead. "Once they see what she can do..."

Was there something a little more than friendly about that smile? Synnamon asked, "When will you start to work, Nicole?"

"I have to give a month's notice to my current employer."

Synnamon frowned.

"Is something wrong?" Conner asked.

"I was just thinking that it might have been wiser to wait to make the announcement," Synnamon mused. "Giving them a month to think about it, without the new boss present..."

"Oh, Nick will be in and out. And I have no doubt she can handle anything that bunch might do or say."

Nicole looked less certain, Synnamon thought. That was odd. At the New Year's Eve party she'd seemed to ooze confidence. But of course, things had changed since New Year's—and not only where the job was concerned.

"The situation will have difficulties," Nicole said. "But I'm looking forward to the challenge."

"I'm sure you'll do very well," Synnamon said. It was almost a throwaway line, a social nicety, but it was true, she realized. It had always been the other members of the team she was concerned about, not Nicole herself. For no matter what Conner thought of her personally, he wouldn't have given her the job if she wasn't an able chemist.

Synnamon was startled when Nicole looked up from her grapefruit with a sudden smile that lit her eyes and turned her good looks into stunning beauty.

"You wouldn't like to put that in the company newsletter, I suppose?" Nicole said.

Still a bit bemused by the woman's sparkle, Synnamon said slowly, "I don't quite know what you mean."

"You see, it's obvious that your opinion is very important to everyone at Sherwood."

Involuntarily, Synnamon's gaze slid down the length of the table to find Conner watching her thoughtfully over the rim of his wineglass.

Almost everyone, she nearly said. *Except perhaps the boss*. Instead, she shrugged. "Since I'm not officially on the payroll any more, I can't see it making much of a difference. But if I can help—''

"Of course you can," Conner said. "A few simple things should do it. You could have lunch together a few times, maybe."

Synnamon would have given anything to be able to glare at him and announce that she had no intention of becoming friends with Nicole Fox. But to say so would be to admit that she wasn't any more comfortable with the situation he'd created than Conner was.

In fact, she thought irritably, at the moment she was probably less at ease. How did the man do it, anyway? It wasn't fair that he could turn the tables on her so completely and so effortlessly.

Somehow talking about the new job had broken the ice, and Nicole seemed to relax. Suspiciously, Synnamon replayed the conversation as she served the bourguignonne. She couldn't help wondering if the whole thing had really been coincidence or if she'd been conned— manipulated into a public position of friendship.

Despite her best efforts to stay aloof, however, she found herself liking Nicole Fox. Though she was still quiet, the woman displayed a dry sense of humor, and under the influence of the bourguignonne she laughed now and then.

Eventually, Synnamon put her napkin down and began to clear the table. "I'll be happy to help," Nicole offered.

"Oh, no." Synnamon smiled. "You've been very restrained, both of you, in not discussing chemistry over dinner, and I appreciate it. So I'll leave you to it for a few minutes while the coffee brews."

She loaded the dishwasher and sliced the chocolate cheesecake, and as soon as the coffee was finished, she loaded a tray and carried it into the living room.

She honestly wasn't trying to be silent, but she succeeded better than she could have hoped. Conner and Nicole had moved to the wide bay window, where only a darker line marked the Rockies in the distance and a golden web of lights spread out across the high plain below the apartment tower. The redhead's hand was on Conner's sleeve, and she was looking at him intently. Her voice was low, but Synnamon had no trouble catching the words. "Are you quite sure you want to go through with this, Conner? You're obviously miserable, and it isn't likely to get easier."

Conner didn't answer. Something caught his attention—Synnamon's reflection in the window glass, perhaps—and he shook Nicole's hand off his sleeve and came hastily across the room to take the tray from Synnamon's hands. "You shouldn't be carrying things like this," he said.

"Why not? It weighs less than my briefcase does."

"Then you shouldn't be carrying **that**, either."

The irritation in his voice pleased Synnamon beyond all reason. Nicole's question had obviously ruffled his composure, and that alone made the strain of the evening worthwhile.

Nicole looked uncomfortable. "I'm surprised you don't have someone to help around the house," she said finally.

So we're all just going to ignore that leading question, Synnamon thought with satisfaction, *and pretend it was never asked*. Well, that was all right with her—a question with no answer was an even more haunting one. It wouldn't bother her any if it kept Conner awake all night.

"Only during the day," she said. "Mrs. Ogden has never lived in. We treasure our privacy—I'm sure you understand. Do you take cream and sugar in your coffee, Nicole?''

Synnamon was sorry to see the evening end. She had to admit, however, that it wasn't entirely because of that spark of liking that had sprung to life between her and Nicole Fox, but because she wasn't looking forward to facing the music once she and Conner were alone.

She left him to finish the good nights, even suggesting that he walk Nicole down to her car, and retreated to the kitchen to attack the mess. She'd put the silver flatware to soak and was in the dining room, stacking the last of the china on a tray, when Conner returned.

It hadn't been as long a farewell as she'd expected, and she had to bite her tongue to keep from asking what had brought him back so quickly. But it was best for her plan to appear not to notice at all.

He brushed her aside and picked up the tray. "You aren't to be lifting things like this any more."

The order annoyed her. "Says who? I'm not handicapped, I'm having a baby. And if you think me lifting a few pieces of china is going to hurt *your child...*"

"Would you rather I call Phoenix and ask the Hartfords to move up here and take over?"

"Of course not."

"Then you'll behave yourself."

Synnamon went on as if he hadn't said anything. "There's no room for them."

"There's a housekeeper's suite."

"*Suite?* A bedroom and a tiny bath are hardly the sort of accommodation they're used to." She followed him to the kitchen and cleared a spot on the counter for the tray. "If what you're really saying is that you'd be more comfortable with someone else around all the time so we're never alone—''

His eyebrows drew together. "Is that why you invited Nick to dinner? Because you don't want to be alone with me?"

Synnamon bit the tip of her tongue. It was just like him to take a straightforward comment and turn it around. "I didn't say anything of the sort. I just thought it would be nice to get to know her better. I had no idea you'd object. But as long as we're getting things straight, perhaps you'll let me know what rules you'd like to set up."

"Does that mean you have some in mind?"

"Well, yes. They're not much different from the ones you'd propose, I'm sure. For instance, don't feel that you have to account for yourself to me, any more than you do to your secretary."

"Oh, I'll happily keep you informed of all my plans," Conner murmured.

What if I'd rather not know what you're up to? Synnamon almost said it, but she bit the words off in time. That was hardly the way to convince him there would be no satisfaction in sacrificing his freedom just to annoy her.

"If you like," she said mildly. "I'll be happy to listen, of course." She started to wash the silver flatware. "I thought you were going to get your clothes and things tonight."

"I did. I left them downstairs with the doorman, because I didn't think you'd be pleased if I staggered in carrying a load of suitcases while Nick was here. Which reminds me, I'll have to call and have him bring them up."

He picked up the house phone.

The soapy silver was sensually slick in Synnamon's hands, and the rhythmic motion of cleaning each piece combined with the rise and fall of Conner's voice in a pleasant pattern.

Overall, she decided, she was happy with the evening. It hadn't turned out quite as she'd hoped, that was true, mostly because of Conner's uncomfortable tendency to twist anything she said around to his own interpretation. But even the fact that he was suspicious and prone to attack surely illustrated the effectiveness of her campaign. He was off-balance and ill at ease. Obviously he didn't know quite what to think.

Perhaps, Synnamon thought dreamily, *if I can keep on giving him the sweetly reasonable, noninterfering, slightly dull wife he seems to want, he might soon decide he doesn't want her after all.*

She finished the flatware and reached for the first crystal wine goblet, laying it carefully in the soapy water.

Or maybe she should go one step further. If she could convincingly portray a clinging vine who was threatening to smother him in unwanted attention, Conner would probably run for cover.

No, she decided, she could never carry that one off.

Conner put the house phone down. ''Jack's on his way up. Where shall I have him put my things, Synnamon? In the guest suite—or in our bedroom?''

The wineglass Synnamon had just picked up slipped out of her soapy hands and shattered against the edge of the sink. Crystal fragments sliced through the bubbles and rattled against the stainless steel. Almost automatically Synnamon scooped both hands into the water to retrieve the pieces.

Instantly, Conner was beside her, pulling her away from the sink. "Stop it, Synnamon! The goblet is gone, and you'll cut yourself to ribbons for nothing."

"That was Waterford crystal. And it was a wedding gift."

"Well, now it's only broken glass. Watch out for your hands." He gathered her hands into his, cupping them between his palms to inspect each line, each joint for cuts.

His fingers felt cool against her skin after the intense heat of the dishwater. The contrast was like a sudden wave of cold running straight up Synnamon's arms to paralyze her brain.

"I'm dripping suds all over the floor," she said, only half-conscious of what she was saying.

"The floor will survive." Conner raised her hands almost to his face, turning the palms as if to cup them against his jaw. Synnamon thought a bit breathlessly that it was almost as though he intended to kiss her fingertips, soap and all.

"Your hands are like silk," he said, and stroked the edge of her palm with a gentle fingertip.

Synnamon had never realized that the band of skin between her wristbone and the base of her little finger was so sensitive. His touch was as soft as a whisper, but the rhythmic movement sent sensation up her arm in a pattern as distinct and unavoidable as ripples of water across the surface of a pond. Except this rhythm, instead of fading slowly away, intensified with each wave.

"So soft," Conner whispered.

The door bell chimed. To Synnamon's ears, the notes sounded flat and almost harsh, as if the bell had developed a chest cold. Or was it her hearing that had gone berserk?

Idiot, she told herself. He was only holding her hands because of her accident. It was crazy to let herself get carried away. She drew back.

For a moment Conner didn't move. Then he cleared his throat and said pragmatically, "Of course, your hands won't be soft for long if you keep doing dishes without rubber gloves."

"I like to feel what I'm doing."

"But that's Mrs. Ogden's job, isn't it?" He turned toward the foyer and paused. "Guest suite or master bedroom?" She couldn't get a good look at his eyes, and there was not a hint of emotion in his voice—nothing to give her a clue to which answer he would prefer.

Synnamon's fingertips were twitching. With the urge to hit him, she told herself. He'd set her up with absolute perfection. If she asked him to use the guest room, he'd no doubt make some comment about it being a silly choice not to want to share a *room*, since she'd caused the whole problem in the first place by sharing a *bed*. And if she was crazy enough to suggest that he return to the master bedroom—well, wouldn't he have a field day with that invitation!

She had to take a very deep breath before she could say, steadily, "Guest suite."

He didn't answer for a long moment. "Very well. Whatever you prefer."

That's all? Synnamon thought in astonishment. *No smart remarks*? She stared down the hall after him.

She felt almost chilly. The temperature in the kitchen had seemed to drop with his departure, and cool air teased her flushed skin. The twitch in her fingertips hadn't gone away, but she no longer had the urge to strike him. Instead, she could almost feel the smooth strength of his jaw, the faint stubble of his beard, the warmth of his cheek against her palm.

She shook her head in disbelief and turned to the sink, carefully fishing out the broken bits of crystal to discard.

I can't want to touch him, she told herself. *It's insane even to think about holding him, caressing him...making love with him.*

She left a note for Mrs. Ogden to warn her about the bits of broken glass that might remain, dried her hands and started down the long hall to her bedroom.

The door to the guest suite was open. On the bed a suitcase lay open, and Conner was stacking shirts in the armoire. Obviously he heard her, for he paused and turned toward the door as Synnamon approached.

She couldn't just ignore him, of course. That didn't fit at all with the image she was trying to maintain. An image, she reminded herself, that she had come close to ruining a few minutes ago. Standing in the middle of the kitchen going all soft in the head because he was holding her *hands*, for heaven's sake.

She paused in the doorway and said, "I hope you'll be comfortable here, Conner. Good night."

"Synnamon."

"What is it?"

"About this bedroom business," he said gently. "Just let me know when you change your mind."

Mrs. Ogden was so tight-lipped she hardly said good morning at all, and she mopped out the kitchen sink with irritable efficiency.

Synnamon drank her first cup of coffee in silence, studiously ignoring the housekeeper's glare. She was still thinking about Conner's parting shot last night. The sheer gall of the man, to suggest that she would inevitably invite him back into her bed. Hell would freeze before that happened—she'd make good and sure of it.

It didn't help, however, to know that a good deal of her annoyance rose not from Conner's confidence but from her own reactions last night. She wouldn't be nearly as furious if she hadn't caught herself woolgathering about the way his face would feel, slightly rough and bristly against her heat-sensitized hands. . . .

And she was doing it again right now, she reminded herself in exasperation. What on earth was wrong with her?

Mrs. Ogden cleared her throat. "It's not my place to ask, of course," she began.

Synnamon sighed. "Probably not," she agreed. "But what's the problem?"

"I was just wondering if you had a nice evening."

"Just lovely," Synnamon murmured. Her mind slid once more to Conner. *If you keep this up*, she told herself, *there's no longer going to be any doubt about who won the first round. And it's not you, my girl.*

"And did your guest enjoy the bourguignonne?"

Synnamon snapped back to the present. "Guest?"

"There's an extra napkin—covered with lipstick, I might add. *And* you didn't put the silver back quite the way I always do."

So that was what was bothering Mrs. Ogden this morning, Synnamon realized, not the bit of additional laundry, but the fact that the romantic little twosome she'd envisioned hadn't turned out quite as she thought it should. Well, Synnamon thought philosophically, the sooner the housekeeper realized her employers were not exactly Cinderella and her prince, living happily ever after together, the less aggravation she'd cause herself by trying to treat an ordinary apartment as if it was an enchanted castle!

"Yes, she did enjoy it," Synnamon said mildly. "There was plenty, and the flavor was outstanding. It would have been such a shame to waste the extra serving."

Mrs. Ogden grumbled. Synnamon was glad the sudden shrill ring of the telephone kept her from hearing clearly. She ignored the housekeeper and picked up the cordless phone.

"Good morning," Conner said. "Sorry I couldn't stay for breakfast with you."

I'll try to survive the disappointment, Synnamon wanted to say. But sarcasm was guaranteed to get her nowhere. "I hope Mrs. Ogden took good care of you."

"It wasn't the same, of course. I waited as long as I could, but you were sound asleep when I looked in."

He'd looked in on her? *Make a note to put a lock on the bedroom door*, Synnamon ordered herself.

Conner went on, "I was just talking to Hartford, and—"

She exploded. "Dammit, Conner, I told you I don't want them! If you bring them up here, I—I'll fire them!"

"Then it's just as well the subject didn't come up."

She was startled and almost ashamed of herself. "Then why did you call him?"

"I didn't. He phoned me. Actually, he asked for you, but since Annie's new secretary didn't know what to do with him, she transferred the call to my office." His voice dropped into a starkly sober tone. "He asked me to tell you that the Contessa's ashes have been delivered."

Synnamon bit her lip, and tears stung her eyes.

There were times now, six weeks after the Contessa's death, that she could forget the sadness for a few minutes and revel in the happy memories. Sometimes she forgot for a little while that the Contessa was gone. She could pretend that the woman was still only a phone call away, enjoying a balmy winter in Phoenix.

Always, however, something happened to remind her that she could never confide in the Contessa again. This particular reminder was the most painful of blows. The only good thing she could think of was that she could escape from Denver—from Conner—for a few days, and have a chance to think. In Phoenix, surrounded by the Contessa's things and the Contessa's spirit, perhaps she could get hold of herself once more.

"Synnamon? Are you all right?"

She cleared her throat. "Just jolly. What did you expect?"

"I'm sorry."

His voice was husky, and Synnamon regretted her sharp tone. "I'll be all right. I'll need to go to Phoenix, though. She wanted me to take her ashes out to the desert, to a special place she always loved."

"Of course," Conner said. "I'll have Carol get the tickets right away. When shall we go?"

CHAPTER SEVEN

CONNER must have taken her startled silence for assent, for the next thing Synnamon heard was the rustle of pages in his desktop appointment calendar. "It looks to me as if this weekend will work," he said. "I'll have to check with Carol, though, to be sure she hasn't scheduled anything."

Synnamon shook her head, trying to clear her mind. "Conner," she began carefully. "I certainly didn't expect—"

"That I'd let you go alone on such a sad errand," he finished. "Besides, I'd like to pay my final respects, too. I wouldn't feel right, somehow, if I didn't. If I wasn't there, it would seem as if I'd violated the code of ethics that was so important to the Contessa."

Synnamon was left speechless. How could she possibly counter that argument? Of course, the Contessa could probably have punctured his reasoning with her typical good humor. The very thought made Synnamon's eyes sting with tears.

"I'll ask Carol to call you later with the flight details," Conner finished briskly. "And I'll see you this evening. Unless you're planning to come into the office today?"

"I wasn't, but—"

"It's probably as well. Giving Annie a hand is one thing, but she shouldn't start relying on you being here to rescue her every day."

"I'm not rescuing her," Synnamon said crisply. "I'm only lending a hand till she finds her way. And if what you're really saying is that you've already decided she isn't up to the job—"

"Not at all. She seems to be doing fine, with your guidance."

Synnamon didn't answer. While that actually sounded like a compliment, she couldn't quite keep from looking for hidden meanings.

"Sorry," Conner went on. "It was a poor choice of words."

Synnamon sighed. She wondered if her moodiness was because of the pressures of the situation or the raging hormones of early pregnancy. Did she really want to know? One would be over in a few months. The other—if Conner had his way—would go on forever.

"I was a little too sensitive," she said. "I'm sorry, too."

There was a brief silence on the other end of the phone line before Conner said, "Would you like to go out for dinner tonight?"

The invitation startled her, and before she stopped to think Synnamon had answered. "No!" Her tone was harsh, and she hastily tried to soften the refusal. "I mean, thank you—but I don't feel like being in public, exactly."

"I understand. Sometimes in the midst of grief it feels good to have something else to concentrate on, and sometimes it's more comfortable to be alone."

He could say that again, Synnamon thought. Except she was morally certain Conner's definition of alone didn't mean *solitary*, just *private*. If he had the vaguest understanding of her desire to be completely by herself, he wouldn't insist on going to Phoenix, would he? And he'd know that her wish to stay at home tonight instead of going out wasn't entirely on the Contessa's account, but was partly because she didn't feel up to explaining to every friend they ran into that yes, they had reconciled....

She growled as she put the phone down. She'd just have to make it clear over dinner that he wasn't invited to Phoenix, that was all, without letting him realize that she was desperate for a couple of days alone. Though exactly how she was going to convince him...

You might as well argue with an influenza germ, Morea had said.

Hoping that Morea might have some wisdom, Synnamon called the law office to leave a message. "You're actually in?" she said when Morea's secretary put her straight through. "And not busy?"

"I wouldn't go that far," Morea said. "You got through because you're on the list of people I need to call today, anyway. I'm doing my part for the Have a Heart Club, working on the Valentine's Ball. So if you want to buy tickets—"

"Not particularly."

"It's all in a good cause. Of course, I'm sort of glad you put off the purchase till now."

"Why?"

"Because last week you could have gotten by with one ticket, and this week you'll have to buy two. Which makes a cool thousand bucks for the organ transplant program."

Synnamon groaned. "So send me two tickets and I'll write a check. Just don't expect me to show up for the dance."

"Why on earth not? Valentine's Day is for lovers, and—"

"Make that one ticket. Conner can buy his own."

Morea made a sympathetic clucking noise. "But now that you're back together and acting like a pair of cooing doves—"

"Where did you get *that* idea?"

"Overheard it at the Pinnacle last night."

"Since when did the grapevine work that fast?"

"Apparently the diner in question was coming through the hotel lobby downstairs on his way to the restaurant just as Conner was checking out, overheard the address where his luggage was being sent and assumed the rest. Unless you *have* been acting like doves?"

"Certainly not in public. Maybe I won't buy any tickets at all."

"Be a sport, Synnamon. Have a heart, as the organizers would say. At least one ticket—"

"All right, one. No, on second thought, send me two."

"Will you make up your mind?"

"Definitely two," Synnamon said. "That way I can bury them in my lingerie drawer and forget all about the ball. If I don't buy two, you'll call Conner, and he'd not only spring for a pair of tickets, he'd want to go."

"Maybe I should call him anyway," Morea mused. "I might end up with another thousand for the cause."

"And one less friend and client."

"You mean you *are* still my client? In that case, it's a good thing I haven't obeyed Conner's orders to send a bill for my services and cancel you out of my computer."

"A very good thing. I'm trying my best to apply your advice, Morea—"

"Now that's a first," Morea muttered.

Synnamon ignored her. "And be the most flexible and cooperative of wives, so Conner will get tired of the whole thing."

"And how's it working out?"

"It's driving me crazy, and he hasn't even noticed."

"Are you sure he hasn't noticed? Maybe he's trying to be the most flexible and cooperative of husbands with the specific intention of driving you crazy."

"If that's what he's doing," Synnamon said glumly, "it's working. And if that's the best suggestion you can give me—"

She heard the door bell chime, and Mrs. Ogden's footsteps faded away down the hall toward the foyer.

"At the moment it is," Morea said. "Frankly, darling, in my experience, you two are breaking virgin ground where divorce is concerned."

"Oh, that's reassuring."

"But if you decide to give up the making nice, I can always file an injunction to get him thrown out of the apartment."

"And wouldn't that look great in court?" Synnamon muttered. "He hasn't laid a hand on me. No verbal assaults, not even an implied insult."

"Mental cruelty," Morea said helpfully. "Playing games with your mind."

Mrs. Ogden cleared her throat, and Synnamon turned to face her. The housekeeper was standing in the doorway, a long florist's box in her arms. "Excuse me, but you've got a visitor, Mrs. Welles."

"All right, thanks." The housekeeper went into the kitchen, and Synnamon uncupped her hand from the telephone. "Morea, this effort to be cheerful and cooperative is wearing on me. I don't know if it's the stress of having Conner around all the time or my howling hormones, but—"

"Personally, I'd bet on the stress. But then," Morea mused, "I don't know anything about the other, so—"

"But if it keeps up, I'm going to have to check myself into a clinic. That, or just turn into a roaring werewolf."

"Well, maybe that's the answer. Give Conner one long look at the real, honest you, and he might take to his heels."

"Screaming all the way? I couldn't be so lucky. Stick to the law, Morea. Your psychological advice seems to lack a little reality, somehow."

"You asked," Morea said cheerfully. "I'll send the tickets over this morning by special messenger."

"Just in case I'm in the asylum by afternoon?"

"Well, when there's a thousand dollars at stake, it does pay to be careful of these things. Not that I have any real doubts about your sanity, of course."

"That," Synnamon said wryly, "makes one of us. While you're at it, send an extra book of tickets. I'll make a few phone calls myself and see if I can sell them."

"Thanks, darling. It *is* a good cause, after all."

"Besides, misery loves company," Synnamon finished. "If I have to go to this dance, maybe I can at least cajole all my friends into going, too."

Mrs. Ogden had gone to the kitchen, so Synnamon couldn't ask who her visitor was. She was startled, therefore, when she looked into the big living room and saw Nicole Fox seated on the edge of a chair.

Nicole jumped up the instant she saw Synnamon. "I didn't mean to intrude this morning," she said hastily. "I just brought some flowers by as a thank-you gift for last night, and when I asked about you—"

"Mrs. Ogden practically dragged you in," Synnamon added, "and abandoned you before you could say you were only asking in order to be polite."

Nicole nodded. "Something like that," she admitted. "She took the flowers and went that way before I could tell her..." She took a deep breath. "It's not that I didn't want to see you, but I didn't intend to barge in like this."

She looked unusually pale, Synnamon thought. She was a little surprised at the sympathy that trickled through her. The young woman was courageous, that was sure. Nicole could have had the florist make a delivery. What had made her brave the personal contact?

Nicole took two steps toward the door.

It would have been very easy for Synnamon to stand still and do nothing, and in a couple of minutes the woman would be gone. But she couldn't help feeling curious.

"Then you *did* want to see me?" Synnamon asked. Did Nicole intend to ask for Conner's freedom, perhaps? Well, if it was anything like that, they might as well get it out in the open. "Sit down, please. I'll ask Mrs. Ogden to make coffee."

"Oh, no—don't bother with coffee. I don't want to put you to any trouble." Nicole perched on the edge of a chair. "I hope you'll like the flowers as much as I enjoyed myself last night."

"It's very kind of you to bring them yourself," Synnamon said.

"You know, you're not at all..." Nicole's voice trailed off, and a tinge of color crept into her cheeks.

"What you expected," Synnamon said flatly.

"Well, no. Conner told me, you see—"

Synnamon could almost imagine *that* conversation. Didn't a wandering husband always have a tale of woe about his wife, a tale guaranteed to win sympathy from the other woman? Surely Nicole wasn't naive enough to repeat it to her. And why had she been dim-witted enough to invite Nicole to sit down and discuss it, anyway?

"He said that you were practically raised by somebody who was even more a stickler on good behavior than Emily Post," Nicole said. "So of course I thought—"

"That I'd be overbearing and rude to anyone who might not be as knowledgeable?" But Synnamon's mind was only half on the question. That was unusual, for Conner to be talking to Nicole about the Contessa. Of course, he'd cared for her, too. Perhaps, in his grief, he'd turned to Nicole for comfort. "I think Conner overstated the case, however. The Contessa was certainly concerned about proper behavior, but she never criticized anyone else's manners. It's extremely impolite to notice anyone else's bad behavior, she always said."

Nicole considered that and smiled. "It does make sense, doesn't it? But Conner didn't ever say anything negative about her. I'm sorry if I made it sound as if he had. He obviously respected her very much."

Synnamon looked straight at her. "And you're very fond of him, aren't you, to defend him like that to me?"

"Oh, yes." Nicole toyed with the cording on the wing chair she sat in and sighed. "He's—wonderful, that's all. I wish..."

Her eyes were so dilated and full of tears that Synnamon was sure Nicole could no longer see her. And there was a tremor in the woman's voice that expressed her feelings for Conner more convincingly than actual words of love could. The combination left Synnamon feeling as if there was a boulder lodged at the base of her throat.

"You're a very lucky woman," Nicole went on, in a low voice that was next door to tears, "to have him. And now your baby, too."

And how, Synnamon thought helplessly, *would the Contessa have answered that*? "Thank you," she said crisply.

Nicole stood up. "I must go. I'm due at work soon—we're doing some around-the-clock tests, and I'm taking the late shift so I can spend some time at Sherwood, as well. And since I'm sort of leaving the company in the lurch by changing jobs in a busy season—" She paused. "But I'm babbling, and you don't want to hear the details. Thanks again for having me over last night. It really opened my eyes..." Her voice dropped almost to a whisper, so soft that Synnamon wondered if she knew she was speaking aloud. "About everything I'm missing."

Synnamon showed her out, then closed the door and leaned against it.

So, in Nicole's opinion, she was a lucky woman. The very thought made her feel hollow.

She wondered what Nicole would have said if she'd announced she'd happily give Conner back to her, wrapped up in hearts-and-flowers gift paper...if only she could.

Conner came home on the dot of six, and a little later, over Mrs. Ogden's chicken Angelique, Synnamon braced herself to bring up the Phoenix trip. She'd rehearsed her little speech in front of her mirror off and on all afternoon, and she was as ready as she could ever be.

The Contessa had asked her to go alone, she'd tell him, so the secluded spot she'd chosen would always remain secret.

The question was whether Conner would fall for the excuse. Or if, at least, he'd pretend to agree, and let her go to Phoenix by herself. She had to admit to having her doubts. Morea might well have a point. If Synnamon could think up this game, so could Conner—and they could no doubt play it with equal facility.

She couldn't quite see what Conner had to gain from the stunt, though, unless he was hoping to make her so tired of him that she'd give up their child into his care and disappear. But of course he needn't have any such elaborate plan as that in mind. It was nothing new, Morea said, for a divorcing couple to try to wear on each others' nerves, for no other reason than just to prove they *could*.

Synnamon only hoped she was being half as successful at driving Conner nuts as he was at making her feel crazy.

She raised a forkful of chicken Angelique to her lips and said, "Conner—"

At the same moment, he said, "I talked to Luigi today."

She was interested despite herself. And also, she admitted, just a little glad for the excuse to put off broaching what was likely to be an uncomfortable discussion. "Did you get him soothed down?"

Conner shook his head. "Not as well as I'd hoped."

"What's the problem?"

"He seems to be convinced I'm going to run the company into the ground without you there to oversee my actions."

"Oh, for heaven's sake." Synnamon's voice was full of disgust. "I've never heard anything so silly."

He looked at her for a long moment, his eyes dark and intense in the dancing light of the candle flames.

Synnamon felt as if he was staring straight through her, and her hands began to shake.

"Thank you for the compliment," he said softly.

Her trembling fingers steadied, and embarrassed warmth rose from the pit of her stomach and suffused her entire body. She hadn't intended to flatter him—she'd only been telling the truth. But it was an odd, uncomfortable feeling to find praise for him rising so automatically to her tongue—without even considering what she wanted to say or the effect it might have.

"At any rate," Conner went on, "I think I need to see him in person."

"And as soon as possible," Synnamon agreed. "Where Luigi is concerned, it's important to control the damage before it gets worse."

"Exactly. I'm glad your assessment of the situation agrees with mine. I've made arrangements to visit him this weekend."

Instead of going to Phoenix. Now Synnamon was glad she hadn't rushed into the discussion. He'd handed her a trump card, and if she played it carefully... "I understand," she said quickly. "Sherwood's concerns come first, and you must do whatever you feel is necessary for the business." She looked at her plate and then gave him the most sincerely troubled look she could manage. "I do want to go to Phoenix, though, Conner. I don't want to put the trip off any longer. So if you don't mind, while you're off seeing Luigi—"

"Of course," Conner said. "Carol already has tickets for us both on the Friday afternoon Denver to Phoenix flight."

Us? "But..." She stopped and tried again. "I thought you said you need to see Luigi right away."

Conner nodded. "That's what makes it perfect. Luigi's spending the winter in his house in Scottsdale—right next door to Phoenix." He cut another bite of chicken Angelique. "Which means we have a wonderful excuse to be in his neighborhood—and also that you can help convince him Sherwood is in good hands."

The Contessa's villa looked just the same. Synnamon got out of the rental car and stood for a moment staring at the quiet facade of the house. It took no imagination at all to picture the Contessa at ease on the chaise longue in her morning room, basking in the soft, filtered sunshine she favored and waiting for them to arrive. There would be hugs and happy greetings, followed by excellent coffee—or more probably sherry, since it was already cocktail hour—and some of Mrs. Hartford's gourmet snacks, and delightful conversation....

Synnamon sighed and let her shoulders slump. Conner, who was lifting luggage from the trunk of the car, turned his head quickly to look at her. She said quietly, "The Contessa always called this the city of new beginnings— but I had no idea how difficult this would be."

The front door opened and Hartford bustled out to help with the luggage. Over Conner's protests, he gathered up the two largest pieces and smiled tentatively at Synnamon. "Welcome home, Mrs. Welles."

She closed her eyes in pain. She didn't want to think of this as her home instead of the Contessa's. Then she squared her shoulders and picked up a flight bag.

Conner took it out of her hand. "I told you not to carry things."

"I'm only trying to make myself useful," she muttered.

"So you don't have to think about the Contessa? This is the hardest part, Synnamon—going in the first time without her being there. Get that behind you and you'll be all right. Remember going into your father's penthouse right after he died?"

She nodded. "It's different, though," she said, almost under her breath.

"A little, perhaps. But after this first time, it will never be quite as difficult again."

It was a *lot* different, she wanted to say. She had mourned Silas Sherwood, of course, but even more she had grieved the father she'd have liked to have—a father who thought she was special, who wanted to spend time with her. And because Silas hadn't been the sort of father she'd longed for, she had to admit—even though she was a bit ashamed of the fact—that there had been a little relief mixed in with her shock and sadness. Relief that the lifelong effort to please him was over at last.

The villa smelled of something spicy. But there was another scent, too—the almost-stale aroma of a room that had been closed up too long. It seemed more like a photograph than a real room, Synnamon thought, as if the image of a single instant had been captured and frozen, never to recur. There was no dust, of course, but there was also no air of human occupation. Each dainty pillow sat squarely in place as if a body had never leaned against it. The piano's music rack was empty, the strings silent. And for the first time in all the years she had known this room, there were no fresh flowers anywhere.

The lack of roses brought home the Contessa's absence as nothing else could have. Tears welled in Synnamon's eyes and overflowed. She tried to control them, turning her back in the hope that Conner wouldn't see, but the effort was futile.

He said something under his breath that she didn't quite catch and came across the room to her.

Synnamon willed herself not to tense, but he didn't touch her, just pulled a white handkerchief from his pocket and put it in her hand.

"I apologize for offending you with my expressions of grief," she said. She knew her tone was just short of nasty, and at the moment she didn't care.

Conner's voice was calm. "Feeling sorry about the Contessa is one thing. Feeling sorry for yourself is another. Which is this?"

I hate it, Synnamon thought, *when he's so logical— and so right*. "The least you could do is let me take it out on you," she grumbled. "I'd feel ever so much better."

The corner of his mouth turned up slightly. "No doubt. What did it, anyway? I can't see anything different."

"The roses," she said. "The Contessa always had roses." She mopped at her eyes.

"Don't—you'll smear your mascara." Conner took the handkerchief out of her hand.

"No, I won't. It's your new nonstreaking kind."

"Well, nothing's guaranteed if you scrub at it like that." He touched the folded edge of the handkerchief gently to her swollen eyelids. "Would you feel better if there were roses?"

Synnamon considered. "I don't think so. That would just be pretending."

"Then we won't have roses. Perhaps— Oh, here comes Hartford, and I smell coffee."

Coffee, she thought. Not sherry. "Did you tell him I'm not drinking alcohol these days?"

Conner looked thoughtful. "No. I thought you might have. Or perhaps he's a mind reader. Are you, Hartford?"

"A mind reader, sir? Not at all. But Mrs. Hartford made gingersnaps this afternoon, and she thought coffee would go better. But if you'd prefer a Scotch and water—"

"No. The coffee will be fine. We've made a dinner date for tomorrow, by the way, so would you tell Mrs. Hartford she doesn't need to worry about feeding us?"

"With Luigi?" Synnamon asked.

Conner nodded. "At his estate, no less." He poured cream into his cup and added, "You look disappointed, Hartford."

"My wife will be, sir. She's been looking forward to a couple of healthy appetites. I must say I sympathize. Life is a bit dull now."

"I'd think you'd enjoy the peace and quiet," Conner said.

"But we feel so unnecessary, sir. In fact, we'd hoped to talk to you both about that very thing."

"Sit down," Conner said.

Hartford didn't seem to hear the invitation. "We thought, perhaps, if you could use us in Denver..."

Conner looked thoughtful.

The silence drew out uncomfortably till Synnamon could stand it no longer. "I'm sorry, but you know it's not a terribly large apartment, and Mrs. Ogden is already in place. I'm afraid no one would be very happy, all tripping over one another. And there is only a single room and bath, not even a butler's suite—"

Conner interrupted. "However, we may buy a house before long. With the baby coming, we could really use the space. And once we make the move—"

"A baby? What wonderful news! Wait till I tell Mrs. Hartford. She'll be thrilled." Hartford's smile faded. "I only wish the Contessa could have known."

After he had hurried toward the kitchen, Synnamon eyed Conner with distaste. "You had to tell him, didn't you?"

"About the baby? That isn't the sort of secret one can keep indefinitely. And we could use more space than we have in the apartment."

"Well, that's certainly true enough. We could *use* the entire planet of Mars. You can have the top hemisphere, I'll take the bottom." She saw the quizzical quirk of his eyebrows and thought better of the outburst. "You must admit, Conner, that it would be polite to tell me these things before you start making announcements to the butler."

"You're right, of course, though the notion actually hadn't occurred to me till right at that moment. But since you think it's a good idea, too—"

Mrs. Hartford bustled in. "How delightful! A baby... And Hartford tells me we're coming to Denver, too."

Synnamon gave up and sipped her coffee. She couldn't possibly fight them all—at least, not just now, when the only thing she felt was overwhelmingly tired.

"I think," she said, "I'll go up for a nap." She pushed her cup away.

"You must take care of yourself," Mrs. Hartford said. As Synnamon left the living room, she heard the housekeeper exclaiming, "Of course you'll want a boy first, Mr. Welles. Every man thinks in terms of a son first, I think."

"Perhaps you're right," Conner said. His voice was slow, lazy, almost dreamy. "A son."

Of course, Synnamon thought. *First, last and always, no doubt*. And if the baby was a girl instead, just how disappointed would he be?

The guest room had been rearranged since their last visit, and instead of the primly separated twin beds it was once more a king-size rectangle. Synnamon shook her head and considered calling Hartford upstairs and asking him to change it. But it seemed like far too much effort—not only for him to do the work, but even for her to make the request.

Besides, if she asked to have the beds rearranged—or if she used the Contessa's boudoir instead and left Conner in the guest room—she might as well announce that the supposedly fairy-tale marriage had hit the shoals some time ago. That was hardly something she wanted to do now that the Hartfords knew about the baby.

And what was the point, after all? Two months ago, the beds had been separated by the width of the room, but it hadn't prevented her from making a mistake that would resonate through the rest of her days.

The biggest mistake, she told herself grimly, of a lifetime.

CHAPTER EIGHT

"THERE'S Luigi's house," Synnamon said. "At least, the number on the gatepost matches what's written in your notebook."

The rental car pulled slowly between the gates and paused at the end of the drive as if Conner was hesitant to go any closer. "*That's* what you call a house?"

"In polite company, yes."

He cast a curious glance at her. "The Contessa's philosophy sank in deep, didn't it?"

"You're surprised?"

"By you, no. By the house—yes, a bit. I expected grandiosity from Luigi. A Roman style villa, perhaps. But I must say the minaret atop the chalet roof is just a little more than I was prepared for."

Synnamon glanced at his notebook, still open in her lap, and said hopefully, "I don't suppose Luigi could have given you the wrong house number?"

"No. And I'm afraid I didn't turn the digits around when I wrote them down, either." The car edged forward.

"I didn't think so. Actually, I'm not at all surprised. It's exactly the sort of thing Harold Henderson would think up."

"Who's Harold Henderson?"

"Luigi." She looked at him in surprise. Conner was still staring at the house, his hands lying loose on the steering wheel. The shadowed light cast by the gatepost lamps cut his face into sharp angles. "Didn't my father ever tell you about him? He's about as Italian as pizza."

Conner frowned. "Wasn't pizza invented in Chicago?"

"Or New York City, at the moment I can't remember which. But it surely wasn't Rome, and that's my point. Luigi was invented—for lack of a better term—in the south Bronx. I can't believe my father never told you."

"Perhaps Silas was keeping a few secrets back to maintain his value to the company," Conner mused.

"I wouldn't put it past him."

"Do you realize," Conner went on, "that you never refer to Silas as anything but 'my father'?"

She shot a sideways look at him, but he was staring straight ahead. "Really?" Synnamon kept her tone polite but flat.

"It's very interesting. Even to his face, I never heard you say 'Dad' or 'Papa' or even 'Father'."

She deliberately widened her eyes, feigning shock. "How about 'Daddy, darling'?"

"Don't try to be flippant. You know perfectly well you've never—at least in my hearing—called him anything of the sort."

"Well, you knew my father. It shouldn't be too hard to figure out." She closed his pocket notebook and held it out. "Here—you'd no doubt be lost without this."

"Possibly. And Carol would be devastated if she had to start from scratch." His palm brushed the back of her hand as he took the small leather book. The contact sent a shiver up Synnamon's arm, but Conner didn't seem to notice. He tucked the book into his breast pocket, parked the car in the enormous concrete circle in front of the house and reached for the door handle. Then he settled into his seat with a frown.

"On second thought," he said, "is this a parking lot or a sculpture garden? I don't see any evidence of cars, and there's the strangest piece of metal I've ever seen planted right in the middle.''

''I'm willing to take my chances. If Luigi gets offended and throws us out, we can go to Emilio's for a hamburger.''

Conner came around the car. ''Where's that?''

''It's a little dive in a very bad neighborhood—but the food is ambrosia. The Contessa used to take me there.''

''The Contessa was quite the woman, wasn't she?'' His tone was admiring.

Synnamon had to clear her throat. ''I always thought so. You know, a lot of people expected her to be a snob, but she was a genuine lady. She probably wouldn't even have winced at Luigi's minarets.''

''Now that,'' Conner muttered, ''would be a challenge.'' He tucked her hand into the bend of his elbow.

Luigi himself came to greet them in the entrance hall.

Synnamon could feel Conner's muscles trembling under her fingertips. Not from nervousness, though, she was positive of that. She wouldn't be surprised if it was repressed laughter that was causing those tremors. And she had to admit that Luigi was a sight to behold.

The shiny wallpaper—pure gold leaf, Synnamon was sure—reflected the light from the dozen torch-shaped sconces and made his hair look like polished amber. The shiny gold tunic he wore was a cross between a toga and Hollywood's idea of an Arab chieftain's robe, and he bowed ceremonially from the waist as he greeted them.

Black, beady eyes flickered over Conner and came to rest approvingly on Synnamon. ''My dear,'' he said. ''You're as sinfully lovely as ever. Silas was right—he told me once that you'd mature beautifully.''

''No doubt he added that it would be entirely due to constant use of Sherwood cosmetics,'' Synnamon said.

"But of course—our Silas was a man who was proud of his product. Conner, I don't believe we've met except over the telephone, have we? What a happy occasion this is, then. I'm glad you made the effort to come all this way just to see me."

The small black eyes had sharpened, Synnamon saw, as if he was calculating his worth to the Sherwood corporation. If two senior officers and shareholders gave up an entire weekend to placate him...

She gave a tiny shake of her head. "I'm sorry to disappoint you, Luigi, but we had some family business here, as well."

"Of course," he murmured. "But I shouldn't keep you standing here. Come in, come in."

The lounge to which he led them managed to make the front entrance look underdecorated. Every wall was draped with rich brocade, and the folds of heavy fabric stirred uneasily with every movement. The room, Synnamon thought, was positively creepy—as if there were secret listeners behind every panel.

She turned down a poisonous-looking cocktail offered by a young woman wearing a skimpy uniform, which looked more like a costume, and asked for club soda with a twist of lime.

Luigi frowned. "Just club soda? I'm sure my staff could find anything you'd like."

"Not right now, thanks."

Conner looked up from a dubious appraisal of his glass. "We're expecting a child later in the year, so of course Synnamon is watching very carefully what she eats and drinks."

"I see," Luigi said. "So the Sherwood empire will be in safe hands for another generation? A fine, strong boy to fill Silas's shoes?"

"We certainly hope so," Conner agreed. "Don't we, darling?"

Synnamon forced herself to nod and look as enthusiastic as she could manage.

Luigi monopolized the conversation all the way through dinner, talking of his chain of spas and the new beauty treatments he was introducing. Synnamon listened with half an ear. She was trying to figure out the contents of her entree and wishing she could send it to Sherwood's lab for analysis before she risked another bite. She didn't realize how far her mind had wandered until Luigi said, "Perhaps after dinner I can show you, Synnamon."

Her gaze flew from her plate to Conner's face, trying to telegraph her panic. Surely he wouldn't ignore her plight. He simply had to rescue her or risk the outcome of the entire evening. But his expression was smoothly noncommittal—or was that the most infinitesimal nod she'd ever seen? She hated to bet on it, but she had no other choice.

"That would be lovely, Luigi," she managed. "And Conner, too, of course?"

"Of course," Luigi said smoothly. "Are you finished, my dear? Didn't you like my chef's creation?"

"It was excellent. But I have a very small appetite these days."

"Then let's go back to the lounge for our coffee and dessert." Luigi tossed down his napkin and led the way. "Take this chair, my dear," he told Synnamon, indicating a long chaise. "It'll make your massage easier."

He strolled across to a drapery panel, which looked no different than the others, pulled it aside and pressed a button on a huge control panel.

"Massage?" Synnamon asked under her breath.

Conner shrugged. "You agreed to it."

Synnamon had to take a deep breath, count to a hundred and remind herself that kicking was forbidden—no matter how much he deserved it.

The same scantily clad young woman who had served drinks came in with a silver tray that contained something that would have looked more at home in an emergency room. Luigi intercepted Synnamon's look and said, as he picked it up, "A wonderful new development, I think. This is the only silicone gel face mask that exists. It allows us to do facial massage without disturbing the client's makeup. Fingers alone are so untidy, don't you think?" He advanced on her. "If you'll just lean back and let me drape this over your face—"

She shot a look at Conner.

With deceptive ease, he moved into position at the head of her chaise. "Why don't you show me the techniques, Luigi?"

Luigi smiled. "Very well. But without the mask, you can't reproduce the results. And the mask is going to be exclusively available at Luigi Salons."

"Of course," Conner said genially. "But if you were to allow us to manufacture them for you..."

"That remains to be seen." Luigi draped the gel envelope over Synnamon's face. "Put your fingertips right here. Now press gently and draw them upward, like so." He nodded. "That's it."

The pressure of Conner's hands against her face was almost nonexistent, but the silicone mask seemed to magnify the effect, sending tiny surges of energy through each muscle.

"Have you already made arrangements with another manufacturer?" Conner asked.

"Not just yet. But I must be honest. I don't like what I see going on at Sherwood these days. The contamination in the manufacturing plant, for instance—"

"That could have happened anywhere," Synnamon tried to say. But the words came out garbled, and for a split-second Conner's fingertips pressed against her jawline on both sides of her chin. Not a very subtle way to tell her to keep her mouth shut, Synnamon thought—but it was effective. She sank a little deeper into the lounge.

"I understand your concern," Conner said. "We knew we were taking a risk, Synnamon and I, by announcing what was going on. I think most of our competition would have tried to hide the fact—but we had faith in our customers. We knew they'd understand the situation and would appreciate our honesty."

Luigi sniffed. "That's just a fancy-dress way of saying that you *couldn't* keep it secret. In Silas's day, things like that wouldn't have happened."

"Oh, no—they happened. He just managed to keep the news away from the customers. You're right about one thing, Luigi. I'm not Silas."

Conner's fingers didn't stop moving in soft patterns over Synnamon's face, and despite her intense interest in the conversation going on over her head, she couldn't stop herself from surrendering to the gentleness of his touch.

It was odd, though. Her face was relaxing under the soft stroking pressure, the tenseness in her temples was gone, and her cheek muscles felt as soft as butter under a summer sun. But instead of vanishing altogether, the tension felt as if it had sunk deep inside her body. Far from the sensitive touch of his fingertips, there seemed to be a coiled spring, and it was winding tighter with every stroke of his hands.

"I don't have anything against you, exactly," Luigi said. "But when an old family firm goes out of the family, something's lost."

"But Sherwood hasn't gone out of the family," Conner pointed out.

"Technically, no. But it's not like you were Silas's son. And with Synnamon leaving—"

"Who said she's leaving?" Conner's voice held a note of mild curiosity.

Synnamon almost sat up straight in shock, but his fingertips pressed her into the soft lounge.

"She's chosen for the moment to concentrate on a healthy baby," Conner went on, "but that doesn't mean she's less interested in Sherwood just because she's not holding down a day-to-day job there. In fact, she may take more real interest in policy-making now that she can focus on the big picture instead of the details of servicing customer accounts."

Very smooth, Synnamon thought. She almost believed him herself. Though maybe he was completely serious. He hadn't said anything about taking her advice, just that she'd have more time to offer it.

"Besides," Conner mused, "who knows? Maybe once the baby's born Synnamon will decide to run Sherwood all by herself, and I'll stay home and raise him."

"Very funny," Luigi said, grunting. "But of course we'll have to wait and see what happens when the time comes, won't we? For right now, I just want you to know I'm keeping a close eye on things. And if I see one more piece of evidence that Sherwood is falling short of Silas's standards, you won't get another chance to sweet-talk me—either one of you."

For a moment, Synnamon thought she could detect in the blunt tones the last traces of a Bronx accent. Then Luigi's voice regained its usual oily charm. "And if Synnamon decides to throw you out altogether, Conner, I'd be happy to take you on."

Conner's fingers slipped, and a corner of his fingernail jabbed Synnamon's face under the edge of the mask. It wasn't a scratch. If she hadn't been so sensitized by the massage, she might not have felt it. And she understood why he'd slipped. She'd been a bit stunned herself by the idea that Luigi wanted to hire him.

"I'd say you're a natural at facial massage," Luigi went on easily, "and I know a lot of ladies who'd be happy to let you practice on them."

As soon as she thought she could get by with it, Synnamon pleaded exhaustion. It wasn't entirely a ploy, either—she *was* dead tired. But she was also horribly keyed up. Even after she'd sat up and taken the mask off, the effects of the massage lingered. She could still feel not only the soft stroking of Conner's fingertips but the tension that had retreated inward, tension that refused to go away.

Once safely out of Luigi's driveway, she put her head back against the seat of the rental car and said, "That was pretty smooth, Conner."

"Likewise. I couldn't have pulled it off without you."

She didn't believe that for a moment, but she didn't feel like arguing. "How long do you think you can keep him believing that I'll be back to work before long?"

"You might want to return."

"To what? Annie's doing fine."

Conner shrugged. "There are other jobs."

"I don't think so." She sat up. "I'm starving. Do you think Mrs. Hartford would mind if we raided the refrigerator?"

"Mind? I think she'd be more likely to empty it for you. But I thought you told Luigi you had a very small appetite these days."

"Only where unidentified food is concerned. What *was* that main dish, anyway?"

"I don't think you want to know."

"In that case, don't tell me."

The corner of his mouth quirked. "What was that place you were telling me about? The dive with the great burgers?"

"Emilio's?"

"That's it. Let's go there. I could stand a thick, hot, all-American cheeseburger right now."

Synnamon hesitated. Surely there wasn't any reason not to go. Besides, the alternative was to return to the Contessa's, invade the refrigerator and sooner or later retreat to that shared king-size bed. The longer she could put that off, the better she'd feel. "All right. Head toward downtown, and I'll give you directions when we get close."

Emilio's was even more of a dive than on her last visit. Though it was clean, the decor ran to vinyl, paper and sturdy glass, and there were even more neon signs in the windows and above the bar than Synnamon remembered. The jukebox was playing, and two couples occupied the tiny dance floor. But despite the hour, only one of the high-backed booths was empty, and without waiting to be noticed by the waitress, Synnamon led the way to it.

Conner slid into the seat across from her and looked around. "The Contessa actually came here?"

"Not only did she come, but Emilio would cook her hamburgers himself and keep her up to date on the doings of all his various nieces and nephews. I got the sweetest note from him after she died—complete with grease stains."

The waitress set a half-sheet of paper in front of each of them.

Synnamon glanced at the smeared photocopy and looked up in surprise. "A menu? What's Emilio's coming to?"

The waitress shrugged. "Some of the tourists get nervous without one. What can I get you?"

"Hot tea, please. And I'll have a medium burger with everything."

Conner didn't even look at his menu. "I'll take your word for it. The same for me, but with coffee."

"I don't mind if you have a beer or something, Conner. Just because I'm being careful what I drink these days—"

He shook his head. "No, that concoction at Luigi's was enough to put me off alcohol for life. I don't know what was in it, but it tasted like the inside of a bat cave."

The waitress returned with their drinks, and Synnamon toyed with her spoon while she waited for her tea to brew. It felt odd, being out with him like this. Almost as if it was a first date.

In fact, she thought, she hadn't been this anxious on their first date. Of course, that evening more than a year ago had been a company function, and they'd only gone together at Silas's suggestion—so Synnamon hadn't really looked at it as a date at all. It was only later that she realized the quiet young man in the long white lab coat was paying a great deal more attention to her than she had expected him to.

She looked up from her tea and found his attention focused on her, his eyes intent and thoughtful. There were two tiny frown marks between his eyebrows, she noted. For the first time she realized that there were other lines in his face, as well. Were they new, or had she just never noticed them before?

She was chastened by the knowledge that it had been a long time since she had really looked at him—at the chiseled face, the strong, lean body, the graceful hands. So long, in fact, that in a way he hardly looked familiar at all.

And what was he thinking as he looked at her?

There was an odd twinge in the pit of her stomach as she wondered what he was feeling. Curiosity, perhaps, at how they had come to this pass. Sadness, no doubt. And probably regret.

Nervously, she raised a hand to brush her cheek. "I was so frazzled that I forgot to ask. *Did* Luigi's mask make a mess of my makeup?"

For a moment she thought he hadn't heard. Then, slowly, he shook his head. "No, it performed as promised. You look fine."

"Good." She folded her hands around her teacup. "It was quite a sensation. Are you serious about wanting to manufacture it?"

He shrugged. "We'd have to look at the details, of course. Making a few for Luigi's spas probably wouldn't be profitable."

"He might consent to a home version."

"If you feel like trying to persuade him, go right ahead. Synnamon—"

There was a firmness about his tone as he said her name that Synnamon hadn't heard for a while—not since those first arguments about the baby—and a shiver ran through her at the reminder.

Conner looked at the table while he drew a rectangle with the base of his coffee mug. "I know you want your privacy tomorrow when you go to scatter the Contessa's ashes, and I respect that. I'll stay as far away as you like—even if it's here in Phoenix while you go out in the desert. But is there any chance you'd reconsider? I'd like to go with you."

She didn't answer.

A moment later, he said quietly, "You see, I lost my grandmother when I was a teenager. Nobody told me she was so very sick till she was gone, and then it was too late. I couldn't even go to the funeral. She was very different from the Contessa, of course—and yet the way they loved was so terribly similar."

"And you need to say goodbye?"

"I'd like to. It's up to you, of course."

Synnamon hesitated. "All right. You can come with me, Conner."

Somehow, the simple phrase didn't feel like an invitation. It felt more like a promise.

Suddenly, a question seemed to echo in her mind. *Why can't we make it work?* she asked herself.

If the baby had come along earlier, before they had started the legal paperwork, they'd have tried to go on, and the idea of a divorce might never have come up at all.

There was Nicole, of course. But perhaps that, too, was partly Synnamon's own fault. In the months they'd lived together, she'd never been suspicious of Conner. He'd given her no reason to wonder if there were other women in his life. And even if that was largely because Sherwood itself seemed more attractive to him than any other woman could possibly be—well, that was a fact of life Synnamon had long ago accepted.

Maybe Conner was right, after all, and they could make it work. He seemed willing enough to give Nicole up. That was clear from the way Nicole herself was acting. And once they'd adjusted to the new realities forced upon them by circumstances, they might rub along fairly comfortably together for the rest of their lives.

There was an all-gone feeling in her chest at the idea. She didn't know whether it came from the necessity of giving up the only bit of independence she'd ever experienced, or from uncertainty about the roles she would be called on to play over the years. The only thing she knew for sure was it would take time to truly get used to the idea of being Conner's wife once more, and the mother of his child.

And after all, she reminded herself, there was no rush. She needn't decide anything right away, for time was the one thing they had in abundance.

"You miss him, don't you?" Morea challenged.

Synnamon hardly heard her. She didn't realize how far her thoughts had wandered while Morea studied the dessert tray. "What did you say?"

Morea shook her head at the waiter, then snapped the last bread stick in two and brandished half of it at Synnamon. "Conner's been gone not quite a week and you're mooning around like a—"

"Please," Synnamon begged. "Spare me the comparisons."

"Then you admit that you miss him?"

Synnamon hesitated. Three weeks ago, when she'd been trying to find an excuse to escape to Phoenix by herself for a couple of days, she'd have found the idea of missing Conner laughable. But now that he'd been in Asia for five days, trying to work out a sudden kink in the supply of product packaging...

"Sort of," Synnamon said.

"And you actually think it's going to be happily ever after?"

"I wouldn't go that far. But Conner's right. We made a deal, and there's no reason we can't live with it. Of course we both wish things were different, but where there's a child, sometimes people have to make sacrifices."

"All right, spare me the sermon. And pardon me if I don't throw out your case file just yet."

"You never throw out case files."

"Of course not—but I'm not usually so certain that I'll need them again." She slipped the bill for their lunch from under Synnamon's hand. "My treat. Consider it a good-luck gift."

"Thanks—I think."

Morea grinned. "But don't lose my phone number. You'll need it when Prince Charming makes you break out in warts after all. I have to go, darling. There are half a dozen clients on my calendar this afternoon."

She swirled off, and Synnamon finished her coffee in peace before she strolled to the Sherwood complex. The weather was pleasant for the end of January—in fact, it almost felt like spring—and it was nice not to feel rushed, as she had for so many years.

Annie was doing just fine in her new job, and there was really nothing for Synnamon to do except provide moral support now and then. The only reason she had even come to work today was that Mrs. Ogden was spring-cleaning the apartment with a vengeance. With a baby on the way, she'd announced, there was serious work to be done.

Though to be honest, it would be more accurate to say that was the main reason, not the only one. For Morea was right. She was missing Conner.

The two weeks since their return from Phoenix hadn't been exactly easy. There had been tense moments. She'd been snappish on occasion, and Conner had seemed moody now and then. But there was a growing peace within Synnamon, a sense that she was doing the right thing. It had started, she thought, out in the desert when she had scattered the Contessa's ashes in the out-of-the-way spot she had loved, and Conner had not said a word to break the mood. She had felt closer to him in that moment than ever before.

Just inside Sherwood's lobby, she stopped in the main ladies' room to repair her lipstick and was startled to catch a glimpse in the mirror of Nicole. Her face looked blotchy, her eyes were red-rimmed, and she was pressing two fingers to the center of her forehead as if she was in pain.

Synnamon couldn't help but feel sympathetic toward Nicole and a little annoyed with Conner. She'd known the job wasn't going to be an easy one for Nicole—or any outsider—to take on. And Synnamon knew that feeling of helpless inadequacy, too—the sense that the job was far too big and her talents far too small. But she'd really thought Nicole could handle it.

She carefully outlined her lips, then said, without looking at the other woman, "Is there anything I can do to help?"

Nicole shook her head. "No. Thanks anyway."

Synnamon twisted her lip brush in the tube and began to fill in the outline she'd made. "If you're having trouble with your staff—"

"No," Nicole said drearily. "It's not the job. Believe me, I wish it was."

"Then are you ill? There's a lot of flu going around."

Nicole sighed. "It's not flu."

"Overwork? You've been holding two jobs."

There was a half-hysterical catch in Nicole's voice. "You, of all people, should understand what I'm feeling right now."

"Oh, no." Synnamon's voice was barely a breath.

"Yes," Nicole said flatly. "You see, I'm pregnant, too."

CHAPTER NINE

THE best measure of Synnamon's shock, perhaps, was the fact that her first thought was to wonder how the Contessa would have advised handling a problem like this.

It was a thorny etiquette problem, indeed, so ridiculous that it was almost laughable. But one more look at Nicole's ravaged face removed the last hope that this was someone's sick idea of a practical joke.

As the truth sank in, Synnamon found herself clinging to the edge of the sink, trying to stop her knees from shaking.

"How long?" she said. It was an idiotic question, of course—as if it mattered. As if it was any of her business, really.

"A month. Maybe a little more."

"That's so little time. Are you—" She stopped. Of course Nicole was certain. She was levelheaded and professional, not the sort to panic till the facts were in.

"I ran the test myself," Nicole said drearily. "I thought I was all right. Then a little while ago, it just hit me— the enormousness of it all."

"It does that," Synnamon agreed. There was an irony in their similarities, which under other circumstances would have been deliciously funny, she thought. Well, maybe someday she'd have enough distance and detachment to enjoy looking back on it all. But in the meantime...

Synnamon counted back. *A month. Maybe a little more*. About the time they were in Fargo, she thought.

Conner had sounded so happy when he'd called her from Fargo.

Conner.

There was the tiniest bit of comfort in knowing that when he went to Fargo, he hadn't yet known about Synnamon's child. And he hadn't known about Nicole's baby when he announced that he and Synnamon would stick to the vows they'd made.

Synnamon could feel sympathetic about the trap he was going to find himself caught in. Committed to a woman he didn't love because of an accidental pregnancy, while the woman he cared about was also carrying his child.

Almost sympathetic, she thought dryly.

She asked, half-afraid of the answer, "Have you told Conner?"

Nicole shook her head. "Not yet. I can't. He's already so—"

She stopped, leaving Synnamon wondering exactly what she'd intended to say before she'd thought better of it.

Synnamon could think of half a dozen possibilities. *Busy. Upset. Angry. Miserable.* Maybe it didn't even matter which word Nicole would have chosen.

Nicole said, "He's been under so much stress..." Her gaze met Synnamon's, and she gulped. "With this trip, I mean."

"And everything else," Synnamon said bleakly. "I know. Don't worry about hurting *my* feelings. Just the same, he'll have to know."

Nicole nodded. "Of course. But I need to think it through myself first. I only found out for sure this morning." Something close to panic flared in her eyes. "You don't mean to tell him, do you? Synnamon, please—promise you'll let me handle it."

Synnamon wanted to scream. This was hardly a secret she wanted to share, but now that she was in the middle of it, there weren't a lot of options—and all of them were bad ones. She could make the promise Nicole asked for and trust that the woman would carry through. She could tell Conner herself, and let the fallout rain over them all. Or she could pretend she'd never walked into the ladies' room this morning.

Right, she thought. *And while I'm at it, I'll pretend the sky is chartreuse, too.*

She knew better than to give her word. And yet she knew just as clearly that no matter what Nicole did, she herself wouldn't be the one to tell Conner. Synnamon couldn't bring herself to barge into the middle of what should be a sensitive and private and happy moment.

Poor Nicole, she thought. It was nightmare enough, this situation they were all caught in. But if Synnamon was the one to break this news to Conner, it could only get worse. She wouldn't do that to any of them.

"You'll have to tell him soon," she said.

Relief gleamed in Nicole's eyes. "I will. I promise I will. But I need a little time to think first."

Synnamon could understand that. She'd felt the same need herself. *And look at where it got me*, she thought.

Still almost in a daze, she retreated to the little office she'd adopted. It was down the hall from her old one and around a corner, close enough to be handy if Annie needed her, but out of the way otherwise. She'd never been so glad to be away from Sherwood's bustle. She closed the door behind her and sank into her chair.

"How could he do this to me?" she whispered.

The words seemed to echo in the room and in her brain.

How strange it was, she thought, for her to react that way. After all, wasn't this—in a convoluted and painful sort of way—going to bring about exactly what she'd wanted?

There was no question in her mind that Conner would want to be free now. Offered a choice between building a family with a woman he cared about and one he felt only duty toward, there could be no doubt what his choice would be. And that would leave Synnamon with exactly what she wanted—her freedom, her child . . . and probably no interference at all from Conner.

But that *wasn't* what she wanted.

She stared across the room, not seeing her surroundings as the kaleidoscope in her mind slowly turned, shattering her long-held image of herself and bringing into focus a new and unfamiliar reality.

She didn't want her freedom. She wanted what she had glimpsed in Phoenix, that night in Emilio's bar—a marriage that might not be passionate but was calm and peaceful and caring. A relationship that might not be precisely loving but that included friendship and companionship. A family that took in mother and father and child.

Why don't you stop lying to yourself? she accused. The truth was, she wouldn't begin to be content with that. Even more than she wanted her child, she wanted Conner. His friendship, his passion . . . his love.

Had her love for him sneaked up on her in the few weeks since they'd made this feeble effort to reconcile? Or had she always loved him and hidden the fact from herself?

She looked hard into the hidden corners of her heart and saw a painful truth that she had been trying for weeks to ignore.

Her pregnancy had been purely accidental. She was not calculating or cruel enough to plan to bring a child into the world to serve as a bargaining chip. But the seduction that night in Phoenix—and it had been a seduction, she admitted now—had not been an accident. On some level, she had been trying to prove that there was still something between them, that Conner still desired her, that it wasn't all over, after all.

She had been trying to win him back because deep inside, she had known even then that she loved him.

Synnamon propped her elbows on the desk blotter and put her face in her hands. Her head throbbed worse with every heartbeat.

She'd thought she'd made the mistake of a lifetime— but she'd been wrong. She knew now that hers had been the mistake of *several* lifetimes. Hers. Conner's. Nicole's. And that of not one but two innocent babies.

And now that the trouble had come to light, what on earth were they going to do about it?

Synnamon didn't expect Conner to come directly to the apartment. His plane was due to land at mid-afternoon, and she thought he'd go to the office.

After more than a week in Asia, his in-basket was overflowing. Synnamon knew what it looked like because several times in the past few days his secretary had asked her advice on how to handle the more pressing concerns. And Conner had to know what it would look like, too.

But he had come home instead.

Synnamon knew he was there the moment his key clicked in the door, even though she was at the far end of the apartment in her office alcove, too far away to hear the tiny noise.

He's home, her heart sang. *He came straight home!*

Then the still-sane part of her brain kicked into gear, reminding her that he might live here for a few more days, but it was not his home now, and it would never be again. All she could do was to treasure those last few days.

Or maybe it wouldn't be days. Perhaps he had come straight to the apartment to tell her that he'd talked to Nicole already. Maybe in a matter of minutes he'd break the news to Synnamon that it was all over.

And she would have to hold up her head and smile, and try not to gasp for breath as if she'd just finished a marathon.

She hadn't seen Nicole since they'd parted in the ladies' room four days ago. But Conner's secretary had his itinerary. If Nicole had braced herself to tell him, all she'd have had to do was make an excuse about why she needed to call.

Synnamon could almost feel his footsteps coming closer down the carpeted hall. It was funny, she thought, how quickly she had become sensitized to his presence—and how long it had taken her to become fully aware of it. That fact alone should have warned her that she wasn't indifferent to him, after all. If she'd only had enough brain to wonder why she felt that way...

Conner had shed his jacket and slung it over his shoulder, and he was loosening his tie when he appeared in the doorway of her office.

Synnamon put down the telephone, checked another name off Morea's list of possible Valentine's Ball ticket buyers, and looked at him.

Trying to appear pleasant but unexcited at the sight was one of the hardest things she had ever done. Just looking at him sent tiny darts of painful pleasure through her body. She'd never seen him in quite this way before, with the knowledge that she loved him coloring her vision.

He looked tired. The lines in his face were deeper, and there was a blue shadow under his eyes, so faint that only her newly sensitized gaze could have picked it up.

She wanted to reach up to him, to stroke the lines away, to hold him and force him to rest.

"Hi," he said. "I thought maybe you'd be at Sherwood today."

The low voice reached straight through Synnamon and twisted her heart. She had to force herself to look away and shrug. "I didn't feel like it. I've been in most days."

"I know. Carol told me you'd helped out with some details."

She tensed. "Carol asked for help, so I did what I could. That's all."

"You're a bit touchy today, aren't you? I didn't accuse you of interfering with my job, you know. In fact, I'm damned grateful you stepped in on a couple of those things."

Synnamon forced herself to relax. "You've been to the office already, then?"

"No, I called Carol from the airport." He rubbed the back of his neck and yawned.

"Then..." She knew she shouldn't say it, but the words slipped out before she could stop herself. "Then you haven't seen Nicole."

"No. Why?"

She hesitated, and then prevaricated. "Nothing I can put my finger on."

"But you obviously have a reason—and I'm interested in why you brought up Nick, because she left an odd message for me."

Synnamon's heart felt hollow.

"Something about a crisis at her other job keeping her away from Sherwood this week. I'm starting to wonder, myself, if she really wants to make the change."

"I couldn't possibly judge that." Synnamon toyed with the stack of tickets.

Conner didn't press the point. He reached for one of the bits of heavy bright red paper instead. "What's this?"

"Tickets to the Valentine's Have a Heart Ball."

"Do we really need a dozen of them?"

"Of course not," Synnamon said tartly. "In fact, I didn't plan on going at all, since we're hardly an advertisement for lovers. I'm selling them for Morea."

"Of course," he said. "I should have known."

She wished she could find even a hint of irony in his voice—a bit of sarcasm that she could twist into a belief that he cared—but he sounded perfectly straightforward.

The silence grew. She stacked the tickets neatly and didn't look at him. "How was your trip?"

"Just a business trip—pretty much like all of them. Got a few problems solved and discovered some new ones. Made one good deal, but a couple of others I'd hoped for didn't come through." His hand went to the back of his neck again.

Synnamon's hands ached to rub his muscles till the tension faded away and he was soothed into the rest he so obviously needed. But she no longer had the right to do that...

In fact, she told herself curtly, she'd never really had that right. Even in the early days, the best days, it had never been that sort of marriage, and it would be folly to forget it now. It would only cause more pain in the long run if she were to start editing her memories.

"You'd better get some sleep," she said. She knew her voice was curt, but she couldn't help it.

I'm glad he won't be here long, she told herself. *I hope Nicole doesn't waste any time.*

But that didn't ease the dull ache deep in her chest.

*   *   *

Conner looked better by the time Mrs. Ogden's turkey tetrazzini was ready to serve a couple of hours later. "Thanks for suggesting the nap," he said as he held Synnamon's chair. "I always did have trouble sleeping on airplanes. Even in first class there's really not enough room to get comfortable."

She served his portion and passed his plate across the table. "That's the bad side of being so tall, I suppose." Her voice was carefully casual. "You do look better."

You look wonderful, her heart said. Asleep or awake, rested or tired, sick or well—it wouldn't matter to her, now that she knew how she felt about him. He would always look wonderful.

"I expect it'll take me a couple of days to catch up at the office," Conner said. "But after that, perhaps we could declare an afternoon off and start to look for a house."

Synnamon's hand tightened on her fork. "I don't think that would be a good idea."

"Why not?"

She regretted letting her words outrun her brain. It had been the obvious answer, expecting as she did that by the end of the week he would have talked to Nicole and any house-hunting trip would be called off, anyway. But it might have been simpler and more sensible to agree instead of face the question. What reason could she give, really, for not wanting to go shopping?

She grasped at the first straw she thought of and said, "It's the slow season for real estate. It's hard to show houses in the winter, so—"

"Seems to me that makes it a buyer's market, if the whole world isn't looking along with us."

"But because of that, a lot of people wait till spring to put their homes up for sale."

Conner shrugged. "Well, if we don't find anything we like, we'll just keep looking. If the Hartfords are coming to Denver anytime soon, we'll need the space."

Synnamon couldn't stop herself. "I don't think that's such a good idea, either. Having them move up here, I mean."

Conner put down his fork. "What's gotten into you? They want to come, and we're going to need them."

She folded her hands in her lap, trying to stop her fingers from trembling.

"Are we back to this again?" He sounded more sad than annoyed. "If the next thing you're going to suggest is that I just get out of your life—"

She raised her chin a fraction. *Why not*? she asked herself. It would be far better to ask him to leave now than to wait around for him to end it. Her heart was dangling by a thread as it was—a thread that was more frayed by the moment. If she asked him to go, she could preserve a remnant of her dignity by making the split her choice, not his.

And even if he later found out that she'd known about Nicole and the baby... Well, at least Synnamon wouldn't have to be there. She wouldn't have to see him agonize, or hear him apologize. Or, worst of all, watch in frozen pain as he tried to hide his happiness.

She twisted her hands together till the ache in her fingers helped her deny the agony in her heart. "As a matter of fact, Conner," she said firmly, "why don't we just call it off right now?"

"I'd love to." His voice was cool. "I had a good chance to think this week, too. But that's hardly the question we're dealing with just now, is it? The fact is that as long as we share a child, I'm *in* your life, and there's no getting out. Believe me, if it wasn't for the baby—"

Synnamon's self-control snapped. It was bad enough to know that to him she was no more than an incubator, but for him to come straight out and say it hurt her beyond bearing. "Don't let that affect your choices," she snapped. "I only told you about the baby in the first place because it seemed the fair thing to do. If I'd had any idea what you'd expect me to put up with—"

"More than I should have expected, obviously, from a woman who's so cold that every time she exhales the furnace kicks on."

Synnamon was too furious to let herself admit the hurt that lay buried beneath her anger. "I might be cold around you, but that doesn't mean I *never* feel—"

"Synnamon, you don't know what warm is."

If there had been any pain in his voice—if it had been an accusation rather than a simple, flat statement—the charge might have hurt her less. But the fact that he not only found her unfeeling but so obviously didn't care wounded her like the thrust of a dull knife.

"Obviously I made the wrong choice," she said.

"About what? Telling me about the baby or not having an abortion? You aren't making things any easier for anyone by treating this baby like a life sentence, you know."

"Isn't that what you've made it? And there isn't even any chance of getting time off for good behavior!"

Conner pushed his chair from the table. "Oh, I wouldn't worry about that—since good behavior seems beyond us both these days."

Synnamon had no idea how long Mrs. Ogden had been standing in the doorway between foyer and living room, watching her. Finally the housekeeper cleared her throat, and Synnamon turned from her study of the hazy mountain range. "What is it, Mrs. Ogden?"

"I just wondered if you had any preference on the dinner menu for tonight."

"How about arsenic soup and foxglove salad?" She shook her head. "I'm sorry. I don't like being so sarcastic, but I can't seem to help it."

Mrs. Ogden made a comforting click with her tongue. "Now, now. You'll feel better once the morning sickness is all over. I remember with my first little one, I actually hated my husband for a while because it was his fault I felt so awful. But once the baby starts to move..."

Synnamon tuned her out. Somehow she doubted that the Ogdens, whatever their problems, had lived in the same sort of armed camp she and Conner had been occupying for the past few days. All her fingernails were gone, and if something didn't happen soon she'd probably start chewing her toes.

How long, she asked herself, was Nicole planning to keep the sword suspended above her head? And how long was Synnamon going to stand around and wait for it to drop?

"No longer," she said firmly.

"What?" Mrs. Ogden sounded a bit offended.

"Sorry. Excuse me, please—I just remembered something I have to do."

She called Annie at Sherwood, and said, "Do me a favor?"

"Anything, Mrs. Welles, you know that."

"Two favors, then," Synnamon said firmly. "I'm not your boss any more, so would you please use my first name? And second—I need to call Nicole Fox at her regular job, and I don't want to ask Carol for the number."

There was enough of the perfect secretary left in Annie that she didn't even ask why. "Let me put you on hold," she said, and a moment later Synnamon was reaching for a pen.

She stared at the number for several minutes before she picked up the phone again.

A bored-sounding secretary answered. "Ms. Fox isn't in," she said. "But she'll probably call later. Can I take a message?"

"No." Then Synnamon took a deep breath. "Yes—and get this word for word, please. 'Synnamon Welles called to ask, Would you kindly do something about this situation you're in?'"

The puzzled-sounding secretary repeated it, and Synnamon put the phone down. The tightness in her chest had eased, if only by a fraction. At least, now that she'd done the little she could, she didn't feel quite so helpless any more.

The dinner hour arrived, and Conner with it. He was almost painfully prompt these days, Synnamon had noted.

Mrs. Ogden had made pot roast. Obviously, Synnamon thought, she'd decided a little down-home atmosphere might help smooth things out. She was dishing their entrees up as they entered the dining room together, in silence.

"You don't need to stay to serve that," Synnamon said.

Mrs. Ogden didn't even glance up. "It's quite all right. I just love seeing those sour looks you two give each other curdling my gravy."

Synnamon bit her lip. Obviously her halfhearted excuse this afternoon hadn't sat well with Mrs. Ogden, and she'd have some fences to mend come tomorrow morning. Then there was the fact that Conner hadn't even seemed to notice the exchange. Mrs. Ogden's attitude didn't bode well, but Conner's was positively threatening.

If this keeps up, she thought, *we'll all be nuts*.

She had to force herself to pick at her dinner, and it wasn't until after she heard the back door close behind Mrs. Ogden that she made an effort to start a conversation. Then she pushed her untouched Bavarian cream aside and said, "Tough day?"

She thought for a moment that Conner wasn't going to answer.

"You might say so." He picked up his coffee. "Nick called this afternoon and dropped a bombshell on me."

A bombshell. So her message to Nicole had gotten through and jolted her—finally—into action.

Now that the moment she had been waiting for had arrived, all Synnamon wanted to do was run from it. Suddenly her throat was so tight the air felt too thick to breathe. The soft scent of half a dozen beeswax candles in the table centerpiece seemed as harsh and overpowering as a chemical fire.

"No wonder—" Her voice was little more than a breath. She cut the words off and picked up her water goblet.

"No wonder what?" Conner's gaze sharpened on her.

Synnamon shrugged. "I'd noticed that you were a bit moody when you came in." *And that*, she thought, *was an understatement that deserved a Pulitzer Prize*!

He sipped his coffee, watching her over the rim. "I thought perhaps you knew ahead of time."

She tried to sound interested but detached. "What was the bombshell?"

"She backed out of the job."

The words took an instant to register. Her muscles seemed to understand before her brain did, and with detached interest Synnamon watched her wrist turn and her fingers loosen, letting her goblet tumble to the table. She didn't even jump when the water surged over her, drenching the front of her dress.

She backed out of the job. But that made no sense at all.

Conner set his cup down. "You seemed shocked."

"So do you." She hardly heard what she said. It took the last air in her lungs to form the words. "But—you told me yourself you thought she was considering it."

"I may have said it, but I didn't really believe she'd do it. In fact, I can't believe it now." He was frowning.

It was not the reaction she had expected. It wasn't even close. She would not have been surprised at shock, pain, discomfort, confusion. But anger? Anger that obviously wasn't focused at her, but at Nicole—and not because of a baby, but because of a job.

She said, tentatively, "That's what you're angry about? The job?"

"Wouldn't you be? She hadn't actually signed an employment contract, but we'd agreed on the deal. I held the position to make it convenient for her past the time I wanted the job filled—and then she pulls this." He shook his head.

Synnamon was stunned. One thing was obvious. Nicole hadn't told him about the baby.

But why? What on earth could have made the woman decide to keep such a secret?

For Conner's sake, she thought. *To spare him pain.*

She could understand that. She'd considered doing the same thing herself, when she'd discovered her pregnancy. It wasn't Conner's fault or his responsibility, she'd told herself. Why tell him at all?

She'd ended up doing so, of course, for two reasons. One was her own moral code. She felt it was wrong not to tell the man he was to have a child. But equally important—even though she wouldn't have admitted it at the time—had been her selfish desire to win him back.

But what if her baby had been the second one? If the situation had been reversed, if he'd already known about Nicole's pregnancy before Synnamon had discovered hers, would she have told him?

No, she thought. *I wouldn't, because it would only cause him pain.*

Sadness swept over her. What a noble and generous decision Nicole had made. It was also dead wrong, of course, but noble nonetheless.

How odd it was, she thought, that in the midst of the whole mess she found herself thinking that the two of them—she and Nicole—could have been friends if things had only been different.

"Well?" Conner said.

Synnamon stood up and started to clear the table. "I'm sure she has her reasons," she said softly.

Conner watched her, his gaze brooding, and then abruptly pushed his chair back. In silence, he carried his dishes to the kitchen and then vanished down the hall toward the guest suite.

Synnamon slipped quietly past his door and closed herself into her own room.

No wonder Nicole had wanted time to think things through. But Synnamon, out of her own impatience, had left a curt message and perhaps pushed the woman into a decision she would later regret. Nicole had refused—for reasons that to her were obviously overwhelming—to interfere in an existing marriage.

But that's only going to make all three of us unhappy, Synnamon thought. The sheer weight of numbers dictated a different answer. If there could be two relatively happy people instead of three miserable ones...

She knew what she had to do.

She sat for a little while longer, trying to build up her willpower, and then she crossed the hall and knocked on the guest room door.

CHAPTER TEN

Synnamon knocked, but she didn't hear his step on the thick carpet. She raised her hand to knock again, and the door opened under her touch.

"Well." Conner folded his arms across his chest. "To what do I owe this honor?"

Tears prickled behind her eyes. She couldn't look at him. "I just wanted to say..." Her voice failed, and she had to clear her throat before she could start again. "I'm sorry for everything."

She didn't know how long the silence lasted. She only knew it seemed a hundred years—and even that wasn't long enough. Because the moment he answered, whether he accepted her apology or rejected it, she would have to go away from him, and that was the one thing she didn't want to do.

The tears began to overflow.

Conner didn't speak. He moved, instead, and held out his arms.

Synnamon tried to turn away, but her body wouldn't obey orders. She gave a little whimper and crept into his embrace. She knew it was foolish, stupid, *wrong*—but she could not deny herself a last bit of closeness.

"Oh, Synnamon," he said. He sounded as if he was in pain, too.

If she could have him just a little while longer, she told herself, just long enough to create one last cherished memory, then she would tell him that he could go, with her blessing, to Nicole.

Just a little while longer. Who would it hurt, after all?

She knew she was making excuses that might not stand up even to her own inspection in the light of day. But right now she didn't care. She would do what she had to do—and she had a sneaky suspicion that Nicole would understand.

Conner drew her ever so slightly closer, and Synnamon let herself relax until the softness of her body molded against the strength of his. Slowly, she raised her face to his and let her fingertips brush his cheek.

He had told her once to let him know when she changed her mind about wanting to make love with him. Now she told him, with every nonverbal means at her command. Simply being close to him brought pleasure. Touching him and being touched created glory.

When she gave herself to him, it was, for the first time ever, completely without hesitation, without reservation and with all the love she possessed.

One last loving, she told herself, *to hang onto for the rest of my life...*

And then there was no possibility of coherent thought—only sensation stronger than anything she had ever known. A beauty she had no more than glimpsed before unfolded for her in a panorama of surrealistic color and crashing sound and left her shaking and crying and clinging to him with all the frantic strength of her desire.

He held her afterward, and stroked her hair, and smoothed away her tears, and a long while later he said, "I think we have some things to talk about."

Synnamon tensed and shook her head. "Tomorrow," she whispered, and kissed him again. "Tomorrow."

He held her even after he went to sleep, and she lay in silence for a long while, pressed against his side, watching and listening. She memorized every angle of his face, the curve of each eyelash, the rhythm of his heartbeat.

She waited till the middle of the night to slip away from him. He murmured a little protest and then sank back into sleep, and she left him there and retreated to her bedroom to pack a few of her most precious belongings. She tried a dozen times to write a note, and ended up with three bare sentences.

It's better this way for all of us. Maybe you should talk to Nicole again. I'll be in touch when I can.

She didn't know how to sign it, so she didn't. She folded the page, wrote his name on the outside and left it propped against the coffeepot where he would see it first thing in the morning.

Then, very quietly, she closed the apartment door behind her. The doorman downstairs summoned a cab, but she waited till it was well away from the building before she told the cabby to take her to the airport.

She'd fit right in with all the early commuters, Synnamon thought, on the red-eye flight to Phoenix.

The Contessa had called it the city of new beginnings. Synnamon had hoped that would be true for her, as well, but as the days slid by she found herself doubting that her hopes could ever rise again from the ashes she had made of her life. Perhaps, she thought, once the baby became more real, she would find energy once more, and faith, and an optimistic eye for the future. But in the meantime, it took all the stamina she had just to call Morea and leave a message for her to refile the divorce papers.

The Hartfords were obviously worried about her. Mrs. Hartford cosseted her with every kind of food Synnamon had ever said she liked, and probably would have tucked her into bed each evening if Synnamon had allowed it.

After the first sleepless night, she moved to the Contessa's room. It might hold as many memories as the guest suite, but at least they were more manageable ones.

Still, she lay awake for hours each night while she sorted out the rubbish pile she'd made of her life. She understood now that it hadn't been reluctance to stay married that had prompted her to ask Conner for a divorce. It had been the fear of going on as she was, loving him but unloved in return. She had been afraid that someday he might leave her alone, as her father had, so she had prompted the split herself instead of waiting uncertainly for the day she was sure would come.

She understood, too, why she'd been so generous—despite Morea's strenuous and reasonable objections—in that first, abortive property settlement. By giving Conner full control of Sherwood, Synnamon had been setting him free. She'd separated herself from the company hoping, deep inside the hidden corners of her heart, that he would say the company didn't matter, that he wanted her as much as he wanted Sherwood. That he wanted her *more*...

But it hadn't happened that way, of course, and so she'd moved on. She'd resigned from her job and told herself and Conner and everyone who asked that she was escaping the stress of her father's legacy, the pressures of customer service.

She'd been trying to escape, all right. But it wasn't job stress she'd run from, it was Conner—and the knowledge, no less real even though she hadn't admitted it to herself at the time, that she could never be as important to him as he was to her.

How stupid, she thought. *I had almost everything I wanted, but I threw it away because I wanted more!* She'd had Conner, his name, his promise of fidelity, his honor. But she'd wanted his love, so she'd tossed away the rest as if it had no value.

And now she had nothing at all.

There was no escaping Valentine's Day. It wasn't so much a day any more, Synnamon concluded in disgust, but an entire season. Long before February fourteenth, radio stations began blaring ads for flowers and candy. For a full week, the newspaper headlined the best places in Phoenix to buy exotic gifts, and one of the television talk shows featured daily interviews with the ten longest-married couples in the state. Red hearts and love songs were everywhere.

And it rained. Day after day it rained.

"Don't you dare complain about the rain," Morea said unsympathetically when she called on the twelfth, "because it's snowing like fury here in Denver. And as long as we've brought up fury, that's exactly how I feel about you. I'm speaking as your friend, of course, and not your attorney—but how dare you leave a message like that and then not even call back?"

"I'm sorry, Morea. I've been a little worn down."

"You could be more helpful, you know. You didn't tell my secretary where you are, you didn't even leave a number—"

"How did you find me, anyway? This phone is unlisted."

"It wasn't easy, let me tell you. I had to call Conner to get the number."

Synnamon's heart squeezed. "You didn't tell him I'm here?"

"How could I? I didn't know it myself. I just thought it was worth a try. In any case, if Phoenix was the first hideout I thought of, it's not likely to puzzle Conner for long."

"Stupid question," Synnamon admitted.

Of course, Conner would have had no trouble figuring out where she'd gone. And the fact that he hadn't followed her, hadn't even called, only confirmed that it didn't matter to him what she did. By now he'd no doubt sorted everything out with Nicole.

"Now what's this about the divorce?" Morea asked. "Are we actually going through with it this time? Because if this is only another lovers' spat—"

"It's a far cry from that."

"You know, I ought to refuse to take you back at all."

"Please, Morea. I need a friend."

"You know all my weaknesses, don't you?" Morea sighed. "I suppose we have to start from scratch with the property settlement. And now there'll be child support to negotiate, too."

"No. I don't want any of that. Offer Conner the same deal we agreed to before on the property, and tell him I don't expect anything from him."

"Are you out of your ever-loving *mind*?"

"No," Synnamon said calmly. "I think I've just started to get it back."

Morea groaned. "You're already assured of a place in the hall of fame for difficult clients, Synnamon, you don't have to go for a world's record. All right, I'll get everything organized, and you can sign the papers Friday night at the Valentine's ball. Then if Conner agrees—"

"Now who's lost her marbles? If you think I'm coming back to Denver for a *dance*—"

"Of course you are," Morea interrupted. "The Have a Heart committee is giving you an award for selling the most tickets any one person's ever managed to peddle. How will it look if you don't show up to accept it?"

Synnamon managed a groan—which Morea seemed to interpret as agreement—put the telephone down and went out on the terrace. The rain was only a light mist now, and under the shelter of the terrace roof the air was clean and fresh and almost warm, compared to what she'd left behind in Colorado. She stretched out on a chaise longue and watched scattered raindrops splashing into the pool just off the terrace.

All right, she decided. She'd go to the ball, since Morea apparently was going to insist. She'd make just enough of an appearance to keep the committee happy, she'd sign the papers, and then she'd come back to Phoenix and get on with life. It was time to stop feeling sorry for herself, for her sake and that of her child.

She didn't quite know how she'd start. With simple things, she supposed—a swim, a walk, a little shopping, a call to a friend. The important thing was to begin. If she went through the motions long enough, surely someday she'd feel like living again.

The grand ballroom of the Denver Kendrick Hotel was agleam when Synnamon slipped through the main doors and edged off to a shadowed corner. From this isolated spot, nearly concealed behind a trellis draped with roses and ivy, she could see most of the enormous room. Three huge crystal chandeliers, their multitude of tiny bulbs dimmed, cast a romantic glow over the crowd of dancers. Around the edges of the polished dance floor were rows of tiny tables draped in pink linen, each topped with a single long-stemmed red rose in a glass vase. Red and pink balloons drifted in the shifting air currents. From a stage at one end of the ballroom came the soft strains of a love ballad.

Perfect, Synnamon thought. The ball was well underway, just as she'd planned. The ballroom was a sea of red and pink and white dresses. Her soft pink gown, flattering as it was, wouldn't be noticed from a distance. She could lose herself in the crowd, and no one would know how long she'd been there.

The moment her part was played, she could vanish just as easily. Since she was staying in the hotel, she didn't have to retrieve a wrap. All she had to do was slip up the stairs from the mezzanine to the next floor as if she was seeking out a ladies' room, then vanish into the closest elevator and to her room. No one would miss her, and she could be on a plane to Phoenix first thing tomorrow morning.

It was ironic, though, she thought, to find herself staying even for a single night in the hotel that had been Conner's headquarters during their separation. She wondered which room had been his in those long weeks. Had he been comfortable here?

And was he comfortable now? She wondered if he was with Nicole tonight, celebrating this day for lovers. Perhaps he was remembering, as Synnamon was, that if everything had gone according to plan, their divorce would have been final today. They'd be finished with it now, instead of having to start all over.

Stop thinking about that, she told herself, *and start looking for Morea.*

A voice came from behind her. "Happy anniversary."

She turned too fast, and the slender heel of her shoe skidded on the hardwood floor. Conner's hand closed on her elbow, steadying her till she could regain her balance. Then he took half a step back, as if to better inspect her.

What was she supposed to say? Thanks for the good wishes? It would be an idiotic response, but then his greeting had been, too. He didn't sound happy, and he certainly didn't look happy. His jaw was tight, and his eyes were turbulent.

But he still looked marvelous, she thought. His tuxedo fitted like a dream, and the snowy white of his pleated shirt made him look as if he'd just returned from a few days in the sun. For all she knew, of course, he might have. The thought of him lounging on a beach somewhere with Nicole sent a stab of envy through her heart.

Conner's voice was crisp. "I thought you said you didn't intend to come to this affair."

Synnamon shrugged. "Morea put the pressure on. You know how she can be. I didn't realize you were coming, either."

"Or you'd have warned me to stay away? It's just as well, anyway. You've saved me a trip to Phoenix."

She blinked in surprise.

"You look puzzled. Have you forgotten about that talk we didn't finish?"

Synnamon let her gaze drift across the crowded ballroom. "Well, we can hardly do it here and now, can we?"

"Why not?"

"Oh, come on, Conner. You've known all this time where I was, so why didn't you just pick up the phone if you had something to say?"

"Because by the time Morea told me you'd moved to start the divorce all over again, you were already on your way here."

She sighed. "I'm not going to talk about it right now, Conner."

"Nobody's paying any attention."

That was true enough, she reflected. They were probably as alone in this corner of the ballroom, even though they were surrounded by five hundred people, as it was possible to be. The dancers' attention was focused on the music. The spectators were watching the dancers. No one was paying attention to the isolated corners.

"All right," she said. "Let's get it over with. Surely you can't mean you're surprised that I've filed for divorce again. Why did you think I left, anyway?"

"Because you needed some time to think—even though you did tell me that we'd talk the next day. Or was that just an out-and-out lie? An excuse so you could get away?"

The accusation was close enough to the truth that she couldn't stop the embarrassed flush that rose in her cheeks.

"At any rate," Conner went on, "that's why I didn't hop on the next plane after you. I thought, once you'd had some distance, a chance to consider... And as long as we're asking why, I've got one, too. If you were planning to leave, why did you practically beg to go to bed with me that night? Was it just a nice little farewell gesture? A goodbye gift?"

The accusing note in his voice made Synnamon's heart twist.

"Were you trying to soothe your conscience by giving me something to remember?"

"No!" she snapped.

"Well, that's some comfort, at least. Unless you mean you did it because you finally decided I wasn't so bad in bed after all, and you wanted one last thrill to remember."

Tears of pain came to her eyes. He was making her precious memory sound unbearably stupid and cheap.

"Please, Conner. Going over it all won't do any good." She braced herself. "Did you take my advice?"

"Which bit of it?"

"About talking to Nicole."

"Otherwise known as the spanner in the works? What about her?"

His tone was curt. It was unlike him, Synnamon thought, to be so callous. Upset, certainly. Angry, perhaps. But not uncaring. Not Conner...

"You don't need to be cruel," she said. "What are you going to do about her?"

"I don't have much choice, do I? I'll look for someone else to handle the research and development job."

Synnamon was stunned, and the question was out before she could stop herself. "Then she still hasn't told you about the baby?" She caught her breath, but it was too late.

"Of course she did." He sounded impatient. "That's why she's going back to her other job, because it's less complex. It's also less money, which is why she dithered around so long before making up her mind. But she'll have more freedom for the baby."

The music shifted to a soft and sensual love song, and the ballroom seemed to hush as the dancers slowed to the new rhythm. Synnamon could hear the rustle of air in the balloons above her head. But where Conner's voice was concerned, her hearing seemed abruptly scrambled. He couldn't possibly be saying what she thought she had heard.

"That's all it means to you?" she whispered.

"Why should it..." His gaze sharpened on her face. "Oh, no. You don't think—you can't think Nick's baby has anything to do with me."

"Doesn't it?" she asked crisply.

"No, it doesn't. Nick has a perfectly inadequate jerk of a lover who isn't worth the dust on her shoes. He can't even hold a job, which is why she was so torn between coming to Sherwood and staying where she was."

"And Fargo? You were there together."

"What about it? I needed help. She came up and gave it. She also cried on my shoulder a lot about how sick she was of the boyfriend's behavior. And I—" He stopped.

Synnamon said softly, "You told her how sick you were of me, I suppose?"

"I did my share of crying on shoulders—in a manner of speaking. But that's all the farther it went, I swear. My God, Synnamon, what kind of Lothario do you think I am?"

She shook her head. "It's all right, Conner. Don't think I don't understand, because I do. Our marriage was over, all but the paperwork. Why shouldn't you be seeing someone else? And Nicole told me herself..."

But Nicole hadn't actually said that Conner was the father of her baby, Synnamon realized.

I assumed that because I loved him so much, she must too. I assumed that no woman could overlook him, that no woman could prefer another man if Conner was around. And if she loved him, then of course her baby would be his, as well.

Her stomach was churning. She'd had evidence of Nicole's love, she told herself frantically. She'd never forget the look in Nicole's face that day she'd stopped by the apartment with flowers and told Synnamon what a lucky woman she was. Nicole had meant every word of it. There had been no mistaking the love in her eyes.

And maybe she did love Conner, Synnamon thought. The boyfriend might be no more than a poor substitute for the man she couldn't have. Or maybe the love Nicole felt was a different kind than Synnamon knew but, blinded by her own experiences and prejudices, Synnamon had been unable to distinguish the difference.

"I assumed she *must* love you," she said, almost to herself, "because I did."

Conner might as well have turned to bronze. Not an eyelash twitched.

The music shifted once again, but Synnamon didn't hear it. The realization of what she had said and the implications of that admission crept over her like a cold mist, soaking slowly into her bones. "Not that it changes anything, of course."

Conner moved then, shifting his feet like a boxer about to leave his corner. He put his hands on his hips. *"Did?"* he asked quietly.

She had to go back over what she'd said before she quite understood the question, and then she was forced to admit a grudging respect for the way he'd gone, with a single word, straight to the heart of the matter.

She was already aching from the strain. Surely it couldn't get any worse—unless he were to pry. So why not admit the truth, and at least not add the pain of cross-examination? "No," she said quietly. "I didn't mean past tense. I meant present."

She listened to his long, slow intake of breath and the even longer release. Was he counting to ten, she wondered, or did he have to go even higher? "Is that why you ran away? Because you—" the calmness in his voice gave way for an instant "—love me?"

Synnamon didn't look at him. "Too much to keep you miserable. If Nicole was your happiness..." She stopped, then said, very softly, "Then I wanted you to be happy."

"She's not. We've been friends—no more."

"At any rate, that's sort of beside the point now, isn't it?" Synnamon turned restlessly from him, staring unseeing through the trellis to the ballroom floor.

She couldn't face him. The mere act of looking at him would make it far more difficult to say what she needed to—and it was desperately important that he understand.

"Beside the point," she said huskily, "because I don't think I can do what you want, Conner. I can't live with you, and love you, and know the only value I have for you is the baby. What if it's not the son you want? I couldn't stand to see my little girl rejected as I was—"

He hadn't moved, but she could feel his anger pounding over her as strongly as the sudden hard-rock beat of the band.

His voice was low and rough. "Dammit, Synnamon, I am not your father—and if Silas was still alive, I could cheerfully kill him for what he's done to you."

The cold fury in his voice sent ice chips up her spine.

"I'm sorry," she managed. "But it's always been so clear that you were only interested in Sherwood...." Her voice trailed off.

"Sherwood," he said finally, "was an attraction."

"Tell me something I didn't know." Her tone was bitter.

"So were you, in a very distant kind of way. You're eye-catching, Synnamon. Beautiful, yes—but it's more than that. The way you carry yourself and the air of mystery that hangs around you..." He sighed. "But you were so chilly I didn't seriously consider even trying to get to know you until your father suggested I take you to that party."

"Please, Conner," she begged. "Don't give me the details. I really don't want to know how you fixed it up between you."

He didn't seem to hear. "But there was something different about you that night, when I watched you with the employees—not the management team you worked with all the time, but the line workers, the packers, the kids in the shipping department. And I wanted to find out if there was a real woman under that frosty shell."

She turned slowly to face him, eyes wide.

"That was when I really started watching you and falling for you—but I didn't want to face up to that. It was too painful to admit that I'd tumbled headlong into love with a woman who didn't care if I existed."

Tumbled into love? She couldn't breathe.

"Who only married me to get away from her father—"

"I didn't, really." She could barely whisper.

"You did a good job of faking it, then. You didn't care if it was me in your bed or a stuffed teddy bear—except that the teddy bear would be less demanding and a whole lot more fun to sleep with."

She felt embarrassed color rise in her cheeks. "That's not true. I never rejected you—"

"No, you didn't," he said dryly. "You acted as though you had no say in the matter. You were such a lady in bed that I felt like a criminal every time I thought of making love to you." Conner cleared his throat. "The first time I ever felt you wanted me—really wanted *me*—was the night the Contessa died."

"I was so lonely that night," she admitted.

"But the next morning, you were right back to being the perfect lady. *Thanking* me—my God, Synnamon, you don't know how that hurt. And giving my rings back—"

"I hated the idea that you might be sorry for me. Maybe even feel bound to me because we'd made love."

She put one hand to her temple. Her head was spinning. "Is that why you moved to the guest suite? When we were still together, I mean."

"You call that being together?" he asked dryly. "Of course that's why. I wanted you so much, and it was a little easier that way."

"I thought you'd gotten tired of me." Her body was trembling. "That I hadn't pleased you."

With two steps, Conner was beside her, taking her weight against him. "And I thought you were relieved when I didn't bother you any more."

She shook her head violently and clung to him. "My father taught one lesson well," she said bitterly. "You're only loved for what you can give."

"And since you couldn't be the son he wanted, he found you worthless." He held her a few inches from him and looked intently at her. "What is it going to take to convince you that *I am not Silas*? I don't care if this baby is a boy or a girl. I don't care if there's a baby at all." He paused. "Yes, I do care. If you'd aborted our child—"

"I could never do that."

"I know that now. Anyway, it isn't the baby that matters most. It's you I love, Synnamon. So much that having to face the fact that I couldn't reach you, that my love wasn't enough to break through that wall around you, almost drove me crazy."

She put her head on his shoulder. "Don't, Conner."

"Maybe it's better if I tell you all of it, sweetheart."

She considered, and nodded. He pulled her closer and laid his cheek against the top of her head. His voice, soft and level, stirred her hair.

"To protect myself, I became distant and cold and uncaring. The day you asked for the divorce, it was almost a relief. At least it was over, and I could finally admit that I was a failure at the most important thing I'd ever tried to do.''

She held him tight, wanting to tell him that he wasn't the one who had failed. But her voice was incoherent. It was the closeness of their bodies, the warmth of their embrace that eventually soothed them both. She sensed his muscles relaxing and felt her tension easing away.

A long while later, he raised his cheek from her hair and said, ''Will you wear my rings again, Synnamon?''

She nodded, and was startled when he shifted slightly and reached into the breast pocket of his tux to pull them out.

''I never bothered to put them back in the safe,'' he admitted. ''Sometimes they've been a reminder of unbearable pain, sometimes of a moment when I really believed we had a chance. But always a reminder of you.''

''I know,'' she said. ''You said the diamond was perfect—hard and cold, and just like me.''

''But always with the flash of fire,'' he said softly, ''and the promise of warmth that could keep a man content forever—if I could only reach you and free it.''

''I wouldn't have blamed you for writing me off altogether.'' The knowledge of how close she had come to disaster, through her misguided efforts at self-protection, made her feel sick. ''If it hadn't been for the baby...''

''I don't know what I'd have done,'' he admitted. ''I expect I'd have tried again anyway—because even with my pride in shreds, I couldn't put you out of my mind. And what did I have left to lose?''

He cuddled her closer, and Synnamon let her body melt into his. She'd never known what a comfort it was simply to be held. There was one nice thing about the shadowed corners of a formal ballroom, she thought hazily. The casual observer wouldn't even notice whether a couple was dancing or just embracing.

It was a long while before she remembered that while they'd solved the most important problem, others still awaited attention. "What *are* you going to do about research and development?" she asked. "Look for someone else?"

"I don't want to," he said slowly. "The department has already been without a head for too long. If Nick had procrastinated any longer there wouldn't be anything left."

"No wonder you were grouchy all the time."

"That, along with not knowing where I stood with you from minute to minute." He smiled at her. "I suppose I might have been a little testy."

"A little?" She leaned more comfortably against him.

"Actually," Conner said, "I was thinking I might hire myself. I like research and development, and I miss my lab."

Synnamon frowned. "But can you do it all? Now that I have you back, I'd sort of like to see you once in a while. It's not my decision, of course, but—"

"But you're always sensitive to what's best for Sherwood."

"Well, of course I'm interested."

He smiled. "Don't be touchy, darling—that was a compliment. I was wondering if you might consider a change, too. If you were to come back to work as the head of the whole place..."

"Me?" Her voice was little more than a squeak.

"Of course. You're meant for it, Synnamon. Silas couldn't see it, but he trained you for the job despite himself. You've shown it in a dozen ways. You saw immediately that Nick wasn't right for the job—"

"That," she said wryly, "was mostly because I was jealous."

"Still, you recognized the fact long before I did. And you told me exactly how to handle Luigi."

"True. I'm apparently only blind where you're concerned."

Conner grinned. "And you took care of things while I was in Asia. Carol kept me posted."

"You were thinking of this then?"

"Oh, yes—until I came home to the coldest hello a man ever got."

Synnamon bit her lip.

"Followed by the warmest night of our marriage. That's the thing that hurt worst, actually—to think that you could hold me like that, make love with me, then leave that icy little note and walk away."

Tears were stinging her eyes. "I thought it would kill me to give you up."

"Good." He kissed her softly. "Remember that—so you're never tempted to try it again."

Her tears overflowed, and gently he kissed each one away. After a couple of minutes, however, Synnamon started laughing and tried to push him away.

His arms tightened around her. "What's the matter? Am I tickling you?"

"No—but you have mascara all over you." She traced the line of his lips with her fingertip.

Conner frowned. "I thought you wore the kind that won't come off."

"Well, you guaranteed it against water aerobics, rainstorms and lifeboat rescues—not tears of joy. Obviously, we'll need more tests. Since I'm the boss now—"

He didn't wait for her to finish. "And just as obviously, we can't make an official appearance at the ball with mascara all over us."

"Oh. That *is* a problem, isn't it? I have a room upstairs."

"An inspired idea if I ever heard one." Conner's lips were against her throat, and his breath teased the pulse point under her ear. "You know, I like your suggestion of putting a bed in the president's office, too."

"Even if it's a baby crib?"

"Well, I suppose it'll do for now." He drew her closer yet.

A couple of minutes later, Synnamon emerged from the most thorough kiss she'd ever dreamed of and murmured, "Morea will never forgive me when I tell her this."

"Of course she will. Who'll sell all the tickets for the Valentine's Ball next year if she holds a grudge?"

Synnamon laughed. "But we were going to have the perfect divorce. What a pity we had to go and mess it up!"

"But you're wrong, my love," Conner said firmly. "We're still going to have the perfect divorce."

She pulled away from him, eyes wide with shock.

He tugged a long-stemmed red rose out of the vine-draped trellis, folded her fingers around the stem and raised her hand to his lips. "Because," he said, "the perfect divorce for us is...no divorce at all."

And as he drew her gently into his arms, Synnamon smiled and agreed.

* * * * *

*Look out for the follow-up to this story,
in which Synnamon's best friend and lawyer,
Morea Landon, meets her very own hero!*

It's coming soon!

If you are looking for more titles by

LEIGH MICHAELS

Don't miss these fabulous stories by one of
Harlequin's most renowned authors:

Harlequin Romance ®

brings you

PENNINGTON

a place where dreams come true...

Welcome to Pennington, the fictional town in the heart of England created by popular author Catherine George.

Surrounded by lush countryside, with quaint tearooms and public gardens ablaze with flowers, Pennington is full of charm—the perfect place to find romance!

This delightful English town is the setting for future romances by Catherine George.

Next month watch for:

#3449 THE SECOND BRIDE

Rufus Grierson had married Jo's best friend—but when his wife was taken from him so tragically, Rufus found himself turning to Jo for comfort. Shared grief led to passion...and to pregnancy. Rufus insisted on marriage, but was he only interested in his unborn child—not the love Jo longed to share with him?

Available in March wherever Harlequin books are sold.

Harlequin Romance ®

brings you

SIMPLY THE BEST

Authors you'll treasure, books you'll want to keep!

Harlequin Romance books just keep getting better and better...and we're delighted to welcome you to our **Simply the Best** showcase for 1997, highlighting a special author each month!

Watch for:

#3448 GETTING OVER HARRY
by Renee Roszel

Emily has been jilted at the altar, and her best friend, Meg, convinces her to take a holiday to get over it. But Emily refuses to be persuaded that the best cure for a broken heart is another romance. Enter Lyon Gallant on the scene: he's rich, he's cute—and he wants Emily!

"Renee Roszel heats up your reading pleasure."
—*Romantic Times*

"Fast moving and entertaining, sparkling to the very end!" —*Affaire de Coeur* on *Dare to Kiss a Cowboy*

"Ms Roszel produces exciting characters and dialogue that packs a punch."
—*Rendezvous*

Available in March wherever
Harlequin books are sold.

Mary thought of making a run for the front door, then remembered the phone by her bed. Keeping her eyes on the hall, she slid toward the nightstand.

There was another noise, not so soft this time. A footstep, followed by the sound of something—of someone—brushing against the wall.

Mary's heart bounced in her chest. Fear ran through her body like strong acid. With trembling fingers she lifted the receiver of the phone and brought it up to her ear. In the silence the dial tone seemed impossibly loud. Surely whoever was out in the hallway would hear it. Surely he would know what Mary was trying to do.

24297

Don't miss any books in this thrilling new series
from Pocket Books:

FEARLESS™

#1 Fearless
#2 Sam
#3 Run
#4 Twisted
#5 Kiss
#6 Payback
#7 Rebel
#8 Heat

All Pocket Book titles are available by post from:
**Simon & Schuster Cash Sales, P.O. Box 29,
Douglas, Isle of Man IM99 1BQ**
Credit cards accepted. Please telephone 01624 836000,
Fax 01624 670923, Internet http://www.bookpost.co.uk
or email: bookshop@enterprise.net for details

FEARLESS™

FRANCINE PASCAL

HEAT

POCKET
BOOKS

An imprint of Simon & Schuster UK Ltd
A Viacom Company
Africa House, 64-78 Kingsway, London WC2B 6AH

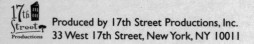
Produced by 17th Street Productions, Inc.
33 West 17th Street, New York, NY 10011

A CIP catalogue record for this book is
available from the British Library

ISBN 0671 77392 5

1 3 5 7 9 10 8 6 4 2

Printed by Omnia Books Ltd, Glasgow

To Sara Weiss

HEAT

a long way from a blizzard

Gaia had no problem understanding his broken-nose English.

THE DEALER SMILED AS GAIA CAME

A Regular Franken-Nazi

close. "Hey," he said. He took the toothpick from between his yellow teeth and waved it through the snowy air. "You're out awful late, little girl."

Gaia Moore shoved her hands down inside her pockets and walked closer. "I'm not a little girl."

"Yeah, babe, whatever." The dealer replaced his toothpick, stomped his feet, and rubbed his hands together. "So what is it you want? I'm freezing out here."

"How sad." Gaia took a long look at the dealer. He was a big man, maybe six-foot three, with big hands, thick arms, an equally thick neck, and hair that had been shaved down to a gray stubble. A regular Franken-Nazi. Exactly the kind of guy Gaia loved to pick a fight with—especially after what had happened over the last couple of weeks. It was easy to see why big boy felt confident enough to be working alone at midnight. Most of the dealers Gaia ran into were wimps, but this guy looked strong enough to pick up a park bench and beat somebody with it.

The dealer scowled. "Hey, girl. You shopping or staring?" His big hands dipped into his pockets and came out with a display of his stock. Clumps of white crystal shoved in tiny bottles. Brown powder in glassine envelopes. "You want something?"

"Yeah." Gaia nodded as she looked at the drugs. "Yeah, I want something." She slowly took her hands from her pockets. "I want you to get out of my park."

The man took a moment to react. "Your park?" He shoved his wares into his coat. "What makes you think this is your park, chicky?"

Gaia jerked her thumb back along the path she had been following. "I live over there," she said. She pointed ahead. "And my favorite doughnuts are over there. I figure that makes everything in between mine."

The dealer was big, but his sense of humor was not. A single heavy black eyebrow crunched down over his squinted eyes. "If you're not making a buy, kid, get out of my face."

It was Gaia's turn to smile. "Make me."

The toothpick fell from the big man's lips. "You got some kind of brain damage? Hell, girl, I clean bigger things than you off my boots."

Gaia glanced down at the man's stained coat, then back at his face. "From the look of you, I wouldn't think you ever cleaned anything."

The dealer opened his mouth as if he was going to reply, then he stopped and shook his head. "You want to be nuts, you be nuts on your own time. I got business to do." He turned his big shoulders and started across the park toward the empty, snow-covered chess tables.

"You afraid of a girl?" Gaia called after him.

The dealer kept walking.

Gaia cupped her hands beside her mouth. "Police!" she shouted. "You better come arrest this asshole!"

The dealer froze. He spun around to face Gaia. "Shut up."

"Police!" Gaia shouted again. "You better hurry! He's wearing a black coat, and he's got a pocket full of crack!"

"Shut the hell up!" The dealer stomped back along the snowy path. "You want to be hurt? If that's what you want, I'll—"

"Police!"

For a big man, the dealer moved fast. He charged and swung a knotted fist at Gaia with enough force to drop a horse. Only Gaia wasn't standing there anymore. She stepped left, ducked under the man's arm, caught his thick wrist, and gave a hard tug.

Gaia's move pulled the dealer off balance. He staggered forward past the place where Gaia was crouching. Before he could turn, Gaia planted her hands against the man's broad back and gave a shove. The dealer tripped and fell facedown on the frozen ground.

The big man scrambled back to his feet. There was snow on his stubble-covered head and more caught in his shaggy unibrow. "I hope you like this snow," he said. "Because I'm gonna make you lick it all up."

He lunged at Gaia, but she dodged again. This time she rose up on the ball of one foot, carefully aimed a kick at the man's ribs—and slipped in the snow.

Ten thousand lessons had taught Gaia how to fall. They didn't help this time. Her feet went up, and Gaia went down. She landed on her butt with enough force to knock most of the air from her lungs and send a jolt of pain running up her spine.

The big man was on her in a moment. One big hand closed around Gaia's right arm and jerked her from the ground. The other hand drove into her gut.

The muscles in Gaia's stomach spasmed. What little air remained in her body hissed out between her teeth. Gaia gasped and strained to pull in a breath. The man tossed her back to the ground and gave her a kick that pounded into her shoulder.

He grunted in satisfaction. "I don't think you're going to make any more trouble for me, babe." He drew back his leg and aimed a second kick at Gaia's head.

Gaia rolled, put her hands under her chest, and flipped onto her feet. Before the man had recovered from his missed kick, Gaia spun and planted a punch in the center of his stomach. She punched again, backed away, and followed up with a high kick that spun the man's head around.

Even though it was the guy who was getting hit, Gaia was the one feeling dizzy. She still couldn't breathe. She was fighting on nothing but the oxygen in her lungs, and that was running out fast.

If the drug dealer had been smaller, that kick would have been enough to send him flying. The fight would have been over in five seconds flat. Instead the big man only staggered for a moment, then lunged toward Gaia again.

Gaia dropped onto her hands and swept the big man's legs out from under him. As he was falling, she landed a fresh kick square in the middle of his face. Blood sprayed from his shattered nose. It arced away from the blow and laced across the snow in a dark red line.

For a moment Gaia froze. She looked at the snow with its stain of blood, and her mind went spinning back. A gunshot echoed through her memory. She saw her mother lying on the kitchen floor. . . .

The oxygen gauge in Gaia's body reached *E*. She dropped out of her memories and onto her knees. Air. She needed air.

The dealer groaned and started to get up. He fumbled at Gaia with sausage-sized fingers.

Gaia's stomach muscles relaxed, and she managed

to grab a lungful of air. She threw off the guy's hand, rolled away across the snow, and got up. She squeezed down another breath. The oxygen flowed into her muscles like cool water.

The dealer stood and faced her across the snow. "Ooh liddle bidch," he said.

Gaia had no problem understanding his broken-nose English. She pulled in enough air to answer him. "Let's get this over with. I want to get my doughnuts."

The big man came for her. He was more cautious this time. Gaia could see the way his eyes danced back and forth as he tried to anticipate her move. It didn't help.

Gaia waited until he grabbed for her, slipped away, and drove a kick into his side. Before he could turn, she drove another kick into his back. It was a kidney shot, illegal in any karate tournament. This wasn't a tournament.

The dealer made a deep grunt and fell to his knees. Gaia kicked him again. And again.

"Top," said the dealer. "Pweez top."

Gaia took a step back. "You going to get out of my park?"

The dealer nodded, sending fresh blood dripping from his nose.

"And you'll never come back."

"Neba. I swear. Neba."

Gaia nodded. "All right, then, go."

The dealer got slowly to his feet and stumbled away. Gaia stood and watched him until the big man was only a smudge in the snowy distance. Then she fell onto the nearest park bench.

For the space of sixty seconds Gaia was completely paralyzed. It was the cost of being stronger and faster during the fight—the price she paid for running her muscles at two hundred percent. She lay there on the bench, unable to move a muscle. She was glad that the park was deserted. The only thing worse than being helpless was having someone else see her when she was helpless.

She turned her head and saw the dealer's blood on the ground. Once again, images flooded her mind. Night. Snow. Blood. Her mother.

Gaia shook the images from her head. She propped herself up on her hands, took in a deep, cold breath, and tried to forget.

My mom loved snow, but she didn't like snowball fights. Or at least, she'd make you believe she didn't like snowball fights. Oh, no, she only came outside to enjoy the beauty of a winter's day. Snow on the tree branches. The way everything sparkled in the sun. All that shit.

She was a good actress, my mom. And if you believed her long enough to look away—pow! You'd catch a cold one right on the ear.

The best thing I remember about those snows was that the snow stayed white for a month at a time. Cloud white. White like things are in dreams. All clean and perfect.

I know that things can seem a lot better when you're remembering than they really were. But those snows really were great. Really.

City snow is not pretty snow. That's the truth. And that's the closest thing to a poem you're going to get out of me.

Back when I was a kid. Before my mom . . . I mean, before my dad . . . Let's just say before. Before I came to New York City. Back then I used to see real snow.

I know, this is already starting to sound like one of those stupid stories your fat uncle Pete tells about the good old days. You know, the "when I was a little kid it snowed all year long and I had to walk ten miles to school and we couldn't afford shoes so I had to wear bread wrappers on my feet and it was all uphill both ways" story.

Old people say things like this because they're way into this nostalgia thing. They want to look back at the past and make it so everybody was braver and nicer and better than they are now. They had it tough, but they stuck together. They didn't get anything but an orange for Christmas, and they were happy.

They ate dirt six days a week,
and they liked it.

   My story's not like that. For
one thing, I'm only seventeen, so
I didn't grow up with dinosaurs
or go hunting mastodons. The
other difference is, no nostalgia.

   Let me tell you right now:
Nostalgia sucks.

   All those old stories are
nothing but dressed-up lies. Who
wants to look back, anyway? I
mean, do you want to look back
and see how your mom died? Do you
really want to think about how
your father disappeared and never
bothered to so much as write? Do
you want to remember how you got
shuffled off from one place to
another and end up being forced
to live with two people you
barely know? No. Believe me,
thinking about the past is just
plain stupid.

   That's why I'm just talking
about snow.

   It snowed in the mountains.

Back then, I had a mom and a dad just like a regular girl. That part of the story seems like a fairy tale now, even to me, but it really did happen. I had a mother. I even have the pictures to prove it.

Of course, if you look at the pictures, you probably wouldn't think they were very good evidence. On one side you have my mom: always stylish, completely charming, totally beautiful. And then there's me. I'm . . . not my mother.

Even back in those days of yore, the Moore family wasn't exactly typical. First off, my dad was like a major government spy. Half the time he was off to some jungle or desert or foreign capital. I never knew which one because he could never talk about it. Then when he was home, Dad dedicated himself to my little problem. The Gaia-don't-get-scared-of-anything problem.

Which wouldn't have been such

a problem at all except my dad
was afraid that I wouldn't get
scared when I should. Which was
completely wrong. Just because
I'm fearless doesn't mean I'm
stupid. I don't go jumping off
cliffs. I don't get into a fight
with more than two or three idiots at a time. Usually.

But Dad made me study every
martial art in creation so I
could stomp the crap out of the
people I should have been afraid
of but wasn't. By the time he was
through, he had turned me into
the muscle-bound freak girl I am
today.

Snow. This is about snow.

In the mountains it snowed for
weeks at a time. Not wimpy little
flurries. Serious snow. And when
it stopped, we would build snow-
men and snow forts and snow anything else you could think of. My
dad would even stop telling me
about "the sixteen deadly pressure points on the human body"
long enough to come outside and

take part in snowball Armageddon.

Of course, not every snow was perfect. I mean, it was snowing on that night, too. The last night.

Blood melts into the snow. You might think it would spread out and fade. Maybe it would even turn some shade of pink. It doesn't. Blood is dark against the snow. That night, that last night, it looked almost black.

Okay, now let's talk about city snow. Let's talk about snow in New York.

First off, it doesn't snow that much here. People talk about this place like it's the north slope of Alaska, but we're lucky to have two decent snows a year. Every little flurry here is treated like an emergency. Two flakes get together, half the city runs for home.

When the snow does fall, it starts out white, just like mountain snow. But give it two hours on the ground, and it turns into

certified City Snow™, pat. pend-
ing.

City Snow is not a product of
nature. It looks like a mixture
of wet cement and motor oil. Ever
see a Coke Slurpee? That's pretty
close. Not the kind of stuff you
want someone to wad up and throw
at you.

I guess you could make a snow
fort in the park—if you worked
fast enough to get it done before
the snow turned to goo. You might
get in a few decent snowballs.
Maybe make a snowman, too.

But some jerk would probably
come along and mug it.

Just one
little line
would be
like   an
ten unforseen
pounds of
Dove dark effect
chocolate.

ELLA DROPPED THE GLOWING STUB OF

a pastel-colored cigarette and heard it hiss into the snow at her feet. She shivered as she tightened the sable-edged hood around her face. The plush fur coat kept her arms and body warm, but it did nothing for the frigid wind that crept under her skirt.

Her Nature

There were at least a hundred decent restaurants in the city and another hundred that were passable. Ella fantasized about a plate of steaming alfredo at Tony's. Perhaps some black crab cake at Opaline. To get out of the wind, she would have settled for coffee at the nearest Chock Full o' Nuts. Instead she was stuck, shivering in the park, watching a little idiot who didn't have the brains to get in out of the cold.

"All right," she said. "Your little protégé finished her fight, and now she's eating her dessert. Do we have to stay out here and freeze all night?"

Beside her, a tall form shifted in the deep shadows of the winter trees. "We're watching. Isn't that your assignment?"

Ella glanced at the girl resting on the cold park bench. Was there some law that said Gaia couldn't go inside like a civilized person? For the ten-thousandth time, Ella wished she had never taken on this assignment. Not that she had been given any choice. "I watch Gaia every day. How long are we going to stay out here?" she asked.

"As long as we have to," said the tall man.

Loki stepped forward, and the light from a distant streetlamp cast sharp shadows across his rugged features. He stood with his hands jammed into the pockets of his black trench coat and his deep-set eyes focused on Gaia. "We wait until we know what we need to know."

Ella scowled. "But she's not doing anything," she said, allowing a note of complaint to creep into her voice. It irritated Ella that Loki would rather spend time out here just watching Gaia when they could be spending that time in a much more intimate way.

"Exactly." Loki turned his face toward Ella for a moment. In the dim light his eyes looked as dark as the winter sky. "And that's what we're here to observe."

"Nothing?"

Loki made an exasperated growl. "You've had months to study this girl," he said. "How many times have you seen her sit quietly and do nothing?"

Ella thought for a moment. "Not many," she said carefully.

"Not many? Try none. Not even after a fight like that. She's usually up and running as soon as she gets her energy back." Loki nodded toward the distant bench where Gaia sat in the falling snow. "The girl is restless. Headstrong. It's part of her nature." He pulled his hands from his pockets and ran gloved fingers along the rough bark of an ancient elm. "Gaia goes hunting for something to eat. Gaia goes looking for another fight. Gaia does not sit quietly and think."

Ella shivered again. "She just finished beating up some guy three times her size. Isn't that enough for you?"

Loki made a noise of disgust. "Did you see how she fought? She was slow. Clumsy. Her heart wasn't in the fight." He shook his head. "That fool should have been no problem, but Gaia came close to being seriously injured."

That thought made Ella smile inwardly. If only Gaia would hurry up and get herself killed. Ella was so tired of hearing Loki talk about the little blond-haired beast. If the girl got herself shot or stabbed or, even better, slowly and painfully beaten to death, Loki would be angry for a time, but he would recover. Best of all, Ella could leave her sham marriage and be with him all the time. That was sure to speed his recovery.

"Maybe she's sick," said Ella.

"If she has an illness, it's not caused by any bacterium or virus," replied Loki. "No. I have a good idea of what's gone wrong with our girl."

She's not my *girl.* Ella knew that Loki had something in mind. She wished he would just spit it out. It was far too cold for drama. "What is it?" she asked.

"Mary Moss."

It took Ella a moment to place the name. "The little junkie girl? Is that what you're worried about?"

Loki was slow to reply. "The relationship between Gaia and this Moss girl is certainly something that we must consider." Loki put his hands back into his coat pockets. "Moss and the other friends that Gaia has made. They're making her . . ." He paused for a moment, a frown turning down the corners of his mouth. "They're having an unforeseen effect."

Ella stared at him. Loki was hiding something. That wasn't surprising—Loki was always hiding some secret. It was part of his job. But this secret involved Gaia, and that made it Ella's business, too.

She clenched her teeth in frustration. Ella couldn't see what difference it made that Gaia had picked up a few pitiful friends, and she certainly didn't like the idea that Loki wouldn't tell her what was going on. "The Moss girl is nothing but a whining little addict, and that other kid, Fargo, is a cripple. Neither of them seems dangerous."

"They're far more dangerous than you know, my dear." He turned to Ella and took a step toward her. "Have you forgotten the goal of this project?"

The intensity of the look in Loki's eyes made Ella take a step back. "No, I—"

21

"Then you'll understand that for things to end up as they should, Gaia must not feel close to anyone," he said. "It's important that she not form any deep attachments."

"I understand." The explanation sounded reasonable enough, but Ella still had the feeling that Loki was hiding something. Something serious.

Loki nodded. "I have to admit that I underestimated this problem myself. I was looking for physical dangers to Gaia, not for this sort of difficulty."

A fresh gust of wind blew in among the trees. Ella shook from head to toe. "Now that we've seen her, couldn't we go somewhere?" Ella stretched her hand toward Loki's. "We don't get enough time together. We could go to your place in the Village and—"

"Not now," said Loki.

No matter how many times Loki rejected her, it always seemed to sting. Ella tried to look unaffected, but she could feel anger settling over her features. She could see no reason for them to stand there being cold. It wasn't as if Gaia was suddenly going to jump up and do something interesting.

Ella started to point this out, but quickly shut her mouth. Making Loki angry was definitely on the list of very unhealthy activities. She had already pushed her luck far enough.

"Maybe I can help solve this problem," Ella suggested.

Loki had already turned his attention back to Gaia. "And how will you do that?" he said without looking at her.

"I could forbid Gaia to go out to see these friends," Ella suggested.

Loki laughed. It was a sound as cold as the snow around them. "And exactly what good would that do? Do you really think Gaia would obey your order?"

Ella felt her face grow warm. She didn't like being reminded of the way Gaia refused to respect her commands. And she especially didn't like the tone of Loki's voice. He seemed amused by the whole idea.

"Maybe I could talk to the parents of the Moss girl," she said. "I could hint that Gaia might have trouble with drugs herself. They might keep Mary—"

"No," said Loki with a sharp shake of his head. "That kind of intervention would only cause Gaia to rebel further. I believe that in this case direct action may be required."

That was an answer Ella had no trouble interpreting. "Then what should I do? I could follow Moss and—"

"Leave the girl to me," Loki interrupted. "No, I have something else for you to do." He stopped abruptly and scanned Ella from head to spiked heels. "There's another of Gaia's relationships that concerns me. One that I think you may be particularly well suited to handle."

23

CRIMINALS WERE ALL BIG BABIES.

Just because it was dark, cold, and snowing, they were all off somewhere keeping their little toes warm. The whole park was deserted.

A Lot of Little Things

Gaia folded her legs beneath her, chomped half a chocolate doughnut in a single bite, and watched the snow fall.

The weather doofus on the eleven o'clock news was calling for six inches, but at the moment the snow was barely there. Big, heavy flakes drifted down slowly from a sky that was half clouds and half stars. It was more than a flurry but a long way from a blizzard.

Spots of cold moisture appeared on Gaia's face as the snow stuck and melted. Snowflakes caught in her hair and snagged on her eyelashes. Slow streams of melt water made their way down her cheeks, and damp spots even dared to appear on her sacred doughnut.

Memories of childhood snow were one thing, but Gaia quickly decided that getting hit in the face by real snowflakes wasn't particularly romantic. Instead it was cold and wet. Still, Gaia sat facing into the night until the collar of her sweater was damp and her long, pale hair was a wind-whipped mess.

She felt weird. There had to be a word for the emotion Gaia felt, but she wasn't sure what that word would be. It wasn't fear. She could be sure of that much. She didn't feel afraid. If her father was right, she *couldn't* feel afraid. Not ever. But if she couldn't be afraid, she could still feel sadness. And loneliness. And guilt. In Gaia's opinion, it wasn't a very good deal.

Except this feeling wasn't one of those familiar aches. This was an actual, honest-to-whatever good feeling. This was a lot of little things that added up to something that might almost be happiness. At least Gaia thought it was happiness. She didn't exactly have a great basis for comparison.

Gaia shoved the second half of the doughnut into her mouth, opened her eyes, and watched as the last of the stars vanished behind the advancing clouds. For what seemed like a century, Gaia had been holding all her secrets to herself. Now, for the first time since being forced to move to New York, she had friends she could share with.

They probably weren't friends her parents would have approved of, but Gaia's parents were long gone. Out of the picture. Mary Moss was a recovering coke addict with something of a wild streak. Ed Fargo had been a daredevil nutcase on a skateboard until an accident cured him of being crazy and left him in a wheelchair. They weren't perfect people.

But that was a good thing. Gaia could never have been comfortable with perfect people. No matter what they had been or what they had done, Ed and Mary were what Gaia needed. People that she could relax with. People that made her almost feel normal.

Only the night before, Gaia had gone so far as to tell Mary about what had happened to her mother. It might not sound like a big step, but for Gaia it was huge. Gaia never talked about her mother. Never. Not to anyone.

Talking to Mary had been one of the hardest things she had ever done. Gaia had spent so many years training to fight that taking out some half-stoned mugger barely took an effort. Her father had forced her to study so hard as a kid that high school was more like kindergarten. But telling someone else about her emotions, letting someone in on the things that had happened to her—that was hard.

Now that Gaia had slipped out a little of her past, she felt surprisingly good. Strange, but good. A little bit of the monster-outsider juice had been drained. A little of the pressure in her head was gone.

The world wasn't perfect, of course. Gaia was still an overmuscled freak. She was still stuck living with her foster parents, the Nivens, and particularly with Superslut Ella.

And of course there was the one least-perfect thing

in Gaia's world. The one that divided possible happiness from undeniable joy.

Sam Moon.

It was probably the best thing that Gaia didn't have Sam. She had only kissed him once. At least, she thought she had kissed him once. Only she had been half dead at the time, and there had been this major blow to her head, and it might possibly have been nothing but a hallucination. Anyway, one maybe kiss and Sam had already become this incredible obsession.

Gaia had already spent enough time thinking about Sam to learn a new language or become a piano virtuoso or develop a new theory of relativity. If she actually had him, actually had Sam Moon all to herself, she might short-circuit or blow up or rip his clothes off and—

Yeah, *obsession* was definitely the right word.

Thinking of the no-Sam situation took the edge off Gaia's good mood. He was probably spending his time with Heather. The insidious, ugly, ultimately evil Heather Gannis.

The image of Sam being somewhere with Heather was enough to finally pull Gaia out of her doughnuts-and snow-induced coma. She unfolded her cold legs and slid off the snow-crusted bench. It was very late. If Ella was still awake, she was going to have a fit when Gaia came in.

Gaia didn't care. She leaned back her head and whispered up to the gray clouds, each word emerging in a puff of steam.

"Come on," she said. "For once let's have some real snow."

SAM MOON LEANED BACK INTO THE

cab to pay the driver, careful to give a good tip. After all, it was the holiday season. People were supposed to be cheerful and generous.

Moonman

"Thanks for the ride, Mr. Haq," Sam said as he handed over the money.

The cabbie took it from him with a grin. "Thank you so much, Samuel," he said in English so exact, it could have come straight from the pronunciation guide in *Webster's*. A look of concern crossed the man's wide face. "Are you all right, Samuel? I haven't seen you at the tables as much as usual."

Oh, I'm fine. It's just that I'm having sex with one girl while I'm totally obsessed with another. Sam tried to smile. "Sure, Mr. Haq. As soon as the weather clears up, you'll see me in the park."

"Perhaps we will play a game then?"

Sam nodded. "Absolutely. I'll be looking for you."

"Good! Very good," said Mr. Haq. "I will be quite happy to take even more of your money." He laughed, gave Sam a final wave, and pulled away from the curb.

Sam turned and walked slowly up the steps to the concrete bulk of his dorm at NYU. The trouble with Gaia—the Gaia problem, as he had started to call it—was not exactly the kind of thing he could discuss with Mr. Haq. And it was definitely not the sort of thing he could discuss with his parents. His parents weren't big believers in problems.

There really isn't *a problem,* he told himself as he came to the door of the dorm. *I'm with Heather, not Gaia. I'm supposed to be happy now.*

Sam pushed open the door, stepped inside, and stomped the snow from his shoes. *I've got to stop thinking about Gaia. Gaia Moore is not a part of my life. Enough already.*

There was more life in the building than there had been the night before. When Sam had come scrambling back on Christmas night—in the futile hope that Gaia might stop by—the place had been all but empty. Since then a trickle of students had turned up every day. It was still more than a week before classes started up again, but already the dorms were nearly a third full.

Sam yawned as he tromped up the stairs to his

room. It had been a long day. He had called Heather first thing that morning to see if she wanted to get together, but she had said she wasn't feeling well. Considering how much alcohol she had downed the night before, Sam wasn't surprised. With Heather out of action and Gaia out of the picture, Sam had decided to hustle back home and spend a day with his parents. He didn't know if the few hours he had been able to spend at home were worth it, but at least it made him feel a little less guilty for running off on Christmas Day.

It was close to two in the morning, but when Sam walked out onto his floor, there was the familiar thick, sudsy odor of beer in the air and the ultrasonic thump of a subwoofer jolting through the walls. Someone down the hall was having a party. It shouldn't have been a surprise. The period between semesters was nothing if not an excuse to party. But Sam was way too tired to participate.

He fumbled into the quad and opened the door to his dorm room. Inside, he dropped his things, shrugged off his heavy coat, and staggered to his bed.

He wondered where Gaia was at that moment. Which was a stupid thing to wonder. Obviously Gaia would be asleep. Like any normal person would be at this hour. And wasn't he going to stop thinking about Gaia, anyway?

Sam took off his boots and lay back against the

pillow. The bass from the nearby party pounded up through the bed like some huge heartbeat. Despite the cold outside, the room suddenly felt stuffy and hot. Sam peeled off his shirt and lay on top of the sheets. He balled up the pillow and pushed it over his ears. He kept his eyes closed and did his best to think about absolutely nothing.

The sound of the bass beat kept pounding through the bed. *Thump. Thump. Thump.* `Gaia. Gaia. Gaia.`

Heather, thought Sam. *Not Gaia.*

Gaia. Gaia. Gaia.

Heather. I love Heather.

Liar. Liar. Liar. You. Love. Gaia.

Oh, shut up.

With a groan Sam got out of bed and walked over to his computer. If he couldn't sleep, he had to do something, and there was only one thing he could think of that might take his mind off the Gaia problem.

Sam had been a chess geek since grade school. Only that `inner geek` could save him now. He logged on to the Internet and went to the pogo.com game site. From there he logged in as Moonman and proceeded to the chess area. Sam bypassed the "blue" chess rooms. Those places were full of beginners and low-rated players. Even though he had been on the site only a few times, Sam's rating was already edging three thousand. If he was going to find a challenge, he would have to do it in the site's "red" room.

Sam yawned while the site loaded. It was funny how as soon as he got out of bed, he started to feel like he could sleep. He wasn't fooled. One quick game to clear his mind, then he would give the bed another try.

A scrolling list of chess games appeared on the screen. Even at this late hour most of the tables were already occupied with games in progress. At others a single name beside the board indicated someone waiting for a challenger. Sam passed up a couple of players with ratings under two thousand. He flipped to the bottom of the list and was happy to see the small silhouette of a waiting player who was rated at 2,950. It was a perfect number, within ten points of Sam's own rating.

Sam reached for the mouse and was about to join the game when he noticed the name of this `perfectly matched player`. *Gaia13*. He froze. It could be a coincidence. There had to be other girls in the world with the name Gaia who liked chess.

Sam's fingers began to literally tremble above the mouse button. He wanted to join the game. There was a chat facility that let the two players send messages to each other while playing. If it really was Gaia—his Gaia—Sam would have a chance to tell her some of the things that he had been thinking for the last few days.

He was going to press the button and go in. He was.

It's not her. It can't be her.

His finger touched the plastic of the button. All he had to do was click the button. All he had to do was . . .

The icon that represented a waiting player suddenly disappeared. *Gaia13 has left.*

Sam leaned back in his chair and closed his eyes. It wasn't her. The name players used on pogo was only a nickname. Just because some player used the name Gaia didn't mean it was Gaia Moore. It wasn't her.

Sam didn't believe that for a second.

WHOIS? QUERY RESULTS

Movie of the Week

Moore, Katia
No Records Found.

Whois? Query Results
Moore, Gaia
No Records Found.

Mary Moss frowned and gave her mouse a shove that sent it sliding across the desktop. She had tried a hundred different search engines and a dozen different queries, and she was still no closer to finding out what she wanted to know. There were a zillion people named Moore and at least ten thousand named Katia. But nowhere could Mary find that combination—the combination that was the name of Gaia's mother.

Ever since Gaia had decided to share the story of her mother's death, Mary had been obsessed with finding out more. The story had everything. There was violence. Murder. Mystery. And, of course, heartbreaking tragedy. Gaia Moore was a regular walking movie of the week. And Mary was a sucker for drama.

But of course, it was more than that. Gaia was Mary's friend. Gaia had saved Mary's ass, both physically and emotionally, on more than one occasion. Maybe this was Mary's chance to finally do something for her best friend.

Mary leaned back in her chair and ran her fingers through her ginger red hair. There had to be some way to get the information she was after. There had to be someplace she could go, someone she could ask.

If I only had a little blast of coke, I'd be able to think so, so much better. The idea of the drug was enough to make Mary shiver. A little cocaine would be like a glass of cold water after crossing a desert. Just one little line would be like ten pounds of Dove dark chocolate. It would be like ... like ...

It would be like setting your hair on fire and trying to put it out with gasoline.

Mary knew well enough that there was no such thing as just one little line of coke. One line of coke could turn into a thousand miles of white powder. Mary had only started fishing her life out of the toilet she had fallen into after her last tangle with drugs. The last thing she needed was to jump inside and flush.

Another idea occurred to Mary. She selected another site from the menu and waited until the search box came up.

<u>ALTAVISTA</u> <u>ADVANCED</u> <u>QUERY</u> <u>FACILITY</u>
moore AND katia

—No results. Try another query.—

<u>ALTAVISTA</u> <u>ADVANCED</u> <u>QUERY</u> <u>FACILITY</u>
moore AND death AND fire
—1 Result Found—

Mary almost typed a fresh query before she realized that she had gotten a hit. Quickly she snatched back her mouse and clicked on the link.

The page turned out to be the archives of a small upstate paper. The article was so different from the story that Gaia told, Mary thought for a second it was just a mistake. Then she realized it wasn't a mistake. It was a lie.

35

The west county home of Mr. and Mrs. Thomas Moore burned down in the early morning hours this Tuesday. Mr. Moore, an employee of the State Department, and his young daughter escaped the blaze, but Mrs. Moore was unable to leave the home in time. The county coroner's office indicates that Mrs. Moore died of smoke inhalation.

The article continued for half a column, but there was no mention of any guns. Mary ran her finger along the monitor glass. The article didn't agree at all with the story that Gaia had told her. Not even the stupidest coroner in the world would mistake a gunshot wound for smoke inhalation. And Gaia had never mentioned her house burning down. That meant either the paper was wrong or Gaia was lying.

Mary was willing to bet anything that Gaia had told the truth. That meant someone had created this story. Someone with enough pull to get just what they wanted planted in a local paper. Someone with enough power to convince local officials to lie.

Mary smiled. This story was getting better.

Mary's heart bounced in her chest. a man-shaped shadow Fear ran through her body like strong acid.

THERE WAS NOTHING LIKE A

sleepless night to make morning look like the bottom of a litter box.

Boiled in Beer

Sam brushed his teeth for a solid ten minutes and still couldn't manage to dislodge the fur that was growing on his tongue. He stared at the face in the mirror and winced. He was supposed to meet Heather in only an hour. If he didn't manage to look a little less like a refugee from *Night of the Living Dead,* the Gaia Problem was going to turn into the No-Girlfriend-At-All Problem.

Sam found he could think a little more clearly about Gaia now that the sun was up. It was clear to him that Gaia had moved on. Maybe she once wanted to be with Sam. Maybe she had never given him a passing thought. Maybe she had only kissed him because someone had massaged her brain with a blunt object. One thing was sure—Gaia wasn't thinking about Sam. According to the phone conversation Sam had held with Gaia's stepmother, Gaia had a boyfriend.

Gaia hadn't even bothered to thank Sam for the Christmas present he had bought for her. If there had been a chance for Sam and Gaia the couple, that chance was over.

There were absolutely zero odds that he was ever going to be with Gaia Moore.

So why do I keep obsessing about her?

He splashed cold water on his face and scrubbed it off with a slightly stale towel. It was like he was haunted by Gaia. He wondered if he could find a priest willing to do an exorcism.

At least I have Heather, he told himself. Then he gave himself a mental kick for having the thought. It wasn't like Heather was some sucky consolation prize. Heather was undeniably and totally beautiful. Half the guys at school were chasing Heather, and the other half didn't even feel worthy enough to try.

Oh, yeah, and there was sex. Only a few nights before there had been sex. It wasn't like Sam had a terrific amount of experience with sex, but sex with Heather was fun. It was good, no, *great.* Great sex. Any guy should feel lucky to have Heather. Having Heather was still the best thing in his life. His Gaia-free life.

Once he was cleaned up and dressed, Sam felt a little better. Less like a zombie and more like he was only terminally ill. He slipped on his coat, took a last dismal look into the mirror, and started out the door.

Before he could get all the way into the hall, another door down the way flew open and music spilled out. A short, wide-shouldered guy with curly brown hair and a broad grin stumbled into the hall. "Sam!" he cried in a voice loud enough to be heard in Brooklyn. "My favorite person in the world!"

Sam winced at the volume. "Hey, Brian." From the slurred, overloud voice and the unsteady walk, Sam could tell that Brian Sandford had a very low percentage of blood in his alcohol system.

The other student took a swaying step. "Man, it's good to see you."

Sam forced himself to smile. Something was badly wrong here. Brian Sandford was obviously drunk, but Sam didn't think he was drunk enough to forget one fact—Brian and Sam hated each other.

Brian was a local who had wandered over to NYU from the Village School. He seemed to have the same set of friends as Heather, though Sam knew Brian wasn't in the class of people that Heather would have considered the top rank. It had taken Sam several meetings to figure out that Brian had the flaming hots for Heather Gannis. He seemed to consider the fact that Heather was dating Sam as some kind of personal insult.

From the broad smile on his face, it seemed that Brian had finally recovered from his jealousy. "It's been a long time, huh?"

"I saw you two nights ago, Brian. At the Kellers' party, remember?"

Brian nodded enthusiastically. He stumbled down the hallway toward Sam and put a hand on the wall to steady himself. "Yeah," he said. "Good party. Too bad you left so soon." Brian's breath was so strong that it made Sam's eyes water. It was clear that Brian hadn't been leaving any parties early. He didn't smell like he had been drinking beer. He smelled like he had been *boiled* in beer.

"I'm glad you enjoyed it," Sam said. He closed the door to his room and zipped up his coat. "I'll be seeing you."

A heavy hand came down on Sam's shoulder. "Too bad about you and Heather," said Brian.

Puzzled, Sam turned and looked into Brian's flushed, smiling face. "What?"

"You know," said Brian. "How you guys are breaking up and everything."

He's drunk, Sam thought. *He's drunk, and he doesn't know what he's talking about.* "Did Heather say something to you?"

"Heather? Nah." Brian's red eyes closed for a moment, and his mouth gaped open. Sam could practically see the two sober brain cells in Brian's head scrambling to dredge up the memory. "It was the guys, man. They were saying how Heather was doing maid service."

"Maid service?"

"You know. Going from bed to bed."

A flash of cold ran up Sam's back, and he felt a sudden, metallic tightness in his guts. "They're lying."

Sam tried to put some kind of authority into his voice, but it wasn't enough to stop the flow of words that spilled from Brian's beer-saturated throat. "That's not what Charlie says."

The coldness in Sam's back began to spread into his legs and arms. There was a buzzing noise in his head. "Charlie."

"Charlie Salita. You know Charlie."

Sam did know Charlie. Charlie was a jock and a standard at all the parties Heather attended. "You're saying that Charlie Salita slept with Heather."

Brian's smile grew even wider. "Charlie says she's really hot," he said.

"He's lying."

Brain leaned in closer. "He's got details, man. He knows things about Heather."

"He's making it all up," Sam insisted.

"Charlie says your old girlfriend is a real bunny in the sack."

Sam Moon wasn't a violent person. He played chess, not football. He couldn't remember being in a real fight since junior high. None of that mattered.

He raised his right hand, carefully folded his

fingers, drew back his arm, and drove his fist straight into Brian Sandford's grinning face.

THE TRAIL OF BLOOD STRETCHED

Like a Family

across the frozen ground. Gaia bent and touched her finger to a bright red splash. Cold. The blood was as cold as the snow it was staining.

Gaia stood and looked ahead. The snow was falling so thickly that she could barely see twenty feet, but somewhere up there she could see shadowy movement. Gaia hurried along, jumping over one splash of blood after another.

Cold wind streamed through her tangled hair and brought goose pimples from the bare skin of her arms and throat. Gaia tried to remember why she was outside in such cold weather without a coat. Or shoes.

The blood trail led into a grove of stark, black-trunked trees. The shadowy figure was closer now, and the blood spots were closer together. Gaia moved faster. She had to catch up. She had to catch up before . . . she didn't know what. Something was going to happen, something bad, and Gaia was the only one who could stop it.

A new shape loomed up out of the snow. It was a building. A house.

Gaia ran ahead for a few steps, then skidded to a stop in the ankle-deep snow. It wasn't just any house—it was her house. Not the brownstone she shared with the Nivens. Her real home. The house where she had lived with her parents. With her mother.

No sooner had the thought of her mother crossed Gaia's mind than a figure ran up the steps and into the house. Gaia had only enough time to tell it was a woman before the front door opened and closed with a bang.

"Mom?" Gaia ran toward the door. "Mom!"

Snow dusted the steps leading up to the door and was drifted against the sides of the house. There was blood here, too. Lots of blood. There was blood on the steps. On the porch. On the door.

Gaia pulled at the door, but it refused to open. "Mom!" she shouted. "Mom, let me in!" There was no answer from the house.

She began to hammer on the door. *Bang. Bang.*

Gaia smashed her fist against the door. The whole thing looked too fragile to stand, much less hold up to blows. Gaia struck out again, and the door rattled in its frame. She jumped and planted a solid kick. The bare sole of her foot clapped against the wood. Dust flew into the blood-stained snow.

Thump.

The boards held.

Gaia gritted her teeth. The door didn't look strong. But no matter how she battered at the aged boards, they wouldn't break.

"Gaia," called a voice from inside.

"Mom?" Gaia froze. "Mom, is that you?"

"Gaia." The voice was soft and familiar.

Gaia put her ear against the door. "Mom. It's me. Will you let me in?"

"Gaia!" This time the voice was a scream. And it wasn't Gaia's mother.

Gaia leaped back from the door. "Mary?"

"Gaia!" screamed the voice inside the house. "Gaia, help me!"

Gaia leaped, spun, and kicked the center of the door with all her strength. With a loud crash the door jumped in its frame. A thin crack split the center board from top to bottom. Fragments of wood rained down. Gaia kicked again. And again. Then followed up the kicks with a blow from a stiff right hand.

The crack widened.

"Hang on!" Gaia shouted into the opening. "I'm coming!"

She spun and directed another kick at the door, but before her foot could reach the wood, strength drained from her legs. The blow landed as only a weak thump. Gaia tried again, but this kick was even weaker.

She staggered and fell against the door. Her muscles were failing. This was supposed to happen after the fight, not in the middle. She couldn't collapse now, not when Mary was still in danger.

Gaia pushed herself away from the burned boards, drew in a deep breath, and pounded against the door with everything she had. Left hand. *Thump*. Right hand. *Thump*. Kick. *Thump*.

Blood began to pour out from under the door. Not a few spots of blood or drops of blood. Streams of blood. Buckets of blood.

The blows did nothing. Gaia was weak. Too weak to help Mary. Too weak to help anyone.

Gray fog closed in at the edge of her vision. Gaia was completely drained. Helpless.

"No," she whispered. "No, I have to get it open." She brought her hand down against the wood over and over.

Thump.

Thump.

Knock.

Thump.

Knock.

Knock.

Gaia's eyes flew open. She came off the bed in a

fighting crouch, jumped into the center of the room, and searched for the nearest enemy.

Only there were no enemies. No corpse of a house in the middle of the snowy woods. No locked door. There was only a bedroom with an unmade bed and several careless heaps of clothes.

Gaia stood there for a moment, her breath coming hard. A dream. It had only been a dream.

The knock at the bedroom door came again. "Gaia? Are you up?"

Gaia groaned. It was Ella's voice. "Yes," she admitted. "I'm up."

"Good. I've got breakfast ready."

Gaia frowned at her bedroom door. This seemed real, but she had to be dreaming. "What did you say?"

"Breakfast is ready."

Gaia wondered if that sentence had ever before passed between Ella's overly red lips. Domestic was not Ella's middle name. Gaia decided she would rather face another nightmare than eat breakfast with a bimbo. "No, thanks," she said.

"You're sure you won't grace this event with your presence?" Even through the door Ella's voice carried enough sarcasm to cut steel. "There's French toast."

"No, thanks, I . . ." Gaia blinked. Wait a minute. Replay that last statement. "Did you say French toast?"

"Yes, but if you don't want it—"

Gaia's stomach grumbled. "I, um. I mean, okay. I'll be down in a minute."

"How wonderful." From outside the door came the sound of Ella's high heels going down the steps.

Gaia looked down at her stomach. "Traitor," she mumbled. Eating breakfast with Ella was against all of Gaia's principles. Most days Ella was a bitch, pure and simple. She treated Gaia with all the warmth usually reserved for a social disease.

So what did it say about Gaia that she was willing to ignore those principles just for a little bread and syrup? "I really am weak," she said to the empty room. At least when it came to food.

She peeled off the oversized T-shirt she had worn to bed and slipped into a pair of worn cargo pants. As she rooted through the pile of clothes on the floor in search of a sweatshirt that had been worn less than three times, Gaia's thoughts returned to her nightmare.

Gaia was not a big believer in dreams. Somewhere among the thousand and one books that her father had force-fed to her, she had even digested Freud's book on dreams. Gaia wasn't buying it. Dreams were just little movies in your head, not predictions about the future. If you dreamed you were falling, it didn't mean you were going to fall. If you dreamed you hit the ground, it didn't mean you were about to die.

If you dreamed a friend was trapped, it didn't mean they were really in danger. And no matter what Mr. Freud said, not everything was about sex.

Gaia had been concerned about Mary—concern seemed to come from a different place than real fear. Which was probably why Mary had been in the dream. But there was no reason to worry about Mary anymore.

Skizz, the drug dealer who had been threatening Mary, had been on the receiving end of a patented Gaia Moore ass kicking. He had survived, but he was in the hospital. And when he got out, the police were waiting. There was no way Skizz could be a threat.

Gaia finally managed to locate a khaki green sweatshirt and tugged it over her head. She dragged her long hair free of the shirt and shook her head. It was just a dream. Dreams didn't mean anything.

She exited her room and made it down to the second-floor landing before the smell of cooking stirred her into hyperdrive. From there she took the steps two at a time.

Cooking was definitely rare behavior on Ella's part. When she did cook, Ella usually made obnoxious gourmet dishes with all the taste of old sneakers. Gaia only hoped that Ella's idea of French toast didn't involve bread and snails.

Gaia reached the bottom of the stairs and slowed her walk as she reached the kitchen. No reason to look too anxious.

George Niven sat at the breakfast table with the Sunday edition of *The New York Times* heaped in front of him. He looked at Gaia over the top of the national news section and smiled. "Hey. How are you doing this morning, kiddo? Going to have some breakfast with us?"

Gaia shrugged. "Guess so." She walked across the ceramic tile floor and sat down across the table from George.

Gaia liked George Niven well enough. George had worked with her father at the CIA for years. He had only one serious flaw. For some reason unknown to science, George was in love with Ella. And in Gaia's opinion, that was a pretty big flaw. It made her wonder just how good an agent George could really be when he couldn't even tell that the woman he had married was the world's biggest slut.

Ella marched across the room, her heels snapping on the tiles like rifle shots. Even though it was barely eight in the morning, her scarlet hair was swept up over her head, her makeup was there in all its Technicolor glory, and she was decked out in a teal dress so short, it barely qualified as a blouse.

"Here," said Ella. She inverted a pan, and two

slices of browned toast fell onto a plate. Gaia grabbed for the syrup and doused the toast in a maple-flavored flood. She was a little cautious on the first bite, but the food was actually good. Wonders would never cease.

"So," said George. "You have any plans for New Year's?"

Gaia shrugged. "I'm not sure."

George folded his paper and put it on the edge of the table. "Why don't you come with us?"

Gaia paused with a forkful of French toast halfway to her mouth. "Come where?"

"With Ella and me," said George. "I have an invitation to a New Year's Eve event down in Washington, D.C. It would be great if we all went together."

"All together," Gaia repeated.

George smiled. "Like a family."

A shiver went through Gaia, and the syrup in her mouth seemed to turn sour. Gaia barely held down her breakfast. "Uh, I . . ."

She was saved from answering by the ringing of the phone in the kitchen. A moment later Ella called from the other room, "Gaia, it's for you."

Gaia jumped up from her chair, ran into the kitchen, and took the phone from a scowling Ella. "Hello?"

"Hey," said Mary's voice at the other end. "I dare you to meet me in the park."

"I told you I'm done with truth or dare," Gaia said, smiling. "But you don't have to dare me to do that. You have something planned?"

"I'm going on an errand," said Mary. "And then to do some shopping. Come along and help me pick out something outrageous."

Gaia wasn't exactly the queen of shopping. In fact, she wasn't the princess or the duchess or the lady-in-waiting of shopping. Gaia was a shopping peasant. The trouble with shopping was that it usually involved trying things on. Trying things on usually meant looking at yourself in a mirror. Looking in a mirror meant facing the fact that your legs were as big as tree trunks and your shoulders looked like they were ready for the NFL.

"How about I skip the shops and meet you after?" Gaia suggested.

"Okay," said Mary. "Just as long as you don't try to get out of our plans for tonight."

Gaia winced. Tonight. She had almost forgotten. "Not the dancing."

"Absolutely the dancing," Mary said. "You promised."

"That's what you say. I don't remember any of it."

"You said you would go."

"I was talking in my sleep."

"It still counts," said Mary. "I better get moving if I'm going to find the perfect thing to wear tonight."

"Mary, why don't we try something else tonight? I mean, dancing, that's just not—"

"Hey, do you hear something?"

Gaia frowned. "What?"

"On the phone," said Mary. "I thought I heard something."

"Like what?"

"I'm not sure. Weird." Mary sighed. "Anyway, see you in the park around three?"

"Sure," said Gaia. Meeting in the park would give her at least one more chance to talk Mary out of her plans for the evening.

Gaia hung up the phone and went back to her breakfast. She managed two forkfuls of syrup-soaked toast before George returned to his earlier question.

"So, what about it?" he asked. "A family outing?"

"Uh, that was my friend Mary on the phone," Gaia said quickly, suddenly seeing her way out of the worst New Year's Eve on the planet with George and Ella. "I forgot I already promised to do something with her."

George frowned, but he nodded. "All right," he said. "But I'll keep the offer open. We need to do something to make this family gel."

Gaia dropped her fork and stood up from the table. A family? With Ella? One thing was sure, that was never going to happen. There might be some paper in an office across town that listed Ella as Gaia's foster mother. But paper was as much of a relationship as they would ever have.

The only thing that made Gaia feel a little better was the expression on Ella's face. From the way her forehead was wrinkled and her lips drawn down in disgust, it was clear that Ella liked the idea of Gaia as her daughter just about as much as Gaia wanted this red-haired bimbo as a mother.

THE NEW YORK PUBLIC LIBRARY

The Bat Cave

wasn't exactly Mary's favorite place. The building was a little too official. A little too People's Court. The last time she had been here was on a field trip back in fourth grade. Or maybe it was third. Whenever it was, all Mary really remembered was the lions.

She stopped to pet one of the stone beasts on its cold marble nose and looked up at the huge building. "Wish me luck, Leo. I'm going in."

Mary hurried up the long staircase with a cold wind blowing at her back. Inside, the library was nearly as cavernous as a football stadium. The place wasn't quite as ominous as she had expected or re-membered. Inside there were colorful displays, banks of computer monitors, and lots and lots of people.

She wandered through the stacks until she found an information desk. After getting directions, she spi-raled down a winding marble staircase, walked past an acre of book stacks, then continued downward to a smaller staircase of black wrought iron. It seemed to Mary that the stairs went down a long way. Much longer than they should have. They twisted on and on, past doors marked Archives and Records and Acquisitions, until Mary was sure that she must be several floors below ground level. It seemed to her that `the weight of the whole city was pressing down on her head.`

Finally, around the time Mary was beginning to wonder if the next door might be marked China, the staircase ended. The hallway she now saw had none of the intricacy or character of the building above. It was just a plain gray hall, with a concrete floor and bare walls.

Mary walked ahead cautiously. The whole place smelled of damp paper and dust. The dim light left shadows along the walls.

If I see a rat, I'm going to scream.

There were no rats. Or at least, the rats stayed hidden.

Another twenty feet along the hall Mary reached a door labeled Research. She let out a relieved breath and rapped her knuckles against the door.

"Yes?" said a muffled voice from inside.

"Aunt Jen?" Mary called. "Is that you?"

There was a rattle, and the door opened just enough to admit a head with ringlets of copper hair and round, rimless glasses. "Mary!" she said excitedly. "What are you doing down here?"

Mary shrugged. "I was on my way to the center of the earth and thought I would stop in." She rolled her eyes. "I came here to see you, of course."

"That's great," her aunt replied. Her expression suddenly changed from a smile to a look of worry. "You're okay, aren't you? You're not in trouble?"

Mary sighed. It was clear that her parents had already passed along the terrible story of Mary and her drug addiction. "No, Aunt Jen, I'm not in trouble." She held up a small manila folder. "I wanted to see if my favorite aunt could help me find some information."

Relief spread over her aunt's face. "I'm your only aunt," she said, "but I guess you can come in, anyway." She swung open the door.

Mary stepped in, but as soon as she was through the door she stopped again. "Wow! It's the Bat Cave."

Jen laughed. "Just a few simple tools."

"Yeah, right." Everywhere Mary looked, there was another computer or monitor or some other piece of electronic gear. The whole place glowed. "It looks like I came to the right person."

Aunt Jen plopped into a padded office chair and waved to another. "Have a seat and tell me what's up."

Mary sat down and opened her folder. She hesitated for a moment. What Gaia had told her was a secret. She knew that Gaia would be upset if she knew Mary had told someone else. On the other hand, Mary couldn't help Gaia unless she knew what was going on. She reached into the envelope and pulled out several sheets of computer printout. "I have this friend," she said. "Something happened to her parents."

Mary watched her aunt take the papers and study them with a frown. Aunt Jen had the same hair as Mary's mother, but that was where the resemblance stopped. Aunt Jen was ten years younger and thirty pounds heavier than her mom. And when she smiled, she looked closer to twelve than thirty-two. Even if Mary had a dozen aunts, this one would still be her favorite.

"What do you think?" Mary asked after a minute of silence.

Aunt Jen shook her head. "I don't know what to think." She flipped through the papers one more time, then looked at Mary. "I'm a library scientist. I study how to organize information. I'm not a detective."

Mary leaned forward in her chair. "Yeah, but you've got access to every piece of paper in the world."

"That's not quite true."

"It's close." Mary smiled hopefully. "Can't you make a few searches? Check a few files?"

"For what?"

"Anything you can find."

Aunt Jen gave an elaborate sigh, but there was a smile on her round face. "All right," she said. "I'll see what I can do." She glanced at her watch. "But it will have to be later."

Mary grinned. "That's fine." She got out of her chair and hugged her aunt. "Call me as soon as you find anything."

Aunt Jen led her back to the door. "You stay out of trouble."

Mary nodded. "Don't worry. I'll be fine." She turned and headed back down the gloomy hallway. Once again she felt that terrible sense of being buried under tons of earth.

I'll be fine if I don't have to come back down here, she thought with a shiver. *If I worked down here, I would have to be drugged.*

LOKI WAITED ON THE THIRD LANDING.

He could hear the girl coming closer, her leather-soled shoes clapping against the metal stairs. She was three twists of the stairs below, but she was climbing steadily. This girl had young legs. She would reach him soon.

He flexed his fingers. This would be a good opportunity to prevent any further threat from Mary Moss. A quick push and she would go screaming back to the bottom of the stairs. The fall was only thirty or forty feet, but Miss Moss would not survive. Loki would see to that.

The footsteps were closer now, still rising to meet him. Loki leaned over the railing. He could just make her out—two turns down.

Gaia shouldn't have told her about Katia. True, he still might have been forced to kill the Moss girl eventually. Her friendship with Gaia, if it continued, was too much of a threat. But the knowledge Gaia had shared with Mary had completely sealed her fate.

Loki squeezed his eyes shut for a moment. No one could know the truth. It was unlikely that this girl could learn anything of importance. Unlikely, but not impossible.

Mary was one turn below now. Her head was barely a foot beneath Loki's boots.

Kill her. Stop her from asking any more questions. It was the cleanest way to solve this problem.

Mary rounded the last turn and headed up to the landing.

Loki faded back into the shadows. He moved with absolute silence, and his clothes blended with the darkness. He stood absolutely still. He didn't breathe. He didn't even blink.

Mary passed within five feet of him. She could have reached out and touched him. He could have reached out and sent her to her death. But Loki had decades of experience in being unseen. Mary went on without pausing.

Loki waited until the girl had passed, then started after her. Mary would live through the day. He had decided that he didn't have enough information to act at this point. His surveillance of Mary Moss was incomplete. She might have informed others of Gaia's story.

He would have to tighten the noose around Mary. He would find out exactly what she knew and who she had told. Once those questions were answered, Loki would see that Mary Moss met with an early and tragic end.

ED FARGO HATED SALT.

Not salt on food. As far as Ed was concerned, salt was in its own food group with an importance level that put it right below the all-powerful sugar-and-chocolate group and just above the equally

Bizzaro Heather

vital grease group. Food salt was good. Unfortunately, not every grain of salt was lucky enough to end up decorating a giant pretzel.

As soon as there was the least hint of snow, the storefronts around the Village began to apply liberal amounts of salt to the sidewalk. Not little dashes of salt. Not handfuls. *Tons of salt.* Whole bags of coarse, milky rock salt. So much of the stuff that Ed wondered if there was actually more salt than snow.

There were several reasons to hate the stuff. Most of the year, being in a wheelchair was at least quiet. Now that it was salt season, every pump of his arms crunched so loudly that he sounded like he was rolling over a bag of potato chips. There was also the cleanliness factor. The salt from the wheels got all over his hands and on his clothes. And then there was the mechanical safety factor. Ed could only imagine what all the crud was doing to the chair. Salt rusted cars, and cars were covered over with nice layers of paint and all kinds of expensive antirust coatings. Ed's chair was nothing but bare metal. He wondered if the whole thing was going to melt into a puddle of rust one day and dump him in the middle of an intersection.

Ed was so involved in staring at the salt clinging to the spokes of the wheels that he almost ran over a beautiful girl.

"Hi, Ed."

Ed looked up to see Heather Gannis standing on

the sidewalk in front of him. As usual, Heather was dressed wonderfully, with a cream-colored sweater peeking from under her jacket and a matching cap of soft wool pulled down over her mass of thick brown hair. And as always, Heather looked great.

"Heather," he said. "You, um . . . You look great."
Another brilliant, insightful observation by Ed Fargo.

Heather gave a halfhearted smile. "Thanks." She looked past Ed for a moment. "I wish I felt better."

Ed searched for the right thing to say. Back when Heather was his girlfriend, he knew what to say. Even after he and Heather had broken up, he had his patented collection of smart-ass remarks. Now that Heather was actually being nice to him again, Ed wasn't sure how to play it.

"Well," Heather said with a disappointed tone in her voice. "I guess I'd better—"

"Wait," said Ed. He gave up looking for something clever to say and went for the simple question. "What's wrong?"

Heather shrugged and looked off into the distance. "I'm not sure."

"You feeling okay? You're not sick or anything?"

"It's not me," she said. "I was supposed to meet . . . someone . . . down here, and he didn't show up. And then I saw you and I thought . . ." She stopped again and shook her head. "I probably shouldn't talk about it."

Ed stared up into Heather's face. She was pretty. Maybe even prettier than Gaia. Of course, Heather didn't have the quirky beauty of Gaia Moore, but there was only one Gaia Moore—and that was probably a good thing for the sanity of everyone involved.

Still, there was no doubt that Heather was very pretty, and at one time Ed had been convinced he loved her. Maybe he really had loved her. He had hated her, too, for the way she had left him after the accident. He wasn't sure that either one of those feelings was completely gone.

"I better go," said Heather. She licked at her lips and fidgeted with her wool hat. "It's getting late."

Ed nodded, but as Heather started to step past him he reached out and caught her by the arm. "How about some coffee?"

Heather shook her head. "I don't know if I should."

"Come on," Ed urged. "Let's have a little latte and talk."

For a long second Heather stood with her head hanging down. Then she nodded. "All right," she said. "I guess I need to talk to someone."

Ed followed her down the street to Ozzie's. It was a place famous in Ed's memory because it was the place where Gaia and Heather had first met—the place where Gaia had doused Heather with a full cup of steaming coffee.

"What are you smiling about?" asked Heather.

Ed pushed back the memory and shook his head. "Nothing," he said. "I'm just glad you decided to come with me."

For once he seemed to find the right words. Heather smiled at his response. "I'm glad you asked me."

While Heather grabbed a spot at one of the tables, Ed went to the counter and ordered for both of them. He had no trouble remembering what Heather wanted. She hadn't been Ed's first girlfriend, but she had been his first really serious girlfriend. And his last. Ed could probably remember almost everything Heather had ever ordered on their dates.

With two steaming double lattes clutched carefully in one hand, Ed rolled over to the table where Heather was waiting. She took her drink without a word and lifted the foamy brew to her mouth. As she put down the cup, she sighed. Her eyes slipped closed for a moment. "Thanks," she said. "I needed this more than you can know."

Ed took a quick sip from his own latte. He knew that Heather had been through a lot over the last couple of weeks. In fact, Ed might be the *only* one who knew everything that had happened. For some reason, Heather had trusted him with some pretty heavy secrets. Still, it wasn't like Heather to let down her guard out in public. Heather lived at the top of the high school food pyramid with the truly popular people. It was a nasty place up there, a place where you didn't dare let people know that you were less than perfect.

"Okay, now that we're stocked on caffeine and sugar, are you ready to tell me what's up?" Ed asked.

Heather put her elbows on the edge of the table and rested her face in her hands. "I don't know if I should," she replied, her voice escaping through her slim fingers. "It's not one thing. It's a lot of things. Some of it's not even really my problem."

"If it's bothering you, then I guess it is your problem."

"Maybe." Heather nodded and gave another sigh. "Maybe I do need to talk about it."

"Then tell me." Ed looked at her with what he hoped was a confident, solid expression. Your trustworthy friend Ed. "You know you can tell me anything."

The tightness in Heather's face relaxed a notch. "I always could." Heather lowered her hands and looked around her, as if afraid someone else might hear, but the coffee shop was nearly empty. Finally she looked back at Ed. "Part of it's about Phoebe," she said softly.

"Phoebe?" Ed flushed. A wave of embarrassment washed over him that almost knocked him out of his chair.

Phoebe was Heather's older sister. If anything, Phoebe was even more beautiful than Heather, though until recently she had been a little bit heavier. Not now, though. Ed had seen Phoebe only a few days before, and she had looked fantastic.

What made Ed red with embarrassment was the memory of what he had said about Phoebe. In the middle of an intense game of truth or dare, Ed had said that he wanted to sleep with Phoebe more than any woman in the world. It had been a lie, of course, and Gaia and Mary were the only ones there to hear him. Surely neither one of them would have talked to Heather. Would they?

Ed swallowed hard and tried not to look too terribly guilty. "Is Phoebe still in town?"

Heather nodded. "Just for a couple more days, though. Then she's going back to college."

A little bit of relief edged through Ed's near panic. Heather didn't *sound* like she knew about Ed's big sex-with-Phoebe confession. "So what's wrong?" he asked.

There was a long moment of silence, then Heather shook her head. "I can't talk about it. At least, not yet." A sad half smile settled on her face again. She reached across the table and took Ed's hand. "Thanks for asking me in here," she said. "I really appreciate it."

Ed tried out another reassuring smile. Anybody else at school might not recognize this soft, vulnerable person. This couldn't be Heather Gannis. Where were the biting remarks? Where was the absolute confidence? They would think this girl was biz-zaro Heather. Most of the students at the Village School probably thought Heather's family was rich and Heather was a pampered princess. Ed was one of the few who knew how hard Heather worked to keep up that illusion.

"So if you can't talk about Phoebe and she's only part of it, what's the rest?"

Heather picked up her coffee, took a long drink, then set the cup down hard on the table. "Sam."

Once Ed had seen some science show where people's brains were monitored while someone read words from a list. Different words caused activity in different parts of the brain. If someone had clamped one of those helmets on Ed, the word Sam would have blown out the circuits.

"You and Sam are having trouble?" Ed hoped his voice didn't show as much strain as he felt. He didn't know whether he wanted Sam and Heather to be apart or not. On the one hand, if Sam stayed with Heather that meant Sam wasn't with Gaia. But Ed wasn't completely sure that he was over Heather. All things considered, Ed decided the world would be better if Sam Moon experienced spontaneous combustion. "Sam was the one who was supposed to meet you."

Heather nodded. "Over an hour ago. We were going to have lunch and maybe see a movie. Everything seemed fine."

"Except he didn't show."

"No," said Heather. "He didn't." She looked over Ed's shoulder toward the street outside. "You don't think that he knows about . . . you know."

Ed knew. "Charlie."

Heather looked around the coffee shop again, then brought her face close to Ed's. "Do you think Sam knows?"

Ed wasn't sure what to say. Charlie had gotten Heather into bed. He had bragged about it and had even used Heather for "points" in the little sex game some of the jocks had put together. "I think it's possible," Ed said carefully. "I mean, Sam's not around the Village School, but he's not on the other side of the world. What are you going to do if he finds out?"

Heather closed her eyes and put her hands against her temples. "I don't know what to do," she said. "I mean, no matter how big a jerk Charlie was and no matter what really happened, I went with him into that bedroom. Nobody made me do that."

Ed reached out and touched his hand gently against Heather's cheek. "It's okay," he said. "Sam probably doesn't know, and even if he does, I'm sure he'll understand."

Heather covered Ed's hand with one of her own and leaned against his palm. "You think . . ." She hesitated for a moment, then ventured a tentative smile.

"You think you would be interested in getting something to eat?"

Ed grinned. "When have I ever turned down food?"

Heather's smile brightened. "And after that—"

"A movie," Ed finished. "Sure. I'd love to."

Heather's smile grew wider and lost some of its sad edge. "I can always count on you." Then, much to Ed's astonishment, she leaned across the table and kissed him on the cheek.

MARY MOSS HELD THE HANDLE OF

That Tone

one shopping bag with her teeth, put another between her knees, and bent down to jab her key into the lock. She managed to turn the doorknob and stumble inside before everything tumbled to the floor.

"Little help here!" she called out, but the apartment was dark and quiet. Mary dragged her stuff inside and let the door swing shut.

Actually, it was probably good that her parents weren't home. For one thing, it showed that they were beginning to trust her again—even if it was for only a few hours in the middle of the day.

Since learning of Mary's drug habit, her parents

had been smothering her with everything from video-tapes and brochures on rehab centers to books from famous users who had kicked their addictions. Even her Christmas presents had been heavily loaded with an assortment of such uplifting material.

Mary didn't feel uplifted. She was off the drugs, and it wasn't because she had gone to any trendy center or been inspired by some has-been celebrity. She had kicked cocaine on her own. Well, maybe having Gaia around had helped a little. Maybe more than a little. But the point was, Mary was off the coke. If her parents were looking for the right time to give her books about drugs, they had missed it—by years.

The other reason it was good to find the apartment empty was that now her parents wouldn't see what she had bought.

Mary hefted the bags and made her way up the stairs to her bedroom. She had just enough time to get her things together before going out to meet Gaia. If she was lucky, she might even squeeze in a call to Aunt Jen before she left, in case there was any news on the Gaia's-parents-mystery front.

She gave the shopping bags a shake. Even though most of her Christmas presents had been of the ex-druggie-book variety, there had still been some cash slipped in among the pages. Not as many bills as in previous years, but then, her parents were probably afraid that if they gave her a big wad of cash, she would shove it up her nose.

Even the reduced cash supply had been enough to add some serious punch to Mary's wardrobe. She emptied the contents of the first bag onto her bed and studied the results. There were blouses she had liberated from Classics, a retro clothing store south of the park. There were some jeans that were `completely too squeezy` at the moment but that Mary hoped to wear as soon as she had battled off the holiday bulge. There were three pairs of shoes and a lace camisole in a violet so deep, it was almost black.

Mary smiled down at the pile. The clothes represented four hours of dedicated shopping, but they were definitely worth it. If you knew where to shop, a little bit of cash could buy `a big chunk of cool`.

She reached down, picked up the camisole, and carried it across to the mirror on her dresser. She held it up and was just imagining what her mother would say if she tried to wear it sans shirt when she heard a noise from the hallway.

Mary turned. "Mom?"

There was no reply.

"Mom? Are you guys home?"

For several long seconds Mary heard nothing. Then there was a soft creaking sound—`the sound of boards shifting under someone's weight.`

At once Mary's throat drew tight. "Mom?" she tried again, but this time it was only a faint whisper.

Slowly she let the camisole slide from her fingers and fall into a dark puddle on the floor. Moving as quietly as she could, Mary took a step toward the door. Then another. She peered out through the opening.

There was no sound from the hallway. No creaking boards. But there was a shadow. A man-shaped shadow. Just outside the limits of her sight, someone was standing in the hallway. Even without the shadow Mary didn't have to see him to know he was there— she could *feel* him.

She thought of making a run for the front door, then remembered the phone by her bed. Keeping her eyes on the hall, she slid toward the nightstand.

There was another noise, not so soft this time. A footstep, followed by the sound of something—of someone—brushing against the wall.

Mary's heart bounced in her chest. Fear ran through her body like strong acid. With trembling fingers she lifted the receiver of the phone and brought it up to her ear. In the silence the dial tone seemed impossibly loud. Surely whoever was out in the hallway would hear it. Surely he would know what Mary was trying to do.

Another footstep from the hallway. Louder this time. Closer.

Mary brought her fingers to the dial and pressed down on the nine. The tone was so loud, it made her jump. She had to close her eyes for a second and draw a breath before moving her finger over to press the one. She raised her finger to press the button again.

There was a sudden noise from downstairs. A clatter followed by the squeak of the door being shoved open.

"Mary, honey?" called a voice from downstairs. "Are you home?"

Mary felt a wash of relief so strong, she almost fell. "Dad!" she called out. "I'm up here." But as soon as she spoke Mary realized that her parents could also be in danger. "Watch out!" she shouted. "There's someone else up here!"

Footsteps sounded from the stairs. "What did you say?" called her father.

Mary let the phone drop and jumped to her door. "Stay back, Dad! There's someone—"

But there was no one. In both directions the hallway was empty.

Her father reached the top of the stairs. "Who did you say was here?"

Mary looked along the empty hall and shook her head. "I heard . . . I mean, I thought . . ." She paused, then shrugged. "Nobody, I guess."

Her father's face turned down in an expression of concern. "Are you okay?"

The tone of his voice made Mary wince. It was a tone she had heard all too often lately. No matter what the words, anytime her parents asked her a question in that tone, she knew what they were really asking—was she on drugs?

"I'm fine," Mary said. "Just fine." She backed into her bedroom and closed the door.

THERE HAD TO BE A BETTER PHRASE

than jet lag. Jet lag sounded so harmless. "Oh, I'll be okay in a little while. I just have a touch of jet lag."

What Tom Moore felt wasn't jet lag. This was something more like jet flu, or jet attack, or maybe jet coma.

For almost twenty hours he had been on a series of planes. Moscow to St. Petersburg. From there to Munich. Munich to London. And finally on to New York. By the time the small government Starcraft jet taxied onto the tarmac at JFK, Tom had to look up at the sky to tell if it was day or night. He felt like someone had beaten him on the head with a rock or drugged his coffee. Or both.

As usual, there had been men in dark suits waiting as soon as he stepped from the plane. The debriefing had gone smoothly. Tom's mission in Russia had gone reasonably well—despite a few setbacks and that botched rendezvous right before he'd left. And despite the fact that the whole trip had been overshadowed by memories of the time he had spent there in the company of his wife. The agency people weren't interested in Tom's memories. All they cared about were the dry facts. They wanted to know about the contacts he had seen and the timetable of the assignment.

Tom stayed awake long enough to accept dry congratulations on the completion of the latest mission, then fell into the backseat of a bland government-issue sedan and gave the driver directions to his latest apartment. Before the car even started to move, Tom fell into a gray haze.

Even in the backseat of the sedan, his mind was haunted by images of Katia. Moscow had been her home and the place where she and Tom first met. Going back there left Tom with a heavy weight of memories that clung to him like cobwebs. He wasn't even sure he wanted them to go away. Katia was gone. Memories were all Tom had.

At least he could still see his daughter, even if it did have to be at a distance. Meeting with Gaia wouldn't be safe for either of them, but Tom *had* to see her and make sure that she was all right. See Gaia. That thought cheered him as he climbed out of the car and walked the last couple of blocks to his apartment.

The apartment wasn't much, just a small one-bedroom place tucked above a corner fruit stand. It was far from fancy, but it provided an adequate base for Tom—especially since he was rarely in town. When he considered some of the other places he had called home over the last few years, it was practically paradise.

The fruit stand was doing slow but steady business. Tom waved at the owners as he walked around the building and made his way up the wooden stairs along the side. Even in December the air was scented by peaches and limes from the store.

Tom was nearly asleep on his feet, but he wasn't so tired that he didn't check the door before he went in. Before leaving, he had placed a small scrap of paper at the bottom of the door. Nothing special, just a little piece of newspaper that he had torn off and wedged against the door frame. If someone wasn't looking for it, they would never know it was there. Which was exactly what Tom was counting on. If someone had opened the door while he was away, the paper would have fallen out. He had fancier methods of detection available, but Tom was a great believer in simple methods.

He bent and inspected the door. The paper was still in its place.

Tom smiled in relief. The bed, and eight hours of solid sleep, were waiting inside.

Except.

Tom had his hand on the doorknob before something started to tickle at his brain. For a half a second his tired mind tried to sort out what was wrong. As he did, his fingers continued to turn the knob.

The paper was still there, so everything had to be okay. Only it wasn't because . . . because . . .

Because the paper was turned the wrong way.

Someone had been there. Someone had gone inside, done whatever they wanted, and come back out. They had been careful. They had seen the little scrap of paper and put it back. Only not perfectly.

The doorknob clicked under Tom's hand, and the door cracked open. For the space of a heartbeat he stood there, staring into the darkness on the other side of the door.

Instantly the sleepiness and exhaustion he had felt since leaving Moscow vanished. Before his heart could beat a second time, he had started to turn away. Before a half second had passed, the suit bag had slipped from his left hand and he was at the top of the stairs.

The explosion came before he could take another

step. There was no noise because the force of the blast instantly stunned his ears into silence. It lifted him, stole his breath in white-hot heat, then flung him downward like a singed rag doll.

He hit the bottom of the steps, bounced, and was instantly forced against the wall by an inferno wind.

When it was over, Tom fell. He fell down into darkness. And silence. And the smell of peaches.

Even Gaia
had her
limits.

**about
tonight**

SAM PUT HIS FINGER AGAINST THE

pawn and shoved it forward on its rank. "It wasn't like I did anything."

"Yah." A black knight jumped in from the side of the board to trample the unprotected piece.

"I mean, sure, I thought about someone else. I'll admit that." Sam pushed his bishop toward the center of the board.

The black queen slid up beside the bishop. "Der is nothing wrong with thinking."

Sam reached for his one remaining rook, hesitated, then drew back the bishop instead. "Okay, maybe I even kissed someone else," he said. "But that's not nearly as bad as what she did. Not even close."

"Yah, of course." The knight jumped again, and the rook left the field.

Sam scanned his diminished army and frowned. He shoved another pawn toward the opposite ranks. "And the first chance she gets, the very first chance—"

The black queen swept forward. "Dat is checkmate."

"It is?" Sam blinked and looked across the board. Usually he had a good grasp of the board, but now the chess game seemed as remote as another planet. He had lost. Again. He unzipped his heavy coat, fumbled in his pockets, and came out with a ten.

Zolov reached across the board and took the bill from his hand. "Thank you," said the old man. He stared down his long nose and studied the bill carefully, as if expecting to find a forgery. After the personal inspection Zolov held the ten up in front of two battered Power Rangers that sat beside the chessboard. "What you think?" he said.

Apparently the little plastic people gave their approval. After a few moments Zolov crumpled the bill and shoved it into the depths of his old tweed coat.

Sam shook his head and stared off across the frozen park. "I don't know. I thought maybe Heather really was the one. Now she's completely lied to me, and Gaia doesn't care if I live or not, so—"

"Be good to Ceendy, you," Zolov said suddenly. The old man's face reddened, and he waved an ancient, arthritic finger at Sam. "I like dat girl."

"Cindy?" Sam leaned back in surprise. "You mean Gaia?"

Zolov's bushy eyebrows drew together. "Dat girl, you should be lucky to have her." The old Russian glared at Sam for a few seconds longer, then picked up his chess pieces and began to put them back into position for a new game. "She is not like the others."

Sam tried to think of something to say. He couldn't be sure—maybe Zolov was thinking of Gaia, maybe he was thinking of someone else entirely. Maybe he was thinking of someone who had been gone for half a century. Zolov was never very clear on much. Except for chess. When it came to chess, Zolov was still as sharp as ever.

The Russian finished arranging the pieces and looked over at Sam. If the old man had been angry before, there was no trace of it remaining on his face. "We play again, yah?"

Sam did a quick calculation. Considering the difficulty he was having concentrating on the game, he was sure to lose. Even on his best days he could rarely match Zolov. But he could afford to lose another ten, and he certainly had nowhere better to go. "Sure," he said.

Zolov held out his hands. Sam picked one at random. The Russian unfolded his fingers to reveal a white pawn. "So," he said. "You go first."

Sam started playing again, moving the pieces through a standard opening. He glanced across the board and decided to risk Zolov's anger. "What is it that makes Gaia different?" he asked.

Zolov snorted. "You not know that, you not know Ceendy, do you?" He jumped a knight over a rank of pawns.

Sam had to smile. He still couldn't tell if Zolov was talking about Gaia or just talking. But this was better than sitting around brooding about Heather. "I guess Gaia is special."

Zolov grunted and shoved a pawn forward.

Sam studied the board for a moment before moving in reply. Just because he knew he was going to lose didn't mean he wanted to make it easy. "It doesn't matter how special Gaia is. She isn't mine."

Zolov started to move, stopped, and looked across the board at Sam. "You don't know?"

"Know what?"

The Russian shook his head. "Think he is a smart boy, but he doesn't even know."

"Know what?" Sam repeated.

"Doesn't know Ceendy loves him." Zolov looked down, pushed up his queen, and smiled. "Dat is check!" he cried.

AS EXPECTED, THE SNOW HAD WIMPED

Music from Mars

out again. No more than a dusting remained along the hedgerows that bordered the park. The parks department, which had absolutely no appreciation for snow, had already completely cleared the main paths. Still, Gaia couldn't find much to complain about. The clouds had broken, the day was bright, and she didn't have to spend it *(a)* going to school or *(b)* sitting around the brownstone with Ella.

Gaia was due to meet Mary by the central arch in half an hour, which gave her plenty of time to cross the park. Normally she walked fast no matter where she was going, but now she strolled along the path at a leisurely pace, watching the people as they passed and the kids slipping down the metal slides on the playground.

She was near the center of the park when she heard a scratchy, warbling music drifting along the path. It was a strange sound. Gaia could make out a man's voice, but the words and the tune were utterly alien. Like music from Mars. She picked up her pace and angled toward the source of the weird sound.

A few twists in the path brought Gaia to a small group of people and a contraption just as strange as the sounds it was making. Mounted on what looked like a large version of a kid's red wagon, `the thing spouted odd, angled lengths of plumbing pipe` and a cone that looked like it might have come from a large desk lamp. At the heart of the mess Gaia could just make out a large— and very old—phonograph.

The record playing on the device wasn't any easier to understand from close up than it had been from far away. The singer's voice rose and fell, and alien words poured out. Gaia couldn't tell what the man was talking about, but there was no mistaking the message. This song was sad. This song was lonely. The singer sounded like he had just discovered he was the only person left in the world.

Standing there in the park with her hands in her pockets and her face chilled by the cold breeze, Gaia knew how he must have felt. She'd felt that way for a long time. But instead of thinking of her mother, the image that appeared in Gaia's mind was Sam. What was he doing right now? Did *he* ever feel this lonely? Did *he* ever hear songs that made him think of *her*?

Gaia wondered if she should walk over to the chess tables. She hadn't played in a while, and she really should keep in practice. She might get a chance to talk to Zolov. She might even run into Sam.

That was ridiculous, of course. Sam was with Heather. He was not only with Heather, he was sleeping with her. And Gaia should know: unbelievably, she'd witnessed them having sex not once, but twice. Although she could be a glutton for punishment, even Gaia had her limits. It was time to accept that Sam was never going to be part of her life. It didn't matter how Gaia felt about him because Sam didn't share those feelings.

"Is this song really that sad?" asked a voice at her back.

Gaia spun to find Mary looking at her. "You're early."

"So are you," said Mary. She tilted her head a little to the side and looked at Gaia. "Is something wrong?"

"No, nothing." Gaia was embarrassed to find there were tears blurring her eyes. The combination of the music and her own thoughts of Sam really had been getting to her. Gaia blinked away the tears and smiled. "How did your shopping trip go?"

Mary's lips turned up in a wicked grin. "Great, of course. I found exactly what I need for tonight."

"About tonight," said Gaia. "I don't know—"

"Oh, no, Ms. Moore," said Mary. "You're not getting out of this." She took Gaia by the arm and drew her away from the phonograph cart. "Come on, let's get somewhere we can talk without yelling."

Gaia followed as Mary led the way toward the north end of the park, where a re-creation of the Arc de Triomphe loomed over the people strolling the paths. The music from the weird phonograph faded until it was only a melancholy hum in the winter air. "Where do you want to go?"

Mary waved a hand ahead. "Doesn't matter. Somewhere we can continue our conversation."

"Which conversation is that?"

"You know." Mary gave Gaia a sideways look. "The conversation we were having about your mother."

Gaia stopped dead in her tracks. Mary was the first

person she had ever told about her mother's death. Sharing had made Gaia feel better than she expected, but she was definitely not ready to say more. "That wasn't a conversation," she said. "That was a dare."

"I know," Mary said. "But I thought it might help you feel better to tell me more about it. I'm here for you, Gaia."

"There isn't any more to tell," said Gaia. Images of snow and violence danced on her brain for a painful moment. "I told you everything."

"Everything?" Mary paced back and forth on the sidewalk. "What about your dad? And how did you end up with the Nivens? And why was your mother killed?" She shook her head. "You've barely even started."

Gaia started to answer, stopped, opened her mouth to reply, then shut it again. The problem with most of Mary's questions was that Gaia didn't really know the answers. And even when she did know, there were still things she wasn't ready to tell. "The truth or dare game's over now," she said. "Let me catch my breath before we get into more."

Disappointment creased Mary's forehead, but she nodded. "All right," she replied. "It's just that it's all so . . . so . . . sad and . . . I wish I could help."

Sad wasn't the first word that came to Gaia's mind when she thought about her own life. *Try tragic. Heartbreaking.* "Let's try another subject. Tell me what you found to wear tonight."

Mary raised her chin and struck a pose. "Only something perfect."

"How nice for you," Gaia said with a laugh. "At least one of us will look decent."

"That's the really good news," said Mary. She held up her left hand and revealed a small plastic shopping bag. She let the bag dangle from the tip of her finger and swung it back and forth. "Now for the even better news. I found something for you, too."

"You bought something for me?" Gaia looked at the bag and got a tight feeling in her stomach. "Something to wear?"

Mary nodded. "Something perfect for tonight." She held the bag out where Gaia could take it. "Come on. Take a look."

Gaia squinted at the bag suspiciously. "I don't know about this. I don't think I should even go."

"You promised."

"That's what you say," Gaia replied. "I don't even remember you asking."

Mary shrugged. "So you were mostly asleep. A promise is still a promise." She held up the bag and gave it a little jiggle. "Just look."

Gaia took the bag and peeked inside. "What is it, a top?"

Mary sighed in exasperation. "It's a dress, of course." She grabbed the bag back from Gaia, reached inside, and pulled out the garment.

Gaia's eyes went wide. "You're sure that's a dress?"

"Absolutely," Mary said with a nod. She shook out the dress and held it up against herself. "It's a little black dress. A genuine LBD. A staple of any decent wardrobe."

"Your wardrobe, maybe." Gaia shook her head. "I don't think that's my size."

"It's exactly your size," said Mary. She held the dress toward Gaia. "It'll look great on you."

Gaia took the dress from Mary and stared at it. It made her feel a little queasy to think about wearing the thing. Not that she didn't want to. Gaia could imagine what Mary or another girl might look like wearing the dress. A normal girl.

"You wear that tonight," said Mary, "and every guy in the place will be looking at you."

Yeah, it'd be a regular freak show. "This thing doesn't even have any straps." Gaia turned the dress over in her hands. "What's supposed to hold it up?"

Mary laughed. "You are."

The thought of that was enough to make Gaia want to drop the dress. "Thanks, but no." She started to hand the dress back, but Mary pushed her hands away.

"You're not getting out of it that easy," Mary said. "You're going to wear that dress, and you're . . . you . . ." Mary's voice trailed off, and she stared off into the distance.

"Mary?" Gaia turned and tried to see what had upset Mary, but Gaia couldn't see anything but a handful of people walking along a path. "What's wrong?"

Mary continued to stare for a moment, then shook

her head. "Nothing. Nothing's wrong." She raised one hand and pushed her red hair back from her face. "I'm seeing ghosts. That's all."

Gaia frowned. "You're not still looking for Skizz, are you?"

"No, I—" Mary stopped and shrugged. "Maybe. I don't know."

Gaia wasn't sure what to say. She knew that Mary had been afraid of the drug dealer. And Mary had been right to be scared. Skizz really had tried to hurt her to get back the money Mary owed for drugs. But there was no reason to be scared of the dealer now. Gaia wasn't proud of the beating she had given him, but there was no way he would be a problem to anyone.

"Skizz is in the hospital," said Gaia. "You know that."

"Yeah, I guess so." Mary still looked doubtful. "It's just that this morning . . ."

"What?"

Mary shook her head. "Nothing." The grin returned to her face. "Let's get back to an important topic, like how you are so going to wear that dress tonight."

Gaia thought about it for a second. She could wear the dress. She would look about as attractive as a football player in a tutu, but she could wear it. "I think I'll find something else."

"You won't even try?" asked Mary.

"Not this time."

Mary's bright green eyes locked onto Gaia's. "Coward."

Gaia took a step back. "What?"

"You heard me," said Mary. She jerked the dress from Gaia's hands and shoved it back into the sack. "I buy you a great dress, and you don't even have the guts to wear it."

Anger started to tighten down on Gaia. "If it's so great, why don't you wear it?"

"Maybe I will." Mary narrowed her eyes. "At least I'm not too scared."

"I am not scared," Gaia said in a near shout. "Believe me, I'm not afraid."

"Yeah?" Mary held out the bag. "Then prove it."

ED WAS ON HIS WAY OUT THE DOOR

Checking with Undertakers

when the phone rang for the two hundred and thirty-seventh time that afternoon. He groaned. Every time his parents were gone, it seemed like he spent all his time answering junk phone calls.

He rolled across the kitchen, grabbed the phone, and started talking. "Look, this is an apartment. We don't need insulated windows. We don't need siding. I don't need insurance because I don't own a car, and I don't donate to anybody who calls me on the phone. Clear enough?"

"That's great, Ed," said the voice over the phone. "Now, are you ready to listen?"

Ed fumbled the phone, dropped it, caught it, and shoved it back against his ear. "Gaia?"

"I need a favor," said Gaia. There was a burst of music and background noise.

"What kind of favor?" asked Ed. "Where are you, anyway?"

"I'm at Eddie's."

"Who's Eddie?"

"Eddie's the restaurant," Gaia said. The music started up again, and Ed had to strain to hear her over the driving beat. "I'm here with Mary."

"Yeah?" In his mind's eye Ed had no trouble picturing Gaia and Mary. Gaia's hair was long and pale, buttery blond. Mary's was shorter, wavy, and copper red. Both of them were beautiful. Together the two girls were the hottest pair Ed had ever seen. Just a couple of days before, Gaia had kissed him. True, it had been an exceptional situation, but it had been a kiss. A real kiss. Right on the mouth. He wondered what Gaia was wearing. He wondered what Mary was wearing. Maybe Mary would—

"Ed? Ed, are you there?"

"Uh, yeah." Ed tried to shake off the daydreams and listen. "I'm here."

"There's something I want you to do for me."

"Sure. What is it?"

Gaia made a reply, but Ed couldn't hear her over a sudden increase in noise from the restaurant.

"What was that?"

"Skizz!" Gaia shouted into the phone.

"What?"

"Skizz. Mary's old dealer. I want you to find out where he is."

Ed stared at the receiver. "How am I supposed to do that?"

"Check the hospitals."

"Why would he be in a hospital?"

"Because," said Gaia, "I put him there."

"Oh," said Ed. Then, "Oh!" as he realized the meaning of what she had said. "You sure I shouldn't be checking with undertakers?"

"No. Or at least, I don't think so. If you can't find him, check and see what you can learn from the police."

Ed grabbed a pad from the kitchen counter and made a couple of quick notes. "Okay," he said. "I'll see what I can find. But remember what happened last time we tried to play detectives?"

"We're not talking about going up against a serial killer," said Gaia. "I just want to be sure this particular scuzzy drug dealer is still out of the picture."

"Gotcha. I'll see what I can find out." Ed cleared his throat. "So, Gaia. If I find some information, maybe we can get together and—"

"Thanks, Ed," said Gaia. "I'll check in soon." The phone clicked and went dead.

Ed hung the receiver back on the hook and scowled. "Great," he said to the empty kitchen. "One kiss and she thinks I'll do anything for her."

Then he pulled a phone book out of the cabinet and started to look up hospitals.

MARY HELD THE PHONE CLOSE TO

her mouth. "Aunt Jen? Can you hear me?"

She waited for the reply from the other end and

With a K

frowned at the receiver. Clearly the tales of Mary's terrible drug addiction were still affecting the opinions of her favorite aunt. "Aunt Jen . . . Aunt Jen . . . Aunt Jen! Look, I'm okay. I'm not at a party. I'm at a restaurant."

Mary shifted around on one foot to see if Gaia was watching her. "Eddie's. *E-d-d-i-e-s*. It's near the campus. NYU, okay?"

She nodded as she listened to her aunt's reply. "No

party. No drugs. Just a greasy restaurant. I'm having a cheeseburger."

Even this information generated a lengthy response. Mary began to wonder how many people went back on drugs just because so many people pestered them about staying off. "Look, Aunt Jen, I only wanted to see if you found out anything about that stuff I brought you."

Mary listened for a moment, gritted her teeth, and squeezed her eyes shut. "Yes, I promise it has nothing to do with drugs. Can we please forget the drugs?"

Mary took another glance toward the table and saw that Gaia was looking at her. She cupped her hand over the mouthpiece and tried to speak as softly as she could in the noisy diner. "Yes, I know what the name Gaia means. Uh-huh."

Mary dragged a small pad of paper from her pocket. *Thomas Chaos,* she wrote on the pad.

The Moss Situation

LOKI DIRECTED THE LASER SENSOR at the window of Eddie's diner. In proper situations the device was a wonder. It could take the tiny vibrations that sound caused in the window and use those vibrations to re-create the original sounds. This was not a proper situation. The noise level inside the place made it nearly impossible to sort one sound from the sea of babble. With some difficulty Loki finally managed to locate the voice of the Moss girl.

". . . is Gaia . . . what that means . . . father . . ."

Loki lowered the device in frustration. It was clear that the girl was discussing Gaia, but he couldn't tell what she was saying. Not even Loki could bug every phone in the city.

The situation was becoming intolerable. The girl had information about Katia, and she had shared that information with others. Possibly several others.

Loki dropped the laser detector back into his pocket, took out his phone, and pressed a single button.

"Yes," said an emotionless voice from the other end.

"We'll have to move faster than expected on the Moss situation," said Loki. "She presents too much potential risk."

"I understand," replied the flat voice. "Measures will be prepared."

"You handle the aunt," said Loki. "I'll take care of the girl myself."

ELLA PICKED UP THE PHONE ON

Step Two

the first ring. "Yes?"

"Hi," said the voice from the other end. "This is Sam Moon. Is Gaia there?"

Ella smiled. Sam was a beautiful boy. Nearly perfect, in Ella's carefully considered opinion. He was far better than anything that Gaia deserved. "No, Sam," Ella said sweetly. "I'm afraid Gaia is out."

"Do you know when she'll be back?"

"Not until late. She's out on a date with her boyfriend."

"Oh."

Ella ran a lacquered nail down the side of the phone. This was working out so well. "Do you want me to take a message?"

"No. No, I guess not."

"Should I tell her you called?"

"No," said Sam. "Thanks."

The sadness in his voice was absolutely delicious. "You're welcome, dear."

Ella set the phone back on its hook and brushed her fingers through her scarlet hair. The call couldn't have gone better if she had planned it. Now it was time for step two.

His
fingertips
pressed into **her**
her, pushing **own**
her **heartbeat**

against him.

"YOU LOOK GREAT."

Gaia squinted at the image in the mirror. "I look ridiculous."

Mary rolled her eyes. "Are you kidding?" She moved around Gaia, inspecting her dress from all angles. "I wish I looked half as good as you."

Gaia tugged at the top of the dress. "Half my size is more like it. This thing might fit you, but it's *way* too small for me."

"Are you nuts? It's a perfect fit."

Gaia turned away from the mirror in disgust. "Okay, you've seen me wear the dress. You have to know I can't go out in this thing."

"All I know is that it fits great, you look great, and you should wear it." Mary flipped back her red hair and studied Gaia for a moment. "But if you're too scared—"

"I'm not scared," Gaia said between gritted teeth. "Being scared has nothing to do with it."

Mary nodded. "You just don't want to be embarrassed."

"Exactly."

"You're afraid somebody will make fun of you."

"Right . . . I mean, no." Gaia drew in a deep breath and blew it out through her mouth. "I am not afraid."

"Good," Mary replied brightly. "Then you won't mind wearing the dress."

Gaia lowered her face into her hands and shook

her head. She wondered if being a sociopathic loner was really such a bad thing. On her own, she managed to get into fights only with armed criminals. Somehow that didn't seem nearly as disastrous as wearing this dress out in public. "Please tell me we're going somewhere that nobody knows me."

"Absolutely."

Gaia raised her head. "And we'll never go there again."

Mary shrugged. "If that's what you want. Wait till you get there before you decide something like that."

"Then all right, I may be crazy, but I'll wear the dress." Gaia went to the closet, pulled out her longest coat, and pulled it over the snug dress. "I'm not saying I'll stay long. Once everyone's had a good laugh, I'm leaving."

Mary shook her head. "You really don't see it, do you?"

"See what?" asked Gaia.

"Believe me. When the guys see you in that dress, there is not going to be any laughing." Mary pulled her coat on over the translucent top and short black skirt that made up her own outfit. "Let's get moving."

Gaia wasn't afraid. She *couldn't* be afraid, but she was definitely not looking forward to this evening. Her mood wasn't improved when she saw that Ella was waiting for them at the bottom of the stairs.

Ella folded her arms and leaned back against the stair rail as the girls approached. "Well," she said. "And where are you two going?"

"Dancing," Mary answered before Gaia could open her mouth. "Want to come along?"

Gaia winced. She could read the sarcasm in Mary's voice. She had no doubt that Ella heard it, too. But that didn't mean Ella wouldn't say yes just because she knew how much Gaia would hate it. Gaia looked back over her shoulder and glared at Mary, but Mary only smiled in reply.

Ella gave a short laugh. "I do love to dance," she said, "but no. I'm afraid I have my own duties to attend to tonight."

"That's too bad," Gaia said quickly. "Well, I'll see you later."

She started to step past, but to Gaia's surprise, Ella reached out and laid her hand on Gaia's arm. "Do be careful, dear," she said.

Concern wasn't usual for Ella. "Sure. All right." Gaia walked on, and Ella's fingers slipped away.

"Please tell me you weren't serious," Gaia whispered as she and Mary reached the door.

"What? About Ms. Niven coming with us?" Mary grinned. "It would be something, wouldn't it? I'd love to see if she even can dance on those heels she wears."

"It would be something, all right," said Gaia. She pushed open the door and stepped out into the cold night.

It wasn't until she was outside the brownstone that Gaia realized how happy she was that Ella couldn't see what she was wearing under the coat. For the first time since she had come to New York, Gaia was wearing a shorter dress than her foster mother.

Oh my God. I'm dressed in Ella wear.

"TWENTY-THREE?"

Sam nodded.

Vodka

The woman behind the bar was thin and thirty something, with pink hair piled on her head, a neat gold hoop through the side of her nose, and deep lines around her eyes. She looked skeptically at the ID card, then at Sam, then at the ID again. "You look younger."

"It's a curse," said Sam. He reached out for the card, but the bartender pulled it away.

"I wish I had a curse like that," she said. She gave the card another long look and held it up to the light. "This is a good fake."

Sam jerked the card away from her and put it back in his pocket. "It's not a fake!" he said.

The woman held up her hands. "Hey, don't get so worked up. I didn't say I wasn't going to serve you." A phone rang. The bartender turned and picked it up.

While she talked, Sam spun around on his stool. There was a dance floor in the club, but no one was dancing. Not yet, anyway. Up on the stage a band was just beginning to set up and a couple of men were arranging lights. Sam wasn't sure what kind of music the band played. He thought about asking, but after a moment he decided it didn't matter. He hadn't come into the club for the music.

He pulled out the ID card he had used to get in. These days, with color laser printers, there was almost nothing that couldn't be faked. Making the ID hadn't taken ten minutes.

The bartender finished with her phone call and strolled back over to stand in front of Sam. "You're getting an awfully early start, kiddo."

"Sam."

"Whatever." The woman leaned one elbow on the bar. "What's it going to be tonight, Sam?"

Sam stuffed the fake ID down in his pocket and studied the bottles behind the bar. The range of beverages was a little intimidating. He wasn't a regular drinker. In fact, he usually skipped both the beer and the shots available at campus parties. He just didn't enjoy it that much.

But this time Sam wasn't drinking for enjoyment. He was drinking to take the edge off of Heather's betrayal. He was drinking to wash Gaia out of his mind. He was drinking to smother the pain that cut through him anytime he thought of either girl.

He expected it would take a lot of drinking.

Sam stared at the multicolored bottles for a few

seconds, then shook his head. "Give me a recommendation," he said.

The bartender took a bottle of water-clear liquid down from the shelf. "If I was you, I would go home," she said. "But if you're going to stay here, then go for vodka."

"Why vodka?"

"Because," said the bartender as she pulled out a glass and set it down on the bar. "Vodka is good when you want to do some serious drinking. It doesn't leave you with such a bad hangover." The woman tipped the bottle and filled the glass nearly full of the clear fluid. "And kid, you look like you're here for serious drinking."

ED HELD HIS FINGERS AGAINST THE

One Thing He Knew

bridge of his nose and tried to get his temper under control. "I *understand* you still need insurance information. I don't *have* insurance information. No. No. No! I don't know his Social Security number!" He listened for a moment longer, then slammed the phone back into its cradle.

Four hours before, Ed had been on his way out of the house. Instead of leaving, he had been on the phone for hours. He never even got out of his kitchen.

Ed had been trying to get information from St. Vincent's, where Skizz was staying, by pretending to be everything from the police to Skizz's brother. The workers at the hospital weren't stupid, but they were overworked. If you kept at it long enough and pestered hard enough, you could get them to tell you what you wanted. But it sure took time.

Ed glanced toward the windows and saw it was already dark outside. He thought about going out. He could find something to eat. Wander down to see what was on at the movies.

But the sad truth was, despite all the time he had spent badgering people over the phone, Ed still didn't have all the information he needed. He had the first part. It wasn't much, really, just a sentence or two.

And Ed knew one thing for sure—what he had learned so far wasn't going to make Gaia happy.

"COME ON!" MARY TOOK GAIA by the hand and started dragging her toward the dance floor.

Gaia put on the brakes. "Wait."

Why People Dance

"Wait for what?" Mary let go of Gaia's hand and swayed from side to side in time to the music. "Come on. Let's get out there."

People pushed past them on both sides. The band had been playing for only a few minutes, but already the floor was getting crowded with couples, singles, and assorted groups. The close press of people made Gaia feel more than a little trapped. She was used to being alone, prowling around the park or hiking down the streets at night. Being in the crowded nightclub made her so squeezed, that Gaia almost forgot about the way she was dressed. Almost.

"Gaia!" Mary called. Even from two feet away she had to shout to be heard over the driving music. She spun around on her high-heeled shoes and flashed a bright smile. "Aren't you going to dance?"

Gaia shook her head. "I don't think so. Dancing isn't on my resume."

Mary grabbed her hand again. "You know how. You just don't know that you know." She pulled Gaia toward the center of the floor.

Gaia let herself be pulled. First it was the skimpy dress. Now it was dancing. She wondered if a person could reach a complete overload of embarrassment. A pressure so strong that they collapsed inward, like a star falling into a black hole.

Mary released Gaia's hand. She started to dance slowly, shifting her weight and letting her arms drift back and forth. "Here's the secret," she said. "Guys have to learn how to dance. Girls don't. I mean, sure you have to learn if you want to be really good, but if you just want to have fun and get the guys bothered, all any attractive girl has to do is move."

Gaia looked down at her own feet. "That's great for attractive girls. How does it help me?"

Mary stopped dancing and put her hands on her hips. "Gaia, give it up. You know you're gorgeous."

"I'm not—"

Mary waved at the dancing crowd. "There's not a woman in this place half as hot as you. Why don't you want to believe that?"

"Because it's not true," said Gaia.

Mary frowned. "Then pretend, okay? For tonight just pretend that you're as pretty as . . . as . . . oh, as pretty as you really are!"

The tempo of the music picked up. Mary smiled and started moving again, swinging her hips and moving her body with the beat. "Come on, dance."

Gaia watched Mary for a few seconds. The red-haired girl moved so well. Her pale face and arms seemed to float above her dark clothing. She wasn't doing anything fancy, but her movements were smooth, fluid. The easy way Mary moved her body made Gaia feel jealous. There was no way she could move like that—and no way she would look as good as Mary did.

For long seconds Gaia stood still in the middle of all the dancing. She thought about leaving the floor. She thought about leaving the whole club. Then she thought about what Mary had said.

Gaia knew that Mary was only trying to make her feel better. She knew she wasn't beautiful—her mother had been beautiful, but not Gaia. But what if she was to pretend? Could she think of herself as beautiful for just one night? Could she imagine what it would be like to be a normal girl? An attractive girl without monster legs? A girl like Mary who knew how to dance.

She closed her eyes. Slowly Gaia began to move. Her feet remained almost still, but her legs moved. Then her hips. Then her body and shoulders and arms.

At first she felt awkward, stiff. Gaia knew how to move smoothly—she had gone through a thousand karate training exercises that were more about moving well than hitting anything. But dancing was different. There was no plan, no path to follow. She had to make it up as she went along.

Gaia picked up speed, bringing herself in time with the music. She started to feel a little better. A little looser. She was sure that if she opened her eyes, half the people in the club would be laughing at her. So she kept her eyes shut.

The more she caught up to the music, the more

she could feel it inside her. The drums pounded in her stomach. The guitars sliced along her arms and legs, driving her to move faster, to dance wilder. With her eyes still closed, Gaia raised her hands over her head and spun around.

Maybe everyone was laughing, but it was starting to feel good. Really good. The movements of her body became more confident. There was a jazzy, electric feeling in her limbs. It was something like the buzz she sometimes got before a fight.

When Gaia dared to open her eyes, Mary was gone. Lost somewhere in a sea of dancing bodies. No one was laughing.

But there was someone looking at her.

A young Hispanic man with flashing black eyes and short-cropped hair was dancing right in front of Gaia. He was smiling at her. And he was dancing at her.

The man wasn't very tall, barely as tall as Gaia, but he was well built, with a narrow waist and broad, square shoulders. Gaia guessed he was somewhere in his early twenties. He wore a black jacket that was hanging open at the front and a snug white shirt that pulled in tight against the brown skin at his throat. He was muscular. Not overmuscled, but smooth, firm, fit.

The man didn't say a word, but his eyes never left Gaia. He looked into her face as he danced. Right into her eyes.

Gaia could barely feel herself moving. It was like she was riding the music. It seemed effortless now, like something she had done all her life.

The tune ended, and the music changed, but Gaia never missed a step. For the first time in a long time she felt like she was part of something bigger than herself.

She understood why people danced.

The man moved closer. He leaned toward Gaia, and she leaned away—but not far away. They moved together, so close that the man's jacket brushed against the cloth of Gaia's dress. As soft as a whisper. Gaia's long blond hair sprayed around her shoulders and spilled across the man's face.

Their bodies were inches apart. Less than an inch. Touching. Gaia could feel the heat coming from the man's skin as if there were a furnace in his chest. She couldn't tell if the beat she felt was the music. Or her own heartbeat. Or his.

The man's hand moved around Gaia and settled at the small of her back. His fingertips pressed into her, pushing her against him.

In that moment Gaia forgot that she was wearing a dress that exposed her bulky legs and arms. She forgot that she was supposed to be embarrassed. For that moment she even forgot about her father, and mother, and Sam.

And when the song ended and the man—the man

she had never seen before in her life—brought his face down to hers, Gaia kissed him. Hard.

VODKA DID PACK A PUNCH.

Unfortunately, that punch didn't hit Sam where he wanted. Instead of thinking less about Heather and Gaia, every shot of vodka only seemed to make him think about them more. And it  burned more, as if he were pouring the alcohol straight into a raw wound in his heart.

Still, Sam didn't stop. He was sure that if he only drank enough of the cold, clear liquid, he wouldn't be able to think at all.

Sam leaned over the bar and waved an unsteady hand toward the glass. " 'Nother one," he said.

The pink-haired bartender gave him a quick inspection. "You sure about that, Sam my man?"

"Sure," Sam repeated with a nod.

The woman frowned. "All right, but just one more." She refilled the glass and waited while Sam shakily counted out the cost of the drink. "Whoever she was, she must have hurt you bad."

A girl with short, honey blond hair, big silver earrings, and a very small red T-shirt dropped onto the stool next to Sam. She gave him a quick smile as she ordered a beer. "Great band, huh?"

Sam glanced over the sea of dancing people at the trio up on the band platform. He shrugged. The truth was, Sam had barely noticed the music. Ever since his second drink, all the noise in the place had merged into a kind of hum. Even though the music was loud enough to send ripples across his drink, the vodka kept Sam insulated from everything going on around him. The music seemed dull and distant, like something happening in another town.

"They're okay," he said. "I guess."

The blond girl's smile slipped a bit. "You here by yourself?"

Sam nodded. He picked up his glass and took a drink. The vodka was cold in his mouth but hot in his throat. "All alone."

"Aww, that's too bad." The girl looked him over for a moment, then held out a hand. "Why don't you come out and dance with me?"

Sam started to say no. After all, he was supposed to be with Heather, and that meant not being with anyone else. Then he realized how completely stupid that was. There was nothing wrong with a little dancing. Besides, dancing was nothing compared to what

Heather had done. He certainly wouldn't be cheating on anyone.

But when Sam started to get up, the room began to swirl around him and the floor swayed like the deck of a ship caught in a storm. He stumbled back against the bar, tried to take a step, and stumbled again.

The girl put a hand on his arm. "Man, you're crashed."

"Am not," Sam replied. He tried to stand up straighter, but that only made the room start to spin faster.

The girl laughed at him. "I don't think you're going to be doing any dancing tonight."

Sam frowned. "I can dance."

"Sure, you can," said the girl, "but not with me. Next time hit the dance floor before you hit the bottle." She drained her beer, gave Sam a quick wave, and charged back out onto the dance floor.

Sam watched her go and felt a fresh flood of despair. He carefully sat down on his swaying bar stool and picked up his drink. He was going to be alone forever. That was clear.

He was beginning to think about leaving when someone new settled in next to him. It was a girl—no, a woman, a definite woman—in a skintight emerald green dress. The dress was cut very high on her thighs to reveal long, shapely legs, and it scooped down low at the top to reveal even more pale skin.

Long seconds went by before Sam could manage to raise his eyes from what the dress revealed and look up at the woman's face.

She smiled at him. "Hello." Her lips were very full and very red.

"Hi," Sam managed. He ran a hand across his tangled hair and tried to return the woman's smile.

"So why is someone as cute as you sitting over here all alone?" she asked. Her voice was soft. Throaty. Sexy.

Sam had to swallow hard before he could reply. "It's, um, a long story."

The woman leaned toward him, revealing even more of the contents of her dress. "That's all right," she said. "I've got all night."

ED SCRIBBLED DOWN A NOTE.

The Good Detective

"Thanks, Detective Hautley. That story will be in the paper tomorrow. Oh, absolutely. Page two or better. Yes, I have the spelling. Thanks again."

The phone went back on the hook for the last time, and Ed leaned back in his chair. He had lied so often that night that he felt like

he had taken a crash course in method acting. He could probably go to work on Broadway. Or
head out to Hollywood.

Or make a real killing ripping people off with a
phone scam.

It had taken more hours of pretending to be someone he wasn't, but finally all the lying had paid off. All
it took was finding the right person.

The right person turned out to be Detective
Charles Hautley. Hautley was a vice cop who wanted
to be in homicide, and he was willing to share a few
choice details with a reporter who might make the
poor, hardworking, clean-living detective into a star.
Once Ed got the good detective on the phone, it hadn't
taken him ten minutes to find out what he wanted.

Hautley knew all about Skizz. He knew
the man's record. He knew about the dealer's trip to
jail. And most important, he knew where Skizz could
be found.

And now that Ed knew the answer, he wished he
had never asked.

I always knew that vacation was the best idea in the history of the world. Right up there with the doughnut.

You have to wonder who came up with something so brilliant. It's a shame that this hero isn't in the history book. There should be statues. There should be parades. They ought to give a holiday in honor of the guy who came up with vacations.

Maybe there was some caveman out there who got tired of hunting woolly mammoths. Better yet, maybe it was some cave woman stuck back home, chewing on mastodon blubber and sewing bearskins. One day she wakes up, looks around, and says, "Hell with this—I'm going to Florida." One smart cave woman.

Even little vacations are good. Memorial Day. Columbus Day. Dead Presidents' Day. But when it comes to vacation, size definitely matters. Spring break, good. Christmas break, also good. Summer, very, very good.

    That's all I knew about vaca-
tion until last night.
    But I have made a discovery
every bit as important as that
sun-bathing cave woman's.
Something right up there with
fire, electric lights, and Krispy
Kreme. I have found the New World
of vacations.
    Ever hear someone say,
"Wherever you go, there you are"?
Yeah, it's a stupid saying.
Corny. Stupid and corny.
    It's also wrong.
    Here is my attempt at explanation.

Point 1. I was at the club last
         night.

Fact B. Gaia Moore got left
         behind.

    I don't want to sound like one
of those guys selling self-
improvement books on 3 A.M.
infomercials, but you really can
take a vacation from being you.
You can stop worrying about who's

looking or who's talking about you
or what they might say. Why should
I care what anybody there thinks
of me? I mean, I don't have to
live with those people. I probably
wouldn't like them if I did.

If you run hard enough, you
can outrun yourself. And the only
secret is: Stop running.

Doesn't make any sense, right?
That's because you haven't been
there.

Actually, I can't claim solo
credit for this great, world-
shaking discovery. It was Mary
Moss who blazed the trail to this
hidden continent of vacation.
It's because of her that I
learned how to stop being Gaia
for a few hours and just have
fun. She led me to the land of
Moss. Mary Land. The place where
you don't stress over what other
people think.

All my life I've never been
afraid, but I think this is what
it really means to be fearless.
It means doing the things you

want to do without worrying about being rejected.

So I think it's time to do something I've been wanting to do for a while. I think it's time to talk to Sam.

The real
difference
this morning **gaia**
was that **moore**
Gaia sounded
naked
happy.

GAIA CAME OUT OF THE SHOWER

The Girl in the Mirror

with one of the tunes from the night before running through her head. She walked across the bedroom wrapped only in a towel, but she had a hard time walking. Her feet still wanted to dance.

She had started to rummage through the clothes beside her bed when she noticed the black dress thrown across her chair.

I wore that. I went out in public in that.

No one had laughed. At least, if someone had laughed, Gaia didn't notice them. The guy she had danced with—Inego, his name was Inego—certainly hadn't been laughing.

Gaia paused, stood up, and walked across the room to the mirror. Carefully she studied her reflection in the mirror.

Gaia wasn't prepared to admit that Mary was right—no way was she beautiful. Not by a long shot. Still, maybe things weren't so bad as Gaia had always thought. Sure, her legs were packed with muscle. But were they so awful? Her shoulders and arms were bulked up, too, but this morning they didn't look so terribly hulkish.

Gaia tried to imagine what it would be like if she

didn't know that girl in the mirror. What if she were just to meet this girl on the street or maybe at school? What if she didn't know this was Gaia Moore, fearless expert in all things kung fu and girl freak? Would she really think this blond stranger looked that bad? Could she be normal? Could she even be . . .

The phone rang. Gaia was across the room in a flash, leaving her towel behind as she ran. She grabbed the receiver and, for once in her life, managed to answer before Ella could get to the phone downstairs. "Hello," she said.

"Gaia?"

"Ed!" Still naked and damp from the shower, Gaia threw herself back onto the unmade bed and lay facing the ceiling. "How are you? It's a beautiful morning, huh?"

There was a pause of at least five seconds before Ed spoke. "It's cloudy outside."

"Whatever," said Gaia. "How are you doing?"

"I'm not sure," Ed replied. "I was trying to reach a girl named Gaia."

"That's me."

"Gaia Moore?"

"Don't be an asshole, Ed."

"Hmmm," Ed replied. "That sounds more like it. Okay, maybe I did reach the right girl after all. But you sound different this morning."

Gaia sat up on the bed and ran her fingers through her damp hair. "Different how?"

"I don't know. You sound cheerful, and you're not, I don't know—"

"Not what?"

"Not whining, I guess."

Gaia scowled at the phone. "I do not whine."

"Oh, yeah? Whenever you talk about your foster parents, or Sam, or school, or—"

"Shut up, Ed." Gaia bounced up from the bed, jammed the phone between her shoulder and her ear, and started digging through the available clothes. "If you're so tired of me, you could always call someone else."

ED SHOOK HIS HEAD, THEN REALIZED that shaking your head didn't work when the other person was on the phone. "No," he said. "The Gaia report is the high point of my day."

Dancing Gaia

"All right, then," Gaia replied. "Stop complaining. Or should I say, stop whining?"

Ed grinned. Gaia did sound different, but she was still Gaia. The real difference this morning was that Gaia sounded happy. That was a condition that didn't happen nearly as often as it should. In Ed's opinion, Gaia needed to be happy all the time. And of course, the way to see that Gaia was happy all the time was to see that she fell in love with Ed.

He started to say something else, but his voice caught, and his smile collapsed. Gaia was happy.

And he was about to ruin it.

"Ed? You still there?"

"Yes." Ed cleared his throat. "I'm still here."

"Hang on for a second. I need to get something on. I'm standing here naked."

Ladies and gentlemen, Ed's mental theater presents: Gaia Moore Naked. *Now held over for another extremely popular extended run.* Ed considered it an absolute tragedy that the picture phone had never caught on. He thought of telling Gaia that there was no reason for her to get dressed just to talk on the phone, but he didn't want to give her quite that clear a glimpse into the things that churned in his brain.

"Okay," she said after a few moments. "I'm back."

"So, uh, did you and Mary go to the club last night?"

"Absolutely."

"And what did you do while Mary danced?"

"What do you mean, what did I do?" Gaia shot back, doing a pretty decent imitation of Ed's tone. "I went dancing."

"You?"

"What? Is it so shocking that I can dance?"

Actually, it wasn't shocking at all. It was very easy for Ed to imagine Gaia dancing. She had those incredible long, strong legs. Dancer's legs. In his mind Ed could see Gaia spinning and swaying on those legs. Her blond hair flying. He knew without ever seeing it that Gaia would be an incredibly sexy dancer.

"So," she said. "Do want to hear about it?"

"Sure." *Hearing might not be enough,* Ed thought. *How about coming over and doing a demonstration for me?*

Ed listened as Gaia described going to the club, getting out on the floor, and starting to dance. Every word increased the heat that was growing inside him. He could picture it in his mind almost as if he were really there. A new feature debuted in his personal Gaia Moore multiplex. Dancing Gaia. Of course, in real life Gaia had probably worn clothes while dancing, but Ed thought he could allow a few special effects in his mental movie.

"And when I opened my eyes," Gaia continued, "this guy was there."

The film suddenly broke in Ed's internal cinema and went flipping around the reel. "Sam?"

"No, not Sam. Some guy I never seen before."

"How bad did you hurt him?"

Gaia made a disgusted sound. "I don't automatically hit every guy I meet. I didn't hurt him. We danced together."

"You danced with a strange guy?"

"Did I mention he was really good-looking?" said Gaia. "And he was a really good dancer. We danced together all night. It was great. Maybe better than great. Incredible. I never really . . . I mean, I never danced like that before."

Ed felt a stab of jealousy. He was immediately jealous of any guy who spent time with Gaia. Having Gaia say that the guy was good-looking only opened that wound a little wider. But what really hurt, what really poured the salt into the cut and rubbed it in good, was the fact that Gaia and this good-looking stranger had danced together.

Ed lusted after Gaia twenty-four hours a day. He was pretty sure that he even loved her. One of these days, if he could show her what a great guy he was and stay close, Gaia might even start to love Ed. After all, she had kissed him, even if it was only once. All he had to do was keep at it and wear down her resistance.

But one thing Ed would never be able to do was dance with Gaia. He would never get to be with her the way the guy from the club had been the night before.

There was a new threat here, a threat maybe even bigger than the hurdle of Sam Moon. It was clear that Gaia liked the dancing. And the guy. If she kept going to the clubs, it would mean she saw less of Ed. And more of the guys who were there—guys who could dance.

"Ed?" Gaia called from the other end. "Are you still there?"

"I'm here." The wheelchair suddenly felt very hard

against his back and arms. He adjusted his position, trying to get more comfortable. "So, are you going to see this dancing fool again?"

"No," said Gaia. "At least, I don't think so. I didn't even tell him anything but my first name."

Good. The situation wasn't completely out of control. "So you just left. You and Mary."

"Are you trying to ask if I had sex with this guy?"

"No." *Yes.*

"Well, I didn't. We talked a little bit. And kissed a couple of times. But mostly we danced."

Kissed.

Ed felt like someone had roped a brick to his heart and thrown it in a lake. Gaia had kissed this stranger. Kissing wasn't supposed to be a big deal. People kissed all the time. But Ed had thought Gaia was different. He'd thought that the kiss she had given him was special. Important.

"Ed? You keep going quiet on me. Are you doing something?"

"No." Ed was embarrassed to hear the catch in his voice. "No, just thinking."

"Don't hurt yourself. What's the news? Did you find out anything?"

Ed had almost forgotten the reason for his call. He held the phone away from his face for a second and cleared his throat before speaking. "Yeah," he said. "Yeah, I found out something."

"So, is Skizz still in the hospital?"

"No." Ed picked up a piece of paper and looked at the notes he had scribbled the night before. "According to the nurse I talked to, his injuries weren't as serious as first believed. Plus the guy had no insurance, so they kicked him out."

"I'm not sure whether I should be happy or upset that he's not that hurt," said Gaia. "If he's out of the hospital, I guess he's in jail."

"That's the really fun part," said Ed. He flipped over his page of notes. "It seems that the drugs found on your boy Skizz were judged to be the product of an illegal search. Inadmissible as evidence."

"So how are they going to keep him in jail?"

"They're not," Ed replied. "Skizz is loose."

The Father of Gaia

MARY BENT DOWN AND PICKED UP A broken piece of wood. It was no more than a few inches in length, splintered at both ends, and scorched black. It was all that remained of the door to the apartment leased in the name of Tom Chaos.

"So what did he look like?" she asked.

The fruit stand owner scratched at his thinning hair. "I'm not sure I ever met the man," he said.

"Didn't you rent the place to him?"

The man nodded. "I did, but that was over the phone. I never met this Chaos guy in person." The man's face pulled down in a heavy frown. "If I knew what he looked like, I'd be putting up posters. This bastard blew up my stand."

Mary looked across the pile of rubble. "I thought the paper said it was a gas explosion."

The fruit stand owner snorted. "Oh, yeah, some gas explosion." He waved a thick finger at Mary. "That damn apartment didn't even have gas."

"So what—"

"Who knows." The man kicked at a pile of shattered boards and rotting fruit. "You gonna hang around here, you be careful. I got enough troubles with the insurance guys already." He turned and stomped away.

Mary looked at the ruined fruit stand and the shattered remains of what had once been an apartment. There wasn't much left. The fruit stand had been split down the middle. No one had been killed, but the building was twisted in its frame like a broken toy. Bricks from the back wall had landed as far as two blocks away. Only some of the plumbing still remained where the apartment had been, sticking up into the sky like the picked-over skeleton of some dead beast.

No one had been killed here, and there had been few witnesses to the actual explosion. It was a small story, buried deep in the pages of the *Times.* Except for the search that Mary's aunt had made, it might have stayed buried.

Mary pulled out her notebook and looked at the few lines she had scribbled. Thomas Chaos had rented the broken apartment. Gaia's father's name was Thomas Moore. There was no real connection. Only two little facts had made Mary come to the site of the ruins.

First, Thomas Chaos didn't exist. All the information he had provided in renting the apartment had turned out to be fake.

Second, in some versions of Greek mythology, Chaos was the father of Gaia.

If those two bits of information fit together as Mary thought, it made for interesting results. Gaia Moore's father was somewhere in New York.

That was information Mary thought Gaia might find very interesting.

It's supposed to be a dream. In fact, it's supposed to be the classic dream, something every male in America fantasizes about.

You're sitting alone when this beautiful woman walks up and sits down beside you. You might be drunk enough to think any woman looks good, but you're not drunk enough that you don't recognize gorgeous when you see it. True, this woman might be a little older than you, and she might be a little more slutty than your usual taste, but isn't that part of the way the dream works? This is a woman with a lot of experience when it comes to sex.

This beautiful woman— beautiful, sexy woman—starts to talk to you. She tells you you're cute. She says she likes you. She tells you she's all alone. She puts her hand on your leg. She brings her face so close, you can smell the flavor of her lipstick. And eventually she asks you if

SAM

you want to go home with her.

What are you going to say?

So, the two of you end up in a hotel room, and the dress comes off, and she's just as sexy as you thought she would be. Her body is incredible.

She's as experienced as you thought she was. She knows exactly what do with her hands. And her mouth. And her body. Even if you're half drunk—even if you're ninety-nine and nine-tenths percent drunk—you're not falling asleep on this performance. She moves like no one you've ever met. She bends in places you didn't even know human beings had joints. She keeps you going not just once or twice but until exhaustion catches up with drunk and the room spins. When you fall asleep, she's still pressed against you. Warm, and soft, and sexy.

When you wake up, the woman is gone. There's no note. The hotel room is taken care of. There are

no obligations or commitments.
You get one night of fantastic
sex with one unbelievable woman
and the price tag is zero. That's
the dream, right? The all-
American male sex fantasy.

So why does it feel so much
like a nightmare?

Mary had absolutely no doubt that someone had come to kill her.

The fear of dying

IT WAS AFTER NOON BEFORE SAM

made it back to his dorm room.
As soon as he was inside, he
stumbled across the room and
collapsed on his bed.

Either the bartender was
wrong or Sam didn't have the
typical reaction to vodka. If
there were hangovers worse than the one
he was feeling, Sam didn't want to know
about it. Already he felt like someone had lifted
the top of his skull, poured in a box of thumbtacks,
and put the lid back on. Add in the family of gerbils
that had taken up residence in his stomach, and Sam
was ready to call the Mafia and see if he could hire a
killer to come and shoot him.

Sam crawled up the bed until his face was smashed
against the pillow and tried to keep his head from exploding. The drums down the hall were silent this
time, but they weren't needed. Sam's heart was beating
all on its own. On some scale, he knew that the hangover was getting better. The idea that he might actually
live through it now seemed like a possibility—not that
death wasn't still an attractive option.

The bone-crushing hangover might not have felt
quite so bad if Sam hadn't also felt so guilty.

Heather cheated first.

That was true. In fact, once one partner had

cheated, could you even call what the other did cheating at all? Shouldn't it be like getting a free hit?

Of course, Sam had kissed Gaia when he was still supposed to be with Heather. And there was the little detail of his constant Gaia obsession.

Sam worked at trying to get the right feeling of justification, but he couldn't manage to find it. Even memories of the great sex he had experienced the night before didn't help. Sam couldn't get past the idea that the sex was wrong. Great, but wrong.

It didn't matter that Heather had cheated. Heather didn't know that Sam knew that she had cheated. And Sam hadn't said anything to Heather about breaking up. So no matter what Heather had done, they were still an official couple. Which made sleeping with the woman from the bar absolutely wrong. And all of that was way too much thinking to do with a hangover.

The whole thing didn't make a lot of sense. Sam knew that. He was acting like some character from a book. Real people weren't supposed to think like this. Real people slept around. Everybody said so.

But it didn't feel right. Maybe no one in the world would blame Sam for sleeping with this woman after Heather had cheated on him. Hell, every guy in the dorm would probably congratulate him for scoring with this babe even if Heather hadn't cheated on him. It didn't matter. The only thing that mattered was that Sam felt guilty. What he had done was wrong, no matter how many talk show guests and frat dudes might disagree.

He was going to have to talk to Heather. He was going to have to tell her it was over.

There was a knock at the door.

Every rap of the mystery guest's knuckles went through Sam's skull like a chain saw. He winced and pulled the pillow tighter around his exploding head. "Go away!" he shouted as loudly as he dared.

"Sam?" said a faint voice. "Is that you?"

Sam groaned and rolled to the edge of the bed. The world did a little jumping, twisting lurch. "Who's there?"

"Gaia."

"Gaia?" Sam sat up quickly, bringing a railroad spike of fresh pain to his head. He couldn't imagine why Gaia Moore would be at his door. Especially not when she had been out with her boyfriend only the night before. He got up and stumbled across the room over a floor that pitched and heaved like a ship on the high seas. He fumbled open the door and saw that the impossible was true. Gaia Moore had come to call.

"Why are you . . . ," he started, then he swallowed and tried again. "Uh. Hi, Gaia."

"Hi, Sam." Gaia was dressed in usual Gaia gear, cargo pants and a gray sweatshirt, but there was something different about her hair. It almost looked like it had been combed. If Sam weren't drunk, he would have sworn she was blushing.

"I wanted to ask you something," she said.

"What's that?"

Gaia pushed her hair back from her face, glanced at Sam for a moment, then looked away. "I was wondering if you had anything planned for tonight."

"Tonight?" Sam wondered if this was just part of the hangover. Was it possible to have hallucinations from one night of drinking? If he didn't know better, he would have sworn Gaia Moore was asking him out on a date.

"It's New Year's Eve," said Gaia. "So I thought you'd probably be doing something with Heather."

"No," said Sam. "I'm not doing anything with Heather." In his own ears he could hear both anger and guilt in that statement.

"That's great!" said Gaia. "I mean, it's not great that you don't . . . I mean . . . I thought maybe you would want to get together tonight."

Sam felt a moment of dizziness that had nothing to do with his hangover. Gaia Moore *was* asking him out on a date. The last few days had been an incredible roller coaster. First there was the woman at a bar, now this. His life was getting so strange in all directions. "Sure," he said. "Sure, I could do something tonight." Surely by then the hangover would have faded.

"Cool." For a moment Sam caught a glance of that endangered species, a Gaia Moore smile. "I'm meeting Ed and Mary around eight. If you came over around seven, we could walk over together."

"Ed Fargo and Mary Moss?"

"Uh-huh. We're talking about checking out the fireworks in the park. If the weather's not too crappy, we thought we might even do the whole tourist Times Square thing. After all, this is my first New Year's in New York."

Ed and Mary. Sam knew Ed Fargo well enough and had meet Mary Moss a few times. If Ed and Mary were coming along, then this wasn't so much a date as a kind of group activity. Nothing serious. Gaia might even be asking Sam more as a let's-be-friends kind of thing, not an I-love-you kind of thing. In fact, that seemed like what had to be going on. Ed and Mary were Gaia's friends. Gaia was just inviting Sam to be part of the gang, not to be her boyfriend.

"Sure," said Sam. "Sure. I'll be there." Being friends with Gaia was better than getting no dose of Gaia at all.

"All right," said Gaia. She bounced on the balls of her feet for a moment. "Okay. I guess I'll see you then."

"Right," said Sam. He managed to make what he hoped was a decent smile in reply.

Gaia hesitated for a moment. Then she spun on the soles of her worn sneakers and padded off down the hall.

Sam watched until the top of her blond head had disappeared down the staircase. Maybe for some guys, meeting a beautiful woman in a bar and having a night of sex was their fantasy. But for Sam Moon, Gaia was the real dream.

MAYBE I SHOULD LIE.

Ed stared at the phone and tried to rub away the headache that was building behind his eyes. He had spent so much time on the phone the last couple of days, his right ear felt hot and swollen. If the phone company charged for local calls by the minute, Ed would have been way deep into his college fund.

There was only one more phone call to make now, but Ed wasn't sure he should do it. If he dialed the phone, it would mean putting Gaia at risk. If he didn't dial, it could mean risking Mary.

I could check it out myself, he thought. *I could tell Gaia that I couldn't get the information. Then I could go up there myself and . . . and . . .*

And what? Ed might hate it when people thought he couldn't do something because he was in a wheelchair. But there were a few things that he really couldn't do. This might be one of them.

One dark, deep little part of Ed's brain definitely did not want to make this call. Sure, Mary was pretty. A little wild sometimes, but Ed liked her. And she was a friend. Still, Mary wasn't Gaia. Gaia was beautiful. Gaia had kissed him. He didn't just like Gaia—he was pretty sure he loved her.

The little reptile part of his brain was talking loud and clear. *Forget Mary. Don't do anything that would get Gaia in trouble.*

That reptile brain was hard to resist. The only thing fighting against it was the idea that if he didn't call, he would be breaking Gaia's trust. If he didn't call and Mary got hurt, Ed would have to live with that forever.

Still, it took a good ten minutes before he lifted the phone and reluctantly dialed Gaia's number.

"Hi. This is Ed. I need to speak to Gaia."

A few seconds later her voice came over the phone. "Hey. You going to be there tonight?"

"I'll be there," said Ed. He took a deep breath and continued. "But I found out something that I thought you should know."

"What's that?"

"I found Skizz."

"ARE YOU SURE YOU DON'T FEEL

up to it?" asked George.

Ella summoned up her best suffering-but-devoted-young-wife smile. "I'm sorry, dear. It really does feel like I have a cold coming on." She laid her fingers lightly against her chest. "I shouldn't make a trip right now."

George frowned. "If you're certain."

"I am." Ella nodded sadly, the brave smile still on her brightly painted lips. "You go on. I'll stay here, nurse my cold, and watch the celebrations on television."

George thought for a moment, then shook his head. "Nope. If you're staying here, I'll just stay with you."

Ella sat up quickly. "Now, George, you can't do that. You know you have commitments down in Washington."

"Those commitments can wait." George knelt down beside the couch, and took Ella's hand. "I'm more worried about us."

"Us? What could be wrong with us?" Ella looked at him with mock concern. "Is there something bothering you, dear?"

"What's bothering me is how little time we spend together," said George. Worry creased his forehead. "Half the time my job takes me out of town. And even when I am home, it seems like you have a photography assignment almost every night."

"I'm trying to get established," replied Ella. "It's important that I take any assignment I can get."

George squeezed her hand. "I understand that, but I miss you, Ella. I want to be with you."

Ella reached across with her free hand and patted George softly on the cheek. "Don't worry. We have all our lives to be together." She nodded toward the door. "Now, go on to your party. The last thing I want you to do is to stay here and catch my cold."

George nodded. "All right," he said. "I'll go. But when I get back, we're going to have some reserved time together."

"Wonderful," said Ella. "I can't think of anything better."

With one last look, George turned for the door. "Take care of yourself while I'm gone."

"Don't worry. I'll be waiting right here." Ella waved at him as he went out the front door of the brownstone.

As soon as the door closed, Ella's expression turned into a scowl. She climbed up off the couch and went into the kitchen to wash her hands. It was getting to the point where just the touch of George's hands was enough to make her want to scream. Just the sight of him made her stomach churn.

George Niven was a great agent once. Even Loki said

so. But he wasn't anymore. Now he was just weak and stupid. Ella wasn't sure how much longer she could keep up this charade. She had never expected to be with George this long. Loki had promised her that one day this long project would move into the next phase. When that happened, Ella wouldn't have to pretend anymore. Wouldn't have to be with a man she despised more every day.

At least she would get a chance to see Loki tonight. If she was lucky, she would even spend the night in his bed. Now that George was out of town, everything would be fine.

To: outsider@div13.gov
From: insider@div13.gov

ENCODED TRANSMISSION—256-BIT KEY TO FOLLOW

Request immediate meeting. Location delta.
1900 hours.
Situation degrading.

MARY LOOKED AT HERSELF IN THE

mirror and grinned. She didn't think she was the most beautiful girl in the world. Usually she didn't think much of her looks at all. But she had to admit that the camisole looked very fine.

Everyday Events

The flimsy top would definitely not meet with her mother's approval, but then, Mary's mother had already gone off to her own New Year's event. There was no one left in the house to pass judgment on what she was wearing.

Mary thought for a moment about changing into something else. After all, if they really did end up down at Times Square, this outfit was going to be beyond chilly. But she was also going to be standing next to Gaia Moore all night. Gaia might not realize she was beautiful, but to most guys, that only made Gaia more attractive. Unless she looked her very best, Mary could get overlooked.

She was still debating whether or not to change when the phone rang. Mary picked it up, expecting it to be Gaia or Ed. Instead there was only a crackling, humming sound on the line. The phone had sounded funny for the last couple of days. There was always this strange little hollow tone to everything. But this went way beyond the previous problems.

"Hello?"

"Mary . . . you . . . me." The voice was faint and filled with static.

"Aunt Jen?" Mary spoke into the phone. "Is that you?"

". . . trouble . . . Katia Moore . . ."

A chill ran down Mary's back. "Aunt Jen, there's something wrong with your phone. I can't hear you."

". . . government . . . secret . . ." Then the phone gave one last squawk and went dead in Mary's hand.

"Aunt Jen?" Mary called hopelessly into the silence. "Are you there?" She waited a few seconds, then set the phone down.

Her aunt must have been calling from a car phone. That was the only explanation. She must have gone into a tunnel and lost the connection.

It was clear that her aunt was trying to tell her something about the death of Gaia's mother. Mary was surprised that her aunt would be working on the problem so late on New Year's Eve. The information on Katia Moore must have turned out to be particularly interesting.

Mary stood by the phone for a moment, hoping her aunt might call back, but the phone stayed quiet.

Mary went back to getting ready, but the chill of fear that had arrived with the phone call wouldn't go away. It had to be more than an interesting story to keep her aunt working so late. If she was calling from a car phone, maybe she was on her way somewhere. Maybe she was even coming to talk to Mary in person.

Then Mary remembered a flaw in that theory. Aunt Jen didn't even *own* a car. She might have a portable phone, it sometimes seemed like everyone in Manhattan carried one, but there was no way the reception should have been so bad. Not from anywhere in the city.

Mary ran back across the room and picked up the phone. This time there was no strange hollow sound. This time there was no sound at all. The phone line was dead.

Mary's heartbeat was suddenly racing. She was paralyzed for a moment, the dead phone in her hand. One part of her brain was still trying desperately to fit this into the world of everyday events. Phone lines go out. It's New Year's Eve. A million people probably called each other at the same time and blew the circuits. But the rest of her mind didn't buy it.

She put the phone back on the hook and grabbed her coat from the closet. Gaia was expecting to meet Mary in the park. That was still an hour away, but Mary decided she would rather freeze out in the cold or walk over to Gaia's brownstone. Anything but stay here. She slipped into her coat, picked up her purse, and headed out.

Mary had gotten as far as the kitchen when she

noticed something strange. There was a little case lying on the kitchen table. A small, leather case that looked something like the case for the flute Mary had once played in junior high band. Curious, she walked over to the case and looked inside.

The case was packed with some kind of dense gray foam. There were cutouts in the foam just large enough to hold an assortment of objects. Only a few of the slots were full. Two held small objects the size of a fingernail. They looked something like miniature lollipops, slightly squashed lollipops, only inside the translucent balls Mary could see an array of tiny electrical parts, and where the stick should have been on a piece of candy, there was a bundle of wires.

Mary had never seen anything quite like this, but she immediately had an idea of what it was for. There had been a funny sound on the phone all week. Someone had been bugging her phone, listening in on every conversation.

There was an empty opening at the center of the case that was shaped something like a large cigar. Next to it was a shape that was considerably more frightening. There was no doubt about what it was meant to hold. Mary could make out every detail of the outline—the grip, the trigger guard, the long, slender barrel. The third opening was fitted to hold a gun, and that gun was missing.

But even that wasn't the worst thing in the case.

The worst thing was two small glass vials. One vial was still in its slot. The other of the tiny bottles was sitting out on the counter. Inside it was a thimble full of snow-white powder.

Cocaine.

The sight of it brought an unexpected wave of desire boiling up from somewhere deep in Mary's guts. It had been *so* long.

One quick sniff. One quick sniff and I'll be able to think this through so much better.

Mary took a slow step back. If there was any time in the world when it was a seriously bad idea to get cranked out of her head, this was the time. She shifted her eyes as far to the right and left as she could without turning her head.

Someone was in the house. That someone was carrying a gun. Mary had absolutely no doubt that someone had come to kill her.

THE CROWD ON THE F TRAIN WASN'T the most upscale Gaia had ever seen. There was a high concentration of black dusters and guys with stubbly little beards. Even on New Year's

Some Dogs

Eve, she suspected more of them were interested in getting drunk or getting high than in celebrating.

Perfect customers for Skizz.

Gaia rode in the front of the front car. If she could have, she would have ridden on the outside. She would have pulled or pushed or done anything to make the cars go faster. There was a tension in her legs. An ache in all her muscles. It wasn't fear, but it wasn't quite the same cold energy she felt right before a fight. By the time the train reached the station, the tension was so great that she squeezed out the door and flew up the stairs before anyone else on the train had taken two steps across the platform.

Skizz was loose. Gaia had expected the scumbag to spend a week or more in the hospital. After that, he should have gone to jail for pushing drugs. Mary should have been safe for years.

Now Gaia would have to take care of him. Again.

Gaia knew she could handle Skizz. She had already kicked his flabby ass twice. Three times would be no problem. That didn't mean there wouldn't be complications. There was no telling what kind of mood Skizz was in. Beating up a guy like Skizz was kind of like kicking a feral dog. He might get scared and run away. He might turn around and bite.

Gaia had one mission, one goal. She had to make sure that a simple message got through the dealer's lice-ridden head: Get near Mary Moss and die.

Gaia reached the street and cut across an intersection toward St. Mark's Place. It was nearly dark, and fat snowflakes were drifting down from a deep gray sky. The sun was still shining on the taller buildings, but already the air felt ten degrees colder.

There weren't as many people on the street here as there were back in the Village. The stores and restaurants along the sidewalks were at least a grade below those near Washington Square. Not the swankiest neighborhood in the city.

St. Mark's Place was a park, but it turned out to be considerably smaller than Gaia had expected, little more than a block of green space and a few knots of trees. Gaia stood in one corner of the cold space for a few minutes and watched as two men passed a bottle back and forth. Two girls with spiked hair walked past, and a cloud of pungent pot smoke momentarily swamped Gaia.

She didn't see Skizz.

According to Ed's source in the police department, Skizz had been spotted at this location twice in the last two days. Both times he had avoided arrest, but the park was a known site for drug traffickers. None of which guaranteed that Skizz would show up tonight.

Gaia bit her lip and did a slow scan of the people in the park. It was getting close to seven. Unless she wanted to miss her meeting with Sam, Gaia needed to get back on the train. It looked like `lowlife hunting` was going to have to wait for another night.

She was halfway back to the station when she saw a familiar shape on the street corner ahead. A big guy with a round gut and a big, jutting beard. Gaia smiled a hard smile. *Thar she blows.* There was no mistaking Skizz's bulky silhouette.

Gaia thought about her approach. She could go in cool and casual. She could come in screaming and kicking. She could be sneaky. Sneaky won.

She came up behind Skizz, grabbed him by the back of the coat, and pulled.

The man flew back a step, stumbled, and fell onto the dirty snow. Gaia quickly stepped around in front of him and put a foot on his chest. "Hi, there," she said. "Funny mee ..." She stopped in midword.

She had the wrong guy. This wasn't Skizz. This couldn't be Skizz.

Only it was.

The drug dealer was a wreck. His face was lopsided and swollen. His lips were split, and inside his open mouth Gaia could see several broken or missing teeth. There was a cast on one of his legs and a sling around his left arm. A bandage wrapped his dirty hair. His left eye was covered by gauze and tape. His right eye looked up at Gaia with complete and utter terror.

"You," he croaked. "It's you." His voice shook.

Gaia couldn't feel fear, but she could feel shock. *I did this.* She didn't exactly feel sorry for Skizz. He had only gotten what he deserved. But it was a little stomach

153

twisting to see what she had done to a man using nothing but her hands and feet.

Gaia took a deep breath and tried to get the proper tone of mean back in her voice. "I came to make sure you stayed away from my friend."

Even as she said it, the statement sounded ridiculous. Skizz couldn't be the one who was after Mary. Skizz couldn't be after anyone.

The dealer pushed his hands against the ground and scooted himself back through the snow. "Don't," he blubbered through his torn lips. "Don't hurt me." Tears streamed from his one good eye and rolled into his matted beard.

Gaia stared down at him for a few seconds longer. Then she put her hands in her pockets and started walking for the subway station.

Some dogs ran. Some dogs bit. Some dogs got broken.

At least Gaia could be sure of one thing. Mary was safe.

MARY MOVED SLOWLY ACROSS THE carpeted floor. At every step she paused and looked left and right. She could barely get herself to move. Her knees trembled, and

My Hero

her legs were unsteady. At any moment she expected a bullet to come out of some corner of the apartment. The fear was so bad, she wanted to lie down and just wait until whoever had left the case on the table came to kill her.

She froze at the door to her room and stood trembling there for several seconds, unable to move.

A noise down the hall broke her free from her paralysis. It was a faint sound, but it was enough to propel Mary through the door and into her room. She closed the door behind her and carefully turned the lock.

She didn't have any illusion that the door would actually keep the intruder out. Her parents had managed to open it with nothing more sophisticated than the bent end of a clothes hanger. And the door was thin enough that even Mary could have probably knocked it down with a kick. She only hoped it would buy her time.

Still trying to move as silently as possible, Mary crept across the room and gave the phone another try. No dial tone. Nothing.

That meant there were two choices. Mary could try to go out the front door. She had already passed on that option once. She figured that it was what the intruder expected, and now he would be even more prepared. Hopefully, whoever was in the apartment wouldn't be prepared for option two.

Before she made her escape, Mary had one more

little task. She went to the dresser and grabbed the handles for the lowest drawer. Mary pulled the drawer open slowly, an inch at a time. She held her breath. Any noise. Any noise at all might draw the stranger with the gun.

It took only a few seconds to open the drawer and grab the bottle of pepper spray she had hidden inside, but they were long seconds. The fear of dying seemed to stretch out time, making every moment into an hour.

Mary stuffed the pepper spray into her pocket and hurried across the room to the bed. Under the foot of the bed was a small case made of bright orange plastic. It was one of those stupid things that her parents had bought from some salesman. Some stupid thing that Mary had always thought was a waste of money. She had certainly never expected to use it. But she was glad she had it now.

Mary slipped the case from under the bed and popped open the latches on the sides. She shivered as the case opened with a loud click.

Inside, there was only a bundle of wire and thin metal rods. It looked like a mess, but Mary dragged it free from the case and carried it over to the window. Then, with her heart beating high in her throat, she put her thumbs against the window locks and pressed. There was a terrible moment when she thought the old locks wouldn't open, but a second later the locks popped, the glass shivered, and the window swung slowly inward.

A blizzard of cold air swirled into Mary's bedroom. Snow settled on her head. Wind made the clothes in her closet into dancing ghosts.

Carefully Mary leaned over the edge and looked down. Five floors below, cars hummed past on the street.

She looked at the bundle of wire and located the top. With hands that shook from both fear and cold, Mary hooked the top over the windowsill and hurled the rest out the window. The emergency escape ladder uncoiled with a whine. Far below, she heard the bottom of the ladder clank against the side of the building.

Mary put her head through the window again and looked down. The ladder didn't reach all the way to the sidewalk, but it was close. If she climbed down and hung from the bottom, her feet would be no more than a dozen feet from the ground.

But that climb didn't look too easy. In fact, it looked insane. The narrow ladder seemed as fragile as a bit of spiderweb, and the bitter wind made the whole thing bob and dance. If Mary climbed down the ladder to the bottom and dropped from there, she would probably be okay. But if she fell from the top, or from thirty or fifty feet up, the sidewalk would do the intruder's job as well as any bullet.

Mary stepped back from the window and looked at

the bedroom door. Maybe going out the front wasn't such a bad idea after all. Slipping past the gunman suddenly seemed like a much better idea than trying to climb that toy ladder down five floors.

The bedroom door rattled. The knob turned, stopped, then turned the other way. A moment later there was a clicking metal-on-metal sound.

Picking the lock. *They're picking the lock just like my parents used to do when I was sulking in my room,* she realized.

Without another moment's thought Mary was standing in the window. She grabbed the ladder, gave it a tug to see if it would hold, then started down.

The ladder was even more treacherous than it looked. The rungs were so narrow that they bit into Mary's fingers like knife blades. The way the ladder lay up against the side of the building made it nearly impossible to keep her feet in place. Again and again her toes slid from a rung, sending her on a dozen terrifying minifalls. But she was doing it. She was making it down.

The end of the ladder was twenty feet below. Then ten.

There was a sudden jerk from above. Mary looked up to see the silhouette of a figure leaning from her bedroom window. With impossible strength, that person was pulling up the ladder. Instead of going down, Mary was heading back up.

She scrambled for the bottom of the ladder, moving

as fast as she could, but by the time she reached the last rung, the end of the ladder was nearly twenty feet above the sidewalk. And it was getting farther away with every passing moment.

Mary let herself dangle from the very bottom of the ladder, closed her eyes, and dropped.

It seemed to take a long time to reach the ground. Too long.

The ground hit her like a subway train. A white-hot lightning bolt ran up Mary's right leg. She was on her side, then her face, then her back, then her side again. A sparkle of lights swam across her vision, and everything in the world shrank to a gray point far down a deep well.

When the world came back, Mary was looking at red taillights streaming past in the slushy street. Her face was lying in cold snow. The rest of her felt kind of numb, like that pins-and-needles feeling you get when your arms or legs fall asleep.

She tried to sit up, but that only brought a new explosion of pain from her leg. Mary bit back a scream and slowly turned herself over.

She was still alive. For the moment that seemed like a miracle.

"Miss?" A man came up at a run. "Miss, are you all right?"

Mary started to nod, then changed her mind. "No. I think my leg is hurt."

The man looked at her for a moment, then looked up at the building. "I saw you come down. That was quite a fall."

"Yeah, tell me about it." Mary squinted up at the window, but she could see no one looking down. The ladder was also missing in action.

"Is there a fire?"

Mary shook her head. "A guy broke into our apartment. I think he's trying to kill me."

The man stood and looked in both directions along the sidewalk. "I think you had better come with me," he said. "We should get you to the police."

Mary's long involvement with drugs hadn't exactly made the police her favorite people, but this seemed like an excellent time to make new friends. "Sure," she said. She tried again to get to her feet. Her right leg didn't cooperate. "I think I'm going to need some help."

The man reached down and helped her to her feet. "I have a car parked on the next block. You think you can make it?"

Mary nodded. "Let's go."

She hopped along at the man's side, leaning against him and keeping almost all of her weight on her left foot. As they passed under a streetlight, she saw that the man was older than she thought. Probably somewhere in his forties. He seemed strong, though, and he had a handsome, chiseled face.

"Why would someone be trying to kill you?" the man asked.

"I don't know," said Mary. She stopped for a second to catch her breath, then limped on. "There was this guy who tried to kill me a couple of days ago, but I don't think he has anything to do with this."

"Two different guys tried to kill you in the last few days?" The man gave a surprised laugh. "You're a popular girl."

"Mary," she said between breaths. "My name is Mary."

The man paused. He supported her weight on one arm and reached across with the other to shake her hand. "My name is Loki."

"Loki? Is that from mythology or something?"

"Exactly."

Mary shook his hand and smiled. "It's a weird name, but you're certainly my hero tonight, Loki."

He took the
dark, heavy
bulk of the
Glock pistol
and pressed **rage**
the blunt
barrel
against
Mary's back.

SAM RANG THE BELL ON THE FRONT

of the brownstone and waited. He was more nervous than he wanted to admit. *This isn't a date,* he told himself. *Gaia probably doesn't even think about me like that. She only invited me over as a friend.*

The Body

That didn't do much to help. But at least he was going to get to see Gaia. Since Thanksgiving they had barely spoken. Her visit was the last thing he had expected.

He heard feet coming toward the door at a near run. There was a fumble of latches, and the heavy wooden door swung open. "Sam!" said Gaia. "You came."

"I said I would come," he replied.

"Yeah, but I figured Heather would call, and you would . . ." Gaia stopped and shook her head. "Never mind. Come on in while I grab my stuff. I just got back myself."

Sam followed her inside the brownstone. "Where have you been?"

"I had an errand to take care of," said Gaia. "But it's all worked out now."

Sam nodded and looked around the room. "This is a great place," he said. He looked up at the high ceilings and the heavy molding. The brownstone was authentic and well maintained. Except for some tacky ceramic figures and some modern art pieces that didn't fit the style of the house, it was the kind of a place that made it into the Sunday magazine section on homes.

"Thanks. It's okay," said Gaia.

Sam stopped looking at the room and looked at Gaia. "You look . . . different."

Gaia tilted her head. "If that was a compliment, you need more practice."

"It was," said Sam. "So I guess I do." Gaia did look different. Her hair, which often looked like it had never been introduced to a comb, was glossy and smooth. Her jeans and sweater were nothing fancy, but they were a lot nicer than the baggy cargo pants and sweatshirts that Sam had always seen her wear before. "So, where's the rest of the gang?"

Gaia opened a closet and pulled out a coat. "I told Ed and Mary we'd meet them in the park. We probably should get going."

"Okay," said Sam. He was relieved to hear that the list hadn't been expanded. If Gaia was worried that he might be doing something with Heather, Sam had been equally worried that Gaia might call in the mysterious boyfriend her foster mother had mentioned on the phone. Sam could take being one of Gaia's gang. He didn't think he could stand to see her cuddling with another guy.

165

A voice called from somewhere in another room. "Gaia? Aren't you going to introduce me to your friend before we leave?"

An annoyed look crossed Gaia's face. She finished pulling on her coat and zipped it closed. "We have to go!" she shouted back. "If you want to meet him, you'll have to hurry."

A woman stepped around the corner into the front room. She was wearing a short teal skirt and a tight white top instead of an emerald dress. But there was no mistaking the legs, the face, or the body. It was the same woman that Sam had met at the bar. The woman he had sex with only hours before.

Gaia gave a sigh. She waved a hand at the approaching woman. "Sam, this is Ella Niven."

The woman walked up slowly, a Cheshire grin on her hungry red mouth. She reached out a hand with nails lacquered to the exact shade of her lips. "Hello, Sam. I'm Gaia's foster mother."

Sam wished that fainting were still in fashion. Falling into darkness and having everything just go away sounded like a wonderful idea. Instead his brain seemed to separate from his body and float up to the high ceiling of the room. He saw his self standing there. The body's mouth was open in a stupid expression. Its eyes were wide and glassy.

Sam watched as Gaia stepped around in front of

the body. He saw the woman—Ella—looking at the body with an amazing expression that mingled amusement, playfulness, and a promise that another night might be waiting.

Gaia looked worried. "Sam? You okay?"

The body took a step back. The mouth closed, opened, closed.

From his perch up by the ceiling, Sam thought the body was about the funniest thing he had ever seen. He would have laughed if he still had a mouth to laugh with. It was nice and warm up near the ceiling. He felt fine there. It was good to be free of the body and all the stupid, embarrassing things that it could do.

"Sam?"

The body turned and stumbled to the front door.

Gaia moved after it. "Sam? Where are you going? What's wrong?"

The body made some meaningless sounds. It fumbled at the door, opened it, and fell out into the night.

At once the feeling of floating by the ceiling vanished. Sam was back inside his own skull as he ran down the sidewalk, pushing past people on their way to parties and celebrations. He could feel the cold wind chapping his cheeks and nose. He could feel the freezing tears that streamed from his eyes. He could feel the crushing weight of emotion that squeezed at his chest.

There was no escaping himself. No escaping the awful wreck he had made of his life.

GO AFTER HIM. YOU COULD *catch him.*

It was true enough. The same thing that made Gaia strong also made her fast. The visit to St. Mark's Place hadn't even been enough to

Nothing but a Tramp

dent the energy in Gaia's legs. She could run down Sam in half a block. But she wasn't sure what to do if she caught him. She had no idea what had made him run in the first place.

"I wonder what upset your friend," said Ella.

Gaia spun around and looked into her foster mother's face. As usual, there was a faint trace of a smile on Ella's lips. Except when she was angry, Ella always seemed to find everyone else in the world quite amusing.

"What do you know about it?" asked Gaia.

"Me?" Ella shook her head. "Why should I know anything?"

Gaia narrowed her eyes. "I don't know, but you do."

"Please. How should I know anything about this boy of yours?"

Gaia didn't bother to answer. Gaia was smart, but it didn't take a genius to know that Ella was hiding something. Somehow Ella knew something about Sam. And from Sam's reaction, Sam certainly thought he knew something about Ella.

"Where did you meet Sam?"

"Why, I'm not sure that I ever have," said Ella. "I'm not in the habit of associating with boys that young."

Gaia gritted her teeth. Ella might be in her thirties, but she certainly dressed like she still thought she was a teenager. Gaia knew that Ella was going out almost every night that George wasn't home—and sometimes even when he was. Ella wasn't fooling anybody but George. For some reason, George seemed completely blind to the things his much younger wife was doing. He was the only one who didn't realize Ella was nothing but a tramp.

If Ella was cheating on George, who was to say she was actually cheating with people her own age? Ella liked to dress younger. Maybe she liked to date younger, too. Maybe she was spending her nights running around with younger guys. Guys like Sam.

Gaia decided not to think about it. She turned and ran out the door.

THE UNITED NATIONS BUILDING

gleamed in the darkness. Tom Moore walked slowly along the curving rows of flags and hunched his shoulders against the cold wind, sending a ripple of pain through his rib cage. *I shouldn't be out here on a night like this,* he thought. *Not in this condition.*

Out of the Darkness

The snow that had started at sunset was falling more thickly as the night wore on. It whipped in between the multicolored banners and drifted up against the curb.

By the time Tom reached the meeting point, the snow had already covered the sidewalks. And was beginning to spread into the streets.

A figure came out of the darkness. Tom tensed for a moment, but as the man came closer he relaxed. Tom put out his hand. "It's good to see you."

George Niven gripped Tom's hand tightly. "It's been too long. Way too long." He looked back over his shoulder. "We better walk."

The two men turned and walked side by side along the icy sidewalk. "This is risky, George," Tom said. "You could have been followed."

"I spent the last hour making sure that I wasn't," George replied. "But don't worry. I don't intend to make this a regular event. I heard about what happened at your apartment. You look terrible."

"I'm fine." Tom glanced at the older agent, dismissing the subject. "So why are we out here in the snow? Have you seen Loki?"

"No. I have no doubt he's nearby, but I don't know where."

"Then why—"

"I think Gaia's in serious danger." George shoved his hands deep into the pockets of his coat and stared up at the fluttering flags.

"How do you know?" Tom asked.

George nodded. "I found a hidden microphone on one of her jackets." He lowered his eyes and looked at Tom. "I'd picked the jacket up off the banister, and as I was carrying it up to her room, I felt something prick my finger. I have no idea how it got there, but . . ."

"But it's got to be a Loki job," Tom finished.

George waved a hand through the air. "I'm almost positive." He paused and stared off into the darkness. "I have someone checking the device to see if we can trace it. Someone from the agency. But I'm not optimistic."

The implications of what George was saying swirled through Tom's mind. If Loki had been close enough to Gaia to have her bugged, then Gaia was under even closer observation than Tom had thought. Loki knew when she was home and when she was away. He knew everything, from what kind of music she was listening to what she ate for breakfast.

"You're right," said Tom. "My daughter is in even more danger than I knew."

George drew in a deep breath. "What do we do now, Tom?"

"I'd love to say that I'll come and get my daughter tonight," said Tom. "But I can't. Not in the shape I'm in. And not while we don't know what Loki's next move will be."

"So we keep waiting."

Tom nodded. "And when we get our chance, we act."

George walked over to the nearest flagpole and leaned against the metal base. "You mean we kill him."

"Yes. We'll do whatever we have to."

Tom pulled a gun from his pocket and studied it briefly before returning it to his coat. Then he shook George's hand again, turned, and walked away.

THE WEATHER HAD CUT DOWN ON Innocent Explanations

the crowds, but there were still at least a hundred people milling around near the arch at the center of Washington Square Park. Gaia stood on her tiptoes, looking for Mary—and hoping that she might see Sam—but neither one was among the crowd. Finally Gaia spotted Ed on the far side of the mass of people and hurried over to join him.

Ed was moving back and forth over the same patch of sidewalk. From the deep groves in the snow, it looked like he had been pacing for some time. He spotted Gaia as she approached and stopped. "Hey, I thought you were bringing Sam with you."

"I was." She shrugged and raised her gloved hands. "He weirded out on me." She started to say something about Ella but stopped herself. She didn't even want to think about it herself, much less give Ed a reason to start making theories. "I guess he's not coming."

Ed grunted. "I guess we're even, then. Mary never showed up."

"Maybe she's still waiting at her place."

"Tried it," Ed replied with a shake of his head. "I've called over there twice. No answer. Did you find our pal Mr. Skizz?"

Gaia nodded. "I found him, but I don't think he's the one after Mary." Thinking of Skizz's battered face, Gaia thought that looking in the mirror must be the scariest thing he did all day.

"Then where is she?"

Gaia wished she knew the answer. There could be a hundred innocent explanations. Mary was never the world's most organized person. She might have gotten the time wrong or run off to do some other errand before they got together. Somehow Gaia didn't think so.

"Come on," she said. "We've got to go."

"Where?" asked Ed.

Gaia started walking. "We'll figure that out on the way."

MARY LEANED BACK INTO THE PLUSH

leather seat. "For a government guy, you've got a great car."

Loki laughed. It was a good laugh. Deep and reassuring. "Thanks. It comes with this assignment."

"Nice work if you can get it." The pain in Mary's leg was beginning to ease. After the terror of escaping the apartment and the freezing air outside, it was great to feel safe and warm. She closed her eyes and listened to the soft hum of the car's big engine. She wondered if it would be too rude if she fell asleep on the way to the police station.

Loki took a right-hand turn at the next intersection. "What do you think they wanted?" he asked.

A Very Popular Girl

"Who?"

"Those people who tried to kill you."

"Oh, them." Mary had been so caught up in what the intruder in her apartment had been trying to do that she hadn't put much thought into who or why. The idea that someone was trying to kill her sort of shoved out all the other thoughts. Now that she was thinking about it, she found it was a pretty tough question.

There were a couple of obvious candidates. After all, Mary had been a very popular girl lately when it came to creeps and thugs.

The intruder could have been Skizz. Mary still owed him five hundred dollars for drugs she had taken before Gaia inspired her to drop the coke habit. Only Skizz wasn't exactly the type to bug someone's phone. He would never have been snooping around her apartment in the first place. He might kill her, sure, but the other stuff was too weird to be Skizz.

Mary also gave some thought to the sex-for-points bozos she had caught at the Village School. Two assholes from the gang had already tried to rape her. Now that Mary had helped to expose the ring, she was sure that they would love to get back at her. Except this thing with the case and the electronics wasn't exactly the kind of stunt that a bunch of dumb high school jocks would pull.

"I don't know," she confessed. "It's not like my family's rich or anything. I can't imagine what . . ." Mary stopped. Maybe she *could* imagine. A memory drifted through her head: Aunt Jen on a crackling phone line.

"Did you think of something?" asked the government man.

Mary nodded. "Maybe. It might have something to do with this friend of mine. A girl named Gaia Moore."

"Gaia?" The man slowed the car and glanced over at Mary. "I know Gaia."

"You do?"

"More than know her. She's my niece."

Mary stared at the man behind the wheel. "You're Gaia Moore's uncle?" The idea excited her so much that she nearly forgot the pain in her leg. It was almost too good to be true. In fact, it almost seemed like it *couldn't* be true. She shot the man a doubtful glance. "Man, what are the odds?"

"Actually, it's not all that coincidental," Loki answered. "I came into town especially to check on Gaia. And her foster parents said she might be with you." The man cast another glance at Mary. There was a tense expression on his face. "So what makes you think that these people who were in your apartment have anything to do with my niece?"

Mary started to blurt out a response but realized

there were things she probably shouldn't say in front of Gaia's uncle. "Gaia told me something," she said carefully. "Something about her mom."

The man sighed. "Katia. Gaia told you about how she died." He steered the car through another right turn.

"Yeah."

"And did you share that information with anyone else?"

A twinge of pain ran up Mary's leg. She twisted in her seat. "I told part of it to my aunt Jen. She works at the library. I thought she might be able to find out something that would help Gaia."

"Your aunt. Yes." Loki looked at her with a strange intensity. "Anyone else?"

"No." Mary peeked out her window. It seemed like they had been driving for a long time. "Are we almost at the police station?"

"Soon," said Loki. "You're sure you didn't tell anyone but your aunt?"

Mary nodded. "Only Aunt Jen." A medium-sized apartment building swung into view through curtains of blowing snow. "Hey!"

"What's wrong?" asked Loki.

"That's my building." Mary ignored fresh pain from her leg and brought her face close to the foggy side window. "We've been going around in circles."

"We have?" Loki pulled around a double-parked minivan. "I must have taken a wrong turn."

A tightness began to slowly squeeze

177

Mary's throat. "What police station were you going to, anyway?"

"Actually," Loki replied, "I thought we should do something about your injuries before we went to the authorities."

"Are we going to a hospital?" asked Mary.

"Not necessary." Loki abruptly stopped the car in the middle of the street. He twisted and reached into the car's backseat.

Mary leaned away from him. "What are you doing?"

Loki pulled back a case. A small, leather case, sort of like the one Mary used to carry her flute in for band. Deftly Loki popped the catches at the side of the case and flipped it open.

"I have just the thing for your pain," he said.

Loki reached into the case, pulled out a vial of cocaine, and threw it to Mary.

ED'S ARMS HAD BEEN DOING LEG

duty for over a year, but he couldn't remember his shoulders ever being so tired. "Where are we going now?"

Deep Breaths

Gaia Moore marched ahead of him, her torn

sneakers crunching through the snow. "Back to the brownstone."

Ed groaned. "You can't mean your brownstone."

Gaia nodded without turning. "The one where I stay, yeah."

"But we've already been there," Ed replied. "And we've been to Mary's apartment, and back to the club, and to half a dozen local restaurants and made at least that many trips across the park."

Gaia stopped in her tracks. She didn't say anything at first, but Ed could see her back moving in and out as she took deep, deep breaths.

Somehow I don't think this is going to be good, Ed thought.

"We're going back because Mary might be there," said Gaia.

"I understand, but—"

Gaia spun around and stomped back to Ed. "What's your idea, huh? Where do you think she is?"

"I don't—"

"Because you know what I think?" said Gaia. "I think she's in trouble!" She leaned over Ed and slammed her hands down on the arms of his wheelchair. "I knew she was in trouble, but I didn't help her."

"You tried to," said Ed. He looked up at Gaia and shivered. There was enough tension in her to light half the city. "Look, I'm sure Mary's okay."

179

Gaia let out a breath that whistled through her teeth. "How the hell can you know that?"

MARY LOOKED THROUGH THE CURVING

side of the small glass vial. The powder inside was so white, so fine.

"Go ahead," said Loki. "You want it, don't you?"

Mary wanted to say no, but instead she nodded. "Yes," she said in a harsh, breathy voice.

She reached over and took the vial from his hands. She did want it. Mary wanted the rush, but more than that she wanted the energy and the feeling of being able to think so much better. "You're not really Gaia's uncle, are you?"

"I am." Loki started the car moving again and took a hard left. "Now, take your medicine like a good girl."

Electric wires. Mary felt like all her nerves had been replaced with tight, hot electric wires. She wanted the cocaine. She needed it.

Mary ran her finger along the black plastic top of the vial. A few loose grains of powder stuck to her fingers. Want it. Need it.

"Take it," repeated Loki. "The sooner you're done, the sooner you can see Gaia."

Gaia.

Mary ran her finger over the glass one last time. Then she dropped the vial on the floorboard of the sedan, raised her foot, and crushed the little bottle under her heel.

"I promised I would stay straight." Mary ground the cocaine into the sedan's dark carpet.

"Promises are very important," said Loki. And then he swung his arm in a lightning-fast backhanded slap that drove his knuckles into Mary's mouth.

The blow was like an explosion. Mary's head snapped back. Incredible pain lanced through her mouth.

"Now," said Loki. His voice was flat calm. "Let's go over a few things again. Did you tell anyone?"

Mary raised a trembling hand to her mouth. Her fingers came back covered in blood.

"Did you tell anyone?" said Loki.

He didn't raise his voice, but his tone left no doubt he expected an answer.

"No," Mary mumbled through her torn lips. "Nobody."

The second blow was blindingly fast.

Mary's head went back so hard, sparks ran across her vision.

"I already know you told your aunt," said Loki. "Isn't that right?"

"Yes," Mary cried. "Yes."

Loki nodded. "So you did tell someone," he said as

he turned the car around another corner. "And did you tell anyone else?"

"No."

"You're certain."

Mary nodded. "Yes." She sniffed. "Don't you know that already?"

"If you're referring to the devices I left at your home?" Loki shrugged. "Unfortunately, they don't always pick up everything."

"There was no one else."

Loki nodded. "For the sake of both you and Gaia, let's hope you're telling the truth."

LOKI STEERED THE BLACK SEDAN

around the corner. "Don't worry," he said. "We'll be getting out soon."

Mary sagged against the window. "And then what?"

Loki didn't answer. Instead he pulled the car over to the side of the road and parked. He left the engine at a low, smooth rumble. The windshield wipers continued to drive back and forth, clearing the heavy, wet flakes of snow.

It was time to end the threat posed by Mary Moss. Loki intended to not only ensure that the girl would never share what she had learned about Katia's death but also to put an end to Gaia's experiment in friendship. When this was over, Gaia would never again dare to share her deepest feelings with anyone—except, of course, her dear uncle.

Loki reached into his pocket and pulled out a black stocking cap. "It's time to get out."

The girl looked at him suspiciously. "I don't suppose that means you're letting me go?"

Loki had no intention of letting Mary go free, but he knew well enough how a little hope could make it easier to keep a prisoner under control. "Come with me and answer a few questions. Then you're free to do as you please."

The expression on the girl's face was one of mingled fear, doubt, and hope. It was clear to Loki that she didn't really believe him, but it was just as clear that she desperately *wanted* to believe. "I thought you were going to kill me."

"Answer my questions, and I'll have no reason to kill you." He pulled the black mask over his face and got out of the car.

The heavy blanket of snow softened his footsteps as he circled the car. Loki checked the area to be sure that no observer was too close before opening the door. There was no one. He jerked open the door, letting in a swirl of snow.

The girl tumbled out and tried to stand. Loki looked down at her.

"Don't try to run," he said. He raised one side of his coat and revealed a heavy black pistol attached to a long tube.

"Silencer," mumbled Mary. "That's what the other thing was in the case."

"Come with me," said Loki. "I'd prefer not to use this if I don't have to."

Mary nodded. She began walking along the sidewalk in slow, small steps. Her feet slipped frequently in the snow.

Loki stayed close. "That's good," he said. "Keep moving."

Mary stopped and shook her head. "No," she said softly.

Loki was on her in one quick stride. He grabbed the front of her coat and pulled Mary toward him. "I said I would prefer not to use the gun. I didn't say I would hesitate."

"Are you really Gaia's uncle?" the girl asked.

"Yes." There was no harm in telling her anything now. The girl would never have the chance to spread her information.

"And after you kill me, what are you going to do to Gaia?"

Loki gave a tug on her coat. "I've already told you. Talk and you're in no further danger."

The girl gave a weak nod. She started to move again, but two steps down the sidewalk her knees folded, and she collapsed in the snow.

Loki took her by the arm and lifted her. Mary dangled from Loki's hand like a doll.

He gritted his teeth. "Get up." Mary continued to hang limply from his hand. Loki removed the silencer and put it back into his pocket. He took the dark, heavy bulk of the Glock pistol and pressed the blunt barrel against Mary's back. "Answer my questions, and I'll set you free. Stay here and die."

Mary got her feet back under her and stood. She trembled in Loki's grip, but when he gave her a nudge with the gun, she began to walk.

Loki steered his captive along. "Her death was an accident."

Even in the dim light he could see the girl's eyes grow wide. "You killed her?"

"I loved her," said Loki.

He jerked on Mary's arm. They were in the midst of a small grove. Ordinarily they might have been visible from half the park, but the driving sheets of snow closed in around them like walls. Everything more than a dozen yards away was lost in curtains of white.

"Stop here," said Loki. He released his grip on her. "Turn around and face me."

Mary slowly spun around. "You killed Gaia's mother."

Loki put his gloved hand in the girl's hair and shoved back her head. "It was an accident."

185

"Right, I believe you." Despite her awkward position Mary suddenly smiled. "So, who were you trying to kill?"

Loki took the Glock pistol and leveled it at Mary's forehead. "Gaia's father." His finger slipped inside the trigger guard.

He barely noticed the girl's right hand coming up. It wasn't until her hand was in front of his eyes that Loki realized he had been careless.

And then his face exploded in pain.

GAIA HAD READ THAT SOME BLIND

people developed a better sense of hearing. Or sense of smell. Or touch.

Maybe it was true; maybe it was nothing more than another urban legend. All Gaia knew was that she couldn't feel fear, but she could feel everything else. Sometimes she wondered if she felt them more than normal, frightened people.

At the moment what she felt was rage. Rage and frustration.

You should know better than to think you're normal. You should know better than to think you can have friends. You should know better than to think you might possibly, one day, be happy.

Ed rolled up beside her. His breath steamed in the light of the nearest streetlamp. "If this snow gets any deeper, I won't be able to move."

Gaia kicked at the path. Six inches of snow and it was still falling. The weather would pick tonight for a decent snow. "It doesn't matter," she said. "I don't know where to go."

"What about the park?" suggested Ed.

Gaia glanced at him. "Why?"

Ed spun his chair around and pointed back the way they had come. "That's where we said we'd meet her. If she's looking for us, that's probably where she'll go."

"I thought you were too tired to move."

"Not yet." Ed gave her a tired grin. "But if it keeps snowing, you might have to carry me home."

MARY RAN UNDER THE THIN, BARE

Mummy

branches of the winter trees. She had lost the path. The snow covered everything, obscuring the boundaries between path and field and playground. Everything looked the same. Black trees. White snow.

She struggled along on her injured leg. At every step it seemed that her foot got heavier. After a hundred yards she was limping. After two hundred she dragged the leg behind her, leaving long cuts in the snow like some mummy from an old movie limping across the sand.

"Help!" she shouted, but it seemed that the snow muffled her voice. "Gaia!"

The snow was falling faster than ever. It made it hard to see more than a few feet ahead. Mary knew that she was still in the park, but she didn't know where.

She might be near the chessboards or the fountain. The Arc de Triomphe might be no more than a dozen yards away, cloaked by night and snow.

"Gaia!"

The same thought ran through her head over and over. *I have to find Gaia. I have to warn her about her uncle.*

HALFWAY TO THE PARK GAIA GOT

behind Ed and pushed. Even with her help, getting the chair through the deepening snow was a struggle. It was ridiculous to even try it. The only thing that made sense was to help Ed get home.

Fireworks

But inside, something seemed to hammer at her. Hurry. Hurry.

No more than two dozen people were waiting near the arch by the time they reached the center of the park. None of them looked anything like Mary Moss.

"How long do we wait?" asked Ed.

Gaia shook her head. She was all out of answers. *I have to find Mary.*

"Gaia."

The call was so faint that at first Gaia was sure she had imagined it. Then it came again.

"Gaia."

"Did you hear that?" asked Gaia.

Ed raised his head. "Hear what?"

Before Gaia could reply, the fireworks finally started. Sparkles of gold and silver mixed with and lit the falling snow.

Gaia didn't stop to watch. She turned and ran into the night.

BLOOD WAS FROZEN ON MARY'S

Close

cheek. She could barely breathe. Her eyes teared in the bitter cold. Her leg ached from hip to ankle.

When the colors started in the sky, she

thought it was an illusion. It was only after the second explosion and the third that she realized it was the fireworks at the center of the park.

Gaia was close. All she had to do was follow the fireworks.

"Gaia!" she shouted again.

She limped forward a step. Another step.

A tall, dark figure appeared from behind a tree. "I have to give you credit," said Loki. "You came very close." He raised the gun over his head and brought the handle of the heavy weapon down in a vicious blow.

This time the fireworks were all inside Mary's head.

LOKI'S EYES WERE STILL STREAMING

Blunt Instrument

with tears. He risked removing his mask for a moment, bent, grabbed a handful of snow, and rubbed it across his burning face. Then he carefully replaced his mask. Even with the heavy snow, the park wasn't completely empty. If he were seen, the situation would be severely complicated.

Despite the pain her attack had caused, Loki felt

even more regret about killing the girl. Mary Moss had proved to be quite resourceful. It was true that she had become too close to Gaia, but if Mary could be turned, that closeness could become an advantage. Mary might be used to manipulate Gaia in ways that a blunt instrument like Ella could never achieve.

No. She knows about Katia. She can't be allowed to survive.

Mary groaned and rolled over in the snow. Her eyes blinked open. "Gaia," she groaned.

Before she could do anything more, Loki drove the toe of his boot into her side. The girl let out a little yip. A small hand with bright red nails reached toward his ankle. Loki stomped down hard on the pale fingers, then sent another kick into the girl's body.

This time he was rewarded by a low, whistling moan before his victim passed out. Mary Moss would be giving him no more trouble.

Loki once again put his fingers in the girl's red hair. He pulled her unconscious form to her knees, moved around behind her, and put the Glock at the base of her skull. It would look like a drug hit. That's what the girl's parents would think. That's what the police would think. Most important, that's what Gaia would think.

And Gaia would learn a very important lesson— don't get too close. Otherwise you might get hurt.

Loki put his finger on the trigger.

"No!" came a scream from his left.

Loki felt a sense of movement. The sense of something rushing toward him out of the darkness and snow.

He pulled the trigger.

GAIA COLLIDED WITH THE MAN JUST

as the gun exploded. For the tiniest slice of a second the muzzle flash lit the snow around her, freezing the motion of every snowflake like the world's loudest strobe light.

Frozen Moment

In that moment of light Gaia could see everything. She could see the wool knit of the man's mask. She could see the black pistol in his gloved hand. She could see the bruises on Mary's face, and the blood on her split lips, and how her ginger hair was blown aside by the bullet on its way to her brain.

The frozen moment ended. Gaia's momentum knocked the man from his feet and sent him sprawling in the snow. Gaia didn't go down. She landed on her feet, skidded, and jumped again to find the man already getting up.

Gaia put a sneaker in his hidden face. The man sat back down in the snow. Gaia launched another kick.

When fighting, Gaia usually worked hard not to cause permanent damage. This wasn't usually. She aimed her blow at the man's neck and delivered it with enough force to send his head bouncing all the way to Eighth Street.

The man blocked. It was a fast, efficient flip of his left arm, just enough to send Gaia's foot grazing past its target.

The missed kick sent Gaia flying over him. She tucked down her head, did a quick tumble, and rolled back to her feet. By the time she turned around, the man was also standing.

Gaia circled left, faked right, and went in. She sent a stiff right hand aiming for his face. Blocked. A spin kick at his side. Blocked. A sharp uppercut at his chin. Blocked.

She took a step back and studied the man. He held his hands low, almost too low, but he was fast. Gaia gritted her teeth. He wasn't fast enough. No one was.

Gaia went back another step, then came forward in an electric rush. She flew into the air with her stiff right leg aimed at the man's head.

The man raised an arm to block, but Gaia adjusted her aim midflight. She lowered her foot and drove it square in the center of the man's chest. He staggered back, but before Gaia could follow up her attack, she was forced to duck a whistling right hand that shattered the air only inches from her face.

This guy was good. Most of the idiots Gaia fought were completely clueless. Some of them had packed on a lot of prison muscle, and they probably looked pretty tough. Gaia wasn't impressed by looks. Even the tough guys were slow and easy. Not this guy. He was big and fast. More than that—he was trained.

The man feinted a kick, then withdrew another step.

Gaia followed. She threw a punch. Blocked. Kick. Blocked. Punch. A solid blow to the man's gut. Kick. A glancing shot to his hip but still enough to make him take another clumsy step. Leg sweep. The man in the black ski mask went down.

Gaia took her time. One more shot. That was all it would take. When it came right down to it, people were so easy to kill.

There was movement on her left. Gaia whipped around to face this new attack.

It was Mary. Her outstretched right hand clawed at the snow.

The man in the mask hadn't managed to touch Gaia a single time, but one look at Mary hit her like a bus. Gaia took a step toward her fallen friend. Then she remembered the man in the mask. Gaia turned back to face her enemy.

He was gone.

Gaia hurried forward. There were footsteps in the deepening snow. If she followed, she could catch the man. She was sure of it. All she had to do was leave Mary.

That was not an option.

She ran back to where Mary lay. Blood was spreading in the snow. It was splashed around Mary and speckled for a dozen yards in all directions. Mary's hand had stopped its fitful clawing at the earth. Mary's legs were still.

Images flashed through Gaia's mind. A house in the snow. Her mother. Blood and snow. Over and over, blood and snow. Gaia moved toward Mary as if she was wading through all her worst nightmares.

She's dead. She had to be dead. There was so much blood.

Gaia knelt in the stained snow. Tears made her vision waver, and her hands trembled as she reached out to touch Mary's cheek. Above her, shifting, sparking colors appeared as a fresh round of fireworks burst over the park. "Mary?"

To Gaia's astonishment, Mary's eyes opened. Her face was a mask of blood and pain, but her eyes immediately locked on Gaia's face. "Gaia?" she said in a weak, weirdly distorted voice.

"It's me." Gaia ran a hand over her friend's hair. Her fingers came back warm and sticky with blood. "Don't worry. You're going . . . You'll be okay."

Mary gave a single slow nod. "Gaia."

Gaia leaned in close. "Yeah."

"I was so worried about you," said Mary. Then her eyes slid back, and a final shiver ran through her body.

Gaia threw back her head and screamed into the falling snow.

LOKI STOOD BACK AMONG THE TREES

and watched as Gaia knelt over the fallen girl. He felt a moment of fear when he realized that the Moss girl was still alive, but then he saw the final shudder rack her body and knew that the threat was finally over.

"Where are you!" Gaia screamed at the night. "Where are you, you bastard!"

Loki didn't move. He didn't dare move. There were sharp pains in his hip and chest. He was quite certain that at least one of his ribs was broken. If Gaia found him, he had no doubt the girl would leave him as dead as he had left Mary Moss.

For an uncomfortable moment it seemed like Gaia was peering straight at Loki's hiding place. Then she turned and ran back toward the people at the center of the park.

Loki waited until Gaia was out of sight, then he went back to Mary. He took two glassine envelopes of cocaine from his pocket and slipped them into the dead girl's coat. Then he opened a third envelope and poured a bit of the powder across her frozen face.

He took one last look to satisfy himself that everything was as it should be, then he started out of the park. For the police everything would be neat and easy. Junkie girl dies. Drugs on the body. Even if they never found someone to blame, they would never look very hard for an answer.

As Loki reached the sedan and climbed inside, he wondered how Gaia would react. The situation of the death—the death, the gunshot, the blood—it was bound to conjure images of her mother. Its effect on Gaia should be interesting.

Loki pressed the speakerphone button on the car's dash. "The task is completed," he said. He reached for the button to hang up the phone, then paused. "Have someone standing by to clean up the car," he said. "There's blood on my upholstery."

He hung up the phone and drove away.

here is a

sneak peek of

Fearless™ #9:

BLOOD

So I've been trying to come up with a snappy reply to all the "I'm so sorry's" I've been getting about Mary. Yesterday at school was pretty bad. Most of those people didn't even know Mary, except from seeing her at parties. They didn't know her favorite band (Fearless), her favorite color (fuschia), her favorite food (satay). So why are they all giving me these lame expressions of grief? All yesterday, during class, after class, I felt their eyes boring holes into me—which, frankly, was the last thing I needed.

If it weren't for the fact that I have gone through worse, I would say that I couldn't bear it. But of course, I can. And I will. I am my father's daughter. Just like him, I'm better off on my own. I should know better than to ever think that will change.

I am the invincible, genetic freak Gaia.

I just thank God Mary didn't
go to this school—it would have
made it all a hundred times
worse. Thanks, Mary.

If only she knew
where he hid
during the
day, like vermin.
Then she **never**
could simply
arrive, **again**
announce a
Candygram, and
take him apart.

ED SHOVELED A SMALL FORKFUL OF chicken potpie into his mouth. He glanced across the school cafeteria table at Gaia. Day two after Mary's death and Gaia was still showing no signs of weakness.

What's a chicken pot?

"What is chicken potpie, anyway?" Ed asked. "What's a chicken pot? Like a pot just to make chicken in? Where do they get these names?"

Gaia looked up at him and almost smiled. That is, her lips pressed together in a flat line for a moment. Which was the most he'd gotten out of her in two days.

She shrugged. "It's hot. You didn't have to make it. What's the problem?" She took a bite of her own lunch.

Ed stared back down at the table, defeated. Then he glanced back at Gaia. "You know, I'm glad you're not a vegetarian," he said, desperate to make conversation. "I don't get the whole vegetarian thing. I mean, if we're not supposed to eat animals, why are they made out of meat?"

Not an original line, but Ed had forgotten what comedian had said it first. Still, even though it was the Ed Fargo Entertainment hour, he was not getting any reaction.

He tried again. "Why don't we go see a movie? Get your mind off of stuff."

Gaia met his eyes. Clear blue eyes, as untroubled as a spring morning in Maine. "No thanks," she said. "I've got some stuff to do at home."

Ed's eyes narrowed. Their mutual good friend had been shot and killed three days ago, and Gaia hadn't cried on his shoulder, hadn't expressed regret, hadn't mentioned Mary's name. Gaia had actually been holding Mary when she died. Now it was like Mary had never existed. And like Ed didn't exist, either.

In the four months he had known Gaia, Ed had seen her furious, violent, shy, antisocial, rude, sensitive, generous, forgiving, and reckless. He didn't think he had ever seen her truly happy, and he knew he had never seen her weak—either physically or emotionally. Why was he expecting something different now, just because her other best friend had been gunned down in front of her only two days ago?

Abruptly Ed pushed his lunch tray away. Suddenly, he didn't feel like eating anymore. What was this "stuff to do at home" shit? Gaia didn't consider the Nivens' house her *home*. He leaned across the table, his eyes narrowing. "Who are you, and what have you done with the real Gaia?"

It was an old joke, an ancient joke, but still chuckle-worthy, in Ed's opinion. *Could we at least see a glimmer of a smile, please?*

205

Instead, Gaia looked suddenly inexpressibly sad. It was only for a moment, but a shadow passed over Gaia's features. Then it was gone. Her face twitched back into its beautiful, expressionless mask. "There is no real Gaia," she said softly.

SLITHER. CROSS. SLITHER. ELLA

loved the sound her thigh-high stockings made when she crossed and uncrossed her legs. Sort of slippery and smooth at the same time.

So powerful

"Go on." Loki turned to face her, his back against the anonymous white wall of this apartment. At first Ella had been surprised that Loki had chosen a doorman building for this month's pied-à-terre. Then she realized that the heavy-jowled gorilla in the cheesy maroon uniform was no doubt on Loki's payroll.

Ella shrugged, crossed her legs again, and felt a wave of pleasure and irritation tingling at the base of her spine. "What can I tell you? You offed her friend, right in front of her. But she hasn't been crying, hasn't been doing anything. As a matter of fact," Ella said thoughtfully, examining a one-inch-long spiky fingernail, "she's been slightly less unbearable lately. At least she's coming home for meals and not sneaking out at night. So George isn't quite as worried about her as he usually is."

The force of Loki's intense gaze made Ella's cheeks burn. Damn him. Even after years he could do this to her. She thought about what Loki was like in bed. Blurred images flitted through her mind, Loki sliding next to her, the cord in his neck tightening as he moved. She visualized his almost surgical precision, an almost superhuman control. Loki was so dangerous, so frightening, so powerful. Falling for him had been as intense and as addicting as jumping off a cliff. But for now, Ella had to focus on business.

"Has she been with her other friends?" he asked. "The wheelchair guy? Ed? Anyone from school? Anyone . . . else?"

Like Sam Moon, you mean? Ella thought sarcastically. She had to gulp hard to keep a grin off her face. Sam Moon had been *delicious.* Absolutely delicious. Ladies, you don't need Prozac: you need a young, unstoppable, pretty boy to put the smiles back on your faces. Not only had Sam been fabulous in bed—strong, uncomplicated, and enthusiastic—but there had been an added layer of pleasure in knowing that Ella was sleeping with the object of Gaia's affection. She almost laughed out loud just thinking about it. Gaia, that perverse, hateful, genetic freak, was eating her guts out over Sam Moon. And Ella had bagged him before Gaia did. It was almost too perfect.

"Ella?" Loki demanded.

Ella snapped back to the present and shook her head. "No. Like I said, she's been staying home," Ella said. "Not making phone calls, not sneaking out. Yesterday she stopped for a slice of pizza on her way home from school, but that's hardly unusual. She has the undiscriminating taste of a hyena."

Loki regarded Ella coldly. "She's a survivor. Like a hyena, you could put her down almost anywhere, and she would survive. She would adapt. She is very strong, our Gaia."

A tiny muscle twitched in Ella's smoothly made-up cheek. God, she hated that bitch. To hear Loki salivating over her was nauseating.

"Uh-huh," Ella said, trying to keep the irritation out of her voice. She didn't quite succeed. Jesus, how long was this going to go on? She shivered without meaning to, just thinking of the weather outside. She wanted to be somewhere far away. Somewhere warm. But no, Ella was stuck here, playing baby-sitter to her foster daughter. Daughter. Ella swallowed hard.

LOKI TURNED HIS BACK TO ELLA AND

Worthy

strode over to the windows. It was already dark, at four-thirty. From these windows he could see the big X formed by Broadway and Seventh Avenue as they crossed and reversed positions. He sighed. Ella was rapidly reaching the limits of her usefulness. The open hatred on her face when she spoke of Gaia was more than annoying. Still, he knew Ella was under control. She wouldn't dare touch a hair on that beautiful head.

Loki sighed again, this time with pleasure. In the window's reflection, he could see Ella, behind him, no longer even bothering to pretend to pay attention to him. She looked at her nails, crossed and uncrossed her legs, yawned, gazed at the ceiling. The fact that she failed to be inspired by Gaia was proof of her own inadequacy.

Gaia alone was perfect. Gaia alone was worthy—worthy of her background, her training, her surveillance. Worthy of his attention. Worthy of something more than attention. The fact that Gaia had witnessed the death of one of the pathetic props in her difficult life—had witnessed it and not crumpled, had watched her friend die and yet shown no signs of weakness or trivial human emotion in the days following—well, that just proved how very special his beloved niece was.

GAIA STEPPED OFF THE NUMBER

6 local on 96th Street and started walking west. The February cold whistled down the wind tunnels made by tall buildings on either side of her. It whipped her hair around beneath the sweat-shirt hood that stuck up from beneath her puffy blue ski jacket.

It hadn't been easy ditching Ed. First he'd asked her to a movie. Then after school he had suggested eating together or even—sacrifice of all sacrifices—going shopping.

She'd rejected him flat out. He'd sat, watching her, as she booked east to catch the green line. She hadn't looked back.

Now, reaching Fifth Avenue, Gaia turned left, then crossed the wide street, heading for the huge columns of the Metropolitan Museum of Art. Her plan was simple: first, an hour of culture, then a bowl of potato-leek soup from the soup Nazi, then a couple of hours in and around Thompkins Square Park, enjoying the lovely January weather and looking for her good old pal Skizz. Gaia shivered once, as if someone had just drawn long fingernails down a chalkboard. Skizz had *looked* pretty harmless after the last beating Gaia had given him.

But she had no doubt in her mind that he was the one who ordered the hit on Mary. One of his asshole dealer friends had probably owed him a favor. But Gaia wasn't fooled. She knew who was to blame. She'd been fooled once by Skizz, but never again.

If only she knew where he slept, where he ate, where he hid during the day like vermin. Then she could simply arrive, announce a Candygram, and take him apart. A couple times.

But Gaia was going to wait until the time was right. She would wait until well after night fell. Hence her quest for culture in the meantime.

When she walked through the huge, heavy bronze doors of the museum, a strong, heated blast of air whooshed down on her. It instantly dried the snowflakes clinging to her hair. Inside it was stuffy, overheated, and dry. Gaia shrugged out of the puffy ski jacket and tied its floppy arms around her waist. She snagged a map from the info desk and made her way to a bank of elevators.

An elevator, a couple of long halls, and a wide stairway later, Gaia found herself in a series of rooms devoted to German Expressionists. As Gaia wandered over in front of a Nolde painting, she had a flashback of her mother. Katia. Katia had taught Gaia how to look at art, how to love it, how to let it get inside her. Remembering those lessons, Gaia sank down on a bare wooden bench and stared at the painting in front of her.

The painting was called "Three Russians," and it showed two men and a woman all bundled up, as if, perhaps, they had just strolled down a New York street in the middle of January. The brushstrokes were coarse and broad; the paint clung thickly to the canvas in crusty swaths. Three Russians. All dressed in fur. They had long, thin noses, high cheekbones . . .

Katia Moore had been Russian. Gaia had hated her accent, had been embarrassed by her rolling r's, her formal hairstyle, the clothes she brought from Europe. She had been so unlike other kids' mothers. Gaia's whole family had been so unlike everyone else's. Which is why she was here, now, seventeen years old, a genetic freak made freakier by her father's intensive, relentless training. Training that had ended as abruptly as her mother's life, and on the same night.

Gaia's breath lightly left her lungs as she felt herself sink into the hard bench. It was so hot in here, so dry.

Why? she screamed silently. Why had she been made into such a freak? As a child, when she realized, when she *knew* that she simply never felt fear, it hadn't been a big deal. In fact, she hadn't really stuck out as a kid, except for her height. But lots of kids had seemed reckless and fearless—like that day she and four of her friends climbed up to the roof of the Rosenblitts' shed, jumped from there to the roof of the Stapletons' garage, then crossed over to the other side and leaped seven feet down onto a pile of compost. Paratroopers! Okay, it had been disgusting, landing in all the fruit rinds and eggshells, but it hadn't been scary. Not for any of them. It had been fun.

But now, at seventeen, never feeling fear had become a weight around her neck, relentlessly dragging her down. But then, her fearlessness was also a good thing, because it meant that nothing would stop Gaia from wiping Skizz out. Her intellect surely wasn't going to get in the way. Her emotions were on vacation. And she didn't feel fear. End result? No Skizz. No Skizz ever again. Just like no—

Gaia suddenly felt hungry. Maybe it was time to hit the soup wagon. She took one last quick look around at the German Expressionists. Gotta hand it to them—they were masters at expressing all the agonies of the human condition. Thwarted love, psychic torture, the sheer pain of existence all laid out for the viewer in bright jewellike colors. All these paintings of anguish. It was almost funny. Gaia hiked up her messenger bag, turned, and left the Three Russians behind.

Skizz is lying low. I almost froze my ass off last night in Thompkins Square Park, but after five hours, he hadn't shown his ugly face. But I'll get him. After I got back to George's last night I couldn't sleep. I thought about all the ways I could kill Skizz. Facing him, sideways, from the back. In my mind I heard his shoulder snap as I bent it. I heard the choked scream of pain rip from his throat as I broke his fingers, one by one.

The thing is, it won't be a lesson. Sometimes bullies need to be taught lessons, and if I'm around, I'm happy to do it. Call it my contribution to society. But the statute of limitations for Skizz to learn his lessons ran out a couple days ago. He's failed the exam. He gets no second chance.

He doesn't know it, but every hour he breathes is one less hour until his own personal doomsday. I promise you. I promise you.

She could
feel him
watching
her. It
didn't
matter. It
didn't
matter. It
didn't
matter.

lower
than
low

"I'LL GO WITH YOU."

Gaia's eyes narrowed as she looked at Ed. She leaned back enough to shut her locker door, then dropped her messenger bag to the floor so she could put on her ski jacket. A few limp, grayish feathers leaked out through the hole and fluttered to the ground. Ed watched them fall.

"No thanks," she said, trying not to sound regretful and not quite succeeding. "I think I'll just go do it. I need to get this paper done." Picking up her messenger bag, she slung it over her shoulder and jerked her hair out from beneath the strap.

Ed's wheelchair blocked her way. "What is *with* you?"

Forcing her face to remain calm, Gaia shrugged. She could see the frustration and uncertainty on his face, and for a moment she wished it weren't there.

"What do you mean?"

"The way you're acting." Ed's arms made choppy movements in the air as he struggled to express himself, obviously wary of how far to push her. "I mean, I'm trying to comfort you here, trying to be a good friend. This is a hard time for you—for me too. But you just keep acting like I should go screw myself."

216

"This isn't a hard time for me," Gaia said evenly. "And I'm not acting like you should go screw yourself. But I have this paper due. I'm tired of all the teachers giving me a hard time. I just want to do some stuff, get them off my back. I'm sorry if that's inconveniencing you."

Ed's eyes bored into hers. "Gaia . . ."

"Gotta go," Gaia said briskly. "Bye." She made a quick pivot around his wheelchair and strode toward the east side entrance of the school. The one with stairs. The one Ed couldn't follow her out of. She could feel him watching her. It didn't matter. It didn't matter. It didn't matter.

The non-excited state

NOW, WHY DOESN'T STARBUCKS *have a concession stand right here?* Sam Moon wondered. He stretched and yawned, his heavyweight sweater riding up to expose some smooth skin and a thin strip of stomach hair. What day was it? He looked at his watch. It gave him only a number. Ah! An abandoned newspaper lay crumpled in the deep armchair next to his. It was Thursday. Assuming that this was today's newspaper.

The life of the pre-med student. `All work and no play.` Actually, Sam's life often consisted of too much play and not enough work. His grades had demonstrated just that at the end of last semester. Which had prompted a heartfelt man-to-man with Dad, which had prompted Sam's working his butt off for the last six weeks. He looked around the study room he was in. The NYU library was ten stories tall, with a huge open vertical space in the middle, and floor after floor of books encircling it like a vise. It made him feel nauseated just looking at it.

But down here in one of the first-floor study rooms, he could block out the rest of the cavernous building and experience only the hushed quiet of the room, the sound-deadening camel-colored carpet, the deeply ugly tweed-covered easy chairs that dotted the room `like chicken pox on a first-grader.`

Sam shifted again in his seat, feeling his muscles' achy protest. How long had he been sitting here, wading through the text and class notes for his human sexuality class? At least three hours, with only one bathroom break. He needed coffee. He needed a Danish or something. At the beginning of the year, someone had turned him on to onion bagels with scallion cream cheese. He'd thought they were incredible, until the night he'd thrown one up through his nose after a bout of tequila shots in Josh Seidman's dorm room.

Once you throw something up through your nose, you never want to eat it again. Fact of life.

Human sexuality. What a laugh. The course was required for pre-meds, and he and his pals thought it would be a hoot. Instead, it somehow managed to suck every last bit of titillating humor from the subject, and turn it into something so dry that sometimes Sam wondered if the team who wrote the textbook had ever, ever gotten it on *once* in their whole dreary academic lives.

Not that Sam was an expert. In fact, he was a royal screw-up when it came to sex, pardon the pun. He had a gorgeous, willing girlfriend, who, even though she was only a high school senior, was still so hot that his friends envied him. But she'd cheated on him. And he didn't have the guts to confront her about it. He wasn't even sure it was worth it, especially after what happened the other night. He'd gotten himself shitfaced and, pissed at Gaia, pissed at Heather, so freaking sick of school and studying and ice and snow—he'd done the dirty with a woman he'd met in a bar. They'd been chatting, friendly-like, and then she put her hand on his thigh and suddenly they were leaving the bar together.

Then there had been the soul-destroying event of

finding out that the woman was none other than Gaia's guardian, Ella Niven. Despite himself, Sam groaned out loud. When he'd found out, he'd almost thrown his guts up, all over Gaia's front door. Man, he was lower than low. Lower than a snake's belly. Lower than a—

This was so messed up. First off, he had to break it off with Heather soon. He was treating her like shit, even though he didn't mean to. She was treating him like shit, too.

If he didn't get the balls to break up with her, it would never happen. He wasn't blind. He knew it was a big prestige thing for her to have a college boyfriend. And she probably cared for him. If he didn't break up with her, they would just drift along in this lame-ass way, neither of them happy, until finally, *boom*. They'd be standing at the altar pledging to go through with this sham of a life forever. He couldn't let that happen. He was a man. A man had balls. He would find the balls to break up with Heather.

Mindlessly, Sam's gaze drifted down to the text page before him. It was almost a full-page, head-on view of A Male's Reproductive Organs. The Non-Excited State. Sam stared at it blankly. *Oh, right,* he thought bleakly. Balls.

A Sisterly Thing

HEATHER LOOKED AT THE SEE-through clear plastic princess phone on her bedside table. It was not ringing. It had not rung in much too long. *Maybe Sam has forgotten how to dial,* Heather thought sarcastically. *Maybe Sam has forgotten that phones exist. That bastard, maybe he's forgotten I exist.*

The phone sat there silently. *Okay, I'm a modern woman,* thought Heather. *I can express my needs. Right now I need a boyfriend who adores me. Right now I need to go to bed with Sam and have him hold me. Because when we're in bed, I can forget about everything else for a while. Forget about Gaia, forget about Ed, forget about my family.*

Heather picked up the receiver and punched in memory dial #1. On the other end, the phone in Sam's dorm suite rang and rang. "Pick it up," Heather said softly. "Pick it up, you jerk. Be there."

"Hello?"

Heather instantly assessed it as a non-Sam voice.

"This is Heather," she said.

"Heather, babe, it's Will."

"Hi, Will. Listen, is Sam there?"

"No dice," said Will. "Sam is wearing out the study chairs over at the library. His dad had his hide over Christmas because of his grades."

"Yeah, I know," said Heather. "So he's at the library?"

"Yep. I'll tell him you called, okay?"

"Okay." Heather hung up the phone. Being at the library, studying alone, was perhaps almost a partial excuse for not calling. And Heather did know that Sam's dad, the earnest Dr. Moon, had really gotten on Sam's case about his grades. So Sam was studying at the library. He wasn't somewhere with someone else. Like Gaia. As soon as the thought intruded, Heather quickly shut it out. God, if only Gaia would just get hit by a truck or something, Heather's life would be almost bearable again. For Heather, Gaia's existence was like getting clubbed in the head all the time and still trying to live a normal life.

Flopping over on her pillow, Heather tried to decide if she should go by the NYU library. Just pretend to be popping in. After all, her school had library privileges. She could say she needed to look something up. Then maybe she could convince Sam that he had studied enough, and they could go get coffee, and then they could swing by his dorm room . . . and then she would get home at two o'clock in the morning on a school night and Heather's parents would plotz.

Also, how likely was it that she would find him? How humiliating was it to plan a trip to the library on a Thursday night, hoping to run into a boyfriend who was treating you like shit? It was ridiculously humiliating, that's what. To hell with him. She would go out by herself, or with her sister Phoebe. Then when Sam called, *she* would be out. The ball would be in her court. And she wouldn't call him back for two frigging days, that jerk.

Heather scrambled off her bed. Maybe Phoebe would be into catching an early movie at the Angelika or something. A sisterly thing.

A bathroom connected Heather and Phoebe's bedrooms. When Heather heard the shower water shut off, she gave the door a brief tap and opened it.

"Hey, Feeb, I have a great idea," Heather began.

Phoebe had just stepped out of the shower and was reaching for a fluffy gold towel. It took only moments for Heather's gaze to sweep her sister's body. She blinked as Phoebe quickly wrapped herself in the towel, brushing long wet strands of hair out of the way.

"Whoa," Heather said without thinking. "You're . . . really skinny."

Really skinny didn't begin to describe what Heather had caught a glimpse of. She knew Phoebe had been dieting a lot—an attempt to get rid of the freshman fifteen she'd put on last year. But until now she'd simply thought Phoebe looked fabulous, model-slim in her bulky winter clothes. Naked, Phoebe looked like something else. Her elbows were whitened points. Her knees had sags around them, like an old lady's. Extra skin. Heather had been able to see Phoebe's rib bones through her skin, and her two hip bones jutted out like clothes hangers. She was much too thin.

Phoebe briskly started toweling her hair. "Thanks," she said casually.

"Like maybe you don't need to diet anymore," Heather said carefully. Now that she looked closely, she saw her sister's skin stretched taut over her facial bones. Her eyes looked deep-set, her cheekbones carved and prominent. Without makeup, her sister looked pale, anemic, underfed. With makeup, Heather knew, Phoebe looked stunning.

Bending over, Phoebe combed her hair out with her fingers, then expertly wrapped a towel around her head. She stood up and tucked in the towel ends. She smiled at Heather, and it suddenly seemed garish, skeletal. Heather began to feel as if she was about to freak out. "Heath-er," Phoebe said in an older-sister singsong. "I'm not dieting anymore. I'm just watching my weight. Trying not to go overboard. You won't believe how awful it was when I was practically a size nine! It was like, I couldn't button anything. I'm never going there again, let me tell you."

Phoebe brushed past Heather and went into her own room, but didn't start getting dressed. *She's waiting for me to leave,* Heather thought numbly.

"No kidding, Feeb," Heather said. "I mean, of course you don't want to be a size nine. But you don't want to be a size zero, either. I think you could lighten up, maybe even put on a few pounds."

"Oh, no way," said Phoebe, sounding irritated. "My body is finally the way I want it. No way am I going to sabotage it now." Her eyebrows came together and she looked at Heather with narrowed eyes. "You know, maybe you're just jealous."

Heather didn't know what to say. Her? Heather Gannis? Jealous? Not in a million years. She opened her mouth to say as much to Phoebe, but on second thought, closed it again without a word. Phoebe turned her back on Heather and opened her closet door. "Okay, clear out. I have to get dressed."

It was a dismissal, and Heather cleared out. There was no way she would go to a movie with Phoebe now. Instead, she went to find their mother.

"Mom?" Heather tapped on the door of her mother's bedroom. Mrs. Gannis was stretched out on her bed, reading a magazine.

"Yes?"

Heather took a deep breath. Her mother had never been easy to talk to. It was as if she had done her job by producing three children, and after that, they were kind of on their own. Maybe that wasn't fair. Heather knew it wasn't easy, living with Dad's reversal of fortune. Her mom had signed on for one kind of lifestyle, and now all of a sudden she was practically clipping coupons. But then, it was tough on all of them.

"Mom, have you noticed how Phoebe looks lately?" Feeling like a rat, Heather came in and perched on the end of her mother's bed. If Phoebe knew she was doing this, all hell would break loose.

Mrs. Gannis looked up, smiled. "Yes, she looks marvelous, doesn't she? I'm so proud of her. She looked simply awful when she got back from that college."

"Um, you don't think she looks a little . . . too thin?"

Her mother gave a short laugh. "Oh, you can never be too rich or too thin. Who said that?"

"I don't know," Heather said impatiently. "But you can be too thin, Mom. And Phoebe—you can see her bones. I think she's lost too much weight."

Sitting up, her mother managed to look both insufferably patient and a bit irritated. "Darling, she looks wonderful. There's nothing wrong with her. Heavens, when I was her age, I wore a size two. The women in our family are small-boned, that's all. Now don't worry about Phoebe. I don't want you telling her she's too thin. Next thing you know, she'll be putting on weight again, and we don't want that." She lay back and flipped a page in her magazine.

Dismissed again. Heather went back to her room, feeling more down than she had in oh, about two hours.

How can I express my feelings toward my only brother's only child? I can tell you that I hate my brother, but the word hate doesn't really begin to cover the depth of the feeling I have for him, my identical twin. He is light, I am darkness. He is a plodding government worker—I am exquisitely subtle in my occupation. I have raised what I do to the level of an art. He cannot approach my greatness. Every day that he lives, he taints my own existence. How can I achieve perfection if my identical twin is so flawed, so spineless, so completely lacking in nuance, in grace, in achievement? It is clear that my brother's days must be brought to an end soon. Only by standing alone can I attain my final destiny.

And then there's Gaia. My niece. Katia's child. The child that should have been mine, would have been mine—will someday be mine. Gaia is poised on the brink

of greatness. I can see that now.
Before, I thought she had potential. Now, seeing her reactions
to this latest test, the death of
the girl Mary, I am convinced
Gaia is almost ready to break
free from her restraining
chrysalis. She is showing
strength beyond measure. She is
unclouded by emotion. She is free
of sentimentality. She will come
to me soon.

FEARLESS™

. . . a girl born without the fear gene

People like me don't have friends.

So if Heather wants Ed, she can have him.

I don't care.

Really.

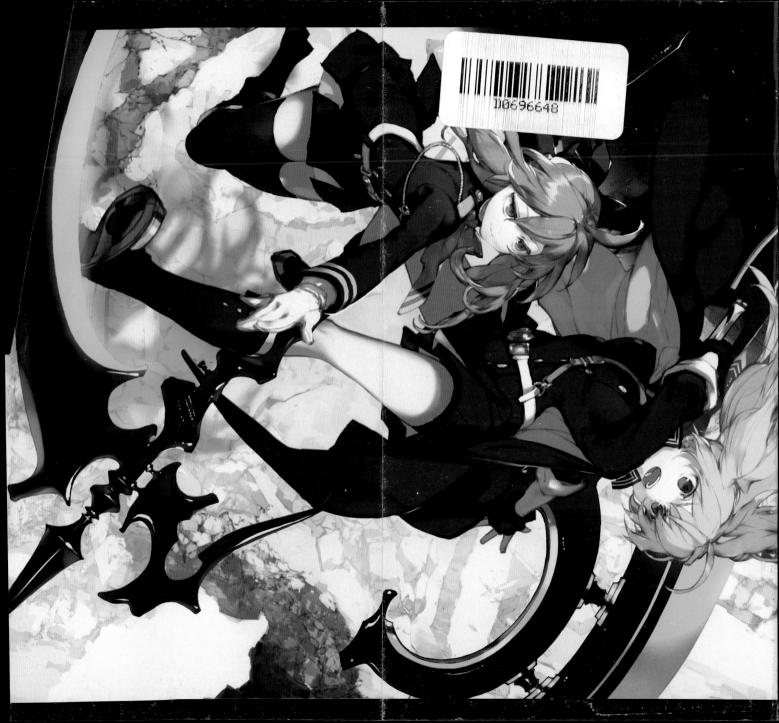

Seraph of the End

—VAMPIRE REIGN—

STORY BY **Takaya Kagami**
ART BY **Yamato Yamamoto**
STORYBOARDS BY **Daisuke Furuya**

CHARACTERS

YOICHI SAOTOME

Yuichiro's friend.
His sister was killed by a vampire.

SHIHO KIMIZUKI

Yuichiro's new companion.
Smart but abrasive.

SHINOA HIRAGI

Guren's subordinate and Yuichiro's
surveillance officer. Member of
the illustrious Hiragi family.

YUICHIRO HYAKUYA

A boy who escaped from the vampire
capital, he has both great kindness and
a great desire for revenge. Lone wolf.

GUREN ICHINOSE

Lieutenant Colonel of the Moon Demon Company,
a Vampire Extermination Unit. He recruited
Yuichiro into the Japanese Imperial Demon Army.

STORY

A mysterious virus decimates the human population, and vampires claim dominion over the world. Yuichiro and his adopted family of orphans are kept as vampire fodder in an underground city until the day Mikaela, Yuichiro's best friend, plots an ill-fated escape for the orphans. Only Yuichiro survives and reaches the surface.

Four years later, after Yuichiro swears revenge against vampires for the death of his family, he is accepted into the Moon Demon Company, a Vampire Extermination Unit in the Japanese Imperial Demon Army. There he meets friends Shinoa, Yoichi and Kimizuki. He also gains Asuramaru, a demon-possessed weapon capable of killing vampires, and finally gets his chance to fight on the front lines.

Meanwhile, Mikaela, thought to be dead, reappears alongside vampires headed to take over the human-held city of Shinjuku.

Seraph of the End
—VAMPIRE REIGN—

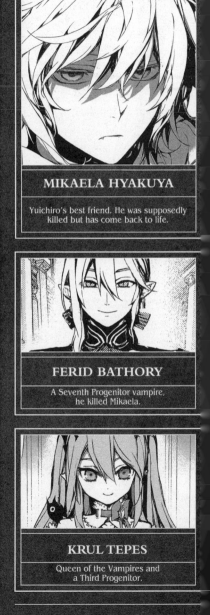

MIKAELA HYAKUYA

Yuichiro's best friend. He was supposedly killed but has come back to life.

FERID BATHORY

A Seventh Progenitor vampire, he killed Mikaela.

KRUL TEPES

Queen of the Vampires and a Third Progenitor.

Seraph of the End
VAMPIRE REIGN

3

CONTENTS

Chapter 8 Mitsuba's Squad

YOU LEFT ME BEHIND, YU...

TO DIE.

THIS DREAM AGAIN.

OH NO.

IT IS A PART OF YOU.

THIS IS THE DARKNESS INSIDE OF YOU.

HA HA!

YOU WILL KEEP HAVING THIS DREAM OVER AND OVER.

AND I...

7

CHAPTER 8
Mitsuba's Squad

YOU HAVE NOTHING TO WORRY ABOUT, LT. COLONEL!

SINCE I'M AN ADULT, I KNOW IGNORING THE WHINY YIPPING OF WEAK, TALENT-LESS LOSERS IS ONLY THE MATURE THING TO DO.

MITSUBA IS PART OF YOUR SQUAD NOW.

NO PICKING FIGHTS, SHINOA.

YES. HERE I AM, MITSU.

KLANG

I'LL CRUSH YOU!!

...

SIGH.

CHING

!!

AHA HA!

CHIK

GRAB

ENOUGH INSUBORDINATION.

CAUSE ANY MORE TROUBLE FOR YOUR *SUPERIOR OFFICER* AND I'LL DUMP YOU BOTH INTO SOLITARY.

OH DEAR.

Urk ....!

I-I'm sorry, sir.

...

SWAT

THERE AREN'T MANY GIRLS OF OUR AGE IN THE MOON DEMON COMPANY, YOU KNOW.

NO, NO. WE GET ALONG VERY WELL!

DON'T YOU TWO GET ALONG?

ANYWAY.

HUH?

I HARDLY CARE ABOUT THAT.

SHE SURE DIDN'T ACT LIKE A FRIEND.

THE MOON DEMON COMPANY GENERALLY OPERATES IN SQUADS OF FIVE.

pat pat

THIS IS YOUR NEW TEAMMATE.

...MEANS SOMEONE WILL BE KILLED.

MOSTLY BECAUSE RUNNING INTO AN ARMED VAMPIRE WITH ANY LESS THAN FIVE...

MITSUBA SANGU.

DON'T GET FULL OF YOURSELF JUST BECAUSE YOU KILLED A FEW OF THOSE.

THE CITY WALLS HAVE PROTECTIVE MAGIC CAST ON THEM, SO ONLY WEAK HORSEMEN CAN COME CLOSE.

HA!

YEAH.

SOME.

SEE, THE MONSTERS WE CALL THE "FOUR HORSEMEN OF JOHN" SUDDENLY APPEARED AFTER THE APOCALYPSE EIGHT YEARS AGO!

ONCE THEY GET A KILOMETER AWAY FROM THE WALLS' MAGIC...

...THEY GET EXPONENTIALLY STRONGER!

WHAT, NERVOUS? YOU'D BETTER BE! YOU WANNA DIE OUT HERE, ROOKIES?!

GOT IT? GOOD! NOW SHUT YOUR MOUTHS, MOVE YOUR FEET AND STAY IN FORMATION!

BLAH BLAH BLAH BLAH

OUT HERE, LOSING YOUR FOCUS FOR EVEN A SECOND INVITES DEATH!

OH!

IT SEEMS SHE'S STARTING TO FEEL RESPONSIBLE FOR THE LIVES OF HER NEW RECRUITS.

ISN'T IT SIMPLY ADORABLE?

AHA HA!

UH, WHAT'S WITH HER?

LOOK. IT'S HARAJUKU STATION.

WHICH MEANS THERE'S BLOOD-SUCKERS HERE—

WE'VE REACHED THE MISSION AREA.

EEEEK!!

THUMP

HELP!!

IF WE TRY TO SAVE THE GIRL, WE WILL BE ATTACKED.

I AGREE.

THIS IS LIKELY A VAMPIRE TRAP.

SHINOA!

SIMPLE.

HOW CAN YOU KNOW THAT?!

WHAT ?!

IT'S IMPOSSIBLE FOR A LITTLE GIRL...

...TO SURVIVE ON HER OWN IN THIS WORLD.

THAT WE SEE HER ALONE NOW MEANS SHE IS BAIT MEANT TO LURE US IN.

THEY AREN'T.

HORSEMEN ONLY ATTACK HUMANS.

HORSEMEN ARE NON-SENTIENT. HOW COULD THEY BE FOLLOWING ORDERS FROM VAMPIRES?

WAIT, HOW CAN SHE BE BAIT?

38

BEAT ME UP TO YOUR HEART'S CONTENT.

SO IF YOU WANNA HIT ME, FINE.

FOR PUTTING YOU ALL IN DANGER.

I DON'T REGRET IT, BUT I DO FEEL BAD.

YOU...!

PEOPLE LIKE YOU...

...THAT I HATE...

IT'S MORONS LIKE YOU...

...WIPE OUT ENTIRE SQUADS.

...MORE THAN ANY-THING!

48

CHAPTER 9 First Extermination

IGNORING ORDERS! ACTING ON HIS OWN!

Shibuya Observation Post

WHO DOES THAT YUICHIRO HYAKUYA THINK HE IS?!

I WON'T STAND FOR IT!

HOW COULD SOMEONE LIKE HIM MAKE IT INTO THE MOON DEMON COMPANY?!

THE TWO CLASHED MIGHTILY AT FIRST.

AND SO...

I CAN'T *BELIEVE* YOU, SHINOA.

!

HUH?

OKAY, I'LL ASK THEN.

HMPH!!

WHA ...?

STMP STMP

CAN YOU TELL ME ABOUT THE VAMPIRES WHO CAUGHT YOU...

...AND WHERE THEY'RE HIDING OUT?

Omotesando Station Entrance, Tokyo

chirp chirp

IT SEEMS THE VAMPIRES ARE HIDING ONE KILOMETER AWAY FROM HARAJUKU...

...IN THE RUINS OF THE OMOTESANDO SUBWAY. THEY KEEP THEIR HUMAN CAPTIVES THERE.

ALL RIGHT.

VAMPIRES TYPICALLY SLEEP BETWEEN EARLY MORNING AND NOON.

THEY OUTNUMBER US AT SEVEN.

THIS IS WHAT THE GIRL YUICHIRO RESCUED HAD TO SAY.

YES, KIMIZUKI?

WE'LL HAVE TO AMBUSH THEM THEN.

...

WHAT IS ALL THIS...?

HUH?

75

I KNEW LT. COLONEL GUREN'S PROTÉGÉ HAD TO BE POWERFUL.

BUT I HARDLY EXPECTED HIM TO BE *THIS* POWERFUL.

OH? PROVE IT!

HE'S STILL WEAKER THAN I AM.

THAT WAS GREAT, YUICHI-RO!

THEY'RE THE LT. COLONEL'S FAVORITE PROBLEM CHILDREN.

TWO BLOCK-HEADS WHO DON'T UNDERSTAND THE MEANING OF "TEAM-WORK."

WHO *ARE* THOSE TWO...?

THAT'S EXACTLY WHY HE CHOSE *YOU* TO TRAIN THEM, DON'T YOU THINK?

...

HEE HEE.

RIGHT.

OKAY EVERY-ONE, FORM UP.

WE'VE STILL GOT FIVE ENEMIES TO—

WHY DID YOU HAVE TO KILL THOSE VAMPIRES ?!

NOW THAT THEY'RE DEAD, WHAT'LL HAPPEN TO US?!

TO OUR CHILDREN ?!

AW. DADDY...

WHAT'S *HIS* DEAL?

YOU DEMON ARMY PEOPLE WON'T EVEN LET US INTO SHIBUYA OR SHINJUKU...

...OR ANYWHERE ELSE, THANKS TO YOUR POPULATION REGULA-TIONS!

HOW ARE WE GOING TO LIVE OUT HERE?!

WHO'S GOING TO PROTECT US FROM ALL THE MONSTERS ?!

LISTEN.

DO YOU THINK YOU'RE HEROES ?!

YOU DAMNED ELITES, LIVING IN YOUR SAFE LITTLE GARDEN BEHIND THOSE MAGIC WALLS...

94

SHIBUYA IS GROWING AND DEVELOPING EVERY DAY.

EXCUSE ME.

YOU SAVED MY DAUGHTER.

I'M THANKFUL FOR THAT.

...

I'M SORRY I SNAPPED.

I AM SURE BY NOW IT HAS ENOUGH ROOM...

...TO ACCOMMODATE THE PEOPLE HERE TODAY.

YES.

COME, LET'S GO.

WHAT?

REALLY?!

CHAPTER 10 **Vampire Attack**

Omotesando, Tokyo

HEY.

CAN YOU REALLY START THE CAR?

QUIET.

THAT'S KINDA AWESOME.

LIKE, REALLY FOR REAL?

108

YEAH, MAYBE WE SHOULDN'T.

MAYBE WE SHOULDN'T MAKE FUN OF SHINOA'S HEIGHT ANYMORE.

Y'KNOW ...

110

112

WHOA!

WHO'S
THAT?!

SKREE

113

114

KLAANG

NOBODY ACT ON THEIR OWN!

OH DEAR. THIS IS BAD.

...!!

wm
wm

TUP

FWOOSH

WE'RE FACING A VAMPIRE ARMED WITH A FIRST-CLASS WEAPON!

HE'S FAR BEYOND ANYTHING WE'VE SEEN—

EH?

....!!

WHAT
?!

WHO DOES THAT BLOOD-SUCKER THINK HE IS?!

THANK GOODNESS...

WE'RE SAVED...

HE MADE FUN OF ME LIKE I WASN'T A THREAT AT ALL!!

OUR ORDERS ARE STILL TO JOIN UP WITH THE SHINJUKU FORCES.

WE NEED TO LEAVE BEFORE THEY CHANGE THEIR MINDS.

CALM DOWN.

WHY?!

WE HAVE CURSED GEAR NOW. HOW CAN THERE STILL BE THAT MUCH OF A POWER GAP?!

DAMN IT...

128

THEN HURRY UP AND TEACH ME!!

...IF YOU LEARN TO USE A FEW CURSES, YOU SHOULD BE ABLE TO FILL IN THAT GAP A LITTLE.

WELL...

WITH YOUR GEAR, YUICHIRO...

HOW-EVER...

ONCE *YOU* ARE ON LEVEL FOOTING WITH A VAMPIRE, THEN WHAT?

MYSELF, MITSU, YOICHI... WE'RE ALL STUCK BEHIND. WE'LL BE KILLED.

THAT IS WHY *ALL* OF US NEED TEAMWORK.

AND I AM PARTICULARLY HAPPY THAT YOU, OF ALL PEOPLE, SUGGESTED A RETREAT.

TODAY'S ENCOUNTER WAS AN EXCELLENT LESSON.

WE WERE EVEN BLESSED TO ESCAPE WITHOUT CASUALTIES.

BUT MOST OF ALL...

Seraph of the End
—VAMPIRE REIGN—

Yuichiro & Co.'s Route

Shinjuku

Route to Shinjuku

Japanese Imperial Demon Army HQ

Omotesando

Shibuya

Battle vs. 9 Vampires

SHINJUKU.

WE FINALLY MADE IT.

CHAPTER 11 Queen's Contract

GWOOO

HURRY!

GRUM

BWROOO

WE ARE UNDER VAMPIRE ATTACK!

EMER-GENCY!

EMER-GENCY!

VAMPIRE FORCES ARE CONCEN-TRATED ON THE WESTERN WALL.

ALL CIVILIANS EVACUATE TO THE EASTERN WALL IMMEDIATELY.

WHAT THE HELL'S GOING ON?!

BWROOO

WHAT ARE THOSE EXTER-MINATION UNITS DOING?!

HOW CAN THEY LET VAMPIRES ATTACK?!

SHINJUKU IS THE JAPANESE IMPERIAL DEMON ARMY'S SECOND CAPITAL!!

...WE HEAD TO THE FRONT LINES!

WOOM

SHIBUYA IS SENDING REINFORCE- MENTS...

THE VAMPIRES ARE ATTACKING IN FORCE!

ALL AVAILABLE SOLDIERS REPORT TO THE WESTERN BATTLE- FRONT!

WHAT'S OUR SQUAD GONNA DO?

WELL?

HOLD OUT UNTIL THEN!

WE ARE A VAMPIRE EXTERMI- NATION UNIT, AREN'T WE?

IF THERE ARE VAMPIRES...

glance

WHOA, CRAP.

HE SPOTTED ME AT *THIS* DISTANCE?

UM, LT. COLONEL GUREN?

I'M NOT SO SURE IT'S A GOOD IDEA TO JUST HANG OUT UP HERE...

2nd Lieutenant Sayuri Hanayori

I'M NOT JUST "HANGING OUT," YOU KNOW.

HUH?

tok

Colonel Mito Jujo

WHAT IS THE MEANING OF THIS, GUREN?

YOU'RE THE ONE WHO ONLY JUST ISSUED THE BATTLE ORDERS.

HARDLY.

YOU'RE LATE, MITO.

LT. COLONEL GUREN.

I HAVE ARRIVED, AS YOU REQUESTED.

LOOKS LIKE SOMETHING BIG'S IN THE OFFING, EH?

2nd Lieutenant Shigure Yukimi

SO WHAT'S THE PLAN?

FROM THE LOOKS OF IT, THE SHINJUKU EXTERMINATION UNITS GOT CAUGHT TOTALLY FLAT-FOOTED.

EXCELLENT.

MY SQUAD'S ALL HERE.

Colonel Norito Goshi

YOUR SQUAD?

I AM A DAUGHTER OF THE PRESTIGIOUS JUJO FAMILY. I AM NOT PART OF *YOUR* SQUAD.

QUIT YOUR YAPPING.

144

146

153

Four Years Ago

THUD

IT SEEMS WE'LL HAVE TO REMIND THESE UPPITY HUMANS OF THEIR PLACE.

LACUS. RENÉ. GATHER EVERYONE AND KEEP ALL BUT THAT MONSTER IN THE MIDDLE BUSY, ALL RIGHT?

AS FOR YOU, MIKA...

GIVE ME MORE POWER...

HERE WE GO.

...DEMON BLADE: "MAHIRU-NO-YO."

* Ed: Mahiru-no-yo = "midday's night"

BECAUSE THAT WAS YOUR LAST SUPPER.

170

172

OKAY.

WE'VE PRETTY MUCH KILLED OFF EVERYTHING BY THE GATE.

IT DOESN'T SEEM SO AT THE MOMENT.

IS THE ENEMY ATTACKING ANYWHERE ELSE?

HAVEN'T ANY OTHER EXTERMINATION UNITS ARRIVED?

YOU THERE. GUARDS.

THE FOLLOWING IS AN ORDER TO ALL ACTIVE UNITS!

ATTENTION! ATTENTION!

...THE HERO WHO RETOOK SHINJUKU FROM THE VAMPIRES WITH ONLY ONE SQUAD, HAS ENTERED THE FIELD!

MOON DEMON COMPANY COMMANDER, LT. COLONEL GUREN ICHINOSE...

JUST NOW...

EVERYONE REDOUBLE YOUR EFFORTS! WE MUST HOLD OUT!

THE TIDE OF BATTLE IS ABOUT TO TURN!

GUREN ...?

THE VAMPIRE COMMANDER IS STATIONED THERE.

PROCEED TO THE 5TH STREET INTERSECTION IMMEDIATELY.

THE FOLLOW-ING IS AN ORDER FROM LT. COLONEL ICHINOSE.

ADDITION-ALLY... ATTENTION SHINOA SQUAD.

REPEAT, PROCEED TO THE 5TH STREET INTERSECTION IMMEDIATELY!

THE 5TH STREET INTER-SECTION? WHERE'S THAT?

NOT FAR FROM HERE!

THEN LET'S GET GOING!

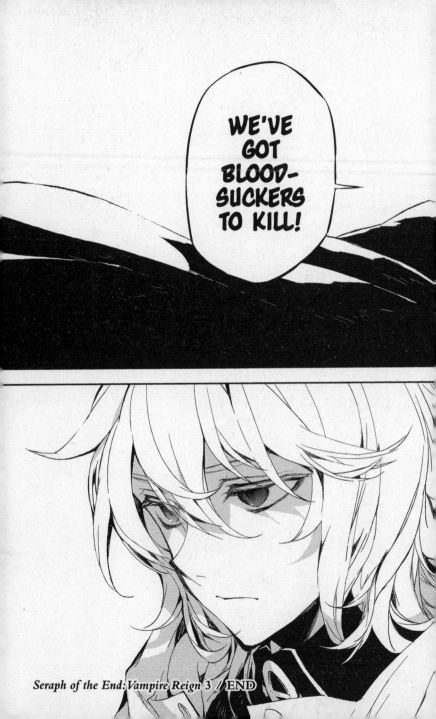

Seraph of the End: Vampire Reign 3 / END

Seraph of the End
VAMPIRE REIGN

HELLO, I'M TAKAYA KAGAMI. HERE'S THE THIRD INSTALLMENT. HOPE YOU LIKE IT!

FERID BATHORY

FERID: "AAH, THE TIME HAS FINALLY COME FOR VAMPIRES TO TAKE THE STAGE. HOW ARE YOU DOING, MY LOVELY LITTLE LAMBS? MY FAVORITE FOOD IS THE BLOOD OF BEAUTIFUL BOYS AND GIRLS. READ MORE ABOUT ME IN MY PROFILE."

A Seventh Progenitor, Ferid is a high-ranking vampire noble. Silver-haired and elegant, he is one of the prettiest characters in the series. However, for some odd reason I wrote that he was golden-haired in the novel, leading Mr. Yamamoto to ask me, via our editor, if there was going to be an event that would turn his hair silver. That was a small moment of panic for me. I don't know why, but that day I was convinced he had golden hair.

FERID: "I SEE. MY BEAUTY HAD SIMPLY BEWITCHED YOU."

Shut up.

KRUL TEPES

A Third Progenitor, she is the queen of the underground vampire city of Sanguinem. She was originally scheduled to appear in Chapter 1, but due to length constraints her introduction was moved to Chapter 5. She was going to show up, kick Ferid's butt and drink Mika's blood, but the storyboards for that looked like they'd run over 100 pages, so we gave up on that idea. (Yeah, that's way too long. ^_^)

KRUL: "THAT FIRST CHAPTER SHOULD HAVE SHOWN ME *KILLING* FERID."

FERID: "AWWW!"

She may look young, but she is as close to the highest rank a vampire can attain, so she is likely the most powerful vampire in this setting.

Character Materials Collection by Takaya Kagami

On Weapon Strength

Because more and more weapons and Cursed Gear have made an appearance in the manga, I thought I would write a little about their relative strengths.

However, if I am going to discuss that in any depth, I will need to start by talking about the equipment available before the apocalypse—in that last year depicted in the *Seraph of the End* novel, *Guren Ichinose's Catastrophe at 16.*

Eight years ago, there were two competing systems of magic. One was a compendium of traditional magic espoused by the religious group known as "The Emperor's Demons," led by the Hiragi family. The other was a hybrid system of world magics put forward by another religious group, the Hyakuya Sect.

Fey Blade: Kujakumaru / Guren Ichinose

Diamond Yasha Spells / Mito Jujo

Hidden Weapons / Shigure Yukimi

However, Cursed Gear was so powerful that it revolutionized the world. Cursed Gear was developed by Guren's lover, the genius spellcaster Mahiru Hiragi. Once a means of mass-producing Cursed Gear was discovered, the old compendium of traditional magics quickly fell into disuse. With their new invention, humanity became a force capable of standing against vampires.

A test subject in Cursed Gear experiments / Mahiru Hiragi

Images from *Seraph of the End: Guren Ichinose's Catastrophe at 16*

Mass–Produced Cursed Gear

Anyone with basic spellcraft knowledge can pick up the downgraded, mass-produced version of Cursed Gear and get a minor boost in strength. The Japanese Imperial Demon Army makes widespread use of it. Yu's weapon in chapter 2 was a mass-produced Cursed Gear sword. One of these weapons gives a regular person three to four times their normal athletic ability.

In comparison, even these downgraded weapons are massively stronger than what Guren and his friends used during the novel timeframe. Cursed Gear is that incredibly powerful.

Seven humans working together and bearing mass-produced Cursed Gear should be able to kill a single unarmed vampire. However, if that vampire is carrying a second-class weapon, then an entire unit of humans with mass-produced Cursed Gear would be necessary to kill it. Even then, it would be a tough fight to win.

Shikama Doji / Shinoa Hiragi

Cursed Gear

Cursed Gear is a weapon with a demon sealed inside of it. Before the apocalypse, confining a demon inside of a weapon had never worked before. Even researching it was forbidden, but that did not stop thousands of human experiments from being conducted on the subject. In the present day not only has a method been discovered, it has been converted to daily use.

Cursed Gear increases a normal person's standard ability sevenfold. Anyone bearing the top rank of Cursed Gear, the Black Demon Series, is easily capable of killing multiple vampires with second-class weapons. However, if the Cursed Gear is not Black Demon Series, a one-on-one match with a vampire carrying a second-class weapon becomes an even battle, if not one still tilted in the vampire's favor. Accordingly, teamwork and formations are necessary.

There remain a few tricks to learning how to use the power of Cursed Gear fully, but those will be introduced at a later date.

Black Demon Series / Shiho Kimizuki

Black Demon Series / Yoichi Saotome

Mitsuba Sangu

Black Demon Series:
Mahiru-no-yo / Guren Ichinose

Black Demon Series:
Asuramaru / Yuichiro Hyakuya

AFTERWORD

HELLO. I'M TAKAYA KAGAMI, AUTHOR OF *SERAPH OF THE END*. THIS TIME I'VE BEEN GIVEN NINE WHOLE PAGES OF BONUS CONTENT TO COVER, SO I THOUGHT I'D TALK A LITTLE ABOUT THE WORLD BEFORE THE APOCALYPSE, AS SHOWN IN THE KODANSHA LIGHT NOVEL SERIES *SERAPH OF THE END: GUREN ICHINOSE'S CATASTROPHE AT 16.* I EVEN BORROWED A FEW ILLUSTRATIONS, LIKE THE ONE BELOW.

THIS IS AN ILLUSTRATION OF WHEN GUREN AND HIS TEAMMATES SAYURI, SHIGURE, MITO AND NORITO WERE ALL IN HIGH SCHOOL. YU AND MIKA WERE ONLY EIGHT YEARS OLD AT THE TIME. WHAT DO YOU THINK? IF YOU LIKE WHAT YOU SEE, I HOPE YOU'LL CONSIDER PICKING UP THE LIGHT NOVEL.

SO, FIVE PAGES ABOUT THE SETTING MEANS I HAVE FOUR PAGES LEFT FOR AN AFTERWORD. LAST VOLUME, THE DESIGNER REALLY SPIFFED UP MY SHORT AFTERWORD, ADDING SOME CHARACTER DESIGNS FROM MR. YAMAMOTO AND ARRANGING IT ALL TO FLOW INTO AN AD FOR THE NEXT VOLUME. I THOUGHT THAT WAS REALLY COOL. YOU NEVER GET NEAT ILLUSTRATIONS LIKE THAT IN A NOVEL'S AFTERWORD. WHEN I FIRST SAW THE ROUGH LAYOUT I WAS STUNNED BY HOW AWESOME IT LOOKED.

I'VE HAD SOME OF MY NOVELS REMADE AS MANGA BY VARIOUS ARTISTS BEFORE, BUT THIS IS THE FIRST TIME I'VE BUILT THE MANGA AND NOVEL FROM SCRATCH, WRITING CHAPTERS FOR BOTH EVERY MONTH. SEEING EVEN MY AFTERWORDS GETTING THE MANGA TREATMENT GIVES ME SOME INSIGHT INTO HOW MANGA WORKS AND WHAT IT'S LIKE. IT'S ENLIGHTENING.

HOW SERIALIZATION WORKS, DEADLINES, THE PROCESS OF PUTTING IT TOGETHER: EVERYTHING IS NEW TO ME, MAKING IT ALL VERY EXCITING.

EXCITING, BUT ALSO BUSY. AND NOT HAVING ANY RECENT HAPPENINGS WORTH TALKING ABOUT IN AN AFTERWORD CAN BE PROBLEMATIC TOO.

SO, YEAH. I'VE RUN OUT OF THINGS TO SAY, BUT I STILL HAVE PAGES LEFT TO FILL. THIS TIME, I THINK I'LL TALK A LITTLE ABOUT HOW *SERAPH OF THE END: VAMPIRE REIGN* IS MADE, AND HOW THE THREE OF US GO ABOUT PUTTING IT TOGETHER. HERE IS HOW IT WORKS:

1. KAGAMI THINKS UP THE CHARACTERS, SETTING AND CONCEPT FOR THE CHAPTER AND KEEPS IT IN LINE WITH THE OVERALL STORY.

2. IF NEW CHARACTERS, SETTINGS, WEAPONS, ETC. ARE INVOLVED, A REQUEST GOES TO YAMATO YAMAMOTO FOR DESIGNS. UTTERLY AWESOME DESIGNS COME BACK, DELIGHTFULLY SURPRISING KAGAMI.

3. KAGAMI WRITES A SCRIPT FOR FOUR CHAPTERS' WORTH OF CONTENT AND PRESENTS IT TO THE EDITOR FOR DISCUSSION. (FOUR CHAPTERS EQUALS ONE VOLUME, SO I TRY TO WORK IN FOUR-CHAPTER CHUNKS, BUT RECENTLY I'M ONLY MANAGING TWO-CHAPTER CHUNKS. (T_T) ONCE THE EDITOR GIVES THE OKAY, IT GOES TO STORYBOARD ARTIST DAISUKE FURUYA.

(CONTINUED ON NEXT PAGE)

4. STORYBOARD ARTIST FURUYA COMES UP WITH MIND-BLOWINGLY AMAZING STORYBOARDS PERFECTLY IN LINE WITH WHAT KAGAMI WANTED. SOMETIMES HE EXPANDS THE IDEAS FAR BEYOND THE EXPECTED, AMAZING KAGAMI FURTHER.

5. YAMAMOTO DRAWS THE MANGA ACCORDING TO THE STORYBOARDS. THIS IS THE FINAL PRODUCT THAT EVERYONE SEES WHEN THEY OPEN THE FINISHED MANGA. IT'S REALLY COOL.

6. TYPESETTING IS DONE ON THE FINISHED ART. THE EDITOR EDITS, RED INK GOING EVERYWHERE. A CALL GOES TO KAGAMI SAYING, "THERE'S NO TIME LEFT, I NEED YOU TO LOOK AT THIS PDF WITHIN THE NEXT HOUR AND GET BACK TO ME!!" KAGAMI JUMPS UP AND PROOFREADS THE WORK FOR ERRORS LIKE MISSPELLINGS AND CHARACTERS USING THE WRONG NICKNAMES. (THIS IS WHY I TRY TO BE AT HOME AT THE END OF EVERY MONTH ^_^)

7. EDITOR REALIZES THERE ARE NO CHAPTER TITLES. KAGAMI QUICKLY CHURNS SOME OUT. (I USUALLY COME UP WITH THE TITLES IN FOUR-CHAPTER CHUNKS, BUT SOMETIMES THERE ARE SLIPS ^_^)

AND IT'S FINISHED! WRITING IT OUT LIKE THIS MAKES IT SEEM PRETTY SIMPLE, BUT SEEING HOW WONDERFUL THE STORYBOARDS, THE MANGA AND EVERYTHING ELSE TURNS OUT EACH TIME REALLY MAKES ME GRATEFUL TO WORK WITH SUCH WONDERFUL PEOPLE. THANK YOU VERY MUCH.

WELL, I THINK THIS TOPIC HAS FILLED A GOOD NUMBER OF PAGES, BUT SINCE, UNLIKE NOVELS, WORD-COUNT AND LINE-COUNT PER PAGE CAN BE DIFFERENT DUE TO LAYOUT, I'M NOT SURE IF THIS WILL BE ENOUGH. I HAVE NO IDEA WHAT I'M GOING TO DO IF THERE'S A LOT OF BLANK PAGES LEFT AFTER THIS. (^_^)

OH, WAIT! I JUST CAME UP WITH AN IDEA THAT'LL FILL MORE SPACE. IN THE MOST RECENT VOLUME OF MY OTHER NOVEL SERIES, *THE LEGEND OF THE LEGENDARY HEROES* (PUBLISHED BY FUJIMI SHOBOKAN), WE DECIDED THAT WE WOULD TRADE PLUGS FOR EACH SERIES, SO I GOT TO DO A FULL TWO-PAGE AD FOR *SERAPH OF THE END: VAMPIRE REIGN* IN THAT VOLUME! AND I HAVEN'T YET DONE A PLUG FOR *LOTLH* HERE! BUT I DON'T THINK I HAVE THAT MANY PAGES LEFT, SO THAT WILL HAVE TO WAIT UNTIL NEXT VOLUME. SORRY! (I REALLY HOPE MY EDITORS FOR THAT SERIES DON'T GET MAD AT ME!)

SO YEAH, THAT'S ALL FOR THIS TIME.

TAKAYA KAGAMI

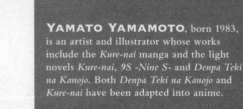

A brilliant sketch of Yuichiro by the author!

TAKAYA KAGAMI is a prolific light novelist whose works include the action and fantasy series *The Legend of the Legendary Heroes*, which has been adapted into manga, anime and a video game. His previous series, *A Dark Rabbit Has Seven Lives*, also spawned a manga and anime series.

❝ I have an office, but I don't go to it. My desk at home is covered in books, so I go to family restaurants to write. But in a burst of determination, I built a home office. So now that I have three places to get three times the work done, I present to you volume 3. I hope you like it! ❞

YAMATO YAMAMOTO, born 1983, is an artist and illustrator whose works include the *Kure-nai* manga and the light novels *Kure-nai*, *9S -Nine S-* and *Denpa Teki na Kanojo*. Both *Denpa Teki na Kanojo* and *Kure-nai* have been adapted into anime.

❝ Yuichiro finally joins the battle against the vampires. He has even more friends. I'm sure they'll grant him even greater power too. I hope you enjoy it. ❞

DAISUKE FURUYA previously assisted Yamato Yamamoto with storyboards for *Kure-nai*.

Seraph of the End

—VAMPIRE REIGN—

VOLUME 3
SHONEN JUMP ADVANCED MANGA EDITION

STORY BY **TAKAYA KAGAMI**
ART BY **YAMATO YAMAMOTO**
STORYBOARDS BY **DAISUKE FURUYA**

TRANSLATION **Adrienne Beck**
TOUCH-UP ART & LETTERING **Sabrina Heep**
DESIGN **Shawn Carrico**
EDITOR **Hope Donovan**

OWARI NO SERAPH © 2012 by Takaya Kagami,
Yamato Yamamoto, Daisuke Furuya
All rights reserved. First published in Japan in 2012 by SHUEISHA Inc., Tokyo.
English translation rights arranged by SHUEISHA Inc.

The stories, characters and incidents mentioned in this
publication are entirely fictional.

Printed in the U.S.A.

Published by VIZ Media, LLC
P.O. Box 77010
San Francisco, CA 94107

10 9 8 7 6 5 4 3 2 1
First printing, December 2014

www.viz.com   www.shonenjump.com

YOU'RE READING THE
WRONG WAY!

SERAPH OF THE END
reads from right to left,
starting in the upper-right
corner. Japanese is read
from right to left, meaning
that action, sound effects,
and word-balloon order are
completely reversed from
English order.

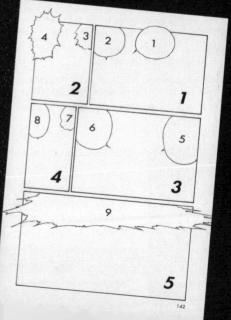

142

Also by Ruth Rendell
Published by Ballantine Books:

THE FEVER TREE AND OTHER
STORIES OF SUSPENSE

THE KILLING DOLL

LIVE FLESH

MASTER OF THE MOOR

THE NEW GIRL FRIEND AND OTHER
STORIES OF SUSPENSE

THE SECRET HOUSE OF DEATH

THE TREE OF HANDS

VANITY DIES HARD

CHIEF INSPECTOR WEXFORD SERIES

THE BEST MAN TO DIE

DEATH NOTES

FROM DOON WITH DEATH

A GUILTY THING SURPRISED

SINS OF THE FATHERS

SPEAKER OF MANDARIN

AN UNKINDNESS OF RAVENS

WOLF TO THE SLAUGHTER

TO FEAR A PAINTED DEVIL

BALLANTINE BOOKS • NEW YORK

the sleeping and the dead
Are but as pictures: 'tis the eye of childhood
that fears a painted devil

MACBETH

ʕʕʕʕʕʕʕ   **PROLOGUE**   ʕʕʕʕʕʕ

HE WAS NINE. IT WAS HIS FIRST MORNING IN EN-
gland and he began to wonder if all English houses
were like this one, large yet with small rooms, full of
things that no one could use: armless statues, vases
with lids to them, curtains as immovably draped as
one of his mother's evening gowns.

They had arrived the night before and he had
passed through the hall wrapped in a blanket and
carried in his father's arms. He remembered only the
great front door, a heavy wooden door with a picture
of a tree on it in coloured glass. They had left him to
sleep as long as he would and someone had brought
breakfast for him on a tray. Now as he descended the
stairs, crossing the half-landing which a bronze sol-
dier guarded with his lance, he saw the hall below
him and his steps faltered.

It was a fine morning but the room looked as

1

rooms do at twilight, dim and still. Instead of being papered the walls were hung with embroideries stretched on frames, and between them curtains that covered—what? Windows? Doors? It seemed to him that they covered things people were not supposed to see. There was a single mirror with a wooden frame and this frame, of carved and polished red wood, looked as if it had grown branches of its own, for strips of wood shaped into leaves and twigs twined across the glass.

Within this mirror he could see not himself but an open door reflected and beyond it the beginning of the garden. The door stood wide and he went through it, seeking the garden where he knew the sun must be shining. Then he saw the picture. He stood quite still and he stared at it.

It was a painting of a lady in an old-fashioned dress of striped silk, bright blue and gold, with a little gold cap on her head. She was holding a silver plate and in the plate was the head of a man.

He knew it must be a very good painting because the artist had made it look so real. Nothing was left out, not even the blood in the plate and the white tube things in the man's neck where it had been cut from his body.

The lady wasn't looking at the thing in the plate but at him. She was smiling and there was a strange expression on her face, dreamy, triumphant, replete. He had never seen such a look in anyone's eyes before but suddenly he knew with an intuition that had in it something of an *a priori* knowledge, that grown-ups sometimes looked at each other like that and that they did so out of the sight of children.

He tore his eyes from the picture and put his hand

up to his mouth to stop them hearing his scream. Then he rushed blindly away, making for the glass place that separated this room from the garden.

He stumbled at the step and put out his hand to save himself. It touched something cool and soft but only for a moment. The coolness and softness were succeeded by a terrible burning pain that seemed to smite him exactly like the shock he had had from his mother's electric iron.

Away in the garden someone laughed. He screamed and screamed and screamed until he heard doors banging, feet flying, the women coming to him from the kitchen.

PART ONE

ʄʄʄʄʄʄʄʄʄʄʄʄʄʄʄʄʄʄ **1** ʄʄʄʄʄʄ

'PRUSSIC ACID?' THE CHEMIST WAS STARTLED. HE had been a member of the Pharmaceutical Society for ten years and this was the first time anyone had made such a request to him. Not that he would grant it. He was a responsible citizen, almost—in his own estimation—a doctor. 'Cyanide of Potassium?' He looked severely at the small man in the suit that was too dark and too thick for a hot day. 'What d'you want that for?'

Edward Carnaby, for his part, was affronted. Mr. Waller was only a chemist, a pharmacist really, not a proper chemist who worked in a laboratory. Everyone knew that doctors poked their noses into one's affairs, trying to find out things that were no business of theirs, but not chemists. You asked for what you wanted—razor blades or shaving cream or a camera film—and the chemist gave it to you. He wrapped it

7

up and you paid for it. When all was said and done, Waller was only a shopkeeper.

'I want it for killing wasps. I've got a wasp nest on the wall of my house under the roof.'

He fidgeted uneasily under Waller's accusing gaze. The fan on the ceiling, instead of cooling the shop, was only blowing the hot air about.

'May I have your name, please?'

'What for? I don't have to have a prescription for it, do I?'

Waller ignored the sarcasm. Responsible professional men must not allow themselves to be ruffled by cheap cracks.

'What gave you the idea of cyanide?' As he spoke the curtain of coloured plastic strips that hung across the entrance to the dispensary parted and Linda Gaveston came out in her pink overall. Her appearance angered Edward, partly because she looked so cool, partly because he felt that a girl whose parents lived on Linchester had no business to be working as an assistant in a chemist's shop. She smiled at him vaguely. Edward snapped:

'If you must know, I read about it in a gardening book.'

Plausible, Waller thought.

'Rather an old-fashioned book, surely? These days we get rid of wasps by using a reliable vespicide.' He paused, allowing the unfamiliar word to sink in. 'One that is harmless to warm-blooded...'

'All right,' Edward interrupted him. He wasn't going to make a scene in front of one of those snooty Gavestons. 'Why didn't you say so before? I'll take it. What's it called?'

'Vesprid.' Waller shot him a last baleful look and

turned round, but the girl—showing off, Edward thought—was already holding the tin towards him. 'Two and eleven.'

'Thanks,' Edward said shortly, taking the penny change.

'The instructions are enclosed.'

Linda Gaveston lifted her shoulders slightly and slipped between the waving strips in the way she had seen a night club girl insinuate herself through a bead curtain on television.

'There goes a nut,' she said to Waller when Edward had gone. 'He lives near us.'

'Really?' Like all the shopkeepers in Chantflower village Waller had a great respect for Linchester. Money flowed from it as from a spring of sweet water. 'Not quite what one has been led to expect.' He watched Edward get into his salesman's car, its back seat full of cardboard boxes. 'It takes all sorts,' he said.

On that hot afternoon Freda Carnaby was the only Linchester housewife who was really working and she was not a wife at all. She was cleaning windows in the single living room of Edward's chalet partly because it was a good excuse for watching the cars coming round The Circle. Linchester business men kept short hours and the man she was looking for might be early. He would wave, even perhaps stop and renew his promise to see her later, and he would notice afresh how efficient she was, how womanly. Moreover he would see that she could look smart and pretty not only in the evenings but also with a wash leather in her hand.

Considering who she was looking for it was ironic

that the first car to appear was Tamsin Selby's. Even if you didn't see the number plate (SIN 1-A) you would know it was Tamsin's Mini because, although it was new, its black body and white roof were already marked with raindrops and with dust, and the back seat was full of leaves and twigs, rubbish from the fields. Freda pursed her lips in happy disapproval. If you had money and you bought nice things (what that monogram of a number plate must have cost!) you ought to take care of them.

Dr. Greenleaf's car followed fast on her tail. It was time, Freda considered, that he bought a new one. A doctor, she had read in one of her magazines, was nowadays the most respected member of a community, and therefore had appearances to keep up. She smiled and bobbed her head. She thought the doctor's kindly grin meant he was grateful to her for being so healthy and not taking up his surgery time.

By the time Joan Smith-King arrived with her shooting brake full of the Linchester children she had fetched from school, Freda had finished the window.

'All delivered in plain vans,' Joan said cheerfully, 'Den says I ought to have a C licence.'

'Can I go to tea with Peter?' Cheryl called. 'Can I, Auntie Free? Please.'

'If you're sure she's no trouble,' Freda said. Cheryl might be only a salesman's daughter, but she had nice manners. She, Freda, had seen to that. But going out to tea was a nuisance. Now Cheryl would come rushing in at seven just when Freda wanted to be relaxed and ready with coffee cups on the best traycloth, paper napkins and sherry in a decanter.

'Ghastly these wasps.' Joan looked up at the chalet roof where the wasps were dribbling out from under the eaves. 'Tamsin said Patrick got a nasty sting on his hand.'

'Did he?' Freda took her eyes from Joan's face and stared innocently at the hedge. 'Don't be late,' she said to Cheryl. Joan moved off, one hand on her wheel, the other pulling Jeremy off Peter, shoving her daughter Susan into Cheryl's lap. The baby in its carry-cot on the front seat began to cry. Freda went round the back and into the spotless kitchen.

She was re-doing her face from the little *cache* of cosmetics she kept in a drawer when she heard Edward's car draw up on the drive. The front door slammed.

'Free?'

She bustled into the lounge. Edward was already at the record-player, starting up The Hall of the Mountain King.

'You might have shut the gates,' she said from the window, but she didn't press the point. A wife could expect small services, not a sister. A sister was only a housekeeper, a nanny to Edward's motherless daughter. Still ... she cheered up. A couple of years and she might have a child of her own.

'How long till tea?'

'Five thirty sharp,' said Freda. 'I'm sure I never keep you waiting for your meals, Ted.'

'Only it's car maintenance at seven.'

Edward went to a different class each night. French on Mondays and Thursdays, accountancy on Tuesdays, carpentry on Wednesdays, car maintenance on Fridays. Freda approved his industry. It was a way, she supposed, of forgetting the wife who had lived just long enough to put the curtains up in the

11

new house and who had died before the first installment was due on the mortgage.

'What are you going to do?'

She shrugged. He was her brother, but he was also
her twin and as jealous of her time as a husband
might be.

'Sometimes,' he said, 'I wonder if you haven't got a
secret boy-friend who pops in when I'm out of the
way.'

Had there been talk, gossip? Well, why not? Only a
few days now and everyone would know. Edward would
know. Funny but it made her shiver to think of it.

He turned the record over and straightened up.
Solveig's Song, music for a cold climate, roared into
the stuffy room. The pure voice pleased Freda, reminding her of large uncluttered rooms she had so far
seen only from the outside as she passed with her
shopping baskets. On the whole, she thought, she
would like to live there. She wouldn't be squeamish.
He loves me, she thought, not thinking of Edward. A
long shudder of pain and anxious happiness travelled
down from her shoulders and along her thighs to her
feet in their tight pointed shoes.

'I wouldn't like that, Free,' he said. 'You're best off
here with me.'

'We shall have to see what time brings forth, shan't
we?' she said, staring through the diamond panes at
Linchester, at ten more houses that encircled a green
plot. How nice, how stimulating it would be next year
to see it all from a different angle. When she turned
round Edward was beside her, flicking his fingers in
front of her face to break up the myopic stare.

'Don't,' she said. Hurt, he sat down and opened his
homework book, *An Outline of Monetary Economics*.

12

Freda went upstairs to lacquer her hair, straighten her stocking seams and spray a little more Fresh Mist under her arms.

DENHOLM SMITH-KING WAS USED TO PERFORMING small and, for that matter, large services for his wife. With five children he could hardly do otherwise. He was already at home when she arrived back, making what he called euphemistically 'a cup of tea.' In the Smith-King household this meant slicing and buttering a whole large loaf and carving up a couple of pound cakes.

'You're early,' she said.

'Not much doing.' He greeted Cheryl vaguely as if he was uncertain whether or not she was one of his own children. 'Things are a bit slack so I hied me to the bosom of my family.'

'Slack?' She found a tablecloth and spread it on what had once been a fine unblemished sheet of teak. 'I don't like the sound of that, Den. I'm always meaning to talk to you about the business. . . .'

'Did you find anyone to sit in with the mob tomorrow night?' he asked, adroitly changing the subject.

'Linda Gaveston said she'd come, I asked her when I was in Waller's.' Joan found the piece of pasteboard from the mêlée on the mantelpiece and read its message aloud: 'Tamsin and Patrick Selby At Home, Saturday, July 4th, eight p.m. Of course I know how affected Tamsin is, but At Home's going a bit far.'

'I reckon you can go as far as you like,' said Denholm, 'when you've got a private income and no kids.'

'It's only a birthday party. She's twenty-seven tomorrow.'

13

Denholm sat down heavily, a reluctant pater-familias at the head of his table. 'Twenty-seven? I wouldn't have put her at a day over twenty.'

'Oh, don't be so silly, Den. They've been married for years.' She had been piqued by his admiration of another woman, but now she looked at him tenderly over their children's heads. 'Fancy being married for years to Patrick Selby!'

'I daresay it's all a matter of taste, old girl.'

'I don't know what it is,' Joan said, 'but he frightens me. I get the shivers every time I see him walking past here with that great German dog of his.' She wiped the baby's chin and sighed. 'It came in the garden again this morning. Tamsin was most apologetic. I'll grant her that. She's a nice enough girl in her way, only she always seems only half awake.'

'Pity they haven't got any kids,' Denholm said wistfully. Uncertain as to whether he was wishing children on to the Selbys from genuine regret for their childlessness or from motives of revenge, Joan gave him a sharp look.

'They're first cousins, you know.'

'Ah,' said Denholm, 'brought up together. One of those boy and girl things, was it?'

'I don't know,' said his wife. 'He's not likely to confide in anyone and she's far too much of the little girl lost.'

When tea was over the children drifted into the garden. Joan handed her husband a tea towel and began to wash up. Jeremy's scream made them both jump and before it had died away Denholm, who knew what it meant, was out on the lawn brandishing the stick he kept in the storm porch for this purpose.

Only Cheryl had not backed away. The other children clung to Denholm as he advanced between the swing and the sandpit.

'Get out of it, you great brute!'

The Weimaraner looked at him courteously but with a kind of mild disdain. There was nothing savage about her but nothing endearing either. She was too autocratic, too highly-bred for that. Haunch-deep in marigolds, she was standing in the middle of Denholm's herbaceous border and now, as he shouted at her again, she flicked out a raspberry pink tongue and delicately snapped off a larkspur blossom.

Cheryl caught at Denholm's hand. 'She's a nice dog, really she is. She often comes to our house.'

Her words meant nothing to Denholm but he dropped the stick. Insensitive as he was, he could hardly beat the dog in the presence of the woman who had appeared so suddenly and so silently on the lawn next door.

'Queenie often comes to our house,' Cheryl said again.

Tamsin Selby had heard. A spasm of pain crossed her smooth brown face and was gone.

'I'm so dreadfully sorry.' She smiled without showing her teeth. 'Please don't be cross, Denholm. She's very gentle.'

Denholm grinned foolishly. The Selbys, both of them, always made him feel a fool. It was the contrast, perhaps, between their immaculate garden and his own cluttered playground; their pale hand-stitched clothes and what he called his 'togs'; their affluence and his need.

'It put the wind up the youngsters,' he said gruffly.

'Come on, Queenie!' The long brown arm rose languidly in an elegant parabola. At once the dog leaped, clearing the hedge with two inches to spare. 'I hope we'll see you tomorrow, Denholm?'

'You can count on us. Never miss a good booze—up.' He was embarrassed and he went in quickly. But Cheryl lingered, staring over the hedge with curious intelligent eyes and wondering why the lady who was so unlike Auntie Free had fallen to her knees under the willow tree and flung her arms round the dog's creamy sable neck.

ffffffffffffffffff **2** ffffff

FIVE YEARS BEFORE WHEN NOTTINGHAMSHIRE
people talked about Linchester they meant the Manor
and the park. If they were county they remembered
garden parties, if not, coach trips to a Palladian house
where you paid half-a-crown to look at a lot of valuable but boring china while the children rolled down
the ha-ha. But all that came to an end when old Marvell died. One day, it seemed, the Manor was there,
the next there were just the bulldozers Henry Glide
brought over from the city and a great cloud of dust
floating above the trees, grey and pancake-shaped, as
if someone had exploded a small atom bomb.

Nobody would live there, they said, forgetting that
commuting was the fashion even in the provinces.
Henry himself had his doubts and he had put up
three chalet bungalows before he realised he might
be on to a better thing if he forgot all about retired

17

farmers and concentrated on Nottingham company directors. Fortunately, but by the merest chance, the three mistakes were almost hidden by a screen of elms. He nearly lost his head and built big houses with small gardens all over the estate, but he had a cautious look at the Marvell contract and saw that there was an embargo on too much tree-felling. His wife thought he was getting senile when he said he was only going to put up eight more houses, eight beautiful architect-designed houses around a broad green plot with a pond in the middle.

And that was what people meant now when they talked about Linchester. They meant The Green with the pond where swans glided between lily leaves as big as dinner plates; The Circle which was a smart name for the road that ran around The Green; the Cotswold farmhouse and the mock-Tudor lodge, the Greenleafs' place that might have been prefabricated in Hampstead Garden Suburb and flown complete into Nottinghamshire, the Selbys' glass box and Glide's own suntrap bungalow. They pointed from the tops of buses on the Nottingham road at the Gavestons' pocket-sized grange, the Gages' Queen Anne and the Smith-King place that had started off as a house and now was just a breeding box. They criticised the chalets, those poor relations and their occupants, the Saxtons, the Macdonalds and the Carnabys.

The two men in the British Railways lorry lived in Newark and they had never been to Linchester before. Now, on the calmest, most beautiful evening of the summer, they saw it at its best. Yet it was not the loveliness of the place that impressed them, the elegant sweep of The Circle, the stone pineapples on the

18

pillars at the Manor gates, nor the trees, elms, oaks and sycamores, that gave each house its expensive privacy, but the houses themselves and their opulence.

Over-awed and at the same time suspicious, they drove between the pillars and into The Circle itself, looking for a house called Hallows.

The lorry rumbled along the road, making ruts in the melting tar and sending white spar chips flying, past the three mistakes, past Shaldom, The Laurels, Linchester Lodge.

'That's the one I'd fancy,' said the driver, pointing to the Cotswold farmhouse with a hint of Swiss chalet in its jade-coloured balconies. 'If my pools come up.' His mate was silent, consumed with envy and with scorn.

'Keep your eyes open, Reg. It's gone knocking-off time.'

'Blimey,' said his mate, throwing his cigarette end into the Gavestons' rhododendrons, 'I haven't got X-ray eyes. It's half a mile up to them front doors, and what with the trees.'

'Now, I'd have them down. Keep out the light, they do. And I'd do something about that empty bit in the middle. You could put up a couple of nice bungalows where that pond is. Here we are. Hallows. I don't know what I brought you for. I could have done better on my tod.'

But he was glad of Reg's help when it came to unloading the parcel. It was heavy and, according to the label, fragile. Something like a door it was or a big mirror. He could just feel a frame thing through the corrugated cardboard.

They humped it up the drive between two rows of

young willows until they came to the paved court in front of the house.

Hallows was beautiful—by most people's standards. Reg and the driver found it on the dull side compared with its ornate neighbours. This house was plain and rectangular, built of York stone and pale unpolished wood; there were no gables and no chimneys, no shutters and not a single pane of stained glass. The windows were huge, backed with white venetian blinds, and the front doors were swing affairs of glass set in steel.

'Are you looking for me?' The voice, delicate, vague, unmistakably upper-class, came from above their heads. The driver looked up to a long undecorated balcony and saw a woman leaning over the rails.

'British Railways, lady.'

'Too dreadful!' Tamsin Selby said. 'I'd forgotten all about it.'

It was true, she had. The delivery of this parcel had been planned in a sprightly, almost malicious mood, very different from her present one. But it had taken so long in coming, so much had happened. She disappeared through the balcony windows back into the bedroom.

'How the rich live,' Reg said to the driver. 'Forgotten, my foot!'

Tamsin came out to them breathlessly. At all costs it must be got in and, if possible, hidden, before Patrick came home. She tried to take it from them but the weight was too much for her. The men watched her efforts with a kind of triumph.

'Would you be terribly sweet,' Tamsin said, 'and carry it upstairs for me?'

'Now, look,' the driver began, 'it's heavy. . .'

She took two half-crowns from the bag she had snatched up in the hall.

'Can't leave it here, can we?' Reg was grinning reluctantly.

'So kind,' said Tamsin. She led the way and they followed her, carrying the parcel gingerly to avoid scraping the dove-grey hessian on the hall walls, the paint on the curled iron baluster rails.

'In here, I think.'

The room was too beautiful for them. Poverty, never admitted, scarcely felt before, scummed their hands with ineluctable dirt. They looked away from the velvet curtains, the dressing-table glass ringed with light bulbs, the half-open door that showed a glimpse of a shower cabinet and tiles hand-painted with fishes, and down at their own feet.

'Could you put it on one of the beds?'

They lowered it on to the nearer of the cream silk counterpanes, avoiding the bed by the window where the turned-back coverlet revealed a lemon lace night-gown folded between frilled nylon pillow and frilled nylon sheet.

'Thank you so much. It won't be in the way here.'

She didn't even bother to smooth the silk where a corner of the parcel had ruffled it, but signed her name quickly and hustled them out of the house. After they had gone she closed the spare bedroom door and sighed deeply. Patrick would be home any minute now and she had meant to use those spare moments checking on everything, making sure she looked her best.

She went into the bedroom with the balcony and looked at herself in the glass. That was all right, just the way Patrick liked her to look, the way he had liked her to look once... The sun—she had spent most of the day in the sun—had done wonders for her dark honey hair. No make-up. To have put on lipstick would have been to spoil the image she liked to create, the facsimile of a smooth teak-coloured mask, straight nose, carved lips, cheekbones that were arched polished planes.

Her hair hung quite straight on to her brown shoulders. Even for him she refused to cut it short and have it set. The dress—that was all right at any rate. Patrick hated bright colours and this one was black and white. Plain as it was, she knew there might be something too casual about it, too suggestive of a uniform for emancipated women. O God, she thought, making a face at her own image and wishing for the first time in her life that it could be transmuted into the reflection of a brisk blonde *Hausfrau*.

Downstairs the table was already laid for dinner: two place mats of blue linen—he had made her give up using the big damask cloths—black Prinknash plates, a long basket of French bread, Riesling dewed from the refrigerator. Tamsin gasped aloud when she saw that she had forgotten to throw away the vaseful of grasses. She grabbed them, scattering brown reeds, and rushed to the kitchen. The dog now, had she fed the dog?

'Queenie!'

How many times in the past months had he scolded her for failing to feed the dog on the dot of five? How many times had he snapped at her for wasting her days dreaming in the garden and the fields, learning country lore from Crispin Marvell, when she should have been at home keeping up with the Gages and the Gavestons.

But she must have done it and, in her panic, forgotten all about it. The plate of congealing horsemeat and biscuit meal was still on the floor, untouched by the dog. Flies buzzed over it and a single wasp crawled across a chunk of fat.

'Queenie!'

The bitch appeared silently from the garden door, sniffed at the food and looked enquiringly at Tamsin with mournful eyes. She is the only thing that we have together now, Tamsin thought, the only thing that we both love, Kreuznacht Konigin, that we both call Queenie. She dropped to her knees and in her loneliness she put her arms round Queenie's neck, feeling the suede-smooth skin against her own cheek. Queenie's tail flapped and she nuzzled against Tamsin's ear.

Of the two female creatures desirous of pleasing Patrick it was the dog who heard him first. She stiffened and the swinging lethargic tail began to wag excitedly, banging against the cooker door and making a noise like a gong.

'Master,' Tamsin said. 'Go, find him!'

The Weimaraner stretched her lean body, cocked her head and stood for a moment poised, much as her ancestors had done listening for the huntsman's command in the woods of Thuringia a century ago. The heavy garage door rumbled and fell with a faint clang. Queenie was away, across the patio, leaping for the iron gate that shut off the drive.

Tamsin followed, her heart pounding.

He came in slowly, not looking at her, silent, his attention given solely to the dog. When he had fondled Queenie, his hands drawing down the length of her body, he looked up and saw his wife.

Tamsin had so much to say, so many endearments remembered from the days when it was necessary to say nothing. No words came. She stood there, looking at him, her hands kneading the black and white stuff of her dress. Swinging the ignition key, Patrick pushed past her, shied at a wasp that dived against his face, and went into the house.

'She hasn't eaten her dinner,' were the first words that he spoke to her. He hated dirt, disorder, matter in the wrong place. 'It's all over flies.'

Tamsin picked up the plate and dropped the contents into the waste disposal unit. Meat juice rubbed off on to her fingers. Patrick looked pointedly at her hand, turned and went upstairs. She ran the tap, rinsed her fingers. It seemed an age since he had gone—the wine, would it get too warm? Ought she to put it back in the fridge? She waited, the sweat seeping into her dress. Presently she switched on the fan.

At last he came in wearing terylene slacks and a tee shirt of pale striped cotton, and he looked handsome if you admired men with ash-blond hair and freckles so dense that they looked like tan.

'I thought you'd like melon,' she said. 'It's cantaloupe.'

Suspiciously Patrick skimmed away the melting golden sugar.

'Not honey, is it? You know I hate honey.'

'Of course it isn't.' She paused timidly. 'Darling,' she said.

He made his way silently through chicken salad, potato sticks, fruit salad (all good hygienic food from tins and packets and deep freezers), eating sparingly,

24

absent-mindedly. The fan whirred and Queenie lay beneath it, paws spread, tongue extended.

'I've got everything for the party,' Tamsin said.

'Party?'

'Tomorrow. It's my birthday. You hadn't forgotten?'

'No, it slipped my mind, that's all.'

Had it also slipped his mind to get a present?

'There's heaps to do,' she said brightly. 'The lights to put up, and we've got to move the furniture in the—' Now it was more than ever important to pick the right word, '—the lounge in case it rains. And— Oh, Patrick, could you do something about the wasps? I'm sure there's a nest somewhere.' She remembered belatedly and reached for his hand. The fingers lay inert in hers, the big red swelling showing at the base of his thumb. 'Too frightful for you. How's it been today?'

'The sting? Oh, all right. It's going down.'

'Could you possibly try to get rid of them? They'll ruin the party.'

He pushed away his plate and his half-finished glass of wine.

'Not tonight. I'm going out.'

She had begun to tremble and when she spoke her voice shook.

'There's so much to do. Please don't go, darling. I need you.'

Patrick laughed. She didn't look at him but sat staring at her plate moving the viscous yellow juice about with her spoon.

'I *am* going out. I have to take the dog, don't I?'

'I'll take the dog.'

'Thank you very much,' he said icily. 'I can manage.' He touched the venetian blind and glanced at the faint patina of dust on his fingertips. 'If you're bored there are things here which could do with some attention.'

'Patrick.' Her face had paled and there were goose pimples on her arms. 'About what you said last night —you've got to change your mind. You've got to forget all about it.' With a great effort she pushed three words from stiff lips: 'I love you.'

She might not have spoken. He walked into the kitchen and took the leash from the broom cupboard.

'Queenie!'

From deep sleep the Weimaraner galvanised into impassioned life. Patrick fastened the steel clip to her collar and led her out through the french windows.

Tamsin sat among the ruins of her meal. Presently she began to cry silently, the tears splashing into the wine glass she held in her cupped hands. Her mouth was dry and she drank. I am drinking my own sorrow, she thought. Five minutes, ten minutes passed. Then she went to the front door and out into the willow avenue. The sky was clear, azure above, violet and apricot on the horizon, thronged with wheeling swallows.

She stopped at the end of the drive and leaned on the gate. Patrick hadn't gone far. She could see him standing with his back to her on The Green staring down at the waters of the pond. The dog had tried, unsuccessfully as always, to intimidate the three white swans. Now she had given up and was following a squirrel trail, pausing at the foot of each tree and peering up into the branches. Patrick was waiting for something, whiling away his time. For what?

As she watched him, a pale green Ford swung into view from behind the elms. That funny little salesman fellow from the chalets, she thought, on his way to his evening class. She hoped he'd pass on with a wave but he didn't. He stopped. Few men passed Tamsin Selby without a second glance.

'Hot enough for you?'

'I like it,' Tamsin said. What was his name? Only one chalet dweller was known to her by name. 'I love the sun.'

'Ah well, it suits you. I can see that.'

Conversation would have to be made. She opened the gate and went over to the car. He mistook her action and opened the door.

'Can I give you a lift? I'm going to the village.'

'No. No, thanks.' Tamsin almost laughed. 'I'm not going out. Just enjoying the evening.'

His face fell.

'As a matter of fact,' he said, stalling, trying to keep her with him long enough for the neighbours to see him talking to the beautiful Mrs. Selby, 'as a matter of fact I'm playing truant. Supposed to be doing a little job of exterminating pests.'

'Pests?'

'Wasps. We've got a nest.'

'Have you? So have we.' She looked up. Patrick was still there. 'My husband—we want to get rid of them but we don't know how.'

'I've got some stuff. It's called Vesprid. I tell you what. When I've done mine I'll bring the tin round. There's bags of it, enough to kill all the wasps in Nottinghamshire.'

'But how kind!'

'I'll bring it round in the morning, shall I?'

Tamsin sighed. Now she would have to have this

wretched man in the way while she was preparing for the party.

'Look, why don't you come to a little do I'm having, a few friends in for drinks at about eight?' He looked at her adoringly and his eyes reminded her of Queenie's. 'If you could come early we could do the wasps then. Bring a friend if you like.'

A party at Hallows! A party at the biggest house on Linchester. Putting on his maudlin widower's voice, he said: 'I haven't been to a party since I lost my wife.'

'Really?' A chord had been struck. 'His wife's dead,' Patrick had said, 'and that's why...' What had she done? 'I'm sorry but I don't think I know your name.'

'Carnaby. Edward Carnaby.'

He looked at her, smiling. She took her hand from the car door and pressed it against her breastbone, breathing like one who has run up a steep hill.

Trust Tamsin Selby to be talking to a man, Joan thought, as she came out of her gate, holding Cheryl by the hand.

'Wave to your Daddy.'

The child was more interested in the man and the dog on The Green. Telling herself that she had meant to go that way in any case, Joan followed her reluctantly.

Patrick had never been one to waste words on the weather and other people's health. His eyes, which had been fixed with a kind of calculating disgust on Edward Carnaby, now turned upon Joan, taking in the details of her limp cotton dress, her sunburned arms and the brown roots of her hair where the rinse was growing out.

'Isn't it *hot*?' She was uncomfortable in his presence and felt the remark had been foolish. In fact, it was no longer particularly hot. A faint breeze was stirring the waters of the pond, ruffling it to match the mackerel sky.

'I don't know why English people make a cult of grumbling about the weather,' he said. He looked very Teutonic as he spoke and she remembered someone had told her he had spent his childhood in Germany and America. She laughed awkwardly and made a grab for Cheryl's hand. He had made it so clear he didn't want to talk to her that she jumped and blushed when he called her back.

'How's business?'

'Business?' Of course he meant Denholm's business, the factory. 'All right, I suppose,' she said, and then because ever since before tea there had been a vague, half-formed worry nagging at her mind, 'Den says things have been a bit slack lately.'

'We can't all get Harwell contracts.' He touched the trunk of a great oak and with a small smile looked up into its branches. 'They don't grow on trees. It's a matter of work, my dear Joan, work and single-mindedness. Denholm will have to watch his step or I'll be taking over one of these days.'

She said nothing. Malice quirked the corners of his thin mouth. She looked away from him and at the dog. Then she saw that he, too, was staring in the same direction.

'Expansion is life,' he said. 'Give it a few months and then we'll make things hum.'

Shivering a little, she drew back from him, feeling a sudden chill that seemed to come not from the scurrying wind but from the man himself.

'We're late, Cheryl. It's past your bedtime.'

'She can come with me,' said Patrick, his curious smile broadening. 'I'm going that way.'

The green Ford had moved away from the Hallows gate but Tamsin was still there, watching. As the man and child walked off towards the chalets, Joan suddenly thought she would go and speak to Tamsin, demand the explanation she knew Patrick would never give to her. But Tamsin, she saw, was in no mood for talking. Something or someone had upset her and she was retreating up the willow drive, her head bent and her hands clenched beneath her chin. Joan went home and put the children to bed. When she came downstairs Denholm was asleep. He looked so like Jeremy, his eyes lightly closed, his cheek pink and smooth against the bunched-up cushion, that she hadn't the heart to wake him.

EDWARD CARNABY KEPT ON TURNING BACK AND waving all the way down to the Manor gates. Tamsin stared after him, unable to smile in return. Her knees felt weak and she was afraid she might faint. When she reached the house she heard Queenie bark, a single staccato bark followed by a howl. The howls went on for a few seconds; then they stopped and all was silent. Tamsin knew what the howls meant. Patrick had tied up the dog to go into someone's house.

She went upstairs and into the balcony room. In the faint bloom on the dressing-table Patrick had written with a precise finger: Dust this. She fell on the bed and lay face-downwards.

Half an hour had passed when she heard the footsteps and at first she thought they were Patrick's. But whoever it was was coming alone. There was no accompanying tip-tap of dog's claws on stone. O God, she thought, I shall have to tell him. Otherwise Patrick might, there in front of everyone at the party.

The doors were unlocked. There was nothing to stop him coming in, but he didn't. He knocked with the prearranged signal. What would he do when he knew it all? There was still a chance she could persuade Patrick. She put her fingers in her ears, willing him to go. He knocked again and it seemed to her that he must hear through glass and wood, stone walls and thick carpets, the beating of her heart.

At last he went away.

'Damnation!' she heard him say from beneath her as if he were looking through the lounge window. The footsteps hurried away down the avenue and out through the footpath on to the Nottingham road. The gate swung, failed to catch and flapped against the post, bang, swing, bang. Tamsin went into the room where the men had put the parcel. She broke her nails untying the string but she was crying too much to notice.

3

THERE ARE PERHAPS FEW THINGS MORE GALLING to one's *amour propre* than to act in a covert, clandestine way when no such discretion is necessary. Oliver Gage was a proud man and now, creeping round the Hallows paths, tapping signals on the glass doors, he felt that someone had made a fool of him.

'Damnation!' he said, this time under his breath.

She had obviously gone out with *him*. Pressure had been put on her. Well, so much the better if that meant she had been preparing the ground. He would make his intentions clear at the party.

He went out into The Circle and made the humiliating detour necessary before he could find his car that he had parked on the ride off the main road. When he entered Linchester for the second time that night it was by the Manor gates and he drove into his own garage drive with a sense of disgruntled virtue and the shame he always felt when he returned to his house. Oliver lived in one of the largest houses on Linchester but it was too small for him. He hated it already. Every Friday night when he came up from his four days in London the sight of the house, magnified perhaps in his mind during his absence, sickened him and reminded him afresh of his misfortunes. For, as Oliver grew older, the sizes of his houses diminished. This was not due to a reversal in his financial life. One of the executives of a national daily, his income now topped the seven thousand mark, but only about a third of this found its way into Oliver's pocket. The rest, never seen by him yet never forgotten, streamed away via an army of solicitors and bank managers and accountants into the laps of his two discarded wives.

When he had married Nancy—pretty, witty Nancy!—and built this, the smallest of his houses to date, he had forgotten for a few months the other pressures on his income. Was not love a Hercules, still climbing trees in the Hesperides? Now, a year later, he reflected that the gods were just and of his pleasant vices had made instruments to plague him.

He unlocked the door and dropped his keys on to the hall table between the Flamenco doll and the Cherry Herring bottle that Nancy by the addition of a shade stuck all over with hotel labels had converted into a lamp. In all his matrimonial career Oliver had never before given houseroom to such an object. He hated it but he felt that, in ensuring it was the first thing his eye fell on when he entered his home, providence was meting out to him a stern exquisite justice.

Nancy's sewing machine could be heard faintly

33

from the lounge. The querulous whine of the motor fanned his ill-temper into rage. He pushed open the reeded glass door and went in. The room was tightly sealed and stifling, the windows all closed and the curtains drawn back in the way he loathed, carelessly, with no attention to the proper arrangement of their folds. Those curtains had cost him thirty pounds.

His wife—to himself and to one other Oliver occasionally referred to her as his present wife—lifted her foot from the pedal which controlled the motor and pushed damp hair back from a face on which sweat shone. Shreds of cotton and pieces of coloured fluff clung to her dress and littered the floor. There was even a piece of cotton dangling from her bracelet.

'My Christ, it's like an oven in here!' Oliver flung back the french windows and scowled at Bernice Greenleaf who was walking coolly about the garden next-door, snipping the dead blossoms off an opulent Zephirine Drouhin. When she waved to him he changed the scowl into a rigid smirk. 'What in God's name are you doing?' he asked his wife.

She pulled a cobbled strip of black and red silk from under the needle. 'I'm making a dress for Tamsin's party.'

Oliver sat down heavily, catching his foot in one of the Numdah rugs. ('If we have wood block flooring and rugs, darling,' Nancy had said, 'we'll save pounds on carpeting.')

'This I cannot understand,' Oliver said. 'Did I or did I not give you a cheque for twenty pounds last Tuesday with express instructions to buy yourself a dress?'

'Well...'

'Did I or did I not? That's all I ask. It's a perfectly simple question.'

Nancy"s babyish, *gamine* face puckered. A curly face, he had called it once, tenderly, lovingly, touching with a teasing finger the tip-tilted nose, the bunchy cheeks, the fluffy fair eyebrows.

'Well, darling, I had to have shoes, you see, and stockings. And there was the milk bill...' Her voice faltered. 'I saw this remnant and this pattern...' She held an envelope towards him diffidently. Oliver glowered at the coloured picture of the improbably tall women in cylindrical cotton frocks. 'It'll be all right, won't it?'

'It will be quite ghastly,' Oliver said coldly. 'I shall be covered with shame. I shall be mortified. Tamsin always looks wonderful.'

As soon as the words were out he regretted them. Now was not the time. Nancy was going to cry. Her face swelled as if the skin itself was allergic to his anger.

'Tamsin has a private income.' The tears sprouted. 'I only wanted to save you money. That's all I think about, saving you money!'

'Oh, don't cry! I'm sorry, Nancy!' She almost fell from her chair into his lap and he put his arms round her with the distaste that was part of his marital experience, the distaste that always came as love ebbed. Every bit of her was damp and clinging and unbearably hot.

'I do want to economise, darling. I keep thinking of all that money going out month after month to Jean and Shirley. And what with both the boys at Bembridge...' Oliver frowned. He disliked the reminder that he had been unable to afford to send the sons of his first marriage to Marlborough. 'And Shirley always so greedy, insisting on sending Jennifer to a private school when state education is so good these days.'

'You know nothing at all about state education,' Oliver said.

'Oh, darling, why did you have to marry such un-attractive women? Any other women would have got married again. Two such disastrous—well, tragic marriages. I lie awake at night thinking about the inroads on our income.'

She was off on a well-worn track, the Friday night special. Oliver let her talk, reaching to the mantel-piece for a cigarette from the box.

'And I haven't got anything exciting for your din-ner,' she finished on a note of near-triumph.

'We'll go out to eat, then.'

'You know we can't afford it. Besides I've got to finish this filthy dress.' She struggled from his lap back to the sewing machine.

'This,' said Oliver, 'is the end.' Nancy, already in-volved once more in fitting a huge sleeve into a tiny armhole, ignored him. She was not to know that it was with these words that Oliver had terminated each of his previous marriages. For him, too, they sounded dreadfully like the mere echoes of happy fin-alities. Must Nancy be his till death parted them? More securely than any devout Catholic, any puritan idealist, he had thought himself until recently, bound to his wife. Hercules had climbed his last tree. Un-less—unless things would work out and he could get a wife with money of her own, a beautiful, well-dowered wife...

He stepped across the rugs, those small and far from luxuriant oases in the big desert of polished floor, and poured himself a carefully-measured drink.

Then he sat down and gazed at their reflections, his and Nancy's, in the glass on the opposite wall. Her remarks as to the unattractiveness of his former wives had seemed to denigrate his own taste and perhaps even his own personal appearance. But now, as he looked at himself, he felt their injustice. Anyone coming in, any stranger would, he thought bitterly, have taken Nancy for the cleaning woman doing a bit of overtime sewing, her hair separated into rough hanks, her face greasy with heat and effort. But as for him, with his smooth dark head, the sharply cut yet sensitive features, the long hands that held the blood-red glass . . . the truth of it was that he was wasted in these provincial, incongruous surroundings.

Nancy got up, shook her hair, and began to pull her dress over head. She was simply going to try on the limp half-finished thing but Oliver was no fool and he could tell from the way she moved slowly, coquettishly, that there was also intention to tempt him.

'If you must strip in the living room you might pull the curtains,' he said.

He got up and put his hand to the cords that worked the pulley, first the french windows, then at the long Georgian sashes at the front of the house. The silk folds moved to meet each other but not before, through the strip of narrowing glass, he had seen walking past the gate, a tall fair man who rested a freckled hand on a dog's head, a man who was strolling home to a beautiful well-dowered wife . . .

With this glimpse there came into his mind a sudden passionate wish that this time things might for once go smoothly and to the advantage of Oliver Gage. He stood for a moment, thinking and planning, and then he realised that he had no wish to be here like this in the darkness with his wife, and he reached quickly for the light switch.

It was fully dark, outside as well as in, when Denholm awoke. He blinked, passed his hands across his face and stretched.

'Ah, well,' he said to his wife, 'up the wooden hill.'

She had meant to save it all for the morning, but the hours of sitting silently beside the sleeping man had told on her nerves. His expression became incredulous as she began to tell him of the meeting on The Green.

'He was pulling your leg,' he said.

'No, he wasn't. I wouldn't have believed him only I know you've been worried lately. You have been worried, haven't you?'

'Well, if you must know, things have been a bit dicey.' She listened as the bantering tone left his voice. 'Somebody's been building up a big stake in the company.' Only when he was talking business could Denholm shed facetiousness and become a man instead of a clown. 'It's been done through a nominee and we don't know who it is.'

'But, Den,' she cried, 'that must be Patrick!'

'He wouldn't be interested in us. Selbys are glass, nothing but glass and we're chemicals.'

'He would. I tell you, he is. He's got that contract and he means to expand, to take you over. And it does rest with him. The others are just—what do you call it?—sleeping partners.'

She would have to say it, put into words the grotesque fear that had been churning her thoughts the entire evening.

'D'you know what I think? I think it's all malice, just because you once hit that dog.'

The shot had gone home, but still he hesitated, the jovial man, the confident provider.

'You're a proper old worry-guts, aren't you?' His hand reached for hers and the fingers were cold and not quite steady. 'You don't understand business. Business men don't carry on that way.'

Did they? he wondered. Would they? His own holding in the firm had decreased precariously as his family had increased. How far could he trust the loyalty of those Smith-King uncles and cousins? Would they sell if they were sufficiently tempted?

'I understand people,' Joan said, 'and I understand you. You're not well, Den. The strain's too much for you. I wish you'd see Dr. Greenleaf.'

'I will,' Denholm promised. As he spoke he felt again the vague indefinable pains he had been experiencing lately, the continual malaise. 'I'll have a quiet natter to him tomorrow at the party.'

'I don't want to go.'

Denholm did. Even if it was cold and there wasn't enough to drink, even if they made him dance, it would be wonderful just to get away for one evening from baby-feeding at ten, from Susan who had to have a story and from Jeremy who never slept at all until eleven.

'But we've got a sitter,' he said and he sighed as from above he heard his son's voice calling for a drink of water.

Joan went to the door. 'You'll have to talk to Pat-

rick. Oh, I wish we didn't have to go.' She went upstairs with the glass and came down again with the
baby in her arms.

Trying to console her, Denholm said weakly,
'Cheer up, old girl. It'll be all right on the night.'

ʄʄʄʄʄʄʄʄʄʄʄʄʄʄʄʄʄʄʄ **4** ʄʄʄʄʄ

WHEN HE HAD BEEN MARRIED TO JEAN, WHEN IN-
deed he had been married to Shirley, he had always
been able to pay a man to clean the car. Now he had
to do it himself, to stand on the gravel like any
twenty-five pound a week commuter, squelching a
Woolworth sponge over a car that he was ashamed to
be seen driving into the office underground car park.
There was, however, one thing about this morning
slopping to be thankful for. Since he was outside he
had been able to catch the postman and take the letters himself. With a damp hand he felt the letter in
his pocket, the letter that had just come from his second wife. There was no reason why Nancy should see
it and have cause to moan at him because of its contents. Those begging letters were a continual thorn in
his flesh. Why should his daughter go on holiday to
Majorca when he could only manage Worthing? Such

a wonderful chance for her, Oliver, but of course she, Shirley, couldn't afford the air fare or equip Jennifer with a suitable wardrobe for a seven-year-old in the Balearics. Fifty pounds or perhaps seventy would help. After all, Jennifer was his daughter as well as hers and she was his affectionate Shirley.

He dropped the sponge into the bucket and bent down to polish the windscreen. Over the hedge he saw that his neighbour was opening his own garage doors, but although he liked the doctor he was in no mood for conversation that morning. Resentment caught at his throat like heartburn. Greenleaf was wearing another new suit! Gossip had it that the doctor was awaiting delivery of another new car. Oliver could hardly bear it when he compared what he thought of as the doctor's miserable continental medical degree with his own Double First.

'Good morning.'

Greenleaf's car drew level with his own and Oliver was forced to look up into his neighbour's brown aquiline face. It was a very un-English face, almost Oriental, with dark, close-set eyes, a large intelligent mouth and thick hair, crinkly like that of some ancient Assyrian.

'Oh, hallo,' Oliver said ungraciously. He stood up, making an effort to say something neighbourly, when Nancy came running down the path from the kitchen door. She stopped and saw the doctor and smiled winningly.

'Off on your rounds? What a pity to have to work on a Saturday! I always tell Oliver he doesn't know his luck, having all these long week-ends.'

Oliver coughed. His other wives had learned that his coughs were pregnant with significance. In

Nancy's case there had hardly been time to teach her, and now...

'I hope I'll see you tonight,' said the doctor as he began to move off.

'Oh, yes tonight...' Nancy's face had taken on its former lines of displeasure. When Greenleaf was out of earshot she turned sharply to her husband. 'I thought you said you left Tamsin's present on the sideboard.'

Oliver had a nose for a scene. He picked up the bucket and started towards the house.

'I did.'

'You bought that for Tamsin?' She scuttled after him into the dining-room and picked up the scent bottle with its cut-glass stopper. 'Nuit de Beltane? I never heard of such extravagance!'

Oliver could see from the open magazine on the table that she had already been checking the price.

'There you are.' Her finger stabbed at a coloured photograph of a similar bottle. 'Thirty-seven and six!' She slammed the magazine shut and threw it on the floor. 'You must be mad.'

'You can't go to a birthday party empty-handed.' Oliver said weakly. If only he knew for certain. There might, after all, be no point in bothering to keep Nancy sweet. He watched her remove the stopper, sniff the scent and dab a spot on her wrist. While she waved her wrist in front of her nose, inhaling crossly, he washed his hands and closed the back door.

'A box of chocolates would have done,' Nancy said. She lugged the sewing machine up on its rubber mat. 'I mean, it's fantastic spending thirty-seven and six on scent for Tamsin when I haven't even got a decent dress to go in.'

'Oh my God!'

'You don't seem to have a sense of proportion where money's concerned.'

'Keep the scent for God's sake and I'll get some chocolates in the village.'

Immediately she was in his arms. Oliver crushed the letter down more firmly in his pocket.

'Can I really, darling? You are an angel. Only you won't be able to get anything nice in the village. You'll have to nip into Nottingham.'

Disengaging himself, Oliver reflected on his wife's economies. Now there would be the petrol into Nottingham, at least twelve and six for chocolates and he'd still spent nearly two pounds on Nuit de Beltane.

Nancy began to sew. The dress had begun to look passable. At least he wouldn't be utterly disgraced.

'Can I come in?'

That voice was Edith Gaveston's. Quick as a flash Nancy ripped the silk from the machine, rolled up the dress and crammed it under a sofa cushion.

'Come in, Edith.'

'I see you've got into our country way of leaving all your doors unlocked.'

Edith, hot and unwholesome-looking in an aertex shirt and a tweed skirt, dropped on to the sofa. From the depths of her shopping basket she produced a wicker handbag embroidered with flowers.

'Now, I want the opinion of someone young and "with it".' Oliver who was forty-two scowled at her, but Nancy, still in her twenties, smiled encouragingly. 'This purse...' It was an absurd word, but Edith was too county, too much of a gentlewoman to talk of handbags unless she meant a small suitcase. 'This purse, will it do for Tamsin's present? It's never been used.' She hesitated in some confusion. 'I mean, of course, it's absolutely new. I brought it back from Majorca last year. Now, tell me frankly, will it do?'

'Well, she can't very well sling it back at you,' Oliver said rudely. 'Not in front of everyone.' The mention of Majorca reminded him of his second wife's demands. 'Excuse me.' He went outside to get the car.

'I'm sure it'll do beautifully,' Nancy gushed. 'What did Linda say?'

'She said it was square,' Edith said shortly. Her children's failure in achieving the sort of status their parents had wanted for them hurt her bitterly. Linda —Linda who had been at Heathfield—working for Mr. Waller; Roger, coming down from Oxford after a year and going to agricultural college! She would feed them, give them beds in her house, but with other people she preferred to forget their existence.

Nancy said with tactless intuition: 'I thought you weren't terribly keen on the Selbys. Patrick, I mean...'

'I've no quarrel with Tamsin. I hope I'm not a vindictive woman.'

'No, but after what Patrick—after him influencing Roger the way he did, I'm surprised you—well, you know what I mean.'

Nancy floundered. The Gavestons weren't really county any more. Their house was no bigger than the Gages'. But still—you'd only got to look at Edith to know her brother lived at Chantflower Grange. I suppose she's only going to the party to have a chance to hob-nob with Crispin Marvell, she thought.

'Patrick Selby behaved very badly, very wrongly,'

45

Edith said. 'And it was just wanton mischief. He's perfectly happy and successful in *his* job.'

'I never quite knew...'

'He set out to get at my children. Quite deliberately, my dear. Roger was blissfully happy at The House.' Nancy looked puzzled, thinking vaguely of the Palace of Westminster. 'Christ Church, you know. Patrick Selby got talking to him when he was out with that dog of theirs and the upshot of it was Roger said his father wanted him to go into the business but he wasn't keen. He wanted to be a farmer. As if a boy of nineteen knows what he wants. Patrick said he'd been forced into business when all he wanted was to teach or some absurd thing. He advised Roger to— well, follow his own inclinations. Never mind about us, never mind about poor Paul with no-one to take over the reins at Gavestons, no heir.'

Nancy, greedy for gossip, made sympathetic noises.

'Then, of course, Roger had to say his sister wanted to earn her own living. Made up some stupid tale about our keeping her at home. The next thing was that impossible interfering man suggested she should work in a shop till she was old enough to take up nursing. I don't know why he did it, unless it was because he likes upsetting people. Paul had a great deal to say about it, I assure you. He had quite a stormy interview with Patrick.'

'But it was no good?'

'They do what they like these days.' She sighed and added despondently, 'But as to going tonight, one has one's neighbourhood, one cannot pick and choose these days.'

'Who else is coming?'

'The usual people. The Linchester crowd and Crispin of course. I think it's splendid of him to come so often considering how bitter he must feel.' Edith's sensible, pink-rimmed glasses bobbed on her nose. 'There was a clause in the Marvell contract, you know. No tree felling. Everyone's respected it except Patrick Selby. I know for a fact there were twenty exquisite ancient trees on that plot, and he's had them all down and planted nasty little willows.'

It was just like Oliver, Nancy thought, to come in and spoil it all.

'If you're looking for your cheque book,' she said innocently, 'it's on my record player. While you're about it you might collect my sandals.'

'Oh, are you going to the village?' Edith got up pointedly.

'I'm going into Nottingham.'

'Into *town*? How perfectly splendid. You can give me a lift.'

She picked up the wicker basket and they departed together.

TWO FIELDS AND A REMNANT OF WOODLAND AWAY Crispin Marvell was sitting in his living room drinking rhubarb wine and writing his history of Chantefleur Abbey. Some days it was easy to concentrate. This was one of the others. He had spent the early part of the morning washing his china and ever since he had replaced the cups in the cabinet and the plates on the walls, he had been unable to keep his eyes from wandering to the glossy surfaces and the warm rich colours. It was almost annoying to reflect what he had been missing in delaying this particular bit of spring-cleaning, the months during which the glaze had been dimmed by winter bloom.

For a moment he mused over the twin olive-coloured plates, one decorated with a life-size apple in relief, the other with a peach; over the Chelsea clock with its tiny dial and opulent figurines of the sultan and his concubine. Marvell kept his correspondence behind this clock and it disturbed him to see the corner of Henry Glide's letter sticking out. He got up and pushed the envelope out of sight between the wall and the Circassian's gold-starred trousers. Then he dipped his pen in the ink-well and returned to Chantefleur.

'The original building had a clerestory of round-headed windows with matching windows in the aisle bays. Only by looking at the Cistercian abbeys now standing in France can we appreciate the effect of the...'

He stopped and sighed. Carried away by his own domestic art, he had almost written 'of the glaze on the apple'. It was hardly important. Tomorrow it might rain. He had already spent two years on the history of Chantefleur. Another few months scarcely mattered. In a way, on a wonderful morning like this one, nothing mattered. He gave the plate a last look, running his fingers across the cheek of the apple—the artist had been so faithful he had even pressed in a bruise, there on the underside—and went into the garden.

Marvell lived in an almshouse, or rather four alms-houses all joined together in a terrace and converted by him into a long low bungalow. The walls were partly of white plaster, partly of rose-coloured brick, and the roof was of pantiles, old now and uneven but made by the hand of a craftsman.

He strolled round the back. Thanks to the bees that lived in three white hives in the orchard the fruit was forming well; they hadn't swarmed this year and he was keeping his fingers crossed. The day spent in carefully cutting out the queen cells had been well worth the sacrifice of half a chapter of Chantefleur. He sat down on the bench. Beyond the hedge in the meadows below Linchester they were cutting the hay. He could hear the baler, that and the sound of the bees. Otherwise all was still.

'All right for some people.'

Marvell turned his head and grinned. Max Greenleaf often came up about this time after his morning calls.

'Come and sit down.'

'It's good to get away from the wasps.' Greenleaf looked at the lichen on the bench, then down at his dark suit. He sat down gingerly.

'There always were a lot of wasps in Linchester,' Marvell said. 'I remember them in the old days. Thousands of damned wasps whenever Mamma gave a garden party.' Greenleaf looked at him suspiciously. An Austrian Jew, he could never escape his conviction that the English landed gentry and the Corinthian aristocracy came out of the same mould. Marvell called it his serfs to the wolves syndrome. 'The wasps are conservative, you see. They haven't got used to the idea that the old house had been gone five years and a lot of company directors' Georgian gone up in its place. They're still on the hunt for Mamma's brandy snaps. Come inside and have a drink.' He smiled at Greenleaf and said in a teasing voice, 'I opened a bottle of mead this morning.'

'I'd rather have a whiskey and soda.'

Greenleaf followed him to the house, knocking his head as he always did on the plaque above the front door that said: 1722. Andreas Quercus Fecit. Marvell's reasons for living there were beyond his understanding. The countryside, the flowers, horticulture, agriculture, Marvell's own brand of viticulture, meant nothing to him. He had come to the village to share his brother-in-law's prosperous practice. If you asked him why he lived in Linchester he would answer that it was for the air or that he was obliged to live within a mile or two of his surgery. Modern conveniences, a house that differed inside not at all from a town house, diluted and almost banished those drawbacks. To invite those disadvantages, positively to court them in the form of cesspools, muddy lanes and insectivora as his host did, made Marvell a curio, an object of psychological speculation.

These mysteries of country life reminded him afresh of the cloud on his morning.

'I've just lost a patient,' he said. Marvell, pouring whiskey, heard the Austrian accent coming through, a sign that the doctor was disturbed. 'Not my fault, but still...'

'What happened?' Marvell drew the curtains, excluding all but a narrow shaft of sunlight that ran across the black oak floor and up Andreas Quercus's squat wall.

'One of the men from Coffley mine. A wasp got on his sandwich and he ate the thing. So what does he do? He goes back to work and the next thing I'm called out because he's choking to death. Asphyxiated before I got there.'

'Could you have done anything?'

'If I'd got there soon enough. The throat closes with the swelling, you see.' Changing the subject, he said: 'You've been writing. How's it coming on?'

'Not so bad. I did my china this morning and it distracted me.' He unhooked the apple plate from the wall and handed it to the doctor. 'Nice?'

Greenleaf took it wonderingly in short thick fingers. 'What's the good of a thing like this? You can't put food on it, can you?' Without aesthetic sense, he probed everything for its use, its material function. The plate was quite useless. Distastefully he imagined eating from it the food he liked best, chopped herring, cucumbers in brine, cabbage salad with caraway seeds. Bits would get wedged under the apple leaves.

'Its purpose is purely decorative,' Marvell laughed. 'Which reminds me, will you be at Tamsin's party?'

'If I don't get called out.'

'She sent me a card. Rather grand. Tamsin always does these things well.' Marvell stretched himself full-length in the armchair. The movement was youthful and the light dim. Greenleaf was seldom deceived about people's ages. He put Marvell's at between forty-seven and fifty-two, but the fine lines which the sun showed up were no longer apparent, and the sprinkling of white hairs was lost in the fair. Probably still attractive to women, he reflected.

'One party after another,' he said. 'Must come expensive.'

'Tamsin has her own income, you know, from her

51

grandmother. She and Patrick are first cousins so she was his grandmother, too.'

'But she was the favourite?'

'I don't know about that. He had already inherited his father's business so I daresay old Mrs. Selby thought he didn't need any more.'

'You seem to know a lot about them.'

'I suppose I do. In a way I've been a sort of father confessor to Tamsin. Before they came here they had a flat in Nottingham. Tamsin was lost in the country. When I gave that talk to the Linchester Residents' Association she bombarded me with questions and since then—well, I've become a kind of adopted uncle, Mrs. Beeton and antiquarian rolled into one.'

Greenleaf laughed. Marvell was the only man he knew who could do women's work without becoming old-womanish.

'You know, I don't think she ever really wanted that house. Tamsin loves old houses and old furniture. But Patrick insists on what are called, I believe, uncluttered lines.'

'Tell me, don't you *mind* coming to Linchester?' Always fascinated by other people's emotions, Greenleaf had sometimes wondered about Marvell's reactions to the new houses that had sprung up on his father's estate.

Marvell smiled and shrugged.

'Not really. I'm devoutly thankful I don't have to keep the old place up. Besides it amuses me when I go to parties. I play a sort of mental game trying to fix just where I am in relation to our house.' When Greenleaf looked puzzled he went on, 'What I mean is, when I'm at Tamsin's I always think to myself, the ha-ha came down here and here were the kitchen

52

gardens.' Keeping a straight face he said, 'The Gages' house now, that's where the stables were. I'm not saying it's appropriate, mind.'

'You're scaring me. Makes me wonder about my own place.'

'Oh, you're all right. Father's library and a bit of the big staircase.'

'I don't believe a word of it,' the doctor said and added a little shyly, 'I'm glad you can make a game of the whole thing.'

'You mustn't think,' said Marvell, 'that every time I set foot on Linchester I'm wallowing in a kind of maudlin *recherche du temps perdu*.'

Greenleaf was not entirely convinced. He finished his whisky and remembered belatedly his excuse for the visit.

'And now,' he said, at ease on his own home ground, 'how's the hay fever?'

IF THE DOCTOR HAD NOT PERFECTLY UNDERSTOOD Marvell's Proustian reference, he had at least an inkling of its meaning. On Edward Carnaby it would have been utterly lost. His French was still at an elementary stage.

Jo-jo monte. Il est fatigué. Bonne nuit, Jo-jo. Dors bien!

He looked up towards the ceiling and translated the passage into English. Funny stuff for a grown man, wasn't it? All about a kid of five having a bath and going to bed. Still, it was French. At this rate he'd be reading Simenon within the year.

Bonjour, Jo-jo. Quel beau matin! Regarde le ciel. Le soleil brille.

Edward thumbed through the dictionary, looking for *briller*.

'Ted!'

'What is it, dear?' It was funny, but lately he'd got into the habit of calling her dear. She had taken the place of his wife in all ways but one. Sex was lacking but freedom and security took its place. Life was freer with Free, he thought, pleased with his pun.

'If you and Cheryl want your lunch on time you'll have to do something about these wasps, Ted.' She marched in, brisk, neat, womanly, in a cotton frock and frilled apron. He noted with pleasure that she had said lunch and not dinner. Linchester was educating Freda.

'I'll do it right now. Get it over.' He closed the dictionary. *Briller*. To shine, to glow, emit a radiance. The verb perfectly expressed his own mental state. He was glowing with satisfaction and anticipation. *Edouard brille*, he said to himself, chuckling aloud. 'I've promised to pass the stuff on to some people.'

'What people?'

'The gorgeous Mrs. Selby, if you must know. I met her last night and she was all over me. Insisted I go to her party tonight.' Now you couldn't say things like that to a wife. 'She wouldn't take No for an answer,' he said.

Freda sat down.

'You're kidding. You don't know Tamsin.'

'Tamsin! That's all right, that is. Since when have you and her been so pally?'

'And what about me? Where do I come in?'

'Now, look, Free, I'm counting on you to sit in with Cheryl.'

The tears welled into her eyes. After all that had

happened, all the love, the promises, the wonderful evenings. Of course it wasn't his fault. It was Tamsin's party. But to ask Edward!

'There's no need to get into a tiz. She said I could bring a friend. I don't know about Cheryl, though.'

'Mrs. Saxton'll sit,' Freda said eagerly. 'She's always offering.' Seeing his face still doubtful, his eyes already returning to the French primer, she burst out miserably, 'Ted, I want to go to the party! I've got a right. I've got more right than you.'

Hysteria in Freda was something new. He closed the book.

'What are you talking about?' She was his twin and he could feel the pull of her mind, almost read her thoughts. A terrible unease visited him and he thought of the previous night, the woman's eyes staring past him towards the pond, her sudden unexplained coldness when he had said who he was.

'Freda!'

It all came out then and Edward listened, angry and afraid. The happy mood had gone sour on him.

5

STRINGS OF LITTLE COLOURED BULBS FESTOONED the willow trees. As soon as it grew dusk they would be switched on to glow red, orange, green and cold blue against the dark foliage of the oaks in the Millers' garden next door.

Tamsin had shut the food and drink in the dining room away from the wasps. Although she had only seen two throughout the whole day she closed the double windows to be on the safe side. The room was tidy, and apart from the food, bare. Functional, Patrick called it. Now, cleaned by him while Tamsin hovered helplessly in the background, it met even his exacting requirements.

'It is, after all, a *dining* room, not a glory hole,' he had remarked in a chill voice to the vacuum cleaner. To his wife he said nothing, but his look meant Please don't interfere with my arrangements. When the tools were put away and the dusters carefully washed, he had taken the dog to Sherwood Forest, smug, silent with his private joy.

It was too late not to bother with a show of loving obedience. Tamsin dressed, wishing she had something bright and gay, but all her clothes were subdued—to please Patrick. Then she went into the dining room and helped herself to whisky, pouring straight into a tumbler almost as if it was the last drink she would ever have. Nobody had wished her a happy birthday yet but she had had plenty of cards. Defiantly she took them from the sideboard drawer and arranged them on top of the radiator. There were about a dozen of them, facetious ones showing dishevelled housewives amid piles of crocks; conventional ones (a family of Dartmoor ponies); one whose picture had a secret significance, whose message meant something special to her and to its sender. It was unsigned but Tamsin knew who had sent it. She screwed it up quickly for the sight of it with its cool presumption only deepened her misery.

'Many happy returns of the day, Tamsin,' she said shakily, raising her glass. She sighed and the cards fluttered. Somehow she would have liked to break the glass, hurl it absurdly against Patrick's white wall, because she had come to an end. A new life was beginning. The drink was a symbol of the old life and so was the dress she wore, silver-grey, clinging, expensive. She put the glass down carefully (her old habits died hard), looked at the cards and blinked to stop herself crying. For there should have been one more, bigger than the others, an austere costly card that said To My Wife.

Patrick was never late. He came back on the dot of

seven in time to bath and shave and leave the bathroom tidy, and by then she had washed her glass, returning it to its place in the sideboard. She heard the bathroom door close and the key turn in the lock. Patrick was careful about propriety.

Tamsin remained in the dining room for some minutes, feeling an almost suicidal despair. In an hour or so her guests would begin to arrive and they would expect her to be gay because she was young and rich and beautiful and because it was her birthday. If she could get out of the house for a few minutes she might feel better. With Queenie at her heels she took her trug and went down to where the currants grew in what had been the Manor kitchen gardens. The dog lay down in the sun and Tamsin began stripping the bushes of their ripe white fruit.

'I will try to be gay,' she said to herself, or perhaps to the dog, 'for a little while.'

Edward and Freda came up to the front doors of Hallows at a quarter to eight and it was Edward who rang the bell. Freda, whose only reading matter was her weekly women's magazine, had sometimes encountered the cliché 'rooted to the spot' and that was how she felt standing on the swept white stones, immobile, stiff with terror, a sick bile stirring between her stomach and her throat.

No one came to the door. Freda watched her brother enviously. Not for him the problem of what to do with one's sticky and suddenly over-large hands that twitched and fretted as if seeking some resting place; he had the Vesprid in its brown paper bag to hold.

'Better go round the back,' he said truculently.

It was monastically quiet. The creak of the

wrought iron gate made Freda jump as Edward pushed it open. They walked round the side of the house and stopped when they came to the patio. The garden lay before them, waiting, expectant, but not as for a party. It was rather as if it had been prepared for the arrival of some photographer whose carefully angled shots would provide pictures for one of those very magazines. Freda had read a feature the previous week, *Ideal Homesteads in the New Britain,* and the illustrations had shown just such a garden, lawns ribbed in pale and dark green where the mower had crossed them, trees and shrubs whose leaves looked as if they had been individually dusted. At the other end of the patio someone had arranged tables and chairs, some of straw-coloured wicker, others of white-painted twisted metal. A small spark of pleasure and admiration broke across Freda's fear, only to be extinguished almost at once by the sound of water gurgling down a drainpipe behind her ankles. A sign of life, of habitation.

The garden, the house, looked, she thought, as if it hadn't been kept outside at all, as if it had been preserved up to this moment under glass. But she was unable to express this thought in words and instead said foolishly:

'There isn't anybody about. You must have got the wrong night.'

He scowled and she wondered again why he had come, what he was going to say or do. Was it simply kindness to her—for he was, as it were, her key to this house—Tamsin's fascination or something more?

'You won't say anything, will you? You won't say anything to show me up?'

'I told you,' he said. 'I want to see how the land lies,

what sort of a mess you've got yourself into. I'm not promising anything, Free.'

Minutes passed, unchanging minutes in which the sleek garden swam before her eyes. Then something happened, something which caused the first crack to appear in Edward's insecure courage.

From behind the willows came a sound familiar to Freda, a long drawn-out bay. Queenie. Edward jerked convulsively and dropped the Vesprid with a clang—a clang like the crack of doom as the dog bounded from a curtain of shrubs and stopped a yard from him. It was an ominous sound that came from her, a throb rather than an actual noise, and Edward seemed to grow smaller. He picked up the tin and held it in front of him, a ridiculous and wholly inadequate shield.

'Oh, Queenie!' Freda put out her hand. 'It's all right. It's me.'

The dog advanced, wriggling now, to lick the outstretched fingers, when the gate opened and a tall fair man entered the garden. He was wearing a green shirt over slacks and Edward at once felt that his own sports jacket (Harris tweed knocked down to eighty nine and eleven) was unsuitable, an anachronism.

'How do you do?'

He was carrying something that looked like a bottle wrapped in ancient yellowing newspaper, and a huge bunch of roses. The roses were perfect, each bud closed yet about to unfurl, and their stems had been shorn of thorns.

'I don't think we've met. My name's Marvell.'

'Pleased to meet you,' Edward said. He transferred the Vesprid to his left arm and shook hands. 'This is my sister, Miss Carnaby.'

'Where is everyone?'

'We don't know,' Freda said sullenly. 'Till you came we thought we'd got the wrong night.'

'Oh, no, this is Tamsin's birthday.' He pushed Queenie down, smiled suddenly and waved. 'There she is picking my currants, bless her! Will you excuse me?'

'Well!' Freda said. 'If those are county manners you can keep them.'

She watched him stride off down the path and then she saw Patrick's wife. Tamsin got to her feet like a silvery dryad arising from her natural habitat, ran up to Marvell and kissed him on the cheek. They came back together, Tamsin's face buried in roses.

'Josephine Bruce, that's the gorgeous dark red one,' Freda heard her say. 'Virgo, snow-white; Super Star —Oh, lovely, lovely, vermilion! And the big peachy beauty—this one—is Peace. You see, Crispin, I *am* learning.'

She stepped on the greyish-gold stone of the patio and dropped the roses on to a wicker table. The Weimaraner romped over to her and placed her paws on the table's plaited rim.

'And look, lovely mead! You are sweet to me, Crispin.'

'You look like one of those plushy calendars,' Marvell said laughing. 'The respectable kind you see in garages on the Motorway. All girl and dog and flowers and liquor, the good things of life.'

'*Wein, Weib und Gesang,* as Patrick says.' Tamsin's voice was low and her face clouded.

Edward coughed.

'Excuse me,' he said.

'O God, I'm so sorry.' Marvell was crestfallen. 'Tamsin dear, I'm keeping you from your guests.'

Afterwards, looking back, Freda thought Tamsin honestly hadn't known who they were. And after all Edward's stupid airs! Tamsin's face had grown dull and almost ugly; her eyes, large and tawny, seemed to blank out. She stood looking at them still holding a rose against her paintless lips. At last she said:

'I know! The man who goes to evening class.'

Freda wanted to go then, to slink back against the stone wall, slither between the house and the wattle fence and then run and run until she came to the chalets behind the elms. But Edward was holding her arm. He yanked her forward, exposing her to their gaze like a dealer with his single slave.

'This is my sister. You said I could bring someone.'

Tamsin's face hardened. It was exactly like one of those African art masks, Freda thought, the beautiful goddess one in the saloon bar of that roadhouse on the Southwell road. Freda knew she wasn't going to shake hands.

'Well, now you're here you must have a drink. Masses of drink in the dining room. Where's Patrick?' She looked up to the open windows on the first floor. 'Patrick!'

Edward thrust the Vesprid at her.

'A present? How very sweet of you.'

She pulled the tin out of the bag and giggled. Freda thought she was hysterical—or drunk.

'It's not exactly a present,' Edward said desperately. 'You said to bring it. You said to come early. We could do the wasps.'

'The wasps? Oh, but I've only seen one or two today. We won't worry about wasps.' She flung back the doors and Patrick must have been standing just within. He stepped out poised, smiling, smelling of bath salts. 'Here's my husband. Do go and check the lights, darling.' And she linked her arm into his, smiling brightly.

Freda could feel herself beginning to tremble. She knew her face had paled, then filled with burning blood. Her hand fumbled its way into Patrick's, gaining life and strength as she felt the faint special pressure and the familiar cold touch of his ring. As it came to Edward's turn her heart knocked, but the handshake passed off conventionally. Edward's spirit was broken and he gazed at Patrick dumbly, half-hypnotised.

'What's this?'

Patrick picked up the Vesprid and looked at the label.

Freda couldn't help admiring his aplomb, the coldly masterful way he shook off Tamsin's hand.

'Doesn't it look horrible on my birthday table?' Tamsin bundled the tin back into the paper and pushed it into Edward's arms. She took his fingers in her own and curled them round the parcel. 'There. You look after it, sweetie, or pop it in a safe place. We don't want it mingling with the drinks, do we?'

Then Marvell rescued them and took them into the dining room.

By THE TIME GREENLEAF AND BERNICE GOT TO Hallows everyone had arrived. He had been called out to a man with renal colic and it was eight before he got back. Fortunately Bernice never nagged but waited for him patiently, smoking and playing patience in the morning room.

'I shall wear my alpaca jacket,' Greenleaf said. 'So

it makes me look like a bowls player? What do I care? I'm not a teenager.'

'No, darling,' said Bernice. 'You're a very handsome mature man. Who wants to be a teenager?'

'Not me, unless you can be one too.'

Well-contented with each other, they set off in a happy frame of mind. They took the short cut across the Green and paused to watch the swans. Greenleaf held his wife's hand.

'At last,' Denholm Smith-King said as they appeared in the patio. 'I was just saying to Joan, is there a doctor in the house?'

'Ha, ha,' said Greenleaf mechanically. 'I hope no-one's going to need one. I've come to enjoy myself.' He waved to Tamsin who came from the record-player to greet him. 'Happy birthday. Nice of you to ask us.' He pointed to the now loaded table. 'What's all this?'

'My lovely presents. Look, chocs from Oliver and Nancy, this marvellous bag thing from Edith.' Tamsin held the gifts up in turn, pointing at the bag as she raised it. 'Sweet delicious *marrons glacés* from Joan, and Crispin brought me—what d'you think? Wine and roses. Wasn't that lovely?'

Marvell smiled from behind her, looking boyish. 'Thy shadow, Cynara,' he said. 'The night is thine. . . .'

'So kind! And Bernice. . .' She unwrapped the tiny phial of scent Bernice had put into her hand. 'Nuit de Beltane! How gorgeous. And I've just been telling Nancy how lovely she smells. Imagine, she's wearing it herself. You're all so good to me.' She waved a long brown hand as if their munificence exhausted her, making her more languid than usual.

Greenleaf crammed himself into a small wicker

armchair. From within the dining room the music had begun the Beguine.

'Your daughter not coming?' he said to Edith Gaveston.

She sniffed. 'Much too square for Linda.'

'I suppose so.'

Tamsin had gone, swept away in the arms of Oliver Gage.

'If you've a minute,' said Denholm Smith-King, 'I've been meaning to ask you for ages. It's about a lump I've got under my arm....'

Greenleaf, preparing for a busman's holiday, took the drink Patrick held out to him, but Smith-King was temporarily diverted. He looked quickly about him as if to make sure that most of the others were dancing, and he touched Patrick's arm nervously.

'Oh, Pat, old man....'

'Not now, Denholm.' Patrick's smile was brief, mechanical, gone in a flash. 'I don't care to mix business with pleasure.'

'Later then?'

Patrick glanced at the ashtray Smith-King was filling with stubs, opened the cigarette box insolently and let the lid fall almost instantly.

'I'm not surprised you've got a lump,' he said, 'but don't bore my guests, will you?'

'Funny chap,' Smith-King said and an uneasy flush seeped across his face. 'Doesn't care what he says.' The red faded as Patrick strolled away. 'Now about this said lump....'

Greenleaf turned towards him and tried to look as if he was listening while keeping his thoughts and half an eye on the other guests.

Most of them were his patients except the Selbys

and the Gavestons who were on Dr. Howard's private list, but he sized them up now from a psychological rather than a medical standpoint. As he sometimes said to Bernice, he had to know about human nature, it was part of his job.

The Carnabys now, they weren't enjoying themselves. They sat apart from the rest in a couple of deck chairs on the lawn and they weren't talking to each other. Freda had hidden her empty shandy glass under the seat; Carnaby, like a parent clutching his rejected child, sat dourly, holding what looked like a tin in one of Waller's paper wrappings.

Beyond them among the currant bushes Marvell was showing Joan and Nancy the ancient glories of the Manor kitchen gardens. Greenleaf knew little about women's fashions but Nancy's dress looked out of place to him, ill-fitting (she'll have to watch her weight, said the medical part of him, or her blood pressure will go soaring up in ten years' time). It contrasted badly with the expensive scent she wore, whiffs of which he had caught while they were standing together by Tamsin's birthday table. Why, incidentally, had Gage looked as black thunder when Bernice handed over their own phial of perfume?

He was dancing with Tamsin now and of the three couples on the floor they were the best matched. Clare and Walter Miller lumbered past him, resolutely foxtrotting out of time. Rather against her will Bernice had been coaxed into the arms of Old Paul Gaveston who, too conscious of the proprieties to hold her close, stared poker-faced over her shoulder, his embracing hand a good two inches from her back. Greenleaf smiled to himself. Gage was without such inhibitions. His smooth dusky cheek was pressed close to Tamsin's, his body fused with hers. They hardly moved but swayed slowly, almost indecently, on a square yard of floor. Well, well, thought Greenleaf. The music died away and broke suddenly into a mambo.

'The thing is,' Smith-King was saying, 'it's getting bigger. No getting away from it.'

'I'd better take a look at it.' Greenleaf said.

A fourth couple had joined the dancers. Greenleaf felt relieved. Patrick was a difficult fellow at the best of times but he could rise to an occasion. It was nice to see him rescuing the Carnaby girl and dancing with her as if he really wanted to.

'You will?' Smith-King half-rose. His movement seemed to sketch the shedding of garments.

'Not now,' Greenleaf said, alarmed. 'Come down to the surgery.'

The sun had quite gone now, even the last lingering rays, and dusk was coming to the garden. Tamsin had broken away from Gage and gone to switch on the fairy lights. But for the intervention of his wife who marched on to the patio exclaiming loudly about the gnats, Gage would have followed her.

'How I hate beastly insects,' Nancy grumbled. 'You'd think with all this D.D.T. and everything there just wouldn't be any more mosquitos.' She glared at Marvell. 'I feel itchy all over.'

As if at a signal Walter Miller and Edith Gaveston broke simultaneously into gnat-bite anecdotes. Joan Smith-King gravitated towards Greenleaf as people so often did with minor ailments even on social occasions, and stood in front of him scratching her arms. He got up at once to let her sit next to her husband but as he turned he saw Denholm's chair was empty.

Then he saw him standing in the now deserted dining room confronting Patrick. The indispensable cigarette was in his mouth. Greenleaf couldn't hear what he was saying, only Joan's heavy breathing loud and strained above the buzz of conversation. The cigarette trembled, adhering to Denholm's lip, and his hands moved in a gesture of hopelessness. Patrick laughed suddenly and turning away, strode into the garden as the lights came on.

Greenleaf, not sensitive to a so-called romantic atmosphere, was unmoved by the strings of coloured globes. But most of the women cried out automatically. Fairy lights were the thing; they indicated affluence, taste, organisation. With little yelps of delight Nancy ran up and down, pointing and exhorting the others to come and have a closer look.

'So glad you like them,' Tamsin said. 'We do.' Patrick coughed, dissociating himself. He was taking his duties to heart, Greenleaf thought, watching his hand enclose Freda Carnaby's in a tight grip.

'Now, have we all got drinks?' Tamsin reached for Marvell's empty glass. 'Crispin, your poor arms!'

'There are mosquitos at the bottom of your garden,' Marvell said, laughing. 'I meant to bring some citronella but I forgot.'

'Oh, but we've got some. I'll get it.'

'No, I'll go. You want to dance.'

Gage had already claimed her, his arm about her waist.

'I'll tell you where it is. It's in the spare bedroom bathroom. Top shelf of the cabinet.'

Joan Smith-King was giggling enviously.

'Oh, do you have two bathrooms? How grand!'

'Just through the spare room,' Tamsin said, ignoring her.

'You know the way.'

The expression in her eyes shocked Greenleaf. It was as if, he thought, she was playing some dangerous game.

'I'm being absurd,' he said to Bernice.

'Oh, no darling, you're such a practical man. Why are you being absurd anyway?'

'Nothing,' Greenleaf said.

Marvell came back holding a bottle. He had already unstoppered it and was anointing his arms.

'Thank you so much,' he said to Tamsin, 'Madame Tussand.'

Tamsin gabbled at him quickly.

'You found the stuff? Marvellous. No, sweetie, that isn't a pun. Come and dance.'

'I am for other than for dancing measures,' Marvell laughed. 'I've been in the chamber of horrors and I need a drink.' He helped himself from the sideboard. 'You might have warned me.'

'What *do* you mean, chamber of horrors?' Nancy was wide-eyed. The party was beginning to flag and she was eager for something to buoy it up and, if possible, prise Oliver away from Tamsin. 'Have you been seeing ghosts?'

'Something like that.'

'Tell, tell!'

Suddenly Tamsin whirled away from Oliver and throwing up her arms, seized Marvell to spin him away past the record player, past the birthday table, across the patio and out on to the lawn.

'Let's all go,' she cried. 'Come and see the skeleton in the cupboard!'

They began to file out into the hall, the women giggling expectantly. Marvell went first, his drink in his hand. Only Patrick hung back until Freda took his hand and whispered something to him. Even Smith-King, usually obtuse, noticed his unease.

'Lead on, Macduff!' he said.

IF IT HAD BEEN EARLIER IN THE DAY OR EVEN IF the lights had been on it would have looked very different. But as it was—day melting into night, the light half-gone and the air so still that nothing moved, not even the net curtains at the open windows—the effect was instant and, for a single foolish moment, shocking.

Marvell pulled a face. The other men stared, Paul Gaveston making a noise that sounded like a snort. Smith-King whistled, then broke into a hearty laugh.

The women expressed varying kinds of horror, squeals, hands clamped to mouths, but only Freda sounded genuinely distressed. She was standing close to Greenleaf. He heard her low gasp and felt her shudder.

'Definitely not my cup of tea,' Nancy said. 'Imagine

forgetting it was there and then coming face to face
with it in the night on your way to the loo!'

Greenleaf was suddenly sickened. Of all the people
in the Selby's spare room he was the only one who
had ever seen an actual head that had been severed
from an actual body. The first one he had encountered as a student, the second had been the subject of
a post-mortem conducted on a man decapitated in a
railway accident. Because of this and for other reasons connected with his psychological make-up, he
was at the same time more and less affected by the
picture than were the other guests.

It was a large picture, an oil painting in a frame of
scratched gilt, and it stood propped on the floor
against the watered silk wallpaper. Greenleaf knew
nothing at all about painting and the view many people take that all life—or all death—is a fit subject for
art would have appalled him. Of brushwork, of colour,
he was ignorant, but he knew a good deal about anat-
omy and a fair amount about sexual perversion.
Therefore he was able to admire the artist for his accuracy—the hewn neck on the silver platter showed
the correct vertebra and the jugular in its proper
place—and deplore a mentality which thought sa-
dism a suitable subject for entertainment. Greenleaf
hated cruelty; all the suffering of all his ancestors in
the ghettos of Eastern Europe was strong within him.
He stuck out his thick underlip, took off his glasses
and began polishing them on his alpaca jacket.

Thus he was unable to see for a moment the face
of the man who stood near him on the other side of
Freda Carnaby, the man whose house this was. But
he heard the intake of breath and the faint smothered
cry.

'But just look at the awful way she's staring at that ghastly head,' Nancy cried, clutching Oliver's hand. 'I think I ought to understand what it means, but I don't.'

'Perhaps it's just as well,' her husband said crisply.

'What is it, Tamsin? What's it supposed to be?'

Tamsin had drawn her fingers across the thick painted surface, letting a nail rest at the pool of blood.

'Salome and John the Baptist,' Marvell said. He was quickly bored by displays of naiveté and he had gone to the window. Now he turned round, smiling. 'Of course she wouldn't have been dressed like that. The artist put her in contemporary clothes. Who painted it, Tamsin?'

'I just wouldn't know,' Tamsin shrugged. 'It was my grandmother's. I lived with her, you see, and I grew up with it, so it doesn't affect me all that much any more. I used to love it when I was a little girl. Too dreadful of me!'

'You're never going to hang it on the wall?' Clare Miller asked.

'I might. I don't know yet. When my grandmother died two years ago she left all her furniture to a friend, a Mrs. Prynne. I happened to be visiting her a couple of months ago and of course I absolutely drooled over this thing. So she said she'd send it to me for my birthday and here it is.'

'Rather you than I.'

'I might put it on the dining-room wall. D'you think it would go well with a grilled steak?'

They had all looked at the picture. Everyone had said something if only to exclaim with thrilled horror. Only Patrick had kept silent and Greenleaf, puzzled, turned now to look at him. Patrick's face was deathly

73

white under the cloud of freckles. Somehow the freckles made him look worse, the pallor of his skin blotched with what looked like bruises. When at last he spoke his voice was loud and unsteady and the icy poise quite gone.

'All right,' he said, 'the joke's over. Excuse me.' He pushed at Edward Carnaby, shoving him aside with his shoulder and stripping the counterpane from one of the beds, flung it across the picture. But instead of catching on the topmost beading of the frame it slipped and fell to the floor. The effect of its falling, like the sweeping away of a curtain, exposed the picture with a sudden vividness. The gloating eyes, the parted lips and the plump bosom of Herod's niece arose before them in the gloom. She seemed to be watching with a dreadful satisfaction the slithering silk as it unveiled the trophy in the dish.

'You bitch!' Patrick said.

There was a shocked silence. Then Tamsin stepped forward and looped the counterpane up. Salome was veiled.

'Oh, really!' she said. 'It was just a joke, darling. You *are* rude.'

Smith-King moved uneasily.

'Getting late, Joanie,' he said. 'Beddy-byes.'

'It's not ten yet.' Tamsin caught Patrick's hand and leaning towards him, kissed him lightly on the cheek. He remained quite still, the colour returning to his face, but he didn't look at her. 'We haven't eaten yet. All that lovely food!'

'Ah, food.' Smith-King rubbed his hands together. It would be another story if a scene could be avoided and Patrick perhaps yet made amenable. 'Must keep body and soul together.'

'The wolf from the door?' Marvell said softly.

'That's the ticket.' He slapped Marvell on the back.

Patrick seemed to realise that his hand was still resting in Tamsin's. He snatched it away, marched out of the room and down the stairs, his dignity returning. With a defiant glance at Tamsin, Freda followed him.

'It's a lovely night,' Tamsin cried. 'Let's go into the garden and take the food with us.' Her eyes were very bright. She linked her arm into Oliver's and as an afterthought clasped Nancy's hand and swung it. 'Eat, drink, and be merry for tomorrow we die!'

They went downstairs and Tamsin danced into the dining-room. Greenleaf thought they had seen the last of Patrick for that night, but he was on the patio, subdued, his face expressionless, arranging plates on the wicker tables. Freda Carnaby stood by him, sycophantic, adoring.

'WELL!' SAID NANCY GAGE. SHE PULLED HER chair up alongside Greenleaf's. 'I thought Patrick made an exhibition of himself, didn't you? Immature I call it, making all that fuss about a picture.'

'It is the eye of childhood that fears a painted devil.' Marvell passed her a plate of smoked salmon rolled up in brown bread.

'Juvenile,' Nancy said. 'I mean, it's not as if it was a film. I don't mind admitting I've seen some horror films that have absolutely terrified me. I've wakened in the night bathed in perspiration, haven't I, Oliver?' Oliver was too far away to hear. He sat on the stone wall in gloomy conference with Tamsin.

Nancy, beckoning to him, raised the salmon roll blindly to her mouth.

'Look out!' Greenleaf said quickly. He knocked the roll out of her hand. 'A wasp,' he explained as she jumped. 'You were going to eat it.'

'Oh, no!' Nancy leapt to her feet and shook her skirt. 'I hate them, I'm terrified of them.'

'It's all right. It's gone.'

'No, it hasn't. Look, there's another one.' Nancy flapped her arms as a wasp winged past her face, circled her head and alighted on a fruit flan. 'Oliver, there's one in my hair!'

'What on earth's the matter?' Tamsin got up reluctantly and came between the tables. 'Oh, wasps. Too maddening.' She was taller than Nancy and she blew lightly on the fair curls. 'It's gone, anyway.'

'You shouldn't have brought the food out,' Patrick said. 'You would do it.' Since he had been the first to do so, this, Greenleaf thought, was hardly fair. 'I hate this damned inefficiency. Look, dozens of them!'

Everyone had pushed back their chairs, leaving their food half-eaten. The striped insects descended upon the tables making first for fruit and cream. They seemed to drop from the skies and they came quite slowly, wheeling first above the food with a sluggish yet purposeful concentration like enemy aircraft engaged in a reconnaissance. Then, one by one, they dropped upon pastry and jelly, greedy for the sweet things. Their wings vibrated.

'Well, that's that,' Tamsin said. Her hand dived for a plate of petit fours but she withdrew it quickly with a little scream. 'Get off me, hateful wasp! Patrick, do something.' He was standing beside her but further removed perhaps than he had ever been. Exasperated

76

and bored, his hands in his pockets, he stared at the feasting insects. 'Get the food in!'

'It's a bit late for that,' Marvell said. 'They're all over the dining-room.' He looked roofwards. 'You've got a nest, you know.'

'That doesn't surprise me at all,' said Walter Miller who lived next door. 'I said to Clare only yesterday, you mark my words, I said, the Selbys have got a wasp nest in their roof.'

'What are we going to do about it?'

'Kill them.' Edward Carnaby had opened his mouth to no one except his sister since, on their arrival, Tamsin had snubbed him. Now his hour had come. 'Exterminate them,' he said. He pulled the tin of Vesprid from its bag and dumped it in the middle of the table where Nancy, Marvell and Greenleaf had been sitting.

'You should have let me do it before,' he said to Tamsin.

'Do it? Do what?' Tamsin looked at the Vesprid. 'What do you do, spray it on them?'

Edward seemed to be about to embark on a long technical explanation. He took a deep breath.

Walter Miller said quickly: 'You'll want a ladder. There's one in my garage.'

'Right,' said Edward. 'The first thing is to locate the nest. I'll need someone to give me a hand.' Marvell got up.

'No, Crispin, Patrick will go.' Tamsin touched her husband's arm. 'Come on, darling. You can't let your guests do all the work.'

For a moment he looked as if he could. He glanced mulishly from Marvell to his wife. Then, without speaking to or even looking at Edward, he started to walk towards the gate.

'Blood sports, Tamsin,' Marvell said. 'Your parties are unique.'

When Patrick and Edward came back carrying Miller's ladder the others had moved out on to the lawn. By now the patio was clouded with wasps. Droves of them gathered on the tables. The less fortunate late-comers zoomed enviously a yard above their fellows, fire-flies in the radiance from the fairy lights.

Edward propped the ladder against the house wall. Making sure his heroics were witnessed, he thrust a hand among the cakes and grabbed one swiftly. Then he unscrewed the cap on the Vesprid tin and poured a little liquid on to the pastry.

'You'd better nip up to the spare bedroom,' he said to Patrick importantly. 'I reckon the nest's just above the bathroom window.'

'What for?' Patrick had paled and Greenleaf thought he knew why.

'I shall want some more light, shan't I?' Edward was enjoying himself. 'And someone'll have to hand this to me.' He made as if to thrust the poisoned cake into his host's hand.

'I am going up the ladder,' Patrick said icily.

Edward began to argue. He was the expert, wasn't he? Hadn't he just dealt efficiently with a nest of his own?

'Oh, for heaven's sake!' Tamsin said. 'This is supposed to be my birthday party.'

In the end Edward went rebelliously indoors carrying his bait. Marvell stood at the bottom of the ladder, steadying it, and when a light appeared at the bathroom window, Patrick began to climb. From the lawn they watched him peer along the eaves, his face white and tense in the patch of light. Then he called out with the only flash of humour he had permitted himself that evening:

'I've found it. Apparently there's no one at home.'

'I reckon they've all gone to a party,' Edward called. Delighted because someone on the lawn had laughed, he licked his lips and pushed the cake toward Patrick. 'Supper,' he said.

Greenleaf found himself standing close by Oliver Gage and he turned to him to make some comment on the proceedings, but something in the other man's expression stopped him. He was staring at the figure on the ladder and his narrow red lips were wet. Greenleaf saw that he was clenching and unclenching his hands.

'Oh, look! What's happening?' Suddenly Nancy clutched Greenleaf's arm and, startled, he looked roofwards.

Patrick had started violently, arching his back away from the ladder. He shouted something. Then they saw him wince, hunch his shoulders and cover his face with his free arm.

'He's been stung,' Greenleaf heard Gage say flatly, 'and serve him bloody well right.' He didn't move but Greenleaf hurried forward to join the others who had gathered at the foot of the ladder. Three wasps were encircling Patrick's head, wheeling about him and making apparently for his closed eyes. They saw him for a moment, fighting, both arms flailing, his blind face twisted. Then Edward disappeared and the light went out. Now Patrick was just a silhouette against the clear turquoise sky and to Greenleaf he looked like a marionette of crumpled black paper whose convulsively beating arms seemed jerked by unseen strings.

'Come down!' Marvell shouted.

'Oh God!' Patrick gave a sort of groan and collapsed against the rungs, swaying precariously.

Someone shouted: 'He's going to fall,' but Patrick didn't fall. He began to slide down, prone against the ladder, and his shoes caught on each rung as he descended, tap, tap, flap, until he fell into Marvell's arms.

'Are you all right?' Marvell and Greenleaf asked together and Marvell shied at the wasp that came spiraling down towards Patrick's head. 'They've gone. Are you all right?'

Patrick said nothing but shuddered and put up his hand to cover his cheek. Behind him Greenleaf heard Freda Carnaby whimpering like a puppy, but nobody else made a sound. In the rainbow glimmer they stood silent and peering like a crowd at a bullfight who have seen a hated matador come to grief. The hostility was almost tangible and there was no sound but the steady buzz of the wasps.

'Come along.' Greenleaf heard his own voice pealing like a bell. 'Let's get him into the house.' But Patrick shook off his arm and blundered into the dining room.

THEY GATHERED ROUND HIM IN THE LOUNGE, ALL except Marvell who had gone to the kitchen to make coffee. Patrick crouched in an armchair holding his handkerchief against his face. He had been stung in several places, under the left eye, on the left wrist and forearm and on the right arm in what Greenleaf called the cubital fossa.

'Lucky it wasn't a good deal worse,' Edward said peevishly.

Patrick's eye was already beginning to swell and close. He scowled at Edward and said rudely:

'Get lost!'

'Please don't quarrel.' No one knew how Freda had insinuated herself into her position on the footstool at Patrick's knees, nor exactly when she had taken his hand. 'It's bad enough as it is.'

'Oh, really,' Tamsin said. 'Such a fuss! Excuse me, will you? It might be a good idea for my husband to get some air.'

For the second time that night Denholm Smith-King looked first at his watch, then at his wife. 'Well, we'll be getting along. You won't want us.'

Marvell had come in with the coffee things but Tamsin didn't argue. She lifted her cheek impatiently for Joan to kiss.

'Coffee, Nancy? Oliver?' She by-passed the Carnabys exactly as if they were pieces of furniture. Oliver rejected the cup coldly, sitting on the edge of his chair.

'Perhaps we'd better go too.' Nancy looked hopelessly from angry face to angry face. 'Have you got any bi-carb? It's wonderful for wasp stings. I remember when my sister...'

'Come *along*, Nancy,' Oliver said. He took Nancy's arm and pulled her roughly. It looked as if he was going to leave without another word, but he stopped at the door and took Tamsin's hand. Their eyes met, Tamsin's wary, his, unless Greenleaf was imagining things, full of pleading disappointment. Then when

Nancy kissed her, he followed suit, touching her cheek with the sexless peck that was common politeness in Linchester.

When they had gone, taking the Gavestons with them, and the Willises and the Millers had departed by the garden gate, Greenleaf went over to Patrick. He examined his eye and asked him how he felt.

'Lousy.'

Greenleaf poured him a cup of coffee.

'Had I better send for Dr. Howard, Max?' Tamsin didn't look anxious or excited or uneasy any more. She just looked annoyed.

'I don't think so.' Howard, he knew for a fact, wasn't on the week-end rota. A substitute would come and—who could tell?—that substitute might be himself. 'There's not much you can do. Perhaps an anti-histamine. I'll go over home and fetch something.'

Bernice and Marvell went with him, but he came back alone. The Carnabys were still there. Tamsin had left the front doors open for him and as he crossed the hall he heard no voices. They were all sitting in silence, each apparently nursing private resentment. Freda had moved a little away from Patrick and had helped herself to coffee.

As if taking her cue from his arrival, Tamsin said sharply: 'Isn't it time you went?' She spoke to Edward but she was looking at Freda. 'When you've quite finished, of course.'

'I'm sure I didn't mean to be *de trop*.' Edward blushed but he brought out his painfully acquired French defiantly. Freda lingered woodenly. Then Patrick gave her a little push, a sharp sadistic push that left a red mark on her arm.

'Run along, there's a good girl,' he said and she rose obediently, pulling her skirt down over her knees.

'Night,' Patrick said abruptly. He pushed past Edward, ignoring the muttered 'We know when we're not wanted.' At the door he said to Greenleaf, 'You'll come up?' and the doctor nodded.

WHEN HE ENTERED THE BALCONY ROOM BEHIND Tamsin, Patrick was already in bed and he lay with his arms outside the sheets, the stings covered by blue pyjama sleeves.

By now his face was almost unrecognisable. The cheek had swollen and closed the eye. He looked, Greenleaf thought, rather as if he had mumps.

Queenie was stretched beside him, her feet at the foot of the bed, her jowls within the palm of his hand.

'You'll be too hot with him there,' the doctor said.

'It's not a him, it's a bitch.' Tamsin put her hand on Queenie's collar and for a moment Patrick's good eye blazed. 'Oh, all right, but I shan't sleep. I feel like hell.'

Greenleaf opened the windows to the balcony. The air felt cool, almost insolently fresh and invigorating after the hot evening. There were no curtains here to sway and alarm a sleeper, only the white hygienic blinds.

'Do you want something to make you sleep?' Prudently Greenleaf had brought his bag back with him. But Tamsin moved over to the dressing-table with its long built-in counter of black glass and creamy wood textured like watered silk. She opened one of the drawers and felt inside.

'He's got these,' she said. 'He had bad insomnia last year and Dr. Howard gave them to him.'

Greenleaf took the bottle from her. Inside were six blue capsules. Sodium Amytal, two hundred milli-grammes.

'He can have one.' He unscrewed the cap and rattled a capsule into the palm of his hand.

'One's no good,' Patrick said. He held his cheek to lessen the pain talking caused him, and Tamsin, white and fluttering against her own reflection in the black glass wardrobe doors, nodded earnestly. 'He always had to have two,' she said.

'One,' Greenleaf was taking no chances. He opened his bag and took out a phial. 'The anti-hista-mine will help you to sleep. You'll sleep like a log.'

Patrick took them all at once, drinking from the glass Tamsin held out to him. 'Thanks,' he said. Tamsin waited until the doctor had fastened his bag and replaced the capsules in the immaculately tidy drawer. Then she switched off the light and they went downstairs.

'Please don't say Thank you for a lovely party,' she said when she and Greenleaf were in the hall.

Greenleaf chuckled. 'I won't,' he said.

The swans had gone to bed long ago in the reeds on the edge of the pond. From the woods between Linchester and Marvell's house something cried out, a fox perhaps or just an owl. It could have been either for all Greenleaf knew. His short stocky body cast a long shadow in the moonlight as he crossed The Green to the house called Shalom. He was suddenly very tired.

* * *

MARVELL, ON THE OTHER HAND, WAS WIDE awake. He walked home through the woods slowly, reaching out from time to time to touch the moist lichened tree trunks in the dark. There were sounds in the forest, strange crunching whispering sounds which would have alarmed the doctor. Marvell had known them since boyhood, the tread of the fox— this was only a few miles north of Quorn country— the soft movement of dry leaves as a grass snake shifted them. It was very dark but the darkness was not absolute. Each trunk was a grey signpost to him; leaves touched his face and although the air was sultry they were cold and clean against his cheek. As he came out into Long Lane he heard in the distance the cry of the nightjar and he sighed.

When he had let himself into the house he lit one of the oil lamps and went as he always did before going to bed from room to room to look at his treasures. The porcelain gleamed, catching up what little light there was. He held the lamp for a moment against the mezzotint of Rievaulx. It recalled to him his own work on another Cistercian abbey and, setting the lamp by the window, he sat down with his manuscript, not to write—it was too late for that— but to read what he had written that day.

Red and white by the window. The snowflake fronds of the Russian Vine and beside it hanging like drops of crimson wax, Berberidopis, blood-red, absurdly named. The moonlight and the lamplight met and something seemed to pierce his heart.

Moths seeing the light, came at once to the lattice

and a coal-black one—Marvell recognised it as The Chimney Sweeper's Boy—fluttered in at the open casement. It was followed by a larger, greyish-white one, its wings hung with filaments, swans-down in miniature. For a second Marvell watched them seek the lamp. Then, fearful lest they burn their wings, he gathered them up, making a loose cage of his hands, and thrust them out of the window.

They spiralled away from yellow into silvery light. He looked and looked again. There was someone in the garden. A shape, itself moth-like, was moving in the orchard. He brushed the black and white wing dust from his hands and leaned out to see who was paying him a visit at midnight.

ffffffffffffffffff **7** fffff

On Sunday morning Greenleaf got up at eight, did some exercises which he told his patients confidently would reduce their waist measurements from thirty-four to twenty-nine, and had a bath. By nine he had looked at *The Observer* and taken a cup of coffee up to Bernice. Then he sat down to write to his two sons who were away at school.

It was unlikely that anyone would call him out today. He had done his Sunday stint on the Chant-flower doctors' rota, the previous week-end, and he intended to have a lazy day. Bernice appeared at about ten and they had a leisurely breakfast, talking about the boys and about the new car which ought to arrive in time to fetch them home for the holidays. After awhile they took their coffee into the garden. They were near enough to the house to hear the phone but when it rang Greenleaf let Bernice answer it, knowing it wouldn't be for him.

But instead of settling down to a good gossip Bernice came back quickly, looking puzzled. This was odd, for Bernice seldom hurried.

'It's Tamsin, darling,' she said. 'She wants you.'

'Me?'

'She's in a state, but she wouldn't tell me anything. All she said was I want Max.'

Greenleaf took the call on the morning room phone.

'Max? It's Tamsin.' For almost the first time since he had met her Tamsin wasn't using her affected drawl. 'I know I shouldn't be ringing you about this but I can't get hold of Dr. Howard.' She paused and he heard her inhale as if on a cigarette. 'Max, I can't wake Patrick. He's awfully cold and I've shaken him but... he doesn't wake.'

'When was this?'

'Just now, this minute. I overslept and I've only just got up.'

'I'll be right over,' Greenleaf said.

She murmured, 'Too kind!' and he heard the receiver drop.

Taking up his bag, he went by the short cut, the diameter of The Circle across the grass. On the face of it it seemed obvious what had happened. In pain from his stings Patrick had taken an extra one of the capsules. I ought to have taken the damned things away with me, Greenleaf said to himself. But still, it wasn't for him to baby another man's patients. Howard had prescribed them, they were safe enough unless... Unless! Surely Patrick wouldn't have been fool enough to take *two* more? Greenleaf quickened his pace and broke into a trot. Patrick was a young man, apparently healthy, but still, three... And the anti-histamine. Suppose he had taken the whole bottleful?

She was waiting for him on the doorstep when he ran up the Hallows drive and she hadn't bothered to dress. Because she never made up her face and always wore her hair straight she hadn't the bleak unkempt look of most of the women who called him out on an emergency. She wore a simple expensive dressing-gown of candy-striped cotton, pink and white with a small spotless white bow at the neck, and there were silver chain sandals on her feet. She looked alarmed and because of her fear, very young.

'Oh, Max, I didn't know what to do.'

'Still asleep, is he?'

Greenleaf went upstairs quickly, talking to her over his shoulder.

'He's so white and still and—and heavy somehow.'

'All right. Don't come up. Make some coffee. Make it very strong and black.'

She went away to the kitchen and Greenleaf entered the bedroom. Patrick was lying on his back, his head at an odd angle. His face was still puffy and the arms which were stretched over the counterpane, faintly swollen and white, not red any more. Greenleaf knew that colour, the yellowish ivory of parchment, and that waxen texture.

He took one of the wrists and remembered what Tamsin had said about the heavy feeling. Then, having slipped one hand under the bedclothes, he lifted Patrick's eyelids and closed them again. He sighed deeply. Feeling Patrick's pulse and heart had been just a farce. He had known when he came into the room. The dead look so very dead, as if they have never been alive.

He went out to meet Tamsin. She was coming up the stairs with the dog behind her.

'Tamsin, come in here.' He opened the door to the room where last night they had looked at the picture. One of the beds had been slept in and the covers were thrown back. 'Would you like to sit down?'

'Can't you wake him either?'

'I'm afraid...' He was a friend and he put his arm about her shoulders. 'You must be prepared for a shock.' She looked up at him. He had never noticed how large her eyes were nor of what a curious shade of transparent amber. 'I'm very much afraid Patrick is dead.'

She neither cried nor cried out. There was no change of colour in the smooth brown skin. Resting back against the bed-head, she remained as still as if she too were dead. She seemed to be thinking. It was as if, Greenleaf thought, all her past life with Patrick was being re-lived momentarily within her brain. At last she shuddered and bowed her head.

'What was it?' He had to bend towards her to catch the words. 'The cause, I mean. What did he die of?'

'I don't know.'

'The wasp stings?'

Greenleaf shook his head.

'I don't want to trouble you now,' he said gently, 'but those capsules, the sodium amytal, where are they?'

Tamsin got up like a woman in a dream.

'In the drawer. I'll get them.'

He followed her back into the other bedroom. She looked at Patrick, still without crying, and Greenleaf expected her to kiss the pallid forehead. They usually did. When instead she turned away and went to the dressing table he drew the sheet up over Patrick's face.

'There are still five in the bottle,' she said, and held it out to him. Greenleaf was very surprised. He felt a creeping unease.

'I'll get on to Dr. Howard,' he said.

Howard was out playing golf. Mrs. Howard would ring the club and her husband would come straight over. When Greenleaf walked into the dining room Tamsin was kneeling on the floor with her arms round the neck of the Weimaraner. She was crying.

'Oh, Queenie! Oh, Queenie!'

The room was untouched since the night before. The drinks were still on the sideboard and out on the patio some of the food remained: heat-curled bread, melting cream, a shrivelled sandwich on a doily. On the birthday table Marvell's roses lay among the other gifts, pearled with Sunday's dew. Greenleaf poured some brandy into a glass and handed it to Tamsin.

'How long has he been dead?' she asked.

'A good while,' Greenleaf said. 'Hours. Perhaps ten or twelve hours. Of course you looked in on him before you went to bed.'

She had stopped crying. 'Oh, yes,' she said.

'It doesn't matter. I don't want to upset you.'

'That's all right, Max. I'd like to talk about it.'

'You didn't sleep in the same room?'

'Not when one of us was ill,' Tamsin said quickly. 'I thought if he were restless it would be better for me to go in the back. Restless!' She passed her hand across her brow. 'Too dreadful, Max!' She went on rather as if she were giving evidence, using clipped sentences. 'I tried to clear up the mess in the garden but I was too tired. Then I looked in on Patrick. It must have been about midnight. He was sleeping then. I know he was, he was breathing. Well, and I didn't wake up till eleven. I rushed into Patrick because I couldn't hear a sound. Queenie had come up on my bed during the night.' Her hand fumbled for the dog's neck and she pushed her fingers into the plushy fur. 'I couldn't wake him so I phoned Dr. Howard. You know the rest.'

Patrick had died, Greenleaf thought, as he had lived, precisely, tidily, without dirt or disorder. Not for him the sloppy squalor that attended so many deathbeds. From mild discomfort he had slipped into sleep, from sleep into death.

'Tamsin,' he said slowly and kindly, 'have you got any other sleeping pills in the house? Have you got any of your own?'

'Oh, no. No, I know we haven't. Patrick just had those six left and I never need anything to make me sleep.' She added unnecessarily: 'I sleep like a log.'

'Had he a weak heart? Did you ever hear of any heart trouble?'

'I don't think so. We'd been married for seven years, you know, but I've known Patrick since he was a little boy. I don't know if you knew we were cousins? His father and mine were brothers.'

'No serious illnesses?'

A petulant cloud crossed her face briefly. 'He was born in Germany,' she said. 'Then, when the war came, they lived in America. After they came back to this country they used to come and see us sometimes. Patrick was terribly spoiled, coddled really. They used to make him wrap up warm even in the summer and

I had swimming lessons but they wouldn't let him. I always thought it was because they'd lived in California.' She paused, frowning. 'He was always all right when he was grown-up. The only time he went to Dr. Howard was when he couldn't sleep.'

'I think you will have to prepare yourself,' Greenleaf said, 'for the possibility of an inquest, or, at any rate, a post-mortem.'

She nodded earnestly.

'Oh, quite,' she said. 'I understand. That'll be absolutely all right.' She might have been agreeing to cancel an engagement, so matter-of-fact was her tone.

After that they sat in silence, waiting for Dr. Howard to come. The Weimaraner went upstairs and they heard her claws scraping, scraping at the closed door of the balcony room.

As THINGS TURNED OUT, IT NEVER CAME TO AN INquest. Greenleaf stood in at the post-mortem because he was interested and because the Selbys had been friends of his. Patrick had died, like all the dead, of heart failure. The death certificate was signed and he was buried in Chantflower cemetery on the following Thursday.

Greenleaf and Bernice went to the funeral. They took Marvell with them in Bernice's car.

'Blessed are the dead,' said the Rector, a shade sardonically, 'which die in the Lord.' Since coming to Linchester Patrick had never been to church.

Patrick's parents were dead; Tamsin had been an orphan since she was four. They had both been only children. Consequently there were no relatives at the graveside. Apart from the Linchesterites, only three friends came to support the widow: the two other directors of Patrick's firm of glass manufacturers and old Mrs. Prynne.

Tamsin wore a black dress and a large hat of glossy black straw. Throughout the service she clung to Oliver Gage's arm. On the other side Nancy, sweating in the charcoal worsted she had bought for her February honeymoon, sat with a handkerchief ready. But she never had to hand it to Tamsin who sat rigid and dry-eyed.

It was only when the coffin was being lowered into the ground that a small disturbance occurred. Freda Carnaby tore herself from Mrs. Saxton's arm and, sobbing loudly, fell to her knees beside the dark cavity. As he said afterwards to Greenleaf, Marvell thought that like Hamlet she was going to leap into the grave. But nothing dramatic happened. Mrs. Saxton helped her to her feet and drew her away.

WHEN IT WAS ALL OVER TAMSIN SLUNG TWO SUITcases into the back of the black and white Mini (SIN A1) and with Queenie in the seat beside her, drove away to stay with Mrs. Prynne.

PART TWO

8

TWO DAYS LATER THE WEATHER BROKE WITH A noisy spectacular thunderstorm and a man died when a tree under which he was sheltering on Chantflower golf course was struck by lightning. The silly season had begun and this was national news. For the Linchester housewives kept indoors by continuous rain, it was for days the prime topic of conversation—until something more personal and sensational took over.

The young Macdonalds had taken their baby to Bournemouth; the Willises and the Millers, each couple finding in the other the perfect neighbours and friends, were cruising together in the Canaries. Tamsin was still away. With four empty houses on Linchester Nancy was bored to tears. When Oliver came home for the week-ends, tired and uneasy, he found his evening programmes mapped out for him.

Tonight the Greenleafs and Crispin Marvell were

invited for coffee and drinks. Opening his sideboard, Oliver found that Nancy had laid in a stock of cheap Cyprus sherry and bottles of cocktails as variously coloured as the liquid that used to be displayed in the flagons of old-fashioned pharmacy windows. He cursed, clinging to the shreds of his pride and remembering the days that were gone.

The mantelpiece was decorated with postcards. Nancy had given pride of place to a peacock-blue panorama from Clare Miller, relegating two monochrome seascapes to a spot behind a vase. He read Sheila Macdonald's happy scrawl irascibly. Tamsin was at the seaside too, but Tamsin had sent nothing...

From where he stood, desultorily watching the rain, he could hear Nancy chattering to Linda Gaveston in the kitchen. Occasionally something clearly audible if not comprehensible arose above the twittering.

'I said it was dead grotty' or 'How about that, doll?' conflicted inharmoniously with Nancy's 'You are awful, Linda.'

Oliver grunted and lit a cigarette. These visits of Linda's, ostensibly made to deliver Nancy's order of tablets of soap or a packet of Kleenex, always put him in a bad temper. They invariably led to petulance on Nancy's part, to dissatisfaction and a carping envy. It amazed Oliver that a village chemist like Waller could stock such an immense and catholic variety of luxury goods, all of which at some time or another seemed so desirable to his wife and at the same time so conducive to the saving of money. The latest in Thermos flasks, automatic tea-makers, thermostatically controlled electric blankets, shower cabinets, all these had in the year they had lived in Linchester, been recommended to Nancy and coveted by her.

'It would be such a saving in the long run,' she would say wistfully of some gimmick, using the suburban colloquialisms Oliver hated.

Moreover it was surprising that behind Waller's counter there stood concealed the most expensive ranges of cosmetics from Paris and New York, scent and creams which were apparently exclusive to him and not to be found in Nottingham or, for that matter, London. He was therefore pleasantly astonished when the door had closed on Linda to see Nancy come dancing into the room, contented, gay and in a strange way, gleeful.

'What's got into you?'

'Nothing.'

'For a poor house-bound, forsaken child bride,' he said, recalling earlier complaints, 'you're looking very gay.'

Indeed she appeared quite pretty again in the honeymoon skirt and a pink sweater, not a hand-knitted one for a change but a soft fluffy thing that drew Oliver's eyes and reminded him that his wife had, after all, an excellent figure. But his words, sharp and moody, had altered her expression from calm to secretiveness.

'Linda told me something very peculiar.'

'Really?' he said. 'Surprise me.'

She pouted.

'Not if you're going to talk to me like that.' For a moment, a transient moment, she looked just as she had when he had first seen her dancing with the man she had been engaged to. It had been such fun stealing her from him, especially piquant because the fiancé had also been Shirley's cousin. 'Nasty Oliver! I shall save it all up till the Greenleafs get here.'

'I can see,' said Oliver in his best co-respondent's voice, 'I can see I shall have to be very nice to you.'

'Very, very nice,' said Nancy. She sat on the sofa beside him and giggled. 'You are awful! It must be the country air.' But she didn't say anything after that and presently Oliver forgot all about Linda Gaveston.

When Marvell rang the door-bell she didn't bother to tidy her hair or put on fresh make-up. There was something of a bacchante about her, exhibitionistic, crudely female. Suddenly Oliver felt old. Her naiveté embarrassed him. He went to dispense drinks from his own stock, leaving the bright mean bottles in the sideboard.

Greenleaf and Bernice had barely sat down when she said brightly:

'Has anyone heard from Tamsin?'

Nobody had. Oliver fancied that Marvell was looking at him quizzically.

'I don't suppose she feels like writing.' Bernice was always kind and forbearing. 'It's not as if we were any of us close friends.'

'What would she have to write about?' Greenleaf asked. 'She's not on holiday.' And he began to talk about his own holiday, planned for September this year, and to ask about the Gages'.

Holidays were a sore point with Oliver who hoped to do without one altogether. He need not have worried. Nancy was obviously not going to let the subject go as easily as that.

'Poor Tamsin,' she said loudly, drowning the doctor's voice. 'Fancy being a widow when you're only twenty-seven.'

'Dreadful,' said Bernice.

'And in such—well, awkward circumstances.'

'Awkward circumstances?' said Greenleaf, drawn unwillingly from his dreams of the Riviera.

'I don't mean money-wise.' Oliver winced but Nancy went on: 'The whole thing was so funny, Patrick dying like that. I expect you'll all think I've got a very suspicious mind but I can't help thinking it was...' She paused for effect and sipped her gin. 'Well, it was fishy, wasn't it?'

Greenleaf looked at the floor. The legs of his chair had caught in one of the Numdah rugs. He bent down and straightened it.

'I don't know if I ought to say this,' Nancy went on. 'I don't suppose it's common knowledge, but Patrick's father...' She lowered her voice. 'Patrick's father committed suicide. Took his own life.'

'Oh, dear,' said Bernice comfortably.

'I really don't know who it was told me,' Nancy said. She picked up the plate of canapés and handed it to Marvell. To his shame Oliver saw that only half a cocktail onion topped the salmon mayonnaise on each of them. 'Do have a savoury, won't you?'

Marvell refused. The plate hovered.

'Somebody told me about it. Now who was it?'

'It was me,' Oliver said sharply.

'Of course it was. And Tamsin told you. I can't imagine why.'

All childish innocence, she looked archly from face to face.

Marvell said: 'I'm afraid I'm being obtuse, but I can't quite see what Patrick's father's suicide had to do with his son dying of heart failure.'

'Oh, absolutely nothing. Nothing at all. You

mustn't think I was insinuating anything about Patrick. It's just that it's one of the funny circumstances. On its own it would be nothing.'

Oliver emptied his glass and stood up. He could cheerfully have slapped Nancy's face. 'I think we're boring our guests,' he said, bracketing himself with his wife and trying to make his voice sound easy. 'Another drink, Max? Bernice?' Marvell's glass was still full. 'What about you, darling?'

'Oh, really!' Nancy burst out laughing. 'You don't have to be so discreet. We're all friends. Nothing's going to go beyond these four walls.'

Oliver felt himself losing control. These people *were* discreet. Would it, after all, ruin his career, damn him as a social creature, if in front of them he were to bawl at Nancy, strike her, push her out of the room?

He stared at her, pouring sherry absently until it topped over the glass and spilled on the tray.

'Damnation!' he said.

'Oh, your table!' Bernice was beside him, mopping with a tiny handkerchief.

'Linda Gaveston was here today,' Nancy said. 'She told me something very peculiar. No I won't shut up, Oliver. I'm only repeating it because I'd be very interested in having an opinion from a medical man. You know that funny little man who's a commercial traveller? The one who lives in the chalets?'

'Carnaby,' said Marvell.

'That's right, Carnaby. The one who was so difficult at the party. Well, the day before Patrick died he came into Waller's shop and what d'you think he tried to buy?' She waited for the guesses that never came. 'Cyanide! That's what he tried to buy.'

Greenleaf stuck out his lower lip. They had only been in the house half an hour but he began to wonder how soon he could suggest to Bernice that it was time to leave. His drink tasted thin. For the first time since he had given up smoking as an example to his patients he longed for a cigarette.

'Waller wouldn't sell anyone cyanide and maybe he managed to get it...' She drew breath. 'Elsewhere,' she said with sinister emphasis. 'Now why did he want it?'

'Probably for killing wasps,' said Marvell. 'It's an old remedy for getting rid of wasps.'

Nancy looked disappointed.

'Linda overheard the conversation,' she said, 'and that's just what this fellow Carnaby said. He said he wanted it for wasps. Linda thought it was pretty thin.'

Thumping his fist on the table, Oliver made them all jump.

'Linda Gaveston is a stupid little trouble-maker,' he said furiously.

'I suppose that goes for me too?'

'I didn't say so,' said Oliver, too angry to care. 'But if the cap fits... I hate all this under-hand gossip. If you're trying to say Carnaby gave Patrick cyanide you'd better come straight out with it.' He drank some whisky too quickly and choked. 'On the other hand, perhaps you'd better not. I don't want to pay out whacking damages for slander.'

'It won't go any further. Anyway, it's my duty as a citizen to say what I think. Everyone knows Edward

Carnaby had a terrific motive for getting Patrick out of the way.'

There was an appalled silence. Nancy had grown red in the face and her plump breasts rose and fell under the clinging pink wool.

'You're all crazy about Tamsin. I know that. But Patrick wasn't. He didn't care for her a bit. He was having an affair with that awful little Freda. Night after night he was round there while her brother was out at evening classes. He used to tie that great dog of theirs up to the gate. It was just a horrid sordid little intrigue.'

As much as Oliver, Greenleaf wanted to stop her. He was immeasurably grateful for Bernice's rich cleansing laughter.

'If it was just a little intrigue,' Bernice said lightly, 'it can't have been important, can it?'

Nancy allowed her hand to rest for a moment beneath Bernice's. Then she snatched it away.

'They're twins, aren't they? It means a lot, being twins. He wouldn't want to lose her. Patrick might have gone off with her.'

But the tension was broken. Marvell, who had taken a book from the fireside shelves and studied it as if it were a first edition, now relaxed and smiled. Oliver had moved over to the record player and the red glaze had left his face.

'Well, what does Max think?' Nancy asked.

How wise Bernice had been, laughing easily, refusing to catch his eye! Greenleaf didn't really want to do a Smith-King and flee at the scent of trouble. Besides, Oliver had some good records, Bartok and the wonderful Donizetti he wanted to hear again.

'You know,' he said in a quiet gentle voice, 'it's amazing the way people expect the worst when a young person dies suddenly. They always want to make a mystery.' He wondered if Bernice and, for that matter Marvell, noticed how dismay was evoking his guttural accent. 'Real life isn't so sensational.'

'Fiction stranger than truth,' Marvell murmured.

'I can assure you Patrick didn't die of cyanide. You see, of all the poisons commonly used in cases of homicide cyanide is the most easily detected. The smell, for one thing...'

'Bitter almonds,' Nancy interposed.

Greenleaf smiled a smile he didn't feel.

'That among other things. Believe me, it's fantastic to talk of cyanide.' His hands moved expressively. 'No, please,' he said.

'Well, what do you really think, then?'

'I think you're a very pretty girl with a vivid imagination and Linda Gaveston watches too much television. I wonder if I might have some more of your excellent whisky, Oliver?'

Oliver took the glass gratefully. He looked as if he would gladly have given Greenleaf the whole bottle.

'Music,' he said, handing records to the discerning Marvell.

'May we have the Handel?' Marvell asked politely. Nancy made a face and flung herself back among the cushions.

The sound of the rain falling steadily had formed throughout the conversation a monotonous background chorus. Now, as they became silent, the music of The Faithful Shepherd Suite filled the room. Greenleaf listened to the orchestra and noted the repetition of each phrase with the appreciation of the scientist: but Marvell, with the ear of the artist *manqué*, felt the absurd skimped room transformed about him and, sighing within himself for something irrevocably lost, saw a green grove as in a Constable landscape and beneath the leaves a lover with the Pipes of Pan.

THE RAIN CEASED AS DARKNESS FELL AND THE SKY cleared suddenly as if washed free of cloud. It was a night of bright white stars, so many stars that Greenleaf had to point out and admire—although he did not know their names—the strung lights of Charles's Wain and Jupiter riding in the south.

'Patines of bright gold,' said Marvell. 'Only they're not gold, they're platinum. Patines of bright platinum doesn't sound half so well, does it?'

'It's no good quoting at me,' said the doctor. 'You know I never read anything but the *B.M.F.*' He drew a deep breath, savouring the night air. 'Very nice,' he said inadequately. 'I'm glad I summoned up the energy to walk back with you.'

'It was a sticky evening, wasn't it?' Marvell went first, holding back brambles for Greenleaf to pass along the path.

107

'Silly little woman,' Greenleaf said, harshly for him. 'I hope Gage can stop her gossiping.'

'It could be awkward.' Marvell said no more until the path broadened and the doctor was walking abreast of him. Then suddenly, 'May I ask you something?' he said. 'I don't want to offend you.'

'You won't do that.'

'You're a doctor, but Patrick wasn't your patient.' Marvell spoke quietly. 'I asked you if I would offend you because I was thinking of medical etiquette. But—look, I'm not scandal mongering like Nancy Gage—weren't you very surprised when Patrick died like that?'

Greenleaf said guardedly, 'I was surprised, yes.'

'Thunderstruck?'

'Like that poor fellow on the golf course? Well, no. You see a lot of strange things in my job. I thought at first Patrick had taken an overdose of sodium amytal. I'd given him an anti-histamine, two hundred milligrammes Phenergan, and one would potentiate...' He stopped, loath to give these esoteric details to a layman. 'He had the sodium amytal and I advised him to take one.'

'You left the bottle with him?'

'Now, look.' Greenleaf had said he wouldn't be offended. 'Patrick wasn't a child. Howard had prescribed them. In any case, he didn't take any more. That was the first thing Glover looked for at the postmortem.'

Marvell opened the orchard gate and Greenleaf stepped from the forest floor on to turf and the slippery leaves of wild daffodils. The petals of a wet rose brushed his face. In the darkness they felt like a woman's fingers drenched with scent.

'The first thing?' Marvell asked. 'You mean, you looked for other things? You suspected suicide or even murder?'

'No, no, no,' Greenleaf said impatiently. 'A man had died, a young, apparently healthy man. Glover had to find out what he died of. Patrick died of heart failure.'

'Everybody dies of heart failure.'

'Roughly, yes. But there were signs that the heart had been affected before. There was some slight damage.'

They had come to the back door. The kitchen smelt of herbs and wine. Greenleaf thought he could detect another less pleasant scent. Mildew. He had never seen mushrooms growing but Marvell's kitchen smelt like the plastic trays of mushrooms Bernice bought at the village store. Marvell groped for the lamp and lit it.

'Well, go on,' he said.

'If you must know,' Greenleaf said, 'Glover made some enquires at Patrick's old school. Tamsin didn't know anything and Patrick's parents were dead. He'd never complained to Howard about feeling ill. Only went to him once.'

'May I ask if you got anything from the school?'

'I don't know if you may,' Greenleaf said severely. 'I don't know why you want to know. But if there's going to be a lot of talk. . . . Glover wrote to the headmaster and he got a letter back saying Patrick had had to be let off some of the games because he'd had rheumatic fever.'

'I see. So you checked with the doctor Patrick had when he was a child.'

'We couldn't do that.' Greenleaf smiled a small, bitter and very personal smile. 'Patrick was born in Germany. His mother was German and he lived there till he was four. Glover talked to Tamsin's Mrs. Prynne. She's one of these old women with a good memory. She remembered Patrick had had rheumatic fever when he was three—very early to have it, incidentally—and that the name of his doctor had been Goldstein.'

Marvell was embarrassed.

'But Dr. Goldstein had disappeared. A lot of people of his persuasion disappeared in Germany between 1939 and 1945.'

'Stopping for a quick drink?' Marvell asked.

Five minutes passed before he said anything more about Patrick Selby. Greenleaf felt that he had been stiff and pompous, the very prototype of the uppish medical man. To restore Marvell's ease he accepted a glass of carrot wine.

The brilliance of the white globe had increased until now only the corners of the parlour remained in shadow. A small wind had arisen, stirring the curtains and moving the trailing violet and white leaves of the Tradescantia that stood in a majolica pot on the window sill. It was rather cold.

Then Marvell said: 'I was curious about Patrick.' He sat down and warmed his hands at the lamp. Greenleaf wondered if Bernice, at home in Shalom, had turned on the central heating. 'Perhaps I have a suspicious mind. Patrick had a good many enemies, you know. Quite a lot of people must be glad he's dead.'

'And I have a logical mind,' said Greenleaf briskly. 'Nancy Gage says Carnaby tried to buy cyanide. Patrick Selby dies suddenly. Therefore, she reasons,

110

Patrick died of cyanide. But we *know* Patrick didn't die of cyanide. He died a natural death. Can't you see that once your original premise falls to the ground there's no longer any reason to doubt it? No matter how much Carnaby hated him—if he did, which I doubt—no matter if he succeeded in buying a ton of cyanide, he didn't kill Patrick with it because Patrick didn't die of cyanide. Now, just because one person appears to have a thin motive and access—possible access—to means *that were never used at all*, you start reasoning that he was in fact murdered, that half a dozen people had motives and that one of them succeeded.' He drank the carrot wine. It was really quite pleasant, like sweet Bristol Cream. 'You're not being logical,' he said.

Marvell didn't reply. He began to wind the clock delicately as if he was being careful not to disturb the sultan and his slave whose fingers rested eternally on the silent zither. When he had put the key down he blew away a monkey spider that was creeping across the sultan's gondola-shaped shoe. Then he said:

'Why wasn't there an inquest?'

Greenleaf answered him triumphantly. 'Because there wasn't any need. Haven't I been telling you? And that wasn't up to Glover and Howard. That's a matter for the coroner.'

'No doubt he knows his own business.'

'You don't have inquests on people who die naturally.' Greenleaf got up, stretching cold stiff legs, and changed the subject. 'How's the hay fever?'

'I've run out of tablets.'

'Come down to the surgery sometime and I'll let you have another prescription.'

* * *

BUT MARVELL DIDN'T COME AND GREENLEAF SAW nothing of him for several days. Greenleaf began to think that he would hear no more of Patrick's death —until surgery time on Wednesday morning.

The first patient to come into the consulting room through the green baize door was Denholm Smith-King. He was on his way to his Nottingham factory and at last he had summoned the courage to let Greenleaf examine him.

'It's nothing,' the doctor said as Smith-King sat up on the couch buttoning his shirt. 'Only a gland. It'll go down eventually.'

'Then I suppose I shall just have to lump it.' He laughed at his own joke and Greenleaf joined in politely.

'I see you've cut down on the smoking.'

He was startled and showed it, but his eyes followed the doctor's down to his own right forefinger and he grinned.

'Quite the detective in your own way, aren't you?' Greenleaf had only noticed that the sepia stains had paled to yellow and this remark reminded him of things he wanted to forget. 'Yes, I've cut it down,' Smith-King said and he gave the doctor a heavy, though friendly buffet on the back. 'You quacks, you don't know the strains a business man has to contend with. You don't know you're born,' but his hearty laugh softened the words.

'Things going better, are they?'

'You bet,' said Smith-King.

He went off jauntily and Greenleaf rang the bell for the next patient. By ten he had seen a dozen people and he asked the last one, a woman with nettle rash, if there were any more to come.

'Just one, Doctor. A young lady.'

He put his finger on the buzzer but no one came so he began to tidy up his desk. Evidently the young lady had got tired of waiting. Then, just as he was picking up his ignition key, the baize door was pushed feebly open and Freda Carnaby shuffled in wearily like an old woman.

He was shocked at the change in her. Impatience died as he offered her a chair and sat down himself. What had become of the bright birdlike creature with the practical starched cotton dresses and the impractical shoes? Even at the funeral she had still looked smart in trim shop-girl black. Now her hair looked as if it hadn't been washed for weeks, her eyes were bloodshot and puffy and there was a hysterical downward quirk at the corners of her mouth.

'What exactly is the trouble, Miss Carnaby?'

'I can't sleep. I haven't had a proper night's sleep since I don't know how long.' She felt in the pocket of the mock suede jacket she wore over her crumpled print dress. The handkerchief she pulled out was crumpled too. She pressed it with pathetic gentility against her lips. 'You see, I've had a great personal loss.' The linen square brushed the corner of one eye. 'I was very fond of someone. A man.' She gulped. 'He died quite recently.'

'I'm sorry to hear that.' Greenleaf began to wonder what was coming.

'I don't know what to do.'

He had observed before that it is this particular phrase that triggers off the tears, the breakdown. It may be true, it may be felt, but it is only when it is actually uttered aloud that its full significance, the complete helpless disorientation it implies, brings home to the speaker the wretchedness of his or her plight.

'Now you mustn't say that,' he said, knowing his inadequacy. 'Time does heal, you know.' The healer passing the buck, he thought. 'I'll let you have something to make you sleep.' He drew out his prescription pad and began to write. 'Have you been away yet this year?'

'No and I am not likely to.'

'I should try. Just a few days would help.'

'Help?' He had heard the hysterical note so often but not from her and he didn't like it. 'Help a—a broken heart? Oh, Doctor, I don't know what to do. I don't know what to do.' She dropped her head on to her folded arms and began to sob.

Greenleaf went to the sink and drew her a glass of water.

'I'd like to tell you about it.' She sipped and wiped her eyes. 'Can I tell you about it?'

He looked surreptitiously at his watch.

'If it would make you feel better."

'It was Patrick Selby. You knew that didn't you?' Greenleaf said nothing so she went on. 'I was very fond of him.' They never say 'love', he thought, always 'very fond of' or 'devoted to.' 'And he was very fond of me,' she said defiantly. He glanced momentarily at her tear-blotched face, the rough skin. When she said out of the blue, 'We were going to be married,' he jumped.

'I know what you're going to say. You're going to say he was already married. Tamsin didn't care for him. He was going to divorce her.'

'Miss Carnaby...'

But she rushed on, the words tumbling out.

'She was having an affair with that awful man Gage. Patrick knew all about it. She used to meet him in London during the week. Patrick knew. She said she was going to see some old friend of her grandmother's, but half the time she was with that man.'

Sympathy fought with and finally conquered Greenleaf's distaste. Keeping his expression a kindly blank, he began to fold up the prescription.

Misinterpreting his look, she said defensively:

'I know what you're thinking. But I wasn't carrying on with Patrick. It wasn't like that. We never did anything wrong. We were going to be married. And Nancy Gage is going about all over Linchester saying Edward killed Patrick because...because...' Her sobs broke out afresh. Greenleaf watched her in despair. How was he to turn this weeping hysterical woman out into the street? How stem the tide of appalling revelations?

'And the terrible thing is I know he was killed. That's why I can't sleep. And I know who killed him.'

This was too much. He shook her slightly, wiped her eyes himself and held the glass to her lips.

'Miss Carnaby, you must get a grip on yourself. Patrick died a perfectly natural death. This is certain. I know it. You'll do your brother and yourself a lot of harm if you go about saying things you can't substantiate.'

'Substantiate?' She stumbled over the word. 'I can *prove* it. You remember what it was like at that awful party. Well, Oliver Gage went back by himself when it was all over. I saw him from my bedroom window. It was bright moonlight and he went over by the pond.

He was carrying something, a white packet. I don't know what it was, but, Doctor, suppose—suppose it killed Patrick!'

Then he got her out of the surgery, bundled her into his own car and drove her back to Linchester.

THREE LETTERS PLOPPED THROUGH THE GAGE letter box when the post came at ten. Nancy was so sure they weren't for her that it was all of half an hour before she bothered to come down from the bathroom. Instead, her hair rolled up in curlers, wet and evil-smelling with home-perm fluid, she sat on the edge of the bath waiting for the cooking timer to ping and brooding about what the letters might contain.

Two bills, she thought bitterly, and probably a begging letter from Jean or Shirley. A saturated curler dripped on to her nose. By this time the whole of the first floor of the house smelt of ammonia and rotten eggs. She would have to use masses of that air freshener stuff before Oliver came home. Still, that was a whole two days and goodness knew how many hours away. Surely Oliver would scarcely notice the smell when he saw how wonderful her hair looked, and all for twenty-five bob.

The timer rang and she began unrolling excitedly. When the handbasin was filled with a soggy mess of curlers and mushy paper she put a towel round her shoulders, a mauve one with Hers embroidered on it in white; His, the other half of the wedding present, was scrupulously kept for Oliver—and went downstairs.

The first letter she picked up was from Jean.

Nancy knew that before she saw the handwriting. Oliver's first wife was their only correspondent who saved old envelopes and stuck new address labels on them. The second was almost certainly the telephone bill. It might be as well to lose that. Now, who could be writing to her from London?

She opened the last envelope and saw the letter heading, Oliver's newspaper, Fleet Street. It was *from* Oliver. She looked at the envelope and the slanted stamp. To her that meant a kiss. Did it mean that to Oliver or had it occurred by chance?

'My darling...' That was nice. It was also unfamiliar and unexpected. She read on. 'I am wondering if you have forgiven me for my unkindness to you at the week-end. I was sharp with you, even verging on the brutal...' How beautifully he wrote! But that was to be expected. It was, after all, his line. 'Can you understand, my sweet, that this was only because I hate to see you cheapening yourself? I felt that you were making yourself the butt of those men's wit and this hurt me more bitterly than I can tell you. So for my sake, darling Nancy, watch your words. This is Tamsin's business and she is nothing to us...' Nancy could hardly believe a letter would make her so happy. '...She is nothing to us. We each possess one world. Each hath one and is one.' Hath, she decided, must be typing error, but the thought was there. 'The merest suggestion that I might be...' Then there was a bit blanked out with x's '...associated with a scandal of this kind has caused me considerable disquiet. We were not close friends of the Selbys...'

There was a great deal more in the same vein. Nancy skipped some of it, the boring parts, and lingered over the astonishing endearments at the end.

She was so ecstatically happy that, although she caught sight of her elated face in the hall mirror, she hardly noticed that her hair was hanging in rats' tails, dripping and perfectly straight.

MARVELL WAS DETERMINED TO GET GREENLEAF interested in the circumstances of Patrick's death and he thought it would do no harm to confront him with a list of unusual poisons. To this end he had been to the public library and spent an instructive afternoon reading Taylor. He was so carried away that he was too late for afternoon surgery—his ostensible mission, he decided, would be to collect another prescription—so he picked a bunch of acanthus for Bernice and walked up to Shalom.

'Beautiful,' Bernice said. Her husband touched the brownish-pink flowers. 'What are they?' Diffidently he suggested: 'Lupins or something?'

'Acanthus,' said Marvell. 'The original model for the Corinthian capital.'

Bernice filled a white stone vase with water. 'You are a mine of information.'

'Let's say a disused quarry of rubble.' The words had a bitter sound but Marvell smiled as he watched her arrange the flowers. 'And the rubble, incidentally, is being shaken by explosions. I've been sneezing for the past three days and I've run out of those fascinating little blue pills.'

Bernice smiled. 'If this is going to turn into a consultation,' she said, 'you'd better go and have a drink with Max.'

She began on the washing up and Marvell followed

Greenleaf into the sitting room. Greenleaf pushed open the glass doors to the garden and pulled up chairs in the path of the incoming cooler air. The sky directly above was a pure milky blue and in the west refulgent, brazen gold, but the long shadow of the cedar tree lapped the walls of the house. The room was a cool sanctuary.

'It might be worth finding out exactly what you're allergic to, have some tests done,' the doctor said. 'It need not be hay, you know. You can be allergic to practically anything.'

Marvell hadn't really wanted to talk about himself but now as if to give colour to his excuse, a tickle began at the back of his nose and he was shaken by a vast sneeze. When he had recovered he said slyly:

'Well, I suppose it can't kill me.'

'It could lead to asthma,' Greenleaf said cheerfully. 'It does in sixty to eighty per cent of cases if it isn't checked.'

'I asked,' said Marvell, re-phrasing, 'if an allergy could kill you.'

'No, you didn't. And I know exactly what you're getting at, but Patrick wasn't allergic to wasp stings. He had one a few days before he died and the effect was just normal.'

'All right,' Marvell said and he blew his nose. 'You remember what we were talking about the other night?'

'What you were talking about.'

'What I was talking about, then. Don't be so stiff-necked, Max.'

They had known each other for two or three years now and at first it had been Dr. Greenleaf, Mr. Marvell. Then, as intimacy grew, the use of their styles

119

had seemed too formal and Greenleaf who hadn't been to a public school baulked at the bare surname. This was the first time Marvell had called his friend by his first name and Greenleaf felt a strange warmth of heart, the sense of being accepted, this usage brings. It made him weak where he had intended to be strong.

'Suppose,' Marvell went on, 'there was some substance, perfectly harmless under normal circumstances, but lethal if anyone took it when he'd been stung by a wasp.'

Reluctantly Greenleaf recalled what Freda Carnaby had told him about the white package carried by Oliver Gage.

'Suppose, suppose. There isn't such a substance.'

'Sure?'

'As sure as anyone can be.'

'I'm bored with Chantefleur Abbey, Max, and I've a mind to do a spot of detecting—with your help. It obviously needs a doctor.'

'You're crazy,' said Greenleaf unhappily. 'I'm going to give you a drink and write out that prescription.'

'I don't want a drink. I want to talk about Patrick.'

'Well?'

'Well, since I last saw you I've been swotting up forensic medicine...'

'In between the sneezes, I imagine.'

'In between the sneezes, as you say. As a matter of fact I've been reading Taylor's *Medical Jurisprudence*.'

'Fascinating, isn't it?' Greenleaf said, in spite of himself. He added quickly: 'It won't tell you a thing about wasp stings or rheumatic fever.'

'No, but it tells me a hell of a lot about poisons. A

positive Borgias' Bible. Brucine and thallium, lead and gold. Did you know there are some gold salts called Purple of Cassius? But of course you did. Purple of Cassius! There's a name to conjure death with.'

'It didn't conjure Patrick Selby's death.'

'How do you *know*? I'll bet Glover didn't test for it.'

'No, and he didn't test for arsenic or hyoscine or the botulinus bacillus, for the simple reason that there wasn't the slightest indication in Patrick's appearance or the state of the room to suggest that he might remotely have taken any of them.'

'I have heard,' Marvell said, 'that a man can die from having air injected into a vein. Now there's a very entertaining novel by Dorothy Sayers . . .'

'*Unnatural Death.*'

'So you do read detective stories!' Marvell pounced on his words.

'Only on holiday.' Greenleaf smiled. 'But Patrick hadn't any hypodermic marks.'

'Well, well,' Marvell mocked. 'Max, you're a hypocrite. How do you know Patrick hadn't any hypodermic marks unless you looked for them? And if you looked for them you must have suspected at the least suicide.'

For a few moments Greenleaf didn't answer him. What Marvell said was near the truth. He had looked and found—nothing. But had he been in possession of certain facts of which he was now cognisant, would he have acted as he had? Wouldn't he instead have tried to dissuade Howard and Glover from signing the death certificate? He had done nothing because Patrick had not been his patient, because it would have been unprofessional to poach on Howard's preserves, because, most of all, Patrick had seemed a reasonably happily married man leading a quite normal life. Happily married? Now, of course, it sounded an absurd description of the mess he and Tamsin had made for themselves, but then... You had to make allowances for the uninhibited way people behave at parties, Tamsin's close dancing with Gage, Patrick's flirtation with Freda Carnaby. The possibility of murder had never crossed his mind. Why, then, had he looked? Just to fill in the time, he thought, almost convincing himself, just for something to do.

And yet, as he answered Marvell, he was fully aware that he was skirting round the question.

'I looked,' he said carefully, 'before Glover began his examination. At the time there seemed nothing to account for the death. It was afterwards that Glover found the heart damage. There were no punctures on Patrick's body apart from those made by wasps. And he didn't die from wasps' stings, unless you might say he had a certain amount of shock from the stings.'

'If by that you mean the shock affected his heart, wouldn't you have expected him to have a heart attack at once, even while he was on the ladder, not three or four hours later?'

The damage caused by the rheumatic fever had been slight. Patrick must have had it very mildly. But in the absence of Patrick's parents and Dr. Goldstein, who could tell? 'Yes, I would,' Greenleaf said unhappily.

'Max, you're coming round to my way of thinking. Look, leaving the cause of death for a moment, wasn't there something very—to use Nancy's word—fishy about that party?'

'You mean the picture?'

'I mean the picture. I went upstairs to get the citronella and there was the picture. Now, it wasn't covered up. It was in a room in Patrick's house. But he didn't know it was there. Did you see his face when he saw it?'

Greenleaf frowned. 'It was a horrible thing,' he said.

'Oh, come. A bit bloodthirsty. By a pupil of Thornhill, I should say, and those old boys didn't pull their punches. But the point is, Patrick was terrified. He couldn't have been more upset if it had been a real head in a real pool of blood.'

'Some people are very squeamish,' said Greenleaf who was always coming across them.

'About real wounds and real blood, yes. But this was only a picture. Now, I'll tell you something. A couple of weeks before he died Patrick was in my house with Tamsin and I showed them some Dali drawings I've got. They're only prints but they're much more horrifying than Salome, but Patrick didn't turn a hair.'

'So he didn't like the picture? What's it got to do with his death? He didn't die from having his head chopped off.'

'Pity,' Marvell said cheerfully. 'If he had we'd only have two-thirds of our present problem. No longer How? but simply Why? and Who?'

He got up as Bernice came in to take him on a tour of the garden.

'I need the advice of someone with green fingers.' She raised her eyebrows at their serious faces. 'Max, you're tired. Are you all right?'

'I'm fine.' He watched them go, Bernice questioning, her companion stooping toward the border

123

plants, his head raised, listening courteously. Then Bernice went up to the fence and he saw that Nancy Gage had come into the garden next door. She evidently had some news to impart, for she was talking excitedly with a kind of feverish desire for the sound of her own voice that women have who are left too much alone. Greenleaf could only remember the last time she had looked like that, but today there was no Oliver to stop her.

His wife's voice floated back to him. 'Tamsin's home, Max.'

Was that all?

He had hardly reached the lawn and heard Bernice say, 'Should we go over?' when Nancy caught him.

'Don't look at my hair,' she said, attracting his attention to it by running her fingers through the strawy mass. 'Something went wrong with the works.'

'Did you say Tamsin was home?'

'We ought to go over, Max, and see if she's all right.'

'Oh, she's all right. Brown as a berry,' said Nancy, and she made a mock-gesture of self-reproach, protruding her teeth over her lower lip. 'There I go. Come back all I said. Oliver says I mustn't talk about the Selbys to anyone, not anyone at all because of you-know-what.'

Marvell tried to catch Greenleaf's eye and when the doctor refused to co-operate, said, 'And what are we supposed to know?'

'Oliver says I mustn't go about saying Patrick didn't die naturally because it wouldn't do him any good.' She giggled. 'Oliver, I mean, not Patrick. He wrote it in a letter so it must be important.'

'Very prudent,' said Marvell.

Greenleaf opened his mouth to say something, he hardly knew what, and closed it again as the telephone rang. When he came back to the garden Nancy had gone.

'Little boy with a big headache,' he called to Bernice. 'Boys shouldn't have headaches. I'm going to see what it's all about and I'll look in on Tamsin on my way back.'

He went to get the car and nearly ran over Edith Gaveston's dog as he was backing it out. After he had apologised she picked up the Scottie and stuck her head through the car window.

'I like your new motor,' she said archaically. 'Only don't blood it on Fergus, will you?'

Fox-hunting metaphors were lost on the doctor. He made the engine rev faintly.

'I see the merry widow's back.' She pointed across The Green. At first Greenleaf saw only Henry Glide exercising his Boxer; then he noticed that the Hallows' windows had all been opened, flung wide in a way they never were when Patrick was alive. The Weimaraner was standing by the front doors, still as a statue carved from creamy marble.

'Poor girl,' he said.

'Tamsin? I thought you meant Queenie for a minute. Poor is hardly the word I'd choose. That house, the Selby business and a private income! In my opinion she's well rid of him.'

'Excuse me,' Greenleaf said. 'I must go. I have a call.' The car slid out on to the tarmac. The Scottie yapped and Edith bellowed:

'Let's hope she hasn't come back to another scandal. One's enough but two looks like...'

Her last words were lost in the sound of the engine

but he thought she had said 'enemy action'. He had no idea what she was talking about but he didn't like it. I'm getting as bad as Marvell, he thought uneasily, compelling his eyes to the road. Then he made himself think about headaches and children and meningitis until he came to the house where the sick boy was.

10

THE DOG QUEENIE TRAVERSED THE LAWN OF HALlows, reacquainting herself by scent with the home she had returned to after a fortnight's absence. She assured herself that the squirrels' dray still remained in the elm by the gate, that the Smith-King's cat had on several occasions crossed the wattle fence and come to the back door, and that a multitude of birds had descended upon the currants, leaving behind them famine and evidence that only a dog could find.

When she had visited the locked garage and peered through the window, whining a little by now, she knew that the man she sought was not on Hallows land. She went back to the house, her tail quite still, and found the woman—her woman as he had been her man—sitting in a bedroom singing and combing her hair as she sang. The dog Queenie placed her head in the silk lap and took a little comfort from the combings that fell upon her like thistle-down.

At first Greenleaf thought that the singing came from the wireless. But then, as he came up to the front doors, he realised that this was no professional but a girl who sang for joy, vaguely, a little out of tune. He rang the bell and waited.

Tamsin was browner than he had ever seen her and he remembered someone saying that Mrs. Prynne lived at the seaside. She wore a bright pink dress of the shade his mother used to call a wicked pink and on her arms black and white bangles.

'I came,' he said, very much taken aback, 'to see if there was anything I could do.'

'You could come in and have a drink with me,' she said and he had the impression she was deliberately crushing the gaiety from her voice. She had put on weight and she looked well. The harsh colour suited her. 'Dear Max.' She took both his hands. 'Always so kind.'

'I saw you were back,' he said as they came into the lounge. 'I've been to see a patient in the village and I thought I'd look in. How are you?'

'I'm fine.' She seemed to realise this was wrong. 'Well, what is it you people say? As well as can be expected. You've had awful weather, haven't you? It was lovely where I was. Hours and hours of sun. I've been on the beach every day.' She stretched her arms high above her head. 'Oh Max!'

Greenleaf didn't know what to say. He looked about him at the room which Bernice used to say was like a set-piece in a furniture store or a picture in *House Beautiful*. Now it was a mess. Tamsin could scarcely have been home more than two hours but there were clothes on the sofa and on the floor, magazines and newspapers on the hearthrug. She had covered the stark mantelpiece with shells, conches, winkles, razor shells, and there was a trail of sand on the parquet floor.

'How's everyone? How's Bernice? If you've been thinking I neglected you, I didn't send a single post-card to anyone. How's Oliver? And Nancy? What have you all been doing?'

Talking, he thought, about your husband. Aloud he said:

'We've all been going on in the same way. No news. Crispin Marvell's with Bernice now giving her some tips about gardening.'

'Oh, Crispin.' There was scorn in her voice. 'Don't you think he rather overdoes this country thing of his?' She caught his astonished eye. 'Oh, I'm being mean, I know. But I just don't care about anyone any more—not you and Bernice, Max—I mean the others. The first thing I'm going to do is sell this place and go far far away.'

'It's a nice house,' he said for something to say.

'Nice?' Her voice trembled. 'It's like a great hot-house without any flowers.' He had never thought her mercenary and he was surprised when she said, 'I ought to get eight or nine thousand for it. Then there's the Selby business.'

'What exactly . . . ?'

'Oh, glass,' she said vaguely. 'Test tubes and things like that. It never did terribly well until recently. But a couple of months ago they got a marvelous contract making stuff for Harwell. The money's rolling in. I don't know whether to stay or sell out to the other directors. Really, Max, I'm quite a rich woman.'

There were such a lot of things he longed to ask her but could not. Where, for instance, if the business hadn't been doing well, had the money come from to buy Hallows? Why had Patrick's father committed suicide? What of Oliver Gage? And why, most of all, was she, a widow of three weeks' standing, singing for joy when she returned to the house where Patrick had died? It struck him suddenly that in their conversation so intimately concerned with him, resulting as it did solely from his death, she had never once mentioned his name.

She took a shell from the mantelpiece and held it to her ear. 'The sound of the sea,' she said and shivered. 'The sound of freedom. I shall never marry again, Max, never.' Freedom, he thought, unaware he was quoting Madame Roland, what crimes are committed in your name!

'I must go,' he said.

'Just a minute, I've something to show you.'

She took his hand in her left one and he sensed at the back of his mind that there was an unfamiliar bareness, something missing. But he forgot about it as they entered the dining room. The french windows were open and beyond them the wicker furniture on the patio was damp from many rains. This room, he remembered, had always been the most austere in the house, its walls painted white, its window hung with white blinds, so that it looked like a ward in a new hospital. But above the long sleek radiator there had once been a plaque of smoky blue pottery, a tiny island in an ocean of ice. It had been removed to lie rejected and dusty on the table, and in its place hung the picture that had frightened Patrick, dominating the room and emphasising its barrenness by contrast with its own crusted gilt, its blue and gold and bloody scarlet.

'The gardener was here when I got back,' Tamsin said. 'He helped me to hang it. Too absurd, but I thought he was going to be sick.' She smiled and stroked the mother-of-pearl conch. His gaze, withdrawn for a moment from Salome, followed the movement of her hand and he saw what he had sensed. Tamsin had discarded her wedding ring.

'She always seems to be looking at you,' Tamsin said, 'like the Mona Lisa.'

It was true. The painter had contrived that Salome's eyes should meet yours, no matter in what part of the room you were standing.

'Is it valuable?' he asked, thinking of the thousands rich men would pay for monstrosities.

'Oh, no. Mrs. Prynne said it's only worth about twenty pounds.'

She was still looking at the picture but with neither gloating nor horror. As he turned curiously to look at her he thought he saw in her eyes only the same pride of possession one of his sons might feel for a tape recorder or an electric guitar. One woman's meat, one man's poison...

'Patrick...' he tried to begin, but he could not speak the name aloud to her.

'WHAT'S THE MATTER, DARLING? NOT THE LITTLE boy?'

'No, no, he'll be all right. I'm looking in again tomorrow.'

'You've been so long.'

Instead of sitting down Greenleaf began to pace the room. The circumstances of Patrick's death were beginning to worry him a lot. If in fact there were sufficient grounds to suspect homicide, wasn't it his duty as the first medical man to have seen Patrick's body, as one of those present at the post-mortem, to see justice done? And if he only suspected shouldn't he, as discreetly as possible, probe just enough to discover whether suspicion was well-founded? Some of the information he had was given in confidence and he couldn't tell Marvell about it. But there was one person he could tell, one from whom he had never felt it necessary to keep the secrets of the consulting room. He could tell his wife.

Bernice might well laugh away his fears and this, he had to confess, was what he wanted. She would tell him he was tired, that he needed a holiday.

The television was on, dancers in some grotesque ballet gyrating like demons. He touched the knob. 'D'you want this?' She shook her head. He switched it off and told her.

She didn't laugh but said thoughtfully:

'Tamsin and Oliver. Yes, I can believe that.'

'You can?'

'I couldn't help noticing the way they danced together at Tamsin's party. I never thought Tamsin and Patrick were very happy together. Except—except until a few days before he died. It was when I called on them collecting for the Cancer Campaign. Tamsin kept calling Patrick darling—she was very sweet to him. I remember thinking how odd it was.'

'But apparently Patrick was in love with Freda Carnaby. Freda Carnaby after Tamsin?'

Bernice lit a cigarette and said shrewdly, 'Did you ever notice how very Teutonic Patrick was? The first four years of his life must have influenced him a lot. Of course, his mother was German. He was an awfully *Kinder, Küche, Kirche* sort of person, house-proud, passionately neat and tidy. But Tamsin's a sloppy girl. Not in her appearance, she's vain about that, but about the house. You could see it narked Patrick.'

Greenleaf's mind went back half an hour. Again he saw the untidy rooms, the shells dribbling sand.

'Now, Freda Carnaby, she'd be different again. Very brisk and practical—or she used to be. All the time they've been here I've never seen her in slacks or without stockings, Max. Time and time again I've noticed it, women who wear those tight little pointed shoes are mad keen on polishing and turning out rooms. Patrick was cruel, too, you know, Max, but I don't think cruelty would get very far with Tamsin. She's too vague and self-sufficient. But Freda Carnaby! There's a masochist if ever I saw one.'

'You may be right,' Greenleaf said. 'But forget the Carnabys for a minute. What about Gage? I can imagine he might want to marry Tamsin.' He grinned faintly. 'He has marriages like other people have colds in the head. But apparently Patrick was going to divorce Tamsin anyway. Would Gage want to'—he almost baulked at the word—'to *kill* him?'

Bernice said unexpectedly, 'He's rather a violent man.'

'Violent? Oliver Gage?'

'Nancy told me something when they first came here. I didn't repeat it because I know how you hate that kind of thing. She was proud of it.'

'So?'

'Well, when Oliver met her she was engaged to

133

some relative of his second wife's. Apparently Oliver just set out to get her. It's a strange way of conducting one's life, isn't it? Oliver and the fiancé were playing billiards in Oliver's house and Nancy came in. Anyway, the fiancé said something to her she didn't like and she told him she'd finished with him and that she was going to marry Oliver. Just like that. Oliver and the fiancé had a violent quarrel and the upshot of it was Oliver hit him over the head with a billiard cue.'

Greenleaf smiled incredulously.

'It isn't really funny, Max. He knocked the fellow out cold.'

'Hitting someone over the head is a long way from poisoning a man in cold blood. Freda Carnaby says she saw him carrying a packet. A packet of what? Glover was very thorough in his tests.' He sighed. 'I've never been interested in toxicology. When I was a student I didn't care much for medical jurisprudence. But I always come back to that in the end. If Patrick was killed, what was he killed with?'

'One of those insecticides?' Bernice asked vaguely. 'You know, you read about them in the papers. I thought they weren't supposed to leave any trace.'

'Not in the body maybe. But there would have been signs. He would have been very sick. The sheets on the bed, Bernice, they weren't clean sheets. I don't mean they were dirty—just not fresh on.'

'Observant of you,' said Bernice. She reached for the cigarettes, caught her husband's eye and let her hand drop.

'Besides, why would Gage want to do away with Patrick? There's always divorce. Unless he couldn't afford two divorces. He'd have to pay the costs of both of them, remember.'

'On the other hand, Tamsin has her private income.'

Greenleaf banged his fist on the chair arm.

'Wherever I go I keep hearing about that private income. What does it amount to, I'd like to know. Hundreds? Thousands? A couple of hundred a year wouldn't make any difference to a man in Oliver's position. Killing Patrick would secure his money too and that might pay for Nancy's divorce. And Tamsin...'

Bernice stared.

'You don't mean you think Tamsin...? Would a woman murder her own husband?'

'They do, occasionally.'

She got up and stood before him. He took her hand and held it lightly.

'Don't worry,' he said. 'Maybe I do need that holiday.'

'Oh, darling. I don't want you to get into this. I'm scared, Max. This can't be happening, not here in Linchester.'

Reading her thoughts, he said gently, 'Whatever we have said no one can hear us.'

'But we have said it.'

'Sit down,' he said. 'Listen. There's something we've got to realise. If someone did kill Patrick, Tamsin must be in it too. She was in the house. I left her and she says she went to bed. You're not going to tell me someone got into the house without her knowing?'

'You say she was happy?'

'Now? Yes, she's happy now. I think she's glad. Patrick's dead. After I told her he was dead she didn't cry, but she cried later. She put her arms round the dog and she cried. Bernice, I think she was crying from relief.'

'What will you do?'

'I don't know,' he said. 'Maybe, nothing. I can't go about asking questions like a detective.' He stopped, listening. A key turned in the lock and he heard the boys come into the hall. And if those women talk, he thought, if Nancy goes about saying Carnaby killed Patrick with cyanide and Freda says Gage killed him with a mysterious white packet, I shall begin to lose my patients.

11

'ONE LARGE JAR OF ZINC AND CASTOR OIL CREAM, half a dozen packets of disposable nappies, a dozen tins of strained food...' Mr. Waller reckoned up the purchases rapidly. 'Gone are the days of all that mashing and fiddling about with strainers, Mrs. Smith-King. I always say you young mothers don't know how lucky you are. A large tin of baby powder and the Virol.' He handed the things to Linda who wrapped each up efficiently and sealed it with sellotape. 'I'm afraid that comes to three pounds seven and tenpence. Say it quickly and it doesn't sound so bad, eh?'

Joan Smith-King gave him a new five pound note.

'It's terrible the way it goes,' she said. 'Still, you can't expect it to be cheap taking five children away on holiday.' She jerked Jeremy's hand from its exploration of Linda's carefully arranged display of bathing caps, each an improbably coloured wig of nylon hair on a rubber scalp. 'I can't tell you how relieved I am to be going at all. My husband's had a very worrying time lately with the business but now everything's panned out well and he'll be able to take a rest.'

'There you are, Mrs. Smith-King. Three pounds, seven and ten, and two and two is ten, and ten and a pound is five pounds. Sure you can manage? What can we do for you, Mr. Marvell?'

'Just a packet of labels, please,' said Marvell who was next in the queue. 'I'm going to start extracting honey in a day or two.' He pocketed the envelope and they left the shop together. Outside, Greenleaf's car was parked against the kerb and the doctor was emerging from the newsagent's with the local paper.

'Have you seen it?' Joan Smith-King asked him. 'On the property page. You have a look.'

Greenleaf did as he was told, struggling with the pages in the breeze. The display box among the agents' advertisements wasn't hard to find: Luxury, architect-designed modern house on the favoured Linchester estate at Chantflower in the heart of rural Notts yet only ten miles from city centre. Large lounge, dining room with patio, superb kitchen, three bedrooms, two bathrooms.

'She doesn't let the grass grow under her feet,' said Joan. 'I'll be glad to see the back of that dog, that Queenie thing. My children are scared stiff of dogs.' Jeremy listened, learning terror at his mother's knee. 'You might not believe it but Patrick Selby was all set to ruin Den's business just because he once hit that dog. I mean, really! Imagine trying to take away someone's livelihood just because he took a stick to an animal.'

Marvell said softly:

'The dog recovered from the bite, the man it was that died.'

'Now look, I didn't mean...' A deep flush spread unbecomingly across her lantern jaws. She stepped back. 'I'm sorry I can't give you a lift. I've got a car full of kids.'

'Come on,' Greenleaf said. He tossed the paper into the back of the car. Marvell got in beside him.

'Sorry,' he said. 'I can see you don't like my detective methods. But it's bloody funny, nobody loved him. His wife was bored with him, he got in the way of his wife's lover—Oh, I've found out about that—his girl friend's brother was afraid of him. Even I was annoyed with him because he cut down my father's trees. Edith disliked him because he played God with her children and now you have Smith-King. I wonder what he was up to there, Max. He told me he was trying to get a Stock Exchange quotation for his shares and expand a bit. Do you suppose he had his old fishy eye on Smith-King's little lot?'

'I'm not listening.'

'Do you happen to know what Smith-King's line is?'

'Chemicals.' Greenleaf said.

'Drugs mainly. And you realise what that means. He must have access to all kinds of lethal stuff. Or there's Linda. She works for Waller and I don't suppose she's above "borrowing" a nip of something for her mother. And what about that Vesprid stuff?'

Bernice had suggested insecticides. Doubt stirred until Greenleaf remembered how he had answered her. 'You'll have to stop all this, you know,' he said.

'Nobody could have got into the house because Tamsin was there.'

'Not all the time. After you'd gone she went out.'

'What?' Greenleaf signalled right and turned into Long Lane. 'How do you know?'

'Because she came to see me,' Marvell said.

GREENLEAF HAD INTENDED TO DROP MARVELL AT the almshouse and drive straight home. But Marvell's statement had suddenly put a different complexion on things. He slammed the car doors and they went up to the house.

'She came,' Marvell said, 'to bring me the currants. You remember the currants? She picked them before the party and put them in a trug.'

'A what?'

'Sorry. I keep forgetting you're not a countryman. It's a kind of wooden basket, a gardener's basket. In all the fuss I forgot them and Tamsin brought them up to me. It must have been all of midnight.'

Midnight, Greenleaf thought, and she walked through the woods alone. She came down here while Patrick—if not, as far as anyone then knew, dying— was at least ill and in pain. She came to bring a basket of currants! It was no good, he would never understand the habits of the English countryside. But Tamsin was accustomed to them. She had learnt in these two years as much from Marvell as she would have from a childhood spent among the fields and hedgerows.

'I was sitting at the window reading through my stuff and I saw her in the orchard.' Marvell knelt down to tie up a hollyhock that the wind had blown

140

adrift from the porch wall. Greenleaf watched him smooth the stem and press back the torn green skin. 'She looked like a moth or a ghost in that dress. Patrick didn't like bright colours. She was carrying the trug and that straw handbag Edith Gaveston gave her for a birthday present. I was—well, somewhat surprised to see her.' He straightened up and stepped into the porch. Greenleaf fancied that he was embarrassed, for, as he lifted the can and began watering the pot plants that stood on the shelves, he kept his face turned away.

'She came all this way to give you some currants?'

Marvell didn't answer him. Instead he said:

'It means, of course, that anyone could have got into the house. Nobody around here bothers to lock their doors except you and Bernice. I walked back with her as far as her gate.' He stroked a long spear-shaped leaf and, wheeling round suddenly, said fiercely: 'My God, Max, don't you think I realise? If I'd gone in I might have been able to do something.'

'You couldn't know.'

'And Tamsin...?'

'Thought he was asleep,' he said, voicing a confidence he didn't feel. 'Why did she really come?'

Marvell was touching with the tips of his fingers a dark green succulent plant on the borders of whose leaves tiny leaflets grew.

'The Pregnant Frau,' he said. 'You see, she grows her children all around the edges of her leaves and each one will grow into another plant. They remind me of the leaves in Jacobean embroidery. And this one...' He fingered the spear-shaped plant, '... is the Mother-in-law's tongue. You see I keep a harem in my porch.'

141

'Why did she come?'

'That,' Marvell said, 'is something I can't really tell you,' Greenleaf looked at him, puzzled as to whether he meant he refused to tell him or was unable to do so. But Marvell said no more and presently the doctor left him.

He hadn't meant to go back to the village and into Waller's shop. He *meant* to turn off at the Manor gates, but something impelled him on down the hill, unease perhaps, or the knowledge that Tamsin had left Patrick alone on the night he died.

'I want a tin of Vesprid,' he said, cutting short Waller's obsequious greeting. Instead of calling for Linda, Waller got it down himself.

'I suppose I shall have to wear gloves and a mask,' Greenleaf said innocently.

'Absolutely harmless to warm-blooded...' Waller's voice trailed away. In this company, and only then, was his confidence shaken. A small voice within his heart told him that to Greenleaf, Howard and their partners, he could never be more than the village medicine man. 'At least... well, I don't have to tell *you*, Doctor.'

When he got home Greenleaf transferred some of the liquid into a small bottle and wrapped it up. It was far-fetched, incredibly far-fetched, to imagine Edward Carnaby going back to Hallows after the party, to wonder if Freda's story of Gage and the white packet was a cover-up for her brother's own trip with a tin of insecticide. Or was it? He went back to the car, drove to the post office and sent the package away to be analysed.

ffffffffffffffffff **12** fffff

THE CHANTFLOWER RURAL COUNCIL DUSTMEN hadn't bargained on the extra load of rubbish that awaited them outside the Hallows back door. They grumbled loudly, muttering about slipped discs and no overtime. Queenie stood on the steps and roared at them.

'Now, if you'll just take these over to Mrs. Green-leaf I'll give you a shilling,' said Tamsin to Peter Smith-King. He was only ten and he looked dubiously at the two suitcases. 'The money'll be useful for your holiday. Come on, they're not really heavy and you can make two journeys. Tell her they're from Oxfam.'

The little boy hesitated. Then he went home and fetched his box barrow. He trundled the cases across the Green, dawdling to throw a stone at the swans, and found Bernice on the lawn giving coffee to Nancy Gage and Edith Gaveston.

'Can we have a peep?' Nancy asked. Without waiting for permission she undid the clasps of the larger case. The lid fell back to reveal, on top of a pile of clothes, a straw handbag embroidered with raffia.

'Oh, dear!' Nancy said.

Edith blushed.

'Of course, I could see she didn't like it,' she said. 'She barely said two words to me when I gave it to her, but really!'

Edith snatched the bag and opened it.

'She hasn't even bothered to take the tissue paper out.'

'Goodness,' Nancy giggled, 'I don't know what use she thinks a handbag is to a starving Asian.' And her eyes goggled as she imagined an emaciated peasant clutching Edith's present against her rags.

'The clothes will be useful though,' Bernice said pacifically.

Nancy stared in horrified wonder as the doctor's wife lifted from the case the slacks and tee-shirt Patrick had worn on the evening of his death. For all their careful laundering they suggested a shroud.

Nancy was on her knees now, unashamedly burrowing.

'Two suits, shoes, goodness knows how many shirts.' She unfastened the other case. 'All Patrick's clothes!'

'Now if it were Paul...' Edith began to describe minutely exactly how she would dispose of her husband's effects in the event of his death. While she was talking Bernice quietly sealed the cases and refilled the coffee pot.

Returning after a few moments, she was aware from Nancy's expression that the conversation had taken a different and more exciting turn. The two women under the cedar tree wore ghoulish lugubrious looks. As she approached she caught the words 'very unstable' and 'a most peculiar family altogether.'

How difficult it was to close one's ears to gossip, how impossible to reprimand friends! Bernice sat down again, listening but not participating.

'Of course I don't know the details,' Nancy was saying.

'Black, please, Bernice,' Edith said. 'Well, that Mrs. Selby—I mean Patrick's mother—it gets so confusing, doesn't it? That Mrs. Selby ran away with another man. We used to call it bolting when I was a girl.' She pronounced it 'gel', snapping her tongue wetly from the roof of her mouth. 'Apparently they'd always been most happily married, married for years. Patrick was grown up when she went off. She must have been all of fifty, my dear, and the man was older. Anyway, she persuaded Patrick's father to divorce her and he did, but...'

'Yes?' Nancy's forlorn, ghoulish face would have deceived no one. Her mouth was turned down but her bright eyes flickered.

'But on the day she got her decree Patrick's father gassed himself!'

'No!'

'My dear, it was a terrible scandal. And that wasn't all. Old Mrs. Selby, the grandmother, too. Dreadful this in-breeding. Look what it does to dogs! She made a terrible scene at the inquest and shouted that her son would still be alive but for the divorce.'

Bernice moved her chair into the shade. 'You're romanticising, Edith. You can't possibly know all this.'

'On the contrary. I know it for certain.' Edith drew herself up, the lady of the manor making her morning calls. 'It so happens I read the account of the inquest in *The Times*. It stuck in my mind and when Nancy mentioned the suicide it all came back to me. Selby, a glass factory. There's no doubt about it being the same one.'

'It's all very sad.' Bernice looked so repressive that Nancy jumped up, scattering biscuit crumbs.

'I must love you and leave you. Oh, Bernice, I nearly forgot to ask you. Have you got the name of that man who put up your summer house?'

'I can't remember. Max would know.'

Nancy waited for her to ask why. When she didn't she said proudly:

'We're going to have that extension done at last, but Oliver says Henry Glide's a bit too pricey. A sun loggia...' She paused. 'And a pram park!'

'Nancy, you're not...? How lovely!'

Nancy pulled in her waist and laughed.

'No, not yet,' she said, 'but Oliver says we can go in for a baby any time I like.'

Trying not to smile at the ludicrous phrase, Bernice found herself saying once more that it was lovely.

'He's been as nice as pie about it and he's all over me. He hasn't been so lovey-dovey for months. Aren't men the end?'

I really ought to thank Tamsin properly for the clothes, Bernice thought after they had both gone. But she felt reluctant to go. Hardly anyone had set eyes on Tamsin since her return. She had become like a sleeping beauty shut up in her glass castle, or like a lurking witch. Bernice couldn't make up her mind whether Tamsin was really bad or whether the gossip had created in her own fancy an unreal Tamsin, a false clever poisoner. Anyway, she must go and be polite.

As she hurried across The Green she encountered Peter sitting on his barrow.

'I went to collect my shilling,' he said, 'but I couldn't find *her*.' He picked up a flat stone and concentrated on sending it skimming across the water. 'The dog's there, though.'

He threw this piece of information out quite casually but Bernice remembered what Max had told her and detected a current of fear.

'I'm on my way over now,' she said. 'Come with me if you like.'

Queenie was indeed there so Tamsin must be too. As she put out her hand to the dog's soft mouth Bernice had a strange feeling that something ought to click. When Tamsin went out without the dog she always shut her in the kitchen. The Weimaraner had been bred as a sentinel as well as a hunter. What was it Max said last night about Tamsin visiting Crispin Marvell? She stopped and pondered. Tamsin's voice from above broke into her reverie.

'Come on in. I was in the bath.'

Peter slunk past the dog.

'Go into the dining room. I won't be a minute.'

Bernice pushed open the double doors and Peter went in first. The dining room door was ajar. Peter went obediently ahead but Bernice waited in the hall. The last thing she wanted was to stay and talk.

She expected Peter to sit down and wait for his wages but he didn't. He stopped and stared at something. She could see nothing inside the room but the child's figure in profile, still as a statue. Then he

147

came out of the room again, backing from whatever it was like someone leaving the presence of royalty. He looked at her and she saw that his face was white but stoical.

'Ughugh,' he said.

At once she knew what he had seen. Surely nothing else Tamsin possessed could summon that squeamish pallor even in a child of ten. She closed the door firmly and turned round. A gasp escaped her before she could control it. Tamsin was behind her, awfully near, clean and gleaming as a wax doll in her pink and white dressing gown. Suddenly Bernice felt terribly frightened. Tamsin had come so silently, the child was silent and now all the doors were closed.

'What's the matter with him?'

If he had been her own child Bernice would have put her arms around him and pressed his grubby cheek against her face. But she could give him no physical comfort. He was too old to hug and too young for explanations.

She felt her voice quiver and jerk as she said, 'I think he saw that picture of yours.'

'Too uncanny,' said Tamsin. She looked at Peter as if she were seeing not him but another child staring out through his eyes. 'Patrick was just about your age when he first saw it, but he wasn't tough like you. He ran away and then *it* happened. The fuss and bother —you can't imagine.'

Bernice was just going to ask what had happened when Peter said sullenly, 'Can I have my shilling?'

'Oh, of course you can. It's there, all ready for you on the table.'

The moment of revelation had passed. Tamsin evidently thought Bernice had come to give Peter moral support, for she opened the door to show them both out.

'I only came to thank you for the things.'

'So glad they're useful. And now I must chase you both away. I've got people coming to look over the house.'

EDITH WAS THE FIRST PERSON ON LINCHESTER TO find out that Hallows was sold and she got it from the gardener the Gavestons shared with Tamsin. As soon as he had told her, over mid-morning tea in the utility room, she slipped out to pass the news on to Mrs. Glide. Henry, after all, ought to be pleased that his handiwork found favour in the sight of buyers. On her way back she met Marvell returning from the shops with his sparse groceries in a string bag.

'Only yesterday, it was,' she said, 'and they made an offer on the spot. These *nouveaux riches* they buy and sell houses like you or Paul might job in and out on the stock market.'

Marvell pursed his lips gravely.

'Now when we were young a house *was* a house. One's grandfather had lived in it and in the fulness of time one's grandson would live in it too.' She ended with sublime insensitivity, 'It was *there*, like the Rock of Ages.'

He smiled, murmured something, his mind working furiously. So Tamsin was leaving soon, escaping...When Edith had left him he walked slowly across The Green towards Shalom. He tried the front door and the back. Both were locked. The Greenleafs were townspeople, fearful of burglars, cautious people who yet declared their absence with fastened bolts and conspicuously closed windows. Marvell scribbled a note on the grocer's chit and left it on the back doorstep weighted down with a stone.

Greenleaf found it when he came in at one.

'Can you drop in this afternoon?' he read. 'I've something to tell you. C.M.'

He suppressed a sigh. Tamsin would soon be gone and with her departure surely the rumours would cease. In a fortnights' time he would be off on holiday and when he came back Nancy would be too preoccupied with plans for the baby, Freda too tranquilised by drugs to bother about the vanished Selbys. And yet, he thought as he began to eat the cold lunch Bernice had left him, Marvell might want him for something quite different. In the past he had often been summoned to have an emergency injection of piriton when Marvell was almost numbed and blinded by hay fever. Without a telephone, Marvell was obliged to call or leave a note. It was even possible that he wanted to show the doctor his manuscript, perhaps finished at last. 'I've something to tell you...' Patrick. He could only mean Patrick. Probably another undetectable poison theory. Well, it was a way of passing his free afternoon.

As he washed his plate and stuck it in the rack to drain, he thought with the small grain of superiority he allowed himself, that when people spoke of the rewards of a medical vocation they ignored this one: the pleasure of shooting the layman's theories down in flames.

On the wooden bench by the back door Marvell sat reading a recipe for ratafia. It was an old recipe, part of a collection his mother had made while still chatelaine of Linchester, and it had been handed down to her, mother to daughter, from a long line of forebears. Brandy, peach kernels, sugar, honey, orange flower water... He had no peaches, or the money to buy them. The recipe said five hundred kernels and, basking in the warm soft sunlight, he imagined with some delight the preliminary labour to the making of ratafia: the consumption of those five hundred ripe peaches.

Presently he got up and began to walk around the house, touching the bricks, themselves peach-coloured. When he came to the side wall where Henry Glide had discovered the fissure, the terrible sign that the whole building was beginning to subside, he closed his eyes and saw only a red mist filled with whirling objects. Then, because he refused to deny facts and deceive himself, he forced his fingers to seek the crack as a man, fearful of cancer yet resolute, compels his hand to probe the swelling in his body.

He jumped when Greenleaf coughed behind him.

'Penny for your thoughts.'

'They're worth more than that,' Marvell said lightly. 'To be precise a thousand pounds.'

Greenleaf looked at him inquiringly.

'That,' said Marvell, 'is the price Glide is prepared to pay me for this land.'

'You're selling? But this place—I thought you were

151

so fond of it.' Greenleaf described with splayed fingers a wide arc that embraced the squat yet elegant house, the shaven lawn, the orchard and the hawthorn hedge over which honeysuckle climbed, a parasite more lovely than its prey. All this meant little to the doctor but by a terrific effort of empathy he had learned its value to his friend. Even he who could scarcely tell a lily from a rose, felt that here the air smelled more sweetly and the sun's heat was moderated to a mellow beneficence. 'The house. It's so old. It's quaint.' He added helplessly, 'People like that sort of thing. They'd want to buy it.'

Marvell shook his head. He was still holding the recipe book and slowly the thought formed in his mind: I will make some ratafia, just a very small quantity, to take away and to remind me. . . .

Aloud he said to Greenleaf: 'It's falling down. The council says it's not safe to live in. I've had Glide here to look at it and all he said was he'd give me a thousand for the land.'

'How long have you known?'

'Oh, about a month now. A thousand's good going, you know. When the Marvells had Andreas Quercus —he was really called Andrew Oakes or something— when they had him build this place for four old persons of the parish of Chantflower, they didn't care that you could only get to it down a muddy lane and the old persons were too grateful to care.'

With what he felt to be tremendous inadequacy, Greenleaf said: 'I'm sorry. Where will you live?' So many questions leapt to his mind, Have you any money? What will you live on? He couldn't dream of asking them. The proximity of Linchester made poverty a more than usually shameful thing.

'I suppose I can get a room somewhere. I can teach. I shall have my thousand pounds. You'd be surprised what a long time I can live on a thousand pounds.' He laughed dryly and Greenleaf, seeing him in the light of this new knowledge, noticed how gaunt he was. This, then, was why Marvell had sent for him, to unburden his soul. I wonder, he thought, if I could rake up a bit, just to tide him over and have the place made water-tight. But Marvell's next words temporarily banished all thoughts of a loan.

'I saw Edith this morning,' he said, 'as I was coming back from the village. She said Tamsin had sold the house. Some people came and made her an offer.'

'Then she'll soon be gone,' said Greenleaf, relieved.

'And since perhaps neither of us will ever see her again I think I can tell you why she came to see me on the night Patrick died.'

HE COULD SEE HER NOW AS SHE HAD COME UP through the orchard, swinging her basket, all pale in the moonlight with her mist-coloured dress, and paler still when she came within the radiance of his lamp. To his fanciful imagination the currants had seemed like beads of white jade veined with crimson. For all her affected speech, the superlatives that came from her lips so often that they lost their meaning and their force, her face had always been a mask, a shield deliberately maintained to hide intellectual cunning or perhaps a chance trick of nature concealing only vacuity.

'I think she is really very clever,' he said to Greenleaf.

He had put his head out of the window and called

153

to her, then gone into the garden and asked after Patrick.

'Oh, Patrick—he spoiled my lovely party. Maddening creature.'

'You shouldn't have come all this way alone. I would have come up tomorrow.'

'Crispin darling, how should I know what you do here in your enchanted cottage? You might have wanted to make your wine tonight at some special witching hour.'

'I'll walk back with you.'

But she had unlatched the door already and pulled him after her into the little damp kitchen. The scent of the night came in with her and as for a moment she stood beside him, very close with her face uplifted, he could smell the rich perfume she wore, Nuit de Beltane, exotic, alien to an English garden. This essence with its hint of witchcraft enhanced the atmosphere of magic unreality.

'So we sat down,' he said, shaking his shoulders as if to shed a memory. 'We sat a long way from each other but the lamp was between us and you know what oil lamps are. They seem to enclose you in a little snug circle. For a while we talked the usual trivia. Then, quite suddenly, she began to talk about us.'

'You and herself?'

'Yes. She said what a lot we had in common, how we both loved country things. She said there had always been a kind of bond between us. Max, I felt very uneasy.'

'And then?'

'I want you to understand how curiously intimate the whole situation was, the darkness around us, the circle of light. After a while she got up and sat beside me on the footstool. She took my hand and said she supposed I realised she hadn't been happy with Patrick for a long time. She's got one of those thick skins that can't blush, but I felt the blush was there.'

'Everyone can blush,' said the doctor.

'Well, be that as it may, she went on to tell me she knew why I came to the house so often. I didn't say a word. It was horribly awkward. She kept hold of my hand and she said she'd only realised how I felt when I brought her the mead and roses. Max, believe me, they were just presents for a pretty woman from a man who can't afford scent or jewellery.'

'I believe you.'

'Suddenly she said very abruptly: "Patrick's leaving me. He wants a divorce. In a year I'll be free, Crispin." It was a blunt proposal of marriage.' Marvell went on quickly: 'I don't want marriage. For one thing I can't afford it. Everybody thinks I'm comfortably off, but the fact is most of the money my father got for Linchester went in death duties. What was left was divided between my brother, my sister and myself and my share went on buying the almshouses. The family had sold them long ago. But I couldn't tell Tamsin all that. I felt she might offer me her own money.'

'That mysterious private income,' Greenleaf said.

'Not mysterious. It amounts to about fifty thousand pounds—the capital, that is—but Tamsin can't touch that. It's invested in oil or something and she has the income for life. I believe it would pass to her children, if she ever had any children. So, you see, I couldn't talk about money to her. Instead I said I was too old for her. I'm fifty, Max. She has a lot of natural dignity, but I thought she was going to cry. I don't mind telling you, it was the most embarrassing experience of my life. I suppose I was weak. I said quite truthfully that she was the most beautiful and most exciting woman I knew. Then I said, "Wait till the year is up. I'll come and see if you've changed your mind." But she only laughed. She got up and stood outside the lamplight and said quite coolly, "Patrick will probably name Oliver Gage. I've been having an affair with him. Did you know?" I realised she was telling me I'd be taking Gage's leavings.'

'And that was all?'

'That was all, or nearly all. I tipped the currants into a bowl and walked back with her, carrying the empty trug. All the way back she was utterly silent and at the gate I left her.'

'Did you see anyone?'

'No one. It was all so extraordinary, like a dream. But the most extraordinary thing was when I saw her the day after Patrick died, the next day. I didn't want to go, Max, but I felt that I should. She was as cold as ice. Not miserable, you understand; the impression she gave was of happiness and freedom. She might never have come to see me the night before. Then, when she came back, I met her out with Queenie in Long Lane. She waved to me and said Hallo. I asked her how she was and she said fine. I'm selling up and leaving as soon as I can. It was as casual as if we'd never been more than acquaintances.'

'Peculiar,' Greenleaf said.

'I don't mind telling you,' Marvell said with a smile, 'it was a hell of a relief.'

PART THREE

13

Two days later Marvell began extracting honey. Greenleaf's jar would be ready for him in the afternoon, he told the doctor, if he cared to come along and collect it. But at half-past three Greenleaf was still sitting in his deckchair under the shade of the cedar tree. Bernice had gone out and he was half-asleep. Each time he nodded off, snatches of dreams crept up on him, bright pictures rather than actual episodes. But they were not pleasant images and they mirrored a subconscious of which he had been un-aware. Worst of all was the hideous cameo of Tam-sin's painting that spiralled and enlarged, twisted and distorted until the head on the plate became Patrick's. He jolted out of sleep to a shrill insistent ringing. Consciousness, reality, came back as with the familiar feel of the canvas, the cool springy grass, he sought tranquillity. Almost in the past days he had found peace of mind. Was it all there still below the surface, a whirlpool of fear and doubt and indecision? The ringing continued and he was suddenly aware that this was not a sound within his head, but the peal of a real bell, the telephone bell.

Reminding himself that he was supposed to be on call, he hastened into the morning room. It was Edward Carnaby.

'I thought I wasn't going to get you,' he said reproachfully. 'It's my Cheryl, my daughter. A wasp got her on the lip, Doctor. Her and Freda, they were having a bit of a picnic on The Green and this wasp was on a piece of cake...'

'Her lip?' From Patrick, Greenleaf's thoughts travelled back to the dead miner. 'Not inside her mouth?'

'Well, sort of. Inside her lip. She's scared stiff. Mind you, Freda's had something to do with that. They're both sobbing their hearts out.'

'All right, I'll come.'

'I thought we'd seen the last of those wasps,' he said as he walked into the Carnaby lounge. Of course it was the only living room they had but it seemed strange to him to cover the entire centre of the carpet with what looked like a dismantled internal combustion engine spread on sheets of newspaper.

'You'll have to excuse the mess,' Carnaby said, blackening his fingers in his haste to remove obstacles from the doctor's path. 'I borrowed it from the class. I can't seem to...'

'Never mind all that!' Freda was on the sofa, squeezing the child in a vice-like hug against her fussy starched blouse. Greenleaf picked his way over to her, stepping gingerly across coils and wheels. He thought he had seldom seen anyone look so tense.

Her mouth was set as if she was grinding her teeth and the tears poured down her cheeks. 'Tell me quickly, Doctor, is she going to die?'

Cheryl struggled and began to howl.

'Of course she isn't going to die.' Greenleaf said roughly while Carnaby fumbled at his feet with bits of metal.

'She is, she is! You're just saying that. You'll take her to the hospital and we'll never see her again.'

He was surprised at so much emotion for she had never seemed to care for the child. Patrick's death must have left a real wound into which a new-found maternal love might pour. Patrick, always back to Patrick... He looked quickly at Carnaby, wondering when the report would come from the analyst, before saying sharply to Freda:

'If you can't control yourself, Miss Carnaby, you'd better go outside.'

She gulped.

'Let's have a look at it, Cheryl.' He prised Freda off her and gently eased the handkerchief from her mouth. The lower lip was bulging into a grotesque hillock and it reminded the doctor of pictures he had seen of duck-billed women. He wiped her eyes. 'You're going to have a funny face for a day or two.'

The child tried to smile. She edged away from her aunt and pushed tendrils of hair from her big characterful eyes, eyes that she must surely have inherited from her mother.

'Mr. Selby had wasp stings,' she said and darted a precocious glance at Freda. 'I heard Daddy talking about it when they got back from that party. I was awake. I never sleep when I have a sitter.' Her lip wobbled. 'It was that Mrs. Staxton. She said wasps were ever so dangerous and she was scared of them, so Daddy said he'd got some stuff and she could take the tin. And she did, she took it home with her and a jolly good thing, because wasps *are* dangerous.' Greenleaf sighed with silent relief. The analyst's report could hardly matter now. Cheryl's voice rose into fresh panic. 'Mr. Selby *died*. Aunty Free said I might die.'

Greenleaf felt in his pocket for a sixpence.

'There's an ice-cream man by The Green,' he said. 'You'll catch him if you hurry. You get a lolly.' Carnaby looked at him, a foolish smile curling his mouth uneasily as if at some inconsequential joke. 'It'll be good for your lip.'

Freda watched her go with tragic eyes. She evidently thought Greenleaf had got rid of Cheryl in order to impart confidential information as to her probable fate. She looked affronted when he said instead:

'Patrick Selby did not die of wasp stings. I thought you had more sense, Miss Carnaby. To talk of dying to a child of eight! What's the matter with you?'

'Everybody knows Patrick didn't die of heart failure,' she said stubbornly.

Greenleaf let it pass. Her bosom quivered. The fallen tears had left round transparent blotches on the thin blouse through which frilly fussy straps and bits of underclothes showed.

'He must have died of the stings,' she insisted, 'and he only had four.'

'Five, but it doesn't matter. Cheryl...'

'He didn't. He only had four. I was sitting with him and I could see.'

Greenleaf said impatiently:

'I should give that a rest, Miss Carnaby.'

Carnaby who had remained silent, ineffectually picking up things that might be ratchets or gaskets, suddenly said rather aggressively, 'Well, it's a matter of accuracy, isn't it, Doctor? It so happens Selby had four stings. I was in the bathroom and I saw the wasps get him. Unless you're counting the one he had a couple of days before.'

'One on his face,' Freda said, 'two on his left arm and one inside his right arm. I thought Cheryl—well, it might have taken her the same way, mightn't it?' The sob that caught her throat came out ludicrously like a hiccup. 'She's all I've got now,' she said. 'Patrick—I could have given him children. He wanted children. I'll never get married now, never, never!'

Carnaby hustled the doctor out into the hall, kicking the door shut behind him. Recalling what Bernice had said, Greenleaf wondered whether Freda's renewed cries were caused by true grief or the possible damage to the paintwork. Then, as he stood, murmuring assurances to Carnaby, the penny dropped. Not the whole penny, but a fraction of it, a farthing perhaps.

'She'll be all right,' he said mechanically. 'There's nothing to worry about.' The worry was all his now.

Then he went, almost running.

Back at Shalom his deck-chair awaited him. He sat down, conscious that on his way round The Circle he had passed Sheila Macdonald and Paul Gaveston without even a smile or a wave. They had been shadows compared with the reality of his thoughts. Before his eyes he could again see Patrick's body in the bed at Hallows that Sunday morning, the thin freckled arms spread across the sheet, sleeves pushed back for coolness. And on the yellowish mottled skin red swellings. One sting on the face, two on the left arm, one on the right arm in the cubital fossa—and a fifth. There *had* been a fifth, about six inches below. Not the old sting; that had been just a scar, a purplish lump with a scab where Patrick had scratched it. The Carnabys could be wrong. Both wrong? They couldn't both be mistaken. Why should they lie? He, Greenleaf, hadn't bothered to count the stings on the previous night and when he had visited Patrick in bed the blue cotton sleeves had covered both arms down to the wrists. Tamsin had been uninterested, the others embarrassed. But Carnaby had watched the wasps attack, he had been there in the line of fire, staring from the bathroom window, and Freda had sat at Patrick's feet, holding his hand. Of all the guests at the party they were in the best position to know. But at the same time he knew he wasn't wrong. *Five* stings, one on the face, two on the left arm...

'Hot enough for you?' It was a high-pitched irritating voice and Greenleaf didn't have to look up to know it was Nancy Gage.

'Hallo.'

'Oh, don't get up,' she said as he began to rise. 'I'll excuse you. Much too hot to be polite. You men, I really pity you. Always having to bob up and down like jack-in-the-boxes.'

'I'm afraid Bernice has taken the boys into Nottingham.'

'Never mind. Actually I came to see you. Don't get me a chair. I'll sit on the grass.' She did so quite gracefully, spreading her pink cotton skirts about her like an open parasol. The renewal of love, strained and contrived though that renewal might be, was

TO FEAR A PAINTED DEVIL

gradually restoring her beauty. It was as if she was a wilting pink and gold rose into whose leaves and stems nourishment was climbing by a slow capillary. 'What I really came for was the name of that man who put up your summer house. We're rather spreading our wings—I don't know if Bernice told you—having an extension to our humble domain, and Mr. Glide—well, he is a bit steep, isn't he?'

'He's in the phone book, Swan's the name. J. B. Swan.'

'Lovely. What a wonderful memory! What do you think? As I was coming across The Green I met that funny little Carnaby girl with an enormous lump in her lip. I asked her what it was and she said a wasp sting. She was sucking one of those filthy lollies. I ask you, the last thing! I said, now you run straight home to Mummy—I forgot she hasn't got a Mummy, just an Auntie and what an Auntie!—and get her to put bicarbonate of soda on it.'

'Not much use, I'm afraid.'

'Oh, you doctors and your anti-biotics. I'm a great believer in the old-fashioned remedies.' She spoke with a middle-aged complacency and Greenleaf thought he knew exactly what she would be like in fifteen years' time, stout, an encyclopaedia of outworn and inaccurate advice, the very prototype of an old wife spinning old wives' tales. 'If I've said it once I've said it a dozen times, Patrick would be alive today if Tamsin had only used bi-carb.' As an after-thought she exclaimed in an advertising catch phrase, 'and so reasonably priced!'

Momentarily Greenleaf closed his eyes. He opened them suddenly as she went on:

'As soon as we got back from that ghastly party I

165

said to Oliver, you pop straight back to Hallows with some bi-carb. He hung it out a bit. Waiting for you to go, I'm afraid. Aren't we crafty? Anyway, he trotted across with his little packet...' It was an absurd description of the movement of that graceful, saturnine man, but Greenleaf was too interested to notice. '... but Tamsin must have gone to bed. She'd forgotten to lock the back door because he tried it, but that Queenie was shut up in the kitchen and she wouldn't let him in. He went round the back and all the food was still out there and Tamsin had left her presents on the birthday table, the chocolates and that bag and Crispin's flowers. She must have been terribly upset to leave it all like that. He hung about for five minutes and then he came home.'

'I expect she was tired,' Greenleaf said, his thoughts racing. So that was the answer to what he had been calling in his mind the Great White Packet Mystery. Simply Oliver Gage taking bi-carbonate of soda to his mistress's husband. And probably, he thought vulgarly, hoping for a little more love on the side. No wonder he waited for me to go.

What Marvell had said about anyone being able to get into Hallows while Tamsin was out had now been shown to be manifestly false. The dog Queenie would guard her master against all comers—against all except one. The feeble motives of Edith Gaveston and Denholm Smith-King evaporated like puddles in the sun. But Tamsin had a motive, or rather many motives which crystallised into a gigantic single drive against Patrick's life. Tamsin was rich now and free. Not to marry Gage whom she had evidently sent about his business, but free to be herself in a glorious scented bright-coloured muddle.

'You're so silent,' Nancy said. 'Are you all right? I'll tell you what I'll do. I haven't got a thing on hand this afternoon. I'll nip indoors and make the poor grass widower a nice cup of tea.'

Greenleaf hated tea. He thanked her, rested his head against the canvas and closed his eyes.

Pᴀᴛʀɪᴄᴋ ʜᴀᴅ ᴅɪᴇᴅ ᴛᴏᴏ ʟᴀᴛᴇ. Gʀᴇᴇɴʟᴇᴀꜰ ʀᴇ-peated the sentence to himself as he came up to the front door of Marvell's house. Patrick had died too late. Not from the point of view of Tamsin's happiness, but medically speaking. Marvell had suggested it at the time the rumors began and Greenleaf had shrugged it off. Now he realised that it was this fact which all the time had been nagging at his mind. Had he died soon after receiving the stings or even if he had had a heart attack on seeing the picture—for Greenleaf was beginning to believe that in Patrick's history it corresponded to the something nasty in the woodshed of Freudian psychology—there would have been no mystery. But Patrick had died hours later.

Why had there been a fifth sting? A wasp in the bedroom? It was possible. Patrick had been heavily sedated. You could probably have stuck a pin in him without waking him. But why should a fifth sting kill him when four had made him only uncomfortable? He banged on the almshouse door for the second time, but Marvell wasn't at home. At last he went round to the back and sat down on the bench.

He had come for his honey, and after much heart-searching, to offer his friend a loan. Talking it over with Bernice after she came back from Nottingham, he had thought he could raise a few hundred, enough perhaps to have the house made habitable according to the standards of Chantflower Rural Council. It was an awkward mission even though he intended to be quite pompous about it, insisting for the sake of Marvell's pride on the money being repaid at the normal rate of interest—Marvell would have to put his back into the history of Chantefleur Abbey. I am a peasant, he thought, and he is an aristocrat (the serfs to the wolves syndrome again). He might hit me. All alone in the garden, he chuckled faintly to himself. He didn't think Marvell would do that.

Presently he got up and walked about, for he was nervous. He hadn't counted on having to wait. Perhaps Marvell would be away for hours and he would have screwed up his courage in vain.

He passed the kitchen window and looking inside, saw that the table was laden with jars of honey, clear and golden, not the sugary waxen stuff you bought in the shops. There would be a pot for them and a pot for the Gages and the Gavestons. Poor though he was, Marvell was a generous man. Last year the harvest had been poor but there had been a jar on almost every Linchester table. Not Patrick's though. Patrick recoiled from honey as if it were poison.

Greenleaf turned away and began to follow the path towards the orchard. Under the trees he stopped and sat down on the stump of a withered ancient apple Marvell had felled in the winter. Apple, plum and pear leaves made a dappled pattern on the turf as the sunlight filtered through gnarled branches. All about him he could hear the muted yet ominous hum of the bees that had been robbed of their treasure. Marvell, he guessed, had reimbursed them, giving them—as he put it—silver for their gold. He had once shown the doctor the tacky grey candy he made for them from boiled sugar. But, just the same, bewilderment over their loss made them angry.

There were three hives made of white painted wood and this had surprised Greenleaf the first time he had seen them for he had expected the igloos of plaited straw you see in children's picture books. Beneath the entrance to each hive—a slit between the two lowest boards—was a wooden step or platform on to which the bees issued, trickling forth in a thin dark stream. There was a suggestion of liquid in their movement, measured yet turbulent, regular and purposeful. Marvell had told him something of their ordered social life, and because of this rather than from the interest of a naturalist, he approached the hive and knelt down before it.

At first the bees ignored him. He put his ear to the wall of the hive and listened. From inside there came the sound as of a busy city where thousand upon thousand of workers feed, love, breed and engage in industry. He could hear a soft roar, constant in volume, changing in pitch. There was warmth in it and richness and an immense controlled activity.

For a moment he had forgotten that these insects were not simply harvesters; they were armed. Then, as he eased himself into a sitting position, one of them appeared suddenly from a tree or perhaps from the roof of the hive. It skimmed his hair and sank on the windless air until it was in front of his eyes. He got up hastily and brushed at it and at the others which began to gather about it. How horrible, how treacherous Nature could be! You contemplated it with the eye of an aesthete or a sociologist, and just as you were beginning to see there might be something in it after all, it rose and struck you, attacked you... He gasped and ran, glad that there was no one to see him. Two of the bees followed him, sailing on the hot fruit-scented air. He stripped off his jacket and flung it over his head. Panting with panic and with sudden revelation, he stumbled into Marvell's garden shed.

The bee-keeper's veiled hat and calico coat were suspended from the roof, taped gloves protruding from the sleeves. The clothes looked like a guy or a hanged man. When he had slammed the door between himself and his pursuers, he sat down on the garden roller, sweating. He knew now how Patrick Selby had died.

'But wouldn't he have swelled up?' Bernice asked. 'I thought the histamine made you swell up all over.'

'Yes, it does.' Greenleaf bent over the kitchen sink,

washing tool-shed cobwebs from his hands. 'I gave him anti-histamine...'

'Why didn't it work, Max?'

'I expect it did, up to a point. Don't forget, Patrick wasn't allergic to wasp stings. But if he was allergic to *bee* stings, as I think he must have been, the histamine reaction would have been very strong. Two hundred milligrammes of anti-histamine wouldn't have gone anywhere. The only thing for people with that sort of allergy is an injection of adrenalin given as soon as possible. If they don't have it they die very quickly.' She shivered and he went on: 'Patrick didn't have that injection. He was heavily sedated, he couldn't call for help and if there was no one near...' He shrugged. 'There would have been a lot of swelling but the swelling would gradually disappear. I didn't see him till ten or eleven hours after he died. His face was a bit puffy and I put it down to the wasp sting under his eye. By the time Glover got to work on him—well!'

'An accident?'

'Too much of a coincidence. Four wasp stings and then you get stung by a bee in your own bedroom?'

'He must have known he was allergic to bee stings.'

'Not necessarily, although I think he did. He hated honey. Remember? He knew about it all right and someone else knew too.'

'You mean he told someone?'

'Bernice, I have to say this. At the moment I can only say it to you, but I may have to tell the police. People with this sort of allergy usually find out about it when they're children. They get stung, have the adrenalin, and afterwards they're careful never to get another. But others know about it, the people who were there at the time.' Turning his back on the window behind which Nature seemed to seethe, he looked at the manufactured, man-made things in the modern kitchen, and at civilised, corseted, powdered Bernice. 'Tamsin and Patrick weren't only husband and wife; they were cousins. They'd known each other since they were children. Even if he half-forgot it, never spoke of it, she might remember.

'So simple, wasn't it? Patrick has the wasp stings and he takes the sodium amytal to make him sleep heavily. When he's asleep she goes to the only place where she can be sure of getting hold of a bee, Marvell's orchard, and she takes with her a *straw* handbag.'

'I see. Straw for ventilation, you mean. The bee wouldn't suffocate. She found the bee before Crispin saw her. But why stay there, why make love to him?'

'I don't know. So it was a good excuse for coming? I tell you I don't know, Bernice. But when she got back Patrick was under heavy sedation. You could have stuck a pin in him.'

'Oh, Max, don't!'

'I'm going over to see her now.' He brushed away the warning hand Bernice rested on his arm. 'I have to,' he said.

SHE WAS LOADING CASES INTO THE BIG CAR, PATrick's car, when he came slowly between the silver-green crinolines of the willows. The car was standing in front of the double doors and Queenie was lying on the driving seat watching the flights of swifts that swooped across the garden, off-course from their hunting ground on The Green.

'I'm leaving tomorrow, Max,' she said. He took the biggest case from her and lifted it into the boot. 'Such a mad rush! I've sold my house and the solicitor's dealing with everything. Queenie and I—we don't know where we're going but we're going to drive and drive. All the furniture—they've bought that too. I shan't have anything but my clothes and the car—I've sold the Mini—and oh, Max! I shall have enough money to live on for the rest of my life.'

The mask had not slipped at all. Only her lips, russet against the egg-shell brown of her face, smiled and swelled the lineless cheeks.

'Leave, Queenie,' she said, for Greenleaf, no lover of animals, was caressing the dog's neck to hide his embarrassment and his fear. 'She thinks she's a bird dog. Come into the house.'

He followed her into the dining-room. The picture had been taken down and was resting against the wall. Was she planning to take it with her or have it sent on? She must have seen him hesitate for she took his hand and drew him to a chair by the window. He sat down with his back to the painted thing.

'You don't like it do you?'

Greenleaf, unable to smile, wrinkled his nose.

'Not much.'

'Patrick didn't like it either.' Her voice sounded like a little girl's, puzzled, naive. 'Really, too silly! He wasn't awfully mature, you know. I mean, people grow out of things like that, don't they? Like being frightened of the dark.'

'Not always.' In a moment he would have to begin questioning her. He had no idea how she would react.

174

In films, in plays, they confessed and either grew violent or threw themselves upon your mercy. His mission nauseated him.

She went on dreamily, apparently suspecting nothing:

'That picture, it used to hang in a room in my grandmother's house in London. The garden room we called it because it opened into a sort of conservatory. Patrick made an awful fuss the first time he saw it—well, the only time really. My uncle and aunt had come home from America and they stayed a couple of nights with my grandmother. Patrick was terribly spoilt.' She swivelled round until her eyes seemed to meet the eyes of Salome. 'He was nine and I was seven. Grandmother thought he was wonderful.' Her laughter was dry and faintly bitter. 'She never had to live with him. But she was fair, my grandmother, fair at the end. She left her money to me. So sweet!'

If only she would tell him something significant, something to make him feel justified in setting in motion the machinery that would send this sprite-like creature, this breathless waif of a woman, to a long incarceration. And yet... Tamsin in Holloway, Tamsin coarsened, roughened in speech and in manners. It was unthinkable.

'That was nice for you,' he said stupidly.

'I loved her, you know, but she was a bit mad. Patrick's father committing suicide, it sent her over the edge. It gave her a sort of pathological fear of divorce.'

This is it, he thought. He needed to hear and at the same time he wanted to stop her. Almost unconsciously he fumbled along the window sill.

'Did you want a cigarette, Max?'

Taking one from the silver box, he said, 'I've given it up,' and lit it with shaking fingers.

'What was I saying? Oh, yes, about Grandmother. She knew I wasn't getting on all that well with Patrick. Funny, she made the match and she wanted us to make a go of it. Just because we were cousins she thought we'd be alike. How wrong she was! After she died we went along to hear the will read—like they do in books. Dramatic, I can't tell you! Patrick wasn't mentioned at all. I don't know if she thought he'd had enough from his father—that went on this house—or perhaps she resented it because he never went to see her. Anyway, she left all her money to me, the income, not the capital, on condition...'

She paused as the dog padded in and Greenleaf listened, cursing the diversion.

'On condition Patrick and I were never divorced!'

O God, he thought, how it all fits, a pattern, a puzzle like those things the boys used to have, when you have to make the ball bearing drop into the right slots.

'As if I wanted to be divorced,' she said. 'I can't support myself. They were too busy educating him to bother about me.'

But Patrick had been going to divorce her. She would have had nothing. Without money from her Oliver Gage would have been unable to marry her, for the costs of her divorce and Nancy's would have fallen on him. Like everyone else he must have been deceived about her income until she got cold feet and told him. He pictured her confessing to Gage; then, when he recoiled from her, running ashamed and wretched—for Tamsin, he was sure, was no nymphomaniac—to Marvell, her last resort. When Marvell refused her there was only one way out...

'Doesn't anybody know?' he asked sharply, not bothering to conceal a curiosity she must take for impertinence.

'It was so humiliating,' she said, whispering now. 'Everybody thought I was quite well-off, independent. But if Patrick had divorced me I would have been—I would have been destitute.'

It was a sudden bare revelation of motive and it recalled him to the real reason of his visit.

'Tamsin...' he began. The cigarette was making him feel a little dizzy, and to his eyes, focusing badly, the woman in the chair opposite was just a blur of brown and bright green. 'I came to tell you something very serious. About Patrick...'

'You mean Freda Carnaby? I know all about that. Please! They were the same kind of people, Max. They really suited each other. If Patrick could have made anyone happy it was Freda Carnaby. But you mustn't think I drove him to it. It was only because of that—Oliver and me... I was so lonely, Max.'

He was horrified that she should think him capable of repeating gossip to her and to stop her he blundered into the middle of it, forgetting his doctor's discretion.

'No, no. I meant Patrick's death. I don't think he died of heart failure.'

Was it possible that, immured here since her return, she had heard nothing of the gossip? She turned on him, quivering, and he wondered if this was the beginning of the violence he expected.

'He must have,' she cried. 'Max, this isn't something that'll stop me going tomorrow, is it? He was so hateful to me when he was alive and now he's dead —I can feel him still in the house.'

So intense was her tone that Greenleaf half-turned towards the door.

'You see what I mean? Sometimes when I go upstairs I think to myself, suppose I see his writing in the dust on the dressing-table? That's what he used to do. I'm not much of a housewife, Max, and we couldn't keep a woman. They were all frightened of Queenie. When I hadn't cleaned properly he used to write in the dust "Dust this" or "I do my job, you do yours". He *did*.'

Were some marriages really like that? Yes, it fitted with what he had known of Patrick's character. He could imagine a freckled finger with a close-trimmed nail moving deliberately across the black glass, crossing the t, dotting the i.

Although he knew her moods, how suddenly hysteria was liable to wistfulness or vague reminiscing, he was startled when she burst out in a ragged voice:

'I'm afraid to go in his room! He's dead but suppose—suppose the writing was there just the same?'

'Tamsin.' He must put an end to this. 'How many wasp stings did Patrick have?'

She was still tense, hunched in her chair, frightened of the dead man and the house he had built.

'Four. Does it matter? You said he didn't die of the stings.' The air in the room was pleasantly warm but she got up and closed the door. It was stupid to feel uneasy, to remember the frightened charwoman, the Smith-King children. She sat down again and he reflected that they were shut in now with the strong watchful dog and that all the neighbours were away on holiday.

'How many did he have when he came in from the garden?'

'Well, four. I told you. I didn't look.'

'And after—when he was dead?'

He stubbed out the cigarette and held his hands tightly together in his lap. His eyes were on her as she coaxed the Weimaraner to her chair, softly snapping her fingers and finally closing them over the pearly fawn snout.

'There, my Queenie, my beauty, my beauty...' Dry brown cheek pressed against wet brown nose, two pairs of eyes looking at him.

'I think he was stung by a bee, Tamsin.'

At a word from her the dog would spring. For armour he had only the long curtains that hung against the window blinds. Wrapped around him they would protect him for a moment, but the dog's teeth would rip that velvet and then...?

'Stung by a *bee*?'

'Perhaps it was an accident. A bee could have got into the bedroom—'

'Oh, no.' She spoke firmly and decisively for her. 'It couldn't happen that way.' Her mouth was close to the dog's ear now. She whispered something, loosening her fingers from Queenie's dew-lap. Greenleaf felt something knock within his chest like a hand beating suddenly against his ribs. But it was ridiculous, absurd, such things couldn't happen! The dog broke free. He braced himself, forgetting convention, pride, the courage a man is supposed to show, and covered his face as the chair skidded back across the polished floor.

179

15

FOR ONE OF THOSE SECONDS THAT TAKE AN AGE TO
live through he was caught up in fear and fettered to
the chair. His eyes closed, he waited for the hot
breath and the trickling saliva. Tamsin's voice came
sweet and anticlimactic.

'Oh, Max, I'm awfully sorry. That floor! The furniture's always sliding about.'

I make a bad policeman, he thought, blinking and
adjusting his chair back in its position by the window.
But where was the dog and why wasn't he in the
process of being mauled? Then he saw her, puffing
and blowing under the sideboard in pursuit of—an
earwig!

'You baby, Queenie. She'll hunt anything, even insects.' It was all right. The drama had been nothing
but a domestic game with a pet. And Tamsin, he saw,
had noticed only that he was startled by the sudden

skidding of a chair. 'Talking of insects,' she said, 'it's funny about the bee. It's a coincidence, in a way. You see, that's what happened when Patrick first saw the picture. I'd never seen him before and I was watching from the garden. He ran into the conservatory and there was a bee on a geranium. He put out his hand and it stung him.'

The shock was subsiding now.

'What happened?' he asked rather shakily.

Tamsin shrugged and pulled Queenie out by the tail.

'Why, nothing happened. It made me laugh. Children are cruel, aren't they? Grandmother and my aunt, they made a dreadful fuss. They put him to bed and the doctor came. I remember I said, "He must be an awful coward to have a doctor for a bee sting. I bet you wouldn't have got the doctor for me," and they sent me to my room. I told him about it when we were older but he wouldn't talk about it. He only said he didn't like bees and he couldn't stand honey.'

'Didn't it ever occur to you that he might be allergic to bee stings?'

'I didn't know you could be,' she said, her eyes wide with surprise.

He almost believed her. He wanted to believe her, to say, 'Yes, you can go. Be happy, Tamsin. Drive and drive—far away!'

Now more than ever it seemed likely that the bee had got there by chance. Hadn't he opened the window in the balcony room himself? Wasps stung when they were provoked; perhaps the same was true of bees and Patrick's killer, alighting on his exposed arm, had been alerted into venom by a twitch or a galvanic start from the sleeping man. If Tamsin were guilty she would clutch at the possibility of an accident and no law could touch her.

'I asked you about an accident,' he said. 'Could a bee have stung him by accident?'

'I suppose so.' Marvell is wrong, he thought. She isn't clever. She's stupid, sweetly stupid and vague. She lives a life of her own, a life of dreams sustained by unearned, unquestioned money. But dreams can change into nightmares...

Then she said something that entirely altered the picture he had made of her. She was not stupid, nor was she a murderess.

'Oh, but it couldn't!' Dreamy, vague children often do best in examinations, drawing solutions from their inner lives. 'I know it couldn't. Crispin told me something about bees once. They're different from wasps and when they sting they die. It's like a sort of hara-kiri, Max. They leave the sting behind and a bit of their own inside with it. Don't you think it's horrid for them, poor bees? The sting would still have been in Patrick's arm if it had been an accident. We'd have seen it!'

Unwittingly he had given her a loophole. A guilty woman would have wriggled through it. Tamsin, in her innocence, was confirming that her husband had been murdered.

'Max, you don't mean you think I...?'

'No, Tamsin, no.'

'I'm glad he's dead. I am. I tried everything I could to make him forgive me over Oliver and give that woman up. But he wouldn't. He said I'd given him the chance he'd been waiting for. Now he could divorce me and Freda's name wouldn't have to be brought into it at all. Oh, outwardly he was perfectly friendly to Oliver, but all the time he was having his flat in town watched. Oliver and Nancy must come to the party. Then, when he'd got everything lined up he was going to drop his bombshell.' She paused and drew a little sobbing breath, rubbing away the frown lines with her ringless fingers. 'He liked to make people suffer, Max. Even the Smith-Kings. Did you see how he was torturing Denholm at the party?' When Greenleaf said nothing she went on in a shaky voice that fell sometimes to a whisper, 'Oh, that awful party! The evening before, he went straight to Freda's house. I was desperate, I cried and cried for hours. Oliver came but I couldn't let him in. All those weeks when we were at the flat he'd been hinting that he'd get Nancy to divorce him. My money would pay for that and keep us both. I had to tell him there wouldn't be any money. I did tell him at last, Max, I told him at the party.'

And Gage had sat beside her gloomily, Greenleaf remembered. There had been no close sensual dancing after that.

'He went on and on about it. He even tried to think of ways of upsetting the will. But d'you know something? I don't want to be married. I've had enough of marriage.' Her voice grew harsh and strident. 'But I'd have married anyone who would have supported me. Can you see me working in an office, Max, going home to a furnished room and cooking things on a gas ring? I'd even have married Crispin!'

'Marvell hasn't any money,' he said. 'His house is falling down and he won't get much for the land.'

She was thunderstruck. The mask slipped at last and her big golden eyes widened and blazed.

'But his books...?'

'I don't believe he ever finishes them.'

To him it was the saddest of stories, that Marvell should have to leave the house he loved, that her nightmare of the room with the gas ring might become real to him. Because of this her ringing laughter was an affront. Peal upon peal of it rang through the room; hot laughter to burn and cleanse away all her old griefs. The Weimaraner squatted, alert, startled.

'What's so funny?'

She no longer cared what he might think or say.

'It's mad, it's ridiculous! He spent the night here, you know, the night Patrick died. He spent it with me. I was so scared when you made me sit on the bed in the back bedroom. I felt you must sense that—that I hadn't been alone. Oh, Max, Max, don't you see how crazy it is?' He stared, his hurt suspicion melting, for he saw that she was laughing at herself. 'I wanted to marry him for his money,' she said, 'and he wanted to marry me for mine, and the mad thing is we hadn't either of us got a bean!'

ffffffffffffffff **16** fffff

SHE WALKED WITH HIM TO THE GATE. HE SHOOK hands with her and impulsively—because he was ashamed of the thoughts he had harboured—kissed her cheek.

'Can I go tomorrow? Will it be all right, Max?' She spoke to him as if he *were* a policeman or a Home Office official. In denying the possibility of accidental death she had declared, if not in words, that Patrick had been murdered. But Greenleaf knew she hadn't realised it yet. Sometime it would reach her, surfacing on to her mind through that rich, jumbled subconscious, and then perhaps it would register no more strongly than the memory of a sharp word or an unfriendly face. By then she might be driving away on the road that led—where? To another terse young company director who would be fascinated for a time by witchlike innocence? Greenleaf wondered as he drew his lips from her powderless cheek.

'Good-bye, Tamsin,' he said.

When he came to the Linchester Manor gates he looked back and waved. She stood in the twilight, one hand upraised, the other on the dog's neck. Then she turned, moving behind the willows, and he saw her no more.

H E ENTERED MARVELL'S GARDEN BY WAY OF THE orchard gate. The bees were still active and he gave the hives a wide berth. It occurred to him that Marvell might still be out but if this were so he would wait—if necessary all night.

By now it was growing dark. A bat brushed his face and wheeled away. For a second he saw it silhouetted against the jade-coloured sky like a tiny pterodactyl. He came to the closed lattice and looked in. No lamps were lit but the china still showed dim gleams from the last of the light. At first he thought the room must be empty. The stillness about the whole place was uncanny. Nothing moved. Then he saw between the wing and the arm of a chair that had its back to the window a sliver of white sleeve and he knew Marvell must be sitting there.

He knocked at the back door. No footsteps, no sound of creaking or the movement of castors across the floor. The door wasn't locked. He unlatched it, passed the honey-laden table and walked into the living room. Marvell wasn't asleep. He lay back in his chair, his hands folded loosely in his lap, staring at the opposite wall. In the grate—the absurd pretty grate that shone like black silver—was a pile of charred paper. Greenleaf knew without having to ask that Marvell had been burning his manuscript.

'I came earlier,' he said. 'I had something to ask you. It doesn't matter now.'

Marvell smiled, stretched and sat up.

'I went to tell Glide he could have the land,' he said. 'You can take your honey, if you like. It's ready.'

Greenleaf would never eat honey again as long as he lived. He began to feel sick, but not afraid, not at all afraid. His eyes met Marvell's and because he couldn't bear to look into the light blue ones, steady, mocking, unfathomably sad, he took off his glasses and began polishing them against his lapel.

'You know, don't you? Yes, I can see that you know.'

Hazily, myopically, Greenleaf felt for the chair and sat down on the edge of it. The wooden arms felt cold.

'Why?' he asked. His voice sounded terribly loud until he realised that they had been speaking in whispers. 'Why, Crispin?' And the Christian name, so long withheld, came naturally.

'Money? Yes, of course, money. It's the only real temptation, Max. Love, beauty, power, they are the obverse side of the coin that is money.'

From his dark corner Greenleaf said: 'She wouldn't have had any if Patrick had divorced her. That was the condition in the will.' The man's surprise was real but unlike Tamsin, he didn't laugh. 'You didn't know?'

'No, I didn't know.'

'Then...?'

'I wanted more. Can't you see, Max? That place, that glass palace.... With the money from that and his money and her money, what couldn't I have done here?' He spread his arms wide as if he would take the whole room, the whole house in his embrace. 'Tell me—I'm curious to know—what did she want from me?'

'Money.'

He sighed.

'I thought I would know love,' he said. 'But, of course, I do see. That kind of sale is a woman's privilege. May I tell you about it?'

Greenleaf nodded.

'Shall we have some light?'

'I'd rather not,' the doctor said.

'Yes, I suppose you would feel that way. I think that like Alice I had better begin at the beginning, go on till I get to the end, and then stop.'

What sort of a man was this that could talk of children's books on the edge of the abyss?

'As you like.'

'When Glide told me about the house I thought I had come to the end of my world. The bright day is done and we are for the dark.' He paused for a moment and rubbed his eyes. 'Max, I told you the truth and nothing but the truth, but I didn't tell you the whole truth. You know that?'

'You told me one lie.'

'Just one. We'll leave that for the moment. I said I'd begin at the beginning but I don't know where the beginning was. Perhaps it was last year when Tamsin was helping me extract the honey. She said Patrick didn't like it. He was afraid of bees and everything associated with them, but he'd only been stung once. That was when he was a little boy at their grandmother's house. He'd been frightened by a picture of a girl holding a man's head on a plate and he'd run into the conservatory. A bee stung him on his hand.'

'Yes, she told me.'

'Max, she didn't know why the doctor had been sent for. She thought it was because Patrick was a spoiled brat. She didn't know why the doctor had given him an injection, had stayed for hours. But at the time I was reading a book about allergies. I was interested because of that damned hay fever. When she'd gone I looked up bee stings and I found why the doctor had stayed and what kind of an injection Patrick had had. He must have been allergic to bee stings. I didn't say anything to Tamsin. I don't know why not. Perhaps, even then . . . I don't know, Max.'

'Some people grow up out of allergies,' Greenleaf said.

'I know that too. But if it didn't come off, who would know?'

'It did come off.'

Marvell went on as if he hadn't spoken.

'It wasn't premeditated. Or, if it was, the meditation only took a few minutes. It began with the picture. I don't know this part—I'm only guessing—but I think that when Tamsin was offered the picture things were all right between her and Patrick, as right as they ever were. Of course she knew he'd hated it when he was a child but she thought he'd grown out of that.'

'When it arrived,' Greenleaf said slowly, 'she must have been trying to patch things up between them. He might think she'd sent for it to annoy him, so she had it put in her room, a room he never went into.'

'I saw it—and, Max, I told them about it in all innocence!'

'Tamsin was past caring then.'

He must be kind, not a policeman, not an inquisitor.

'Go on,' he said gently.

'It was only when Patrick reacted the way he did that I remembered the bee sting. The temptation, Max! I was sick with temptation. I don't know how I got down those stairs.'

'I remember,' Greenleaf said. 'I remember what you said. Something about the eye of childhood fearing a painted devil. I thought it was just another quotation.'

Marvell smiled a tight bitter smile.

'It is. Macbeth. It doesn't mean that in the text. It doesn't mean that Macbeth was looking with a child's memory, but only in a childish way. I suppose it was my subconscious that gave it that meaning. I knew that Patrick feared it because of what had happened when he *was* a child. Then the wasps got him. Even then I couldn't see my opportunity. I wasn't sure of Tamsin. I'd never made love to her. For all I knew I was just an old pedagogue to her, a domestic science teacher. At midnight she came into my orchard.'

'But she wasn't carrying that straw bag,' Greenleaf said quickly. 'It wasn't at all her style. Besides, when Oliver Gage came round with the bi-carb Tamsin was out but the bag was on the birthday table.'

Marvell got up and, crossing to the window, opened the casement. 'My one lie,' he said. Greenleaf watched him drawing in great breaths of the dark blue air. 'Will you be in a draught?'

'It doesn't matter.'

'I felt—I felt suddenly as if I was going to faint.' From shock? From fear? Greenleaf wondered with dismay if for months now Marvell hadn't been getting enough to eat. 'I'll close it now.' He shifted with precise fingers the long wisps of Tradescantia. 'I'd like the lamp. You don't mind?' When Greenleaf shook his head, he said urgently, 'Darkness—darkness is a kind of poverty.'

When the lamp was lit Marvell put his hands round it. They had the opacity age brings and the thought came to Greenleaf that had his son's hands covered that incandescence the light would have seeped through them as through red panes.

'It all happened as I've told you,' Marvell went on, 'except that I didn't say no to Tamsin. I told her I'd walk back with her but that I'd left my jacket in the orchard. I went down to the shed to get my gloves and my veil and a little box with a mesh lid. Someone had once sent it to me with a queen bee in it.

'When we got to Hallows I went in with her. She'd told me you'd given Patrick a sedative and we both knew I was going to stay with her. We didn't say it but we knew. She didn't want to look at Patrick and she went to take a shower. While she was in the bathroom and I could hear the water running I went into Patrick's room. I still wasn't sure the sting wouldn't wake him.

'There was a big pincushion on the dressing-table. I took a pin and stuck it very lightly into him. He didn't stir.'

Greenleaf felt a deathly cold creep upon him, a chill that culminated in a tremendous galvanic shudder.

'Then I put the bee on his arm and I—I teased it, Max, till it stung him.' He slid his hands down the lamp until they lay flat and fan-spread on the table. 'I can't tell you how I hated doing it. I know it's sentimental, but the bees were my friends. They'd worked for me faithfully and every year I took their honey away from them, all their treasure. They'd fed me— sometimes I didn't have anything but bread and honey to eat for days on end. Now I was forcing one of them to kill itself for my sake. It plunged its sting into those disgusting freckles.... My God, Max, it was horrible to see it trying to fly and then keeling over. Horrible!'

Greenleaf started to speak. He checked himself and crouched in his chair. They were not on the same wavelength, a country G.P. and this naturalist who could kill a man and mourn the death of an insect.

Marvell smiled grimly. 'I had to stay after that. I had to stay and see she didn't go into that room. She hated Patrick but I don't think she would have stood by and let him die.' He stood up straight and in the half-dark he was young again. 'I made love to Tamsin under the eyes of Herod's niece.' His shoulders bowed as if to receive age like a cloak. 'At the time I thought it a pretty conceit. I should have remembered, Max, that they might both understand the desires of old men. I thought it was love.'

He sat on the table edge and swung his legs.

'I left at four. She was asleep and Patrick was dead. I checked. The dog came upstairs and I shut her in with Tamsin.

'Perhaps I was vain, Max, perhaps I thought I had a kind of *droit de seigneur*, perhaps I'm just old-fashioned. You see, I thought that still meant something to a woman, that she would have to marry me. When she made it plain she didn't want me, I felt—My God! She'd wanted me before, but I'm fifty and she's twenty-seven. I thought...'

'Crispin, I *do* see.' It was more horrible than Greenleaf had thought it could be. He hadn't anticipated this grubbing into the roots of another man's manhood. 'Please don't. I never wanted to...'

'But it was only money, always money.' He laughed harshly but quite sanely into Greenleaf's face. 'It's all better now, all better. I am Antony still!'

'But why?' Greenleaf asked again. 'Why tell me so much?' He felt angry, but his anger was a tiny spark in the fire of his other emotions: amazement, pity and a kind of grief. 'You led me into this. You made me suspect.' He spread his hands, then gripped the chair arms.

Marvell said calmly: 'Naturally, I intended to get away with it at first.' His face was a gentle blank. He might have been describing to the doctor his methods of pruning a fruit tree. 'But when I knew that I had killed Patrick in vain, for nothing, I wanted—I suppose I wanted to salvage something from the waste. They say criminals are vain.' With a kind of wonder he said: 'I *am* a criminal. My God, I hadn't thought of it like that before. I don't think it was that sort of vanity. All the moves in the game, they seemed like a puzzle. I thought a doctor and only a doctor could solve it. That's why I picked on you, Max.'

He made a little half-sketched movement towards Greenleaf as if he was going to touch him. Then he withdrew his hand.

'I meant to try to get you interested. Then Nancy started it all off for me. I've always thought hatred was such an uncivilised thing, but I really hated Tamsin. When you suspected her I thought, to hell with Tamsin!' He raised his eyebrows and he smiled. 'If it had come to it, perhaps... I don't think I could have let her suffer for what I did.'

'Didn't you think what it would mean if I found out?'

Marvell moved to the fireplace and taking a match from the box on the mantelpiece struck it and dropped it among charred sheets of the manuscript. A single spiraling flame rose and illuminated his face.

'Max,' he said, 'I had nothing to hope for. I've had a fine life, a good life. You know, I've always thought that was the true end of man, tilling the soil, husbanding the fruits of the soil, making wonderful things from a jar of honey, a basket of rose petals. In the evenings I wrote about the things of the past, I talked to people who remembered like me the days before taxes and death duties took away almost everything that made life for people like me a kind of—a kind of golden dream. Oh, I know it was a dream. I wasn't a particularly useful member of society but I wasn't a drag on society either. Just a drone watching the workers and waiting for the summer to end. My summer ended when Glide told me about this house. That's what I meant when I said the bright day was done and I was for the dark.' As the flame died he turned from the fireplace and clasping his hands behind his back looked down at Greenleaf.

'I don't know what to do,' the doctor said. It was the phrase of despair, the sentence desperate people used to him from the other side of the consulting room table.

Marvell said practically: 'There's only one thing you can do, isn't there? You can't be a party to a felony. You're not a priest hearing confession.'

'I wish,' Greenleaf said, a world of bitterness making his voice uneven, 'I wish I'd kept to it when I said I didn't want to hear.'

'I shouldn't have made you.'

'For God's sake!' He jumped up and they faced each other in the circle of yellow light. 'Stop playing God with me!'

'Max, it's all over. I'll have a wash, I'll put some things in a bag. Then we'll go to the police together.' As the doctor's face clouded he said quickly, 'You can stay with me if you like.'

'I'll wait for you. Not here though. In the garden. I'm not a policeman.' How many times had he said that in the past weeks? Or had he in fact said it only to himself in a repetitive refrain that irritated his days and curled itself around his sleep?

Marvell hesitated. Something leaped into his eyes but all he said was: 'Max... forgive me?' Then when the doctor said nothing he picked up the lamp and carried it before him into the passage.

The garden was a paradise of sweet scents. At first Greenleaf was too bemused, too stunned for thoughts. He moved across the grass watching his own shadow going before him, black on the silvered grass. The great trees shivered and an owl flying high crossed the dappled face of the moon.

In the house behind him he could see the lamplight through a single window, the bathroom window. The rest of Marvell's home was as dark and as still as if Glide had already bought it, as if it was waiting with a kind of squat resignation the coming of the men with the bulldozers. A year would elapse perhaps, only six months if the weather held. Then another house would arise, the mock-Tudor phoenix of some

Nottingham business man, on the ashes of the cottages Andreas Quercus had made when George I held court in London.

The light was still on. No shadow moved across it. I must leave him in peace, Greenleaf thought, for a few more minutes. He has lived alone, loving loneliness, and he may never be alone again.

Avoiding the orchard where the bees were, he walked in a circle around the lawn until he came once more to the back door. He went in slowly, feeling his way in the dark. His fingers touched the uneven walls, crept across the plates, the framed lithographs. At the bathroom door he stopped and listened. No sound came. Suddenly as he stood, looking down at the strip of light between door and floor, he thought of another house, another bathroom where Tamsin had showered her slim brown body while her lover gave to Patrick the sting that was his own individual brand of death.

He paced the narrow passage, sickness churning his belly and rising into his throat. When he could stand it no more he called, 'Crispin!' The silence was driving him into a panic. 'Crispin! Crispin!' He banged on the heavy old door with hands so numb and nerveless that they seemed no part of his tense body.

In a film or play he would have put his shoulder to that door and it would have yielded like cardboard, but he knew without trying how impossible it was for him to attempt to shift this two-inch thick chunk of oak. Instead he groped his way back, wondering what that noise was that pumped and throbbed in the darkness. When he reached the open air he realised that it was the beating of his own heart.

He had to make himself look through that lighted window, pulling his hands from his eyes as a man pulls back curtains on to an unwelcome day. The glass was old and twisted, the light poor but good enough to show him what he was afraid to see.

The bath was full of blood.

No, it couldn't be—not all blood. There must be water, gallons of water, but it looked like blood, thin, scarlet and immobile. Marvell's face rested above the water line—the blood line—and the withdrawing of life had also withdrawn age and the lines of age. So had the head looked on Salome's silver platter.

Greenleaf heard someone sob. He almost looked round. Then he knew that it was he who had sobbed. He took off his jacket, struggling with it as a man struggles with clothes in a dream, and wrapped it around his fist and his arm. The window broke noisily. Greenleaf unlatched the casement and squeezed it over the sill.

Marvell was dead but warm and limp. He lifted the slack arms and saw first the slashes on the wrists, then the cut-throat razor lying beneath the translucent red water. Greenleaf knew no history but there came to him as he held the dead hands the memory of a lecture by the professor of Forensic Medicine. The Romans, he had said, took death in this way, letting out life into warm water. What had Marvell said? 'I am Antony still' and 'Max, forgive me.'

Greenleaf touched nothing more although he would have liked to drain the bath and cover the body. He unlocked the door, carrying the lamp with him, and left Marvell in the darkness he had chosen.

Half-way across the living room he stopped and on an impulse unhooked from the walls the olive-co-

loured plate with the twig and the apple. As it slid
into his pocket he felt with fingers that had palpated
human scars the bruise on the underside of the
glazed fruit.

THE WOOD WITH ITS INSINUATING BRANCHES WAS
not for him to-night. He blew out the lamp and went
home by Long Lane.

On Linchester the houses were still lit, the Gages'
noisy with gramophone music, the Gavestons' glowing, its windows crossed and re-crossed by moving
shadows. As he came to Shalom a taxi passed him,
women waved, and Walter Miller's face, brown as a
conker, grinned at him from under a pink straw hat.
Home to Linchester, home to autumn, home to the
biggest sensation they had ever known. . . .

Bernice opened the door before he could get his
key out.

'Darling, you're ill! What's happened?' she cried
and she put her arms round him, holding him close.

'Give me a kiss,' he said, and when she had done so
he lifted her arms from his neck and placed them
gently at her sides. 'I'll tell you all about it,' he said,
'but not now. Now I have to telephone.'

About the Author

Ruth Rendell "the best mystery writer... anywhere in the English-speaking world" (*Boston Sunday Globe*), is the author of *The New Girl Friend, An Unkindness of Ravens, The Tree of Hands, The Killing Doll, Speaker of Mandarin, The Fever Tree and Other Stories of Suspense, Master of the Moor, Death Notes, The Lake of Darkness, From Doon with Death, Sins of the Fathers, Wolf to the Slaughter, The Best Man to Die,* and many other mysteries. She now has five major awards for her work: two Edgars from the Mystery Writers of America for her short stories "The New Girl Friend" and "The Fallen Curtain"; *Current Crime's* Silver Cup for the best British crime novel of 1975, *Shake Hands Forever*; the Crime Writer's Association's Golden Dagger for 1976's best crime novel, *A Demon in My View*; and the 1980 Arts Council National Book Award in Genre Fiction for *The Lake of Darkness*. Her books have been translated into fourteen languages. Ruth Rendell lives in Polstead, England.